Untitled by Shen Chen Hsieh
Digital drawing, 12 inches by 9 inches. 2021.

MOON CITY REVIEW

2021

Moon City Review is a publication of Moon City Press at Missouri State University and is distributed by the University of Arkansas Press. Exchange subscriptions with literary magazines are encouraged. The editors of *Moon City Review* contract First North American Serial Rights, all rights reverting to the writers upon publication. The views expressed by authors in *Moon City Review* do not necessarily reflect the opinions of its editors, Moon City Press, or Missouri State University.

All other correspondence should be sent to the appropriate editor, using the following information:

Moon City Review
Department of English
Missouri State University
901 South National Avenue
Springfield MO 65897

Submissions are considered at https://mooncitypress.submittable.com/submit. For more information, please consult www.moon-city-press.com.

Cover designed by Shen Chen Hsieh.
Text copyedited by Karen Craigo.

moon city press
s p r i n g f i e l d   m i s s o u r i

STAFF

Editor
Michael Czyzniejewski

Poetry Editor
Sara Burge

Nonfiction Editor
John Turner

Assistant Nonfiction Editors
Joel Coltharp
Jennifer Murvin

Fiction Editor
Joel Coltharp

Graphic Narrative Editor
Jennifer Murvin

Assistant Editors

Mackenzie Acup
Steve Booker, Jr.
Nicole Brunette
Alexandria Clay
Ryan Davies
Anna Edwards
Julia Feuerborn
Jessica A. Fox
Amy Gault
Madison Green
Amanda Hadlock
Janel Haloupek
Rebecca Harris
Rebekah Hartensveld
Kristi Hearn
Joshua Henderson

Disney Humphrey
Abigail Jensen
John King
Mikaela Koehler
Ryan LaBee
Jueun Lee
Sarah Lewis
Tayla Mallow-Spears
Alexis McCoy
Shannon McKenzie
Katie McWilliams
Mikayla Mohrmann
Alyssah Morrison
Haley Nelson
Paige Newton
Colleen Noland
Kyle Osredker

Hannah Overby
Sarah Padfield
Sarah Parris
Arial Peat
Annelise Pinjuv
Sujash Purna
Jim Ross
Hannah Rowland
Eli Slover
Cam Steilen
Sean Turlington
Harley Vantuyl
Sabrina Wagganer
Jessica Weaver
Sierra Welch
Grace Willis

Student Editors

Emmalee Barnett
Nicole Brunette
Kyra R. Cook
Braxton Crook

Chloe Hampton
James Heil
Sarah Morgan

Sarah Padfield
Erin Pierce
Anne Roberts
Heather West

Advisory Editors

James Baumlin   W.D. Blackmon   Lanette Cadle   Marcus Cafagña

TABLE OF CONTENTS

Nonfiction

Translations

The Missouri State University Student Literary Competitions

Reviews

Contributors' Notes

NICKALUS RUPERT

Outskirts of the Psiloverse

It's a great misconception that we old folks are wary of experimental supplements. Our feeling is, bring it on. It's April. The sun's dishing up big radiation, squirrels are cussing in the trees, and we're on a sky-high dosage of a mushroom-based compound called Psilovan. Maybe we're all holding out for that miracle pill that'll make time walk backward, though it'd be too embarrassing to say so. It's a wish so thin that even the pressure of speech would knock it to ashes.

Today at Wandering Pines, it's my turn to be captain of the video game machine, so I drop my dose of Psilovan, take up the controller, and pass Morty the headset mic so he can lecture to the other players. This is our only consistent link to young people. I lead our in-game pirate crew to a dense island interior, where I build a fire. Morty cites facts about the moon while flexing his real-life biceps, which are still round as bocce balls thanks to a supplement he tested last year. Different people respond to different meds. A hair growth supplement in December gifted me a blond Barbie-style ponytail that doesn't grow so much as *tide* from the back of my gray-fringed scalp. Someone should've told us that stuff was designed for fashion-conscious paralegals instead of seasoned, sweater-wearing crones like me. Lately, some of the residents look askance at my new hair, but I wouldn't use a word like regret—that's not quite it.

"Correct," Morty tells one of our crewmates, "the moon does, in fact, experience earthquakes. Though maybe *moon*quakes would be more accurate."

Our afternoons may be tame, but after lights-out this place turns into the set of *Caligula*. The nurses are forever trying to distract us with nonsexual forms of stimulation. There's even a jam room with an old set of Gretsch drums and a mint-green Telecaster, but it's no use. We're insatiable—a side effect, probably, of one nutraceutical trial or another.

While Morty lectures, I steer our pirate character to the fire and diddle buttons to make her carve a schooner from driftwood. We think she's supposed to be from Tortuga, and she looks sort of like a younger version of me. It's easy to forget that we all had lives before this place. I remember so little. As our pirate whittles, an in-game sun eases down, and out pops a moon so detailed you can imagine how it'd feel in your palm if you were god-sized. Beside me on the couch, The Suze crochets something racy between sips of iced jungle juice.

Morty is still describing how corrosive moon dust can be when Bertrand rolls up in his brass-plated wheelchair and parks alongside the couch. Bertrand recovered from his knee replacement months ago but can't seem to part with the chariot. With a kingly flourish, he reaches down and thumbs the power switch to our game, darkening the screen.

"I was just about to tell the children how Lagrange points work," Morty says, shuffling a set of loose-leaf lecture notes.

"Ich würde immer lieber glücklich sein als würdig," says The Suze. Ever since the micro stroke she suffered back in November, she can quote from *Jane Eyre* in different languages.

"Yeah, yeah," Bertrand says, "we're all very impressed."

Bertrand pauses to pull a bag of dried goji berries from his shirt pocket. He claims these Himalayan gems are the reason he's staved off cancer and most other chronic ailments. As usual, he offers the bag to everyone, and as usual, everyone declines. Those gojis taste like sweaty raisins, plus they stain your mouth. Bertrand holds up a wooden drumstick he must've stolen from the jam room and tings the side of the wheelchair for attention. A small and reluctant crowd of old folks shuffles toward the couch. Last night, Bertrand says, he took a Psilovan trip to the Cretaceous era, and the experience was too important for him to withhold. Apparently, whatever creature he'd been hadn't made it into textbooks—some kind of clumsy sloth-lizard.

"Where are your authenticating details?" Morty says, flexing his biceps and tracing the veins with his fingers.

"You think that pirate game's noisy?" Bertrand says. "Try walking within earshot of those stinking lizard-birds." He doesn't seem desperate for anyone to believe him, and I envy his indifference.

"How was the weather?" Morty says.

"Think *negative* breeze," Bertrand says, "plus humidity. Only the strongest can make it in that kind of heat."

It's easy to imagine how Bertrand might number himself among the strong, his silver-spun hairdo flashing like plumage among jungle foliage.

"Sounds like a drag," I say, tossing my absurd hair.

Bertrand claims that every passing day saw a more polished version of the dinosaurs, their shapes more balanced and practical, some feathered prototype always hauling itself from the muck. "But just imagine that goddamn *racket*," he says. "You can't, by God, know about that from looking at a fossil."

There's no denying it—he seems changed. The skin around his eyes is tighter, smoother. Bertrand says he'll be experimenting with larger doses of Psilovan. The world, he says, deserves to know more. He performs a kind of bow in his wheelchair, hot-dogs a quick 360, and coasts toward the jam room. The staff doctors always find a way to reward top responders, so it'll be more ritzy wheelchairs, better booze, maybe even pool privileges for Bertrand. He gets big-budget spirit quests while I get bad blood pressure and Barbie hair. It's rumored that he was a commercial pilot before he came to the Pines. No doubt he's used to calling the shots.

"Don't sleep with him anymore," I tell The Suze. "You, either," I tell Morty, just for good measure.

They nod because they're my best friends and they have to, but in time they'll also understand. Bertrand shouldn't get to swim backward in time while the rest of us drown.

My stiff, yet adequate, bed sits in perfect view of a much-envied window. The curtains drop at sundown—it's Pines policy. I sleep soundly, but many of us get animated at nightfall. Every evening we endure the irregular squeaking of bedframes set beneath a chorus of moans that echoes up and down the halls.

Despite all the Psilovan in my system, I dream of squirrels. Even in dream form they're uninteresting. They stand around looking cute and grinding away at windfall nuts. That's it.

I wake to Morty's weight on the mattress. He's lying on his side, smiling at me and doing this very appealing flex-pose so that he becomes a paler version of my dead husband.

"Why the sudden interest?" I say.

"Now that I'm not allowed to screw Bertrand," he says, jiggling the bed, "I can't seem to fall asleep."

"Very funny."

Dark as it is, I can tell he's staring at my hair.

"You never wanted me when I had old-lady hair," I say.

"You never wanted me when I had bony arms," he says, stifling a yawn. I catch a momentary whiff of jungle juice. "Anyway, it's not true. You forgetting the time they caught us on top of the pinball machine?"

I tell him I remember—a lie.

"You prefer me this way," I say, dragging two fingers over his forearms, opening his shirt collar to touch the surgical scar that splits his breastbone. "You dream about dinosaurs. You dream about a platinum blond half a century younger than me."

"I don't dream about dinosaurs," he says, "because I'm not eight years old. And to tell you the truth, I don't know what kind of hair people have in my dreams. Maybe none at all."

That's all I need to hear. I climb aboard Morty and we, too, join the chorus of moans and mattress noises, and we're probably making more commotion than necessary, but that's the way with things at the Pines. After a few minutes, The Suze adds her weight to the mattress, which, if you ask me, is kind of an imposition.

I'm on a commercial flight from Brooklyn to Manhattan. Crowded seats, wailing babies, the whole circus. Hours and hours at cruising altitude. The flight attendants don't appear and don't appear. Our watch dials spin.

Better than squirrels but far from prehistoric.

Encouraged by Bertrand's success, our doctors work with Psilovan reps to increase dosage for all residents. More folks report vivid experiences that sound more like time travel than dreams, though no one reports going as far back as Bertrand. For our cooperation, we're rewarded with long banquet tables of cherrywood bacon, designer apples, champagne grapes, sandwiches of smoked salmon with thick slices of purple tomato.

After my post-lunch nap, I find Bertrand parked in front of the couch with Morty and The Suze, controller in hand. Bertrand was always bad at games—the pirate character appears to be walking in circles—and yet, he's speaking to the in-game pirate crew with great passion.

"Where did you go to *school?*" Bertrand keeps asking. "Ever heard of Eratosthenes? What about Archimedes?"

Apparently Bertrand doesn't play to younger audiences as well as Morty does. The members of his pirate crew take turns dropping their pants to moon him.

"Young man—," Bertrand says, "young man—"

More and more electronic butt cheeks appear.

"Can't believe they programmed that into the game," I say.

"¿Crees que soy un autómata?" says The Suze in a child's voice. "¿Una máquina sin sentimientos?" Fluorescent lighting gives her head a look of terminal electrocution.

"I think she means that they found a hack," Morty says.

The pirate kids take turns describing sex with Bertrand's mother in painstaking detail. Bertrand nudges his wheelchair forward and powers off the system. He stares at us, but really he's staring past us.

"They're convinced that it's *flat.*" He holds one flattened hand aloft. "They claim that all NASA footage is doctored. Hell, they think everything's doctored."

"You can't just preach at them," I say. "You've got to *listen.* You've got to be patient, like Morty."

"I always knew I'd end up disapproving of the youth," Bertrand says, sliding from couch to wheelchair. "But I thought it'd be for good reasons. Sexual politics, maybe, or facial tattoos. These kids have turned their backs on the Enlightenment writ large. Forget teaching them about the Cretaceous. They don't even believe in the Holocene."

"I mean, can anyone actually prove that it's round?" says The Suze. She uses her pinkie finger to stir a glass of jungle juice. "Either way, it's a leap of faith."

"But I've *seen* it," Bertrand says. "Even from the cockpit of a 747 you can see curvature. And thanks to Psilovan, I've seen the Earth from the moon. It's every bit as round as those."

Bertrand points at an onscreen stash of perfectly round cannonballs. Even I can't help feeling a little sorry for him. Unindulged, unheard, the wounded Psilovan champion wheels himself very slowly to the jam room, where he works up the slowest, most depressing drum solo the world has ever heard. Morty gives me a huge wink as he leafs through his lecture notes, contemplating, maybe, which scholastic battle he'd like to wage in Bertrand's stead.

When The Suze rises from the couch, I grab her by the arm and ask where she's going.

"He's in bad shape, Glenda. I'll just bring him a drink, that's all."

"No pity sex," I remind her.

Meanwhile, our neglected pirate hero has wandered into her own campfire and ignited. She waves her hands and yips to capture our attention.

I'm an antelope with a hard-on that won't quit, then I'm a flying fox, then I'm a Tasmanian tiger among a pack of like animals, our noses tuned to the whereabouts of emu and any joeys bold enough to abandon the safety of their mother's pouch. A tapestry of scents displaces the visual world, the savanna breeze coded with layers of olfactory knowing, none of it unpleasant. Not cold data but warm-blooded narrative. Here a whiff of trouble at the watering hole, there a waft of infection that'll soon prove fatal, and there a shiny high note of colostrum. Emergence. The silent traffic of nutrients. Life renewed for another season.

By the second week of May, it's just me left on the couch. The others have little interest in socializing over games—not while there's still Psilovan to be swallowed. They leave bed only to take meals of roast duck and grilled swordfish. Otherwise, they're waiting to board the next dream train into the Psiloverse, where brighter visions await.

There are reports of every stripe. Nancy Hexum says she knows exactly where to find Jean Lafitte's buried treasure, and all she needs is a ride to Texas and a powerboat with an onboard toilet. Pour him a halfway decent Bloody Mary and Drake Schlusser will tell you exactly which island Amelia Earhart washed up on. Pour him another and he'll describe the nine-pound coconut crabs that trailed her blood and picked her meat from the bones. And then there's Elsie Pasillas, who swears The Suze has been making Bertrand's bedsprings sing all night long.

I walk our pirate hero to the center of an island that looks like all the other islands we've explored. No use denying it—Bertrand and Psilovan have ruined whatever joy I might've taken in this. You can't taste the salt on your lips or the chafe of sand against your heels.

There are pixels on the moon and there's redundancy among the waves. While I'm puttering the islands, a Pines orderly drops off a fresh plate: little purple tomatoes, ruby-colored pomegranate seeds, and fresh avocado slices.

My pirate crew sits patiently beside the fire, their pinched little faces eager for the next lesson. No doubt they're waiting for Morty. With much reluctance, I take up the headset mic.

"You're wasting your time," I tell them. "Nothing in here but smoke and mirrors."

Their animated faces turn toward one another as if to confirm a long-suspected point.

"So what should we do?" asks a pirate with purple hair.

"Stop focusing on the screen. Start looking for the projector."

"The fuck is she talking about?" one of them mutters.

"We want the guy who bullshits about moon dust," says another.

I eat some tomato, then some avocado. The young pirates quickly grow bored and blip out of existence. No wonder I never get visitors—I must be a terrible grandmother. But where is it that these computerized shapes go when someone like Bertrand throws the off switch? Does ghost data linger in the shallows? What does it mean that Psilovan dreams are so much more concrete than anything we've experienced on this couch?

I'm an impossibly large, ill-tempered bear, the likes of which I've never seen in *National Geographic*. For several days I trail a young boy who wanders each day to the outskirts of his small village. Inuit? That's not a word that they use. I finally cut him off as he saunters back from an iced-over lake with a trio of fish strung together on a gut line. I stand on my hind feet to terrify him. I show my teeth. Then I maul the kid while he screams for help. I savor the iron of his blood, the salt. His voice pitches up several octaves as I tear into deeper, better-tasting layers. It's deeply disappointing when my teeth finally strike bone. He's just a young kid, but meaty—a little bodybuilder. Nothing has ever felt so correct, so proper. For the first time ever, I belong in my skin.

In my righteousness, I don't notice the boy's father—a sly old trickster. While I'm lapping at various layers and testing my bear strength, he pikes me through the lung. I die without haste at his feet as he curses and wails at the sky. The last thing I see is that string of fish, the eyes already smoky. The father and mother will be eating those fish, but there'll be an empty spot by their fire.

By June we won't leave our beds, won't take visitors. It's all Psilovan, all the time. Sons, daughters, and grandchildren show up to visit or use the weight room and are turned away. Even the judgment-free sex has lost some of its steam. Why rely on your own feeble body when you can experience carnal joy as someone else, or even some*thing* else? Instead of watching soap operas, most of us now live them.

Between handfuls of goji berry, Bertrand speaks of a "prerotic" time before sexual union was even a remote possibility. Today, he's agreed to an interview with a lower-tier TV news team. He's seated before the couch in his wheelchair, and of course the crew wants me planted beside him, along with The Suze and Morty. The crew guys spin the couch around backward so it's no longer facing the TV. We non-Bertrand couch-sitters aren't supposed to do or say anything— we're more like geriatric window dressing, or maybe we're there to show Bertrand's superiority to the average Psilovan user. He rattles off a lot of big talk about the beauty of a black hole's accretion disk when you finally see it face to face. He confirms that it's no violent process when you're drawn in—it's more like stepping into a slow-moving river.

"And what's it like to join the singularity?" says the interviewer.

"What's it *like?*" Bertrand says. "Well, it's like—in fact, it's *a lot* like …." His hands carve at the air, desperate to establish a concrete shape of some kind, but I can tell from the sweat spots on his forehead that he's a goner. For the first time in a long time, Bertrand looks like what he is: an old man straddling the postcard-thin division between his golden years and senility. He tries to start over but can only sputter nonsense and swat at empty space. Finally, the interviewer lady gives his hand a patronizing squeeze and says they'll come back another time. Long after they've packed up their cameras and mics, Bertrand sits among us, upbraiding himself.

"*Ridiculous*," he says. "Just imagine how much knowledge I've cost them."

"I could've talked about being a bear," I say. "I wouldn't have choked."

"I could've told them where to find life on Mars," says The Suze.

"None of that matters," Bertrand says. "You're not engaging the big questions."

"Neither are you, apparently," Morty says. He lifts himself from the couch and uses his powerful arms to spin it back around while The Suze and I are still seated. Now that we've got our backs to Bertrand, Morty moves the TV back into place and fires up the game machine, maybe just for old times' sake.

"But why should I choke?" Bertrand says. "I never choke."

"All that Hawking radiation must've fried your brain," Morty says.

It's Morty's turn to play the game, but he keeps mashing all the wrong buttons, and I must've forgotten how long the game takes to load. It's a lot of waiting. It's a lot of sitting beside The Suze and knowing she's got all the integrity of a pubic louse.

"Aren't you going to put on the headset?" she says.

"You first," I say. "Your tongue's goji-orange and you're covered in old-man stink. Maybe you can tell the children what it's like to have no soul."

For a moment, The Suze ignores me and tries to knit, but before long she dumps the whole project at our feet.

"Non sono un angelo e non lo sarò fino alla morte," she says. Then she drains the rest of her jungle juice and stomps off toward her room.

"They're not really coming back for another interview," Bertrand says. "Are they?"

I'd forgotten that he's still parked behind us.

"The cameras are off," Morty says, spinning around to see Bertrand. "Tell us, what *is* it like to join a singularity?"

Overjoyed, Bertrand runs a blade-like hand through his hair. He starts to speak but gets nowhere. Again, he resorts to wild gesticulations and apelike grunts. Morty and I can only nod and offer apologetic smiles. Whatever's happening to Bertrand is more dangerous than common stage fright. Rejuvenation is one thing, but we're cornering a beast that we don't understand. The human timeline has always run left to right. It's supposed to be consistent. We've plotted a slow rightward course only to hook hard and sloppy to the left.

Later that night, I sneak to Morty's room, slide beneath his covers, and run my fingertips over his arms, but he only snores harder. I move my hand to his thigh and start working my way upward, but he pushes me away before I reach the good parts.

"Who you dreaming of?" I whisper.

"Skin mites," he says with a bawdy wink. "I'm crossing the Bering Strait on the back of a Paleo-Indian."

"In that case," I say, flipping my bangs fetchingly, "lie back and relax. Glenda's here to save you from bug dreams."

I reach for Morty's inner thigh, but he rolls over.

"Not right now," he says.

With his back turned, he gathers the covers into a kind of cocoon, reminding me once more of my dead husband. I'm almost sure he was my husband.

Two days later, orderlies find Morty dead beneath his covers, his face taut with a goonish smile. No one but Bertrand volunteers any words of kindness at his service—they're all too eager to get back to sleep. After the service, I try to stress the dangers of Psilovan, but no one listens.

The autopsy report takes three days because Morty's such a low priority. The coroner mentions the triple bypass Morty had back in the nineties, but he also describes left ventricular hypertrophy consistent with steroid abuse. The Psilovan seems to have played no role in his death, though it probably contributed to the joyous manner in which he departed. It was the muscle supplements that finally put the squeeze on him.

Even so, I begin to flush my daily Psilovan dosages down the toilet. Meanwhile, Bertrand turns the Pines' common room into a makeshift temple. He gets his followers to drag in yoga mats and they all lie on their backs in a pile, Bertrand situated at the core with a heaping bowl of gojis for the whole clan, who call themselves Psilonauts. I complain to the orderlies, but they don't care, and several end up taking their own doses of Psilovan, eating gojis, and joining the pile. I sit at the perimeter and listen to accounts of early life on the planet. Residents describe how it feels to exist as a giant anteater, as a colony of sea salps, as a tardigrade nested inside a pulsar that rotates at 38,000 rpm.

With each passing day, the Psilonauts have less and less need of Bertrand. Some have begun to develop better, more powerful forms of meditation that ferry them deeper yet into the past—to a time before stars, before galaxies, before Morty and Psilovan. It's the followers who figure out that the drug works best when everyone's arms and legs are touching just slightly. The deeper back into time they venture, the more their speech turns into coughs and grunts.

☾

The squirrels in my dreams seem disappointed to see me. I toss peanuts by the pound, but they won't eat.

It takes the Psilonauts three intensive days to reach the cosmic singularity. Afterward, they all claim to have experienced it, but no one will describe what it's like.

"You're all full of beans and wind," I say. "If you'd really experienced it, you'd say it feels like the moment before you're shot from a cannon. You'd say it feels like the instant before you light the fuse to a pile of TNT."

"No cannon," says The Suze. She's lying on her back, grunting like the others, orange teeth exposed. "You're not even really *there*. Hard to explain."

"What about Morty?" I say. "I guess he's not included in your little Psilovan world."

"I remembered," says The Suze in her *Jane Eyre* voice. "Real world wide. Varied field of hopes and fears. Sensations and excitements and so on."

"What's wrong, smart-ass?" I say. "Can't you quote that one in Cantonese?"

She offers a noncommittal grunt.

"Join," Bertrand says. "Ease your Morty pain." He seems to be crying, old Bertrand, as he stuffs another handful of berries into his mouth. As if he actually cared for Morty, as if he feels anything at all. I've known plenty of liars, but either Bertrand's operating on a different frequency or he actually means it this time.

"You're all chickenshit," I say. "You can't escape death by hiding out in a time before life."

"No escape," Bertrand says. "Only experience. Only *witness*."

I stomp to the kitchen and mix up the biggest cup of jungle juice you've ever seen. I drink all I can stomach and carry the rest to the jam room, where I hammer the drums as loudly as I can for as long as I can. When I pry open the door, a few Psilonauts on the perimeter give me eat-shit looks, but most are still deeply entranced—all of them waiting to be born, waiting to explode.

☾

I lie on Morty's bed and wallow in the salty smell of him. But when I dream, I dream of Bertrand. He's riding a wheelchair made of my hair, and for a moment he's finally able to speak easily about a time before everything blew into fragments. As he pontificates, he wheels back and forth, and my hair is forever coming unbound, so that he keeps wiping loose strands from his lap. He says that from where he's sitting there isn't even the idea of singularity because there hasn't yet been more than one of anything. It's a time before matter, before ideas, before *time*. There's no way to observe anything from where he's sitting. You can't even articulate your experience because there's no *you*. You can only *be*, and with that utterance, Bertrand seems to run out of words. He plucks a gray hair from his mouth. It's one of my mine—one of my originals.

Bertrand beckons me to join him in the hairy wheelchair. He wants to get me back there—back to the union. It's what we all want. It's what we've been wanting all our lives, and all the screwing and drinking and gaming have been diversions against the pain of waiting.

I wake at sunrise and snatch up a handful of the Psilovan I haven't been taking. For a long time, I stare into my nightstand mirror and consider swallowing. I watch the woman in the glass and muss her bangs, wondering just who the hell she's supposed to be. The war against Psilovan is a strange one to take up. Even I can't deny that the stuff makes for a pretty good escape. Better than jungle juice, and far better than any of the other supplements we've tried.

I hold the white plastic Psilovan bottle under the vanity light. The company's emblem features a cartoon Eden, tree boughs loaded with glossy red apples. A nice image, but Morty once lectured to the pirate crew about the fact that apples are a relatively new cultivation that never would've existed in the holy garden. They started in Peru as hard, sour little rocks, and only time and experimentation turned them into fruit worth coveting. Even my beloved tomatoes were thought to be poisonous throughout the Middle Ages. Not everything gets better when you push the timeline to the left.

Maybe I don't want to feel better. I want to complain about undercooked bacon and die like I'm supposed to. I want Bertrand to bicker with me and reveal something so personal he'll seem human enough to befriend or maybe even seduce.

☾

I can't make time run backward in the jam room, but I can make it swing on the edge of a cymbal, on the rim of the snare, in the belly of the bass drum.

Bertrand and his dream-lost followers lie on their backs, their arms and legs touching while the game console collects dust. I sit at the perimeter and swallow back jungle juice and frustration. I try to see the Psilonauts as they are. They are not pathetic. They are not the most decrepit yoga troupe of all time. They are me and I am them.

But we are not one—we are not. We are mismatched blocks sifted from a million different toy chests, and there's no getting back to whole.

No one notices when I join the pile to feel the warmth. No one sees me scoop up a handful of gojis and chew. No mystic revelations— they taste as bad as I remember. But I am patient. I am waiting for Psilonauts to return from distant timelines and infinitely compressed states of existence. One day they'll understand that creation is only the tip of a very long arrow. Psilovan might allow you to observe neutrino stars and alien life, but it's like experiencing Jamaica from the balcony of a cruise ship.

Every few hours, someone shuffles off to the restroom with half-closed eyes and a zombie-like gait and returns without speaking. The Psilonauts survive on gojis, and they require very little water. I have an important job here at the Pines: I watch over the pile. I wait to drag everyone's timeline back to the other side.

MELISSA STUDDARD

At Fifty, I Became a Three-Time Finalist for the Darwin Awards

Crashed my car into myself and climbed out of both,
shaking the world off like a short, between-tasks sleep.
Held the year in my mouth like a monk meditating
on a raisin, felt all the ridges and bulges of it, felt
indentations moist with my saliva. Tested
god by walking across a wet floor and cracking my head
on a countertop, tested my body by diving
into a bacteria-laden no-swim-advisory ocean
and cutting my shoulder on a shell. Then,
ate the raisin—how tender,
how merciless, the acrid sweetness, like
fearing death
as death smiles at you
from between your teeth.

MELISSA STUDDARD

Then, sometimes, my body forgets
it's not a peacock

and struts through narrow streets fanning its extravagant
plumage. When I remind it to be human,
it laughs and winks its hundred eyes.
My fortune cookie says to marry the next
person I kiss, but I want to have my fortune and eat it too,
so I kiss an entire shopping mall full of people.
The truth is I love both winter and summer, fall
and the excess pinks of spring. I hoard
snow boots and umbrellas,
surfboards and the gardens that bloom inside my head.
All the trench coats I own, I've embezzled
from myself. When fog
steals the things I love, I hunt down
its opaque ass, kiss it on the lips,
and make love to it
before taking my things back
inside a crushed-velvet bag
that I am also in love with. When waves
lick up the sandals I adore, I dive in and swim until
I'm a tangle of seaweed and froth,
and then I let the sea make love to me,
which doesn't ever feel like cheating
though I'm in love with two men,
one woman, and a non-binary
acquaintance. And sadly,
that makes me less
gay than I thought,

but I'm happy to still be on the continuum.
There can never be too many falling stars,
too many starlings, or blueberries, or foxes.
You must agree. Everyone loves foxes!
Until it's spring and lambs romp through fields
eating clover and forbs. Oh don't make me choose.
I want to take them all home. So, I'll just
move my furniture to the field instead, and god
will promise that it'll never rain again anywhere I stand.
I'll buy all the lambs little
hats for our housewarming party. I'll buy the foxes
diamond necklaces
and mirrors to distract them from the lambs. O,
my little rainbows! My little strange pets! If the fawn
comes leaping over the heartberry bush,
can the love song be far behind?

RENEE EMERSON

A Parable of Memory

Now that all the doors are off the hinges,
all the window glass removed, strangers
pass by and take what they please. Yesterday
an old woman slipped the way your hair felt
into her purse. Last week a young girl carried off
the scent of your skin to play with, let it drop
by the road later. It was unsalvageable.
Sometimes a group will work together
to lift the large and heavy pieces,
like the sound of your voice, scraping
the legs on the hardwood, nicking the paint.
More often I open a drawer to find
small things, like eyelash length and curve
of the upper lip, missing, pocketed. Over time
I've decided the people are not cruel, just blind
to my sitting here, watching. I speak a language
where the only part they understand is
smile and nod; everything else I say sounds
like the sunken spot on a settled grave.
One day I fear there will be nothing left,
but what I carry myself, on my body and in it.

E.J. MORRIS

Their Voices Are in Their Legs

Instead of going home after your time in jail you head to the small cabin on the back of your property. It might not be yours anymore at all. Your husband wasn't there to pick you up. You imagined it could've been your son that pulled up—he should have his learner's by now. Neither of them had been to see you in a while, so you wouldn't really know.

You thumb your way there. A lady picks you up in a Buick. There's an empty car seat in the back and she keeps tucking her hair behind her ear. She definitely thinks you're hurt or homeless. She mentions a women's shelter later in the ride and you know she's just trying to help another woman out, but she wouldn't go further than that. She's safe in her Buick with her suncatcher swooping back and forth from her rearview mirror. She's definitely someone who keeps time.

A song you don't know is on the radio, thrumming low. You ask if you can turn it up and she nods, a little surprised, and you both reach for the dial. She backs off first. You turn it up a little higher than normal volume. You think about how your son asked to dress like a smoke detector the Halloween before you went to jail. How you'd wanted to encourage something more creative and juvenile, but your husband shook his head and said he should be whatever he wants.

The lady drops you at the edge of your property. You think about Timmy, the contractor your husband hired to fix the back porch, and how you'd fucked him in the kitchen a few times, left a chair overturned once and your underwear under the table another time so your husband would put two and two together.

☾

The cabin looks stagnant and you try not to compare it to anything. You grab the spare key from under the lip of the porch and wonder why your husband hasn't been renting it. The inside smells frightened, and there are crayon drawings on the wall from when your son was the age you remember him as.

You also remember some dancing. How your husband would turn on the radio in the main house and spin you. One time you stubbed your toe so hard it bled in your sock. You'd dance and twirl and press your fingers into his ears, lightly, so he couldn't hear anything else; his only sensation would be holding you. You'd twirl until you knocked a lamp over, bumped a picture off the wall, dance, twirl, until it wasn't dancing anymore and both your hands knotted into fists.

You rifle through some drawers in the cabin, find a butter knife, stained coasters, some of your son's old Play-Doh. You lay on the floor, try to knead the dryness out of it, listen to the crickets, the birds outside. Your son's third-grade science textbook said crickets have an incredible ear for music. You drum your fingers to a beat on the floor and listen for them to pick it up. You hum a few lines of a song and wish harder than you've wished for anything in a while that they could sing it back, that you could learn what a cricket's voice sounds like, but then you remember their voices are in their legs.

You also read they are high in calcium. You eat a dead one from the floor. It tastes more complicated than you would've thought, like eggshells and fingernails, the stitches in your gums after an incisor removal, maybe mulch. You think about the word "incarceration," how it sounds like a tongue licking a shard of glass.

You look in the pantry and some coffee mugs are in there, mouths agape at you. You shut it.

You walk out and head for the main house and pretend it's a normal night like eight years ago, that you're just checking on your hydrangeas. When you get close you hear a man's voice, but realize it's your son and that his voice has thickened even without you there. He's throwing a

Frisbee to the dog, that damn dog you'd let outside all the time and it'd always come back wet. Your son still has some baby fat on his frame and he's wearing a black T-shirt. It looks like his nails are also painted black. He rubs the dog's head and flicks the Frisbee. You don't care to look for your husband. He doesn't seem that important right now.

You can't see the scar on your son's forearm from this distance, nor do you look for it, but you know it's there. It was still puckered and scabby when you went away. You rarely think about the woman you T-boned. You got a good look at her face that day, but your vision was blurry because you were so blitzed. Mostly you just think about your son's forearm and the way he'd reached for you after the crash, before he was old enough to realize you'd done that to him.

To distract yourself from the stranger in the yard you walk the mile to the closest convenience store. You ask the cashier what aisle the cereal is on and she says a single number. You wish she'd said something like 349, and that her lips would've started to melt down her chin. Because this can't be real life. But no, you nod as she eyes you, then head in that direction. You avoid stepping on any cracks in the tiles because you've decided you'll be superstitious with your freedom.

There's a man in that aisle and you think he looks like your husband for a second, but certainly not. He's balder, shorter, and definitely older. You ask him if he's alright and he looks at you funny. After a beat, he asks you the same thing. Instead of answering, you pick up a cereal box, give it a shake.

Meagan Cass

Your Amphibious Ex

after Calvino

That summer our houses wavered with heat. Between writing sessions, I researched lakes, creeks, swimming holes. You left your studio early, drove us out of the city, and I told you about rivers that flow over igneous rock, how they can't expand, instead carve shut-ins. What a horrible name, we agreed when we got there. They were beautiful, the rivulets shining, the granite a salmon pink.

You swam in your T-shirt, complaining that my cooking had fattened you up. I was trying to feel hot in a bikini from the Target juniors' section, the top too tight. We must have looked lovely. We found tiny pools, brief depths. You said, "It's good to take a break. Thank you." In the shallows I turned on my stomach, performed a delicate breast stroke. Who knew I could suspend myself in so little?

You hadn't decided if you loved me yet. It had to do with your father, you'd said, how he taught you to crush sadness in your fists like sparrows. It had to do with your sister, the brilliant painter, how she'd crashed her car before showing you the right kind of life, how it felt like you were the ghost. My friends nodded when I explained your distance, gave each other looks over my head.

At the river we were alone. Romantic, I was telling myself. We basked in waterfalls, made out, slid down chutes that reminded us of our teenage water parks. The cannonball was always my favorite slide. A pitch-black tube, a dark spiraling, a rush into blue air. I loved the managed risk of it, the performance of bravery. How I could forget my embarrassing body, my loneliness, my inadequacies at boy-girl parties. Later I would try other things: bulimia, a curriculum vitae, love that had to be earned.

You and your sister floated in manufactured waves, talked Sherman and Gustin. Soon you'd go to the famous school where they crown artists. Then, you planned, New York, scrape by until the right gallery called. Instead you came back to this city that knows you too well, this city that remembers what you couldn't keep from happening, this city where you hadn't meant to meet me, a writer with her own gilded ornaments, your siren wearing too many mirrors. Any year now, you promised, you were moving.

The sun was thick on the water. I could feel it burning my chest and shoulders, memorializing the bikini I wouldn't wear again. You appeared above me on the goldenrod banks, waving but not beckoning. I remember dipping back under, rubbing my belly on the pebbles and sand. A rightness settled in my gut. It was new and also older, before jean sizes and boy-girl relationships, before degrees and awards, all the ways I tried to crown myself, to feel landed.

The next weekend, we biked a trail that belted the whole state. I meant to keep up, to keep track of our miles—you wanted more rigorous exercise—but I couldn't forget that pleasure. You rode ahead, a glint of silver and hunched shoulders, and I slipped into another river. It was a rich gray-green, quieter, slower. A lazy river, the waterpark would have called it.

The way you called what I needed settling down. But what I'd imagined was diving down, then surfacing, then going deeper, a looping motion around each other, into ourselves, into our city, and outward in a hundred directions, then returning. Slow and fast and intimate. A gorgeous risk.

The way existing in a river is hard but luscious work. I could feel my body losing certain capabilities, gaining others. My legs—your best feature, you'd said when I wore dresses for your openings—shortened and widened, became more like paddles. Parts of my heart I'd erased—I don't need you to get sentimental, I'd insisted—began to regenerate. Soon I was crying. My skin, which you'd already told me was too thin—an artist must be a masochist—grew thinner so I could breathe.

The sun sunk into our modest downtown. I was and wasn't afraid. Somewhere you were racing higher, shedding the bulk my love had added. Eventually you would look behind you at my absence. What I mean is we were still together but I was alone in that water.

PAT DANEMAN

Dinner Party With Married Friends

The smell they bring with them to dinner is that of couples—
soap and makeup, shaving foam, and faint perfume.
They arrive together, leave together, in between don't stray
far from each other even if I seat them at opposite ends of my table.

In and out of each other's conversations, answering questions
half-asked, she the nouns and verbs, he the adjectives
and illuminating phrases. In their fresh-pressed clothes,
their black-and-silver hair, they carry the sharpness

and softness of years. They pass bread and pour wine
and wear the jewelry and sweaters they gave each other
last Christmas, thirty birthdays ago. They will get home
in time for the news, then on into flannel and nightlights

and pills, the possibility of sex. Once they didn't know
each other well, but agreed to make the climb—so here they are
tonight, in candlelight, flames ticking down into beads
of white wax that will harden in an instant on the linen cloth.

NANCY CHEN LONG

Another, Bolder Paradise

after Décalcomanie *by René Magritte*

I have studied the painting for years, this faceless man
staring out of a window. The dark mass of him
blots my ability to see

much more than cotton-ball clouds bobbing in a perky blue sky.
He stands next to another version of himself—
a vanished version,

the empty shape of him excised from the window's mahogany curtains.
In both versions, there is his hat. Nothing too fancy,
a derby to elongate the oval of his head.

The flare of the hat's brim draws attention to the symmetry of his ears.
A woman once told me that beauty is nothing
if not symmetry, and I wonder if the man is waiting

for a miraculous message or divine sign,
a beautiful psychopomp to show him the way out
of what I've come to believe is the monotony

of his endlessly perfect days.
A message once arrived to me in a dream, an amber bottle
stuffed with onionskin paper. Nineteen pieces,

each fragment embossed with the sun
and the word *élan*. Not knowing what the word meant,
I tossed the bottle back.

Watched it bob away. But it kept returning to me
like a stray dog.
Another time I thought a message had dropped

from the claws of a crested canary.
I scrambled over hollyhocks and milkweed
to retrieve the dropped napkin—

as if mystics were speaking to me
through a bird as brilliant as the color of happiness,
a songbird that we use to predict death—

stamped with a slice of golden honeycomb
reminiscent of the sun.
When I was a teenager, my father let it slip,

he had been waiting his whole life—
which would mean his children's whole lives as well—
for just one chance at happiness,

his mind always fluttering in some other place
in that future happiness.
Strange, isn't it?

How our bodies can be here,
even when we are not.
My father was ill for years. Before he died,

he told me he was the happiest he had ever been.
Strange, isn't it? How, when we die,
we leave a hole

in the exact shape of our body,
the dark and serious silhouette of ourselves.
My father's hole is the same as the one in the painting:

a swathe of sunny clouds
that divert attention away from the present
storm looming low on the horizon.

A man stands, forever, his back to me.
Faceless and waiting.
I have studied him for years.

(Title is a phrase from "I Have Lived My Whole Life in a Painting Called Paradise" by Diane Seuss.)

NANCY CHEN LONG

Instrument

after Judith Slaying Holofernes *by Artemisia Gentileschi*

A wolf crept into the basement
of my desire. Our howls

for revenge gave way to courage—
I needed to hide no more.

Visibility became my cloak.
Every court is an altar

to the powerful. I rained contempt.
His head in my tortured hands

was too sweet a temptation. Enemy
made small by his own power.

His mistake was thinking
that, if he stripped me to nothing,

I would be weak.

PAIGE POWELL

Infant RealLife

Emmy would really have liked to think there was a God—she would've *loved* to believe it—but sometimes catastrophes happened, like when Ms. Roberts broke her hip and left on medical leave and Coach Mortenberry took over Emmy's child development class, and she knew it was like her mother said, that "It's just us and science out here." The point wasn't that she cared about child development; the point was that, well, her GPA wasn't *necessarily* an indication of her intelligence, and Ms. Roberts, while incompetent, didn't seem to care about Emmy's so-called "behavioral problems," and Emmy was sure she could get out of the class with an A. She could not say the same about Mortenberry's class.

Emmy kept a running list of all the ways Coach Mortenberry was an absolute fuckface:

> 1. He mumbled the word "menstruation" like he was say-ing "gangbang" or "fisting."
> 2. He seemed to be on the abstinence Kool-Aid, and while Emmy could sympathize with having to conform to a fascist core curriculum, she couldn't forgive that he actually seemed to *believe* it.
> 3. Mortenberry's wife was clearly a million times hotter than he was, but Emmy very much got the sense he didn't *know* that.
> 4. He smelled like a dead dog in a sack. Emmy could have forgiven this but see point re.: fuckface.

Emmy had decided to be on her best behavior because after she'd written "Let Them Eat Pussy" on a "Safe Sex" quiz where all the answers were meant to be "Don't have any," the principal had given her three weeks of detention. It was likely she would've been suspended had not both the principal and Mortenberry liked Emmy's mother, who worked as a cafeteria lady.

When they drove home that day, Emmy's mom looked very tired. "You're right, pookie," she said. "It's not that you aren't right. But you've gotta get through the next two years. When you have your college degree you can destroy all the fuckfaces you want."

And so, the next Monday Emmy went to the gym where her child development class now met, because apparently Coach Mortenberry wasn't so much a human man as a poltergeist haunting a high school basketball court. She threw her bag down on the bleachers. She could brainstorm, at least, while he was talking—maybe notes for a story she was working on.

"All right, kiddos. That's bell." Coach Mortenberry clapped his meaty hands. "Listen up. We got a big project coming your way."

He pulled down a screen on the wall behind him, covering a glittery pep rally sign this bitchy student government nerd had made, and plugged his laptop into a projector cart he'd probably borrowed from the AV club. Emmy saw pink bubble letters spelling HEALTHYIMPACT CARES: TEEN PREGNANCY PREVENTION.

"Having a baby? At *your* age?" The video switched to a concerned-looking middle-aged woman shaking her head. She cheerfully walked the class through the statistics: HIV, STDs, the hubris of assuming condoms would do anything at all. "We at HealthyImpact believe that firsthand knowledge of the consequences of premarital sex is the most effective deterrent to teen pregnancy. That's why founder Dr. Michael Jocasta invented Infant RealLife." The screen panned to a baby doll in a pink onesie.

"Oh, God," Emmy said. "It's one of those things." Mortenberry shushed her.

"Infant RealLife does everything a real baby would: eat, cry, even use the restroom! Your instructor will evaluate your care aptitude using our patented sensor technology. And this"—the woman held up a digital wristband—"means nobody else but *you* can take care of your child."

When the video ended, Emmy raised her hand. Coach Mortenberry took a deep breath and said, "Yes, Emmy?"

"Respectfully, what the hell?"

"Language. We talked about this."

"You're putting us on baby house arrest?"

A guy sitting near the front perked up. "Yeah, what? We have a game this weekend."

"All y'all playing the game tomorrow have an alternate essay assignment. For everyone else, this project is worth 20 percent of your grade, and I've already emailed your parents letting them know."

Emmy raised her hand again. "I'll take the essay option, please."

"Too bad, so sad. Any more questions?"

"I'm actually the result of teen pregnancy, so, pretty sure that qualifies me for an exemption."

"Well, the—like the lady said, teen pregnancy is an epidemic. I want y'all to know there are consequences of your actions."

"Mom had me when she was sixteen—you're saying I should never have been born?"

"No, Emmy, that's not—." He shook his head in an abrupt jerk. "Moving on. Fellas, could I get some help?"

Some boys disappeared with Mortenberry into his office and emerged with car seats looped two to an arm, baby dolls nestled neatly inside them like Easter eggs.

"Come get 'em."

Emmy made sure to be at the front of the line. Mortenberry looked at her skeptically before cuffing her with a wristband and thrusting a car seat into her arms. "How come all the babies are white?"

"Emmy—"

"I'm just saying, the video showed *all kinds* of babies. Kind of weird that you just ordered white ones."

"I didn't—." It was hard not to feel a little triumphant as she watched a blotch spread across his stupid nose. "Nope. I'm done. Office. Now."

Fuck, Emmy thought. She hitched her bag onto her shoulder and grabbed her car seat, its unfamiliar weight dragging down the right side of her body.

The problem with being sent to the principal's office was that Emmy had to cut through the cafeteria to get there. She hoped her mother was in the back preparing lunches.

"Emmy?" But of course, Emmy's mother was bussing the tables, and she had a clear view of Emmy's approach. "What are you up to?"

"Taking my child out for a stroll." She turned the seat so her mother could see the baby's puckered lips and empty-eyed stare. "Why didn't you tell me?"

Her mother laughed. "I thought you'd try to get out of it."

"I did."

"Emmy."

"I have *plans* this weekend, Mom. I'm probably not even going to have kids anyway so what's the *point?*"

"The point is that you do it and you get a 100 and it raises your grade." Her mother shoved a pile of Styrofoam trays into the trash. "You didn't answer my question. Why aren't you in class?"

Emmy didn't say anything. She could've lied, but her mother would definitely find out, and then it would be even worse.

"Oh, pookie." Her mother stretched her arm behind her head— she had a habit of stretching when she needed to calm down. "We'll talk at home. Give Hartley my regards."

"OK." As she walked to the office, Emmy wondered why she couldn't seem to help herself.

The bell tinkled as she entered the front office. She waved at the secretary, who was really very nice, and made her way past to Hartley's office. On the wall was a poster: "Only *YOU* can make a difference in the world!" Underneath the lettering was a teddy bear pouring a cup of steaming tea. Emmy puzzled at this while she waited for Hartley to plop herself, breathless and harried, behind her desk.

"All right, Ms. Stewart, fill me in as to why you're here."

"Mortenberry sent me."

"Why?"

"I made a comment."

"Did you curse at him?"

"No. I mean, yeah. But that's not why he sent me. I guess I was being belligerent."

Hartley sighed, not unkindly. Emmy's mom always said Hartley looked so tired because she was actually doing her goddamn job. "You've got to quit pushing his buttons like that, Emmy."

"I'm trying, Mrs. Hartley."

"This is the fourth time you've been in my office this month."

"I come to school. I do my work. I'm not trying to be a problem."

Hartley punched at her keyboard, eyes scrolling over her computer screen. "I'm looking at your grades now," she said. "As and Bs except for that 79 in World History—I assume you're on top of that?" Emmy nodded. "And then Child Development. A *55*? I don't want to disparage any of our electives as *blow-offs*, but, Emmy, come on."

Emmy knew Hartley was being patient, so she attempted to explain her situation rationally. "I can't do work I don't respect."

"Your mom told me you were interested in applying to UT next year."

Emmy nodded, twirling the end of her ponytail.

"You know UT only accepts students in the top 8 percent of their class, yes?" Emmy felt a hot stone sink in her gut—she'd been told, but it hadn't registered, not really. "With your GPA, it's ... *unlikely*. But there are options. If you go to a UT sister school for a semester, for example, you can reapply for admission. But. I know your financial situation. You *need* scholarships, and with this class weighing you down, it's not going to look good. Do you understand?"

Emmy grabbed her face until she could feel her nails imprinting her cheeks. "I hate this class so much."

"There will be things in life you hate more." Her eyes flicked up to the industrial clock. "I'll let Coach Mortenberry know I reprimanded you. Go do some homework."

"Yes ma'am," Emmy said, and left.

The doll didn't cry until Emmy and her mother were driving home. Cry, maybe, was a charitable description: It sounded like a thousand grinding gears from hell. It sounded like the kid who sat in the back of her math class's shitty SoundCloud page. The sound filled the car to bursting. Emmy's mother veered into a pharmacy parking lot. Emmy rocked the doll and it didn't quiet. She clipped a new diaper onto its plastic ass and it continued to scream. She held up the bottle with the sensor to its mouth, and finally, it was quiet.

"Jesus, that's loud," Emmy's mother said.

"Like if you plugged an actual baby into an amphitheater."

"And it could go off all night?"

"You OK'd this. Not me."

With its clothes on, looked at askance, the doll could pass as real. Its soft, rubbery skin smelled like baby lotion. Someone had painted its face to look flushed, as if it had just woken up from a nap. She'd been given a yellow onesie for the doll to wear, so that you could not see its joints or the holes in its chest that broadcast its shrieking cry into the world. She was idly poking at its hard, glassy blue eye when the doll made a sudden, laughing coo. Emmy jumped.

Emmy's mother pulled into their complex. Inside, they both kicked off their shoes. Her mother sank into the couch. In the kitchen, Emmy took out leftover pizza from the refrigerator and nuked a few slices. She grabbed a Coke for herself and a glass of red wine for her mother.

"Thanks, pookie," her mother said. "Happy Friday."

"Cheers," Emmy said.

"Your reading at the library is tomorrow, right?"

Emmy had hoped her mother had forgotten about the library's Creative Writing Youth Reading. "Yeah. I mean, if I go."

"Oh, pookie, you should do it. I think it's really brave. Do you want me to go?"

"No, Mom. It's your day off. Chill."

"I want to. I do."

"We're already up each other's asses twenty-four hours a day," Emmy said. "This isn't really a *parents* kind of thing."

They settled into watching TV. Emmy could tell her mother's feelings were hurt, but she would rather be flayed alive than have her mother hear what she'd written. They leaned into each other, the TV droning as rich families debated which beach house to buy, when Emmy heard her mother snoring. Gently, she laid her mother's head on the couch pillow and went to her room, doll in tow.

Sometimes her mother made her tired. Her mother was unyielding in her love and dedication; she worked two jobs, the one at Emmy's high school and another as a rent-a-maid, and she had raised Emmy alone, with the exception of a few weekends a year when Emmy visited her father, since she'd squeezed out a baby at sixteen. Her life wasn't her own—it had been Emmy's, from the moment she was born. College wasn't in the stars for her mother, but it would be for Emmy. She'd read aloud to Emmy every night until she learned to read, had taken her to any free art, history, or science museum that she could, had always pushed her to try hard. Emmy was appreciative, but it wasn't like she'd asked to be born.

Now that Emmy had the night to herself, she opened her laptop and read what she'd written in the last few days. It was the longest story she'd ever written, and it needed to be good.

She wrote: *Kimberly had him. The Kiddie Killer. She'd have to go rogue on this one, the evidence wasn't there, but she knew it was him. She took the subway to his borough and waited in the dark alley beside the bodega. His apartment was overhead.*

And then she saw him. A weaselly little man—

The doll wailed with an intensity that seemed illogical, *way* louder than in the car, as if its little plastic limbs were being torn from their sockets. Needy little fucker. Emmy had almost forgotten it was there. She cradled it in her arms, swaying from side to side. She had the bizarre impulse to sing it a lullaby. "OK, asshole," she said. "The lady said you'd only go off two or three times a night. You've met your quota."

After a while, she suspected Mortenberry had given her a defective doll on purpose. Every time she settled herself in to write, the doll started wailing, and the sound felt like the tiniest needles inserted in her eyeballs.

Still, she kept writing.

She was outside his door. All Kimberly had thought about for months was catching him, and she'd found him. What if he'd changed? What if he'd turned into a good person? That made her job harder. But no, she thought. If he'd turned into a good person then good for him, but he still had a debt to pay.

It was so late, and she was so tired, that at first she could not understand that there was a voice coming from the corner of her room, and that the voice was saying, "I think it's brave of you."

Emmy sucked in her breath, her toes clenched under her quilt. She could hear her mother snoring. "What the hell?" she muttered.

"Reading that out loud. In front of everybody. Hard-hitting stuff."

Emmy edged herself out of bed, pulling the chain overhead. With the light on, her room looked exactly as it should, the same vanity and piles of dirty clothes and her childhood stuffed animals. She opened her closet door, but there was nothing there.

The voice made a little cough. "*She was outside his door.*" Emmy froze. She could hear where the voice was coming from; she looked at Infant RealLife. "*All Kimberly had thought about for months was catching him.*" She picked the doll up under its arms; she could feel the vibrations of the speaker beneath her palms. "*What if he'd changed? What if he'd turned into a good person?* Kind of amateur prose, but I think they'll figure it out."

"Stop." Emmy looked around, as if someone were playing a *hilarious* joke on her. "I don't under—how are you—"

"Look, I don't know how you need to explain this to yourself—psychosis, LSD in the water—but, hi. It's me. Your baby."

She wanted to be dreaming, even concussed, but she knew she wasn't.

"And if you even *try* to say, 'Oh hey, you guys! My baby doll can talk!,' well, good fucking luck, because not only will I not say a goddamn word but I'll also record in my system that you tried to shake me. They test for that, you know. And you'll fail."

Emmy dropped the doll on her bed. She wasn't in the habit of hallucinating. She cracked her bedroom door to see if anybody had snuck in—Mortenberry, maybe? No; he wasn't half clever enough to pull this off. It had to be something else. She started drafting an email:

> TO: jmortenberry@mihs.edu
> FROM: estewart99@mihs.edu
> SUBJECT: weird doll
> Hi, Coach Mortenberry. I just had a concern about my Infant RealLife. It's talking to me and it seems to know a lot about me. If you could just

She stopped typing. He'd think she'd gone batshit. Maybe she was batshit. She deleted the email. The doll had been silent for a while—long enough for Emmy to laugh. She'd made it all up. What a fucking nut job.

It was the writing. It put her in a weird frame of mind.

"Please," he cried. "Take me to jail. I'll do my time." But Kimberly kept her gun pointed at him. There was something exciting about the thought that she'd be the one to fix the pain that he'd caused. She knew she'd go down for this, but it didn't matter.

A shot to the head was too easy. She needed something more—.

The doll was crying. Emmy got up and snapped a diaper onto its ass. *Her,* she kept thinking, even though that was stupid, even though it was just a hunk of plastic. But its voice—it was a woman's. Deep, raspy, sarcastic as hell—she sounded like some comedian Emmy had seen on Netflix—but unmistakably a woman's voice.

But there hadn't *been* any voice.

"Let's dish," the doll said. "Let's talk *secrets*."

Emmy wanted to puke. "This isn't happening."

"Look, kiddo—I know you backwards and forwards. That's the second week in a row you've been wearing that bra. You figured out how to orgasm at, what, fourteen? Your mom didn't go to college, even though she was *so* smart, and you know it's your fault. I know how much you haven't told her."

"Shut up," Emmy said. Her face felt feverish; maybe that's all this was, a fever, an angry delusion. "Shut your fucking mouth, I swear to god."

The doll didn't respond, and Emmy felt the first hint of tears. She found a roll of duct tape and a T-shirt. She grabbed the doll off the bed, and it was strange, even though she knew it wasn't real, to handle a baby with such aggression. She wrapped the shirt around its fat little gut and taped it up tight, covering the speakers. She took a deep breath.

"Nice try, kiddo," the muffled voice said. It began to cry, but angrier, full of rage—its cries no longer a sound but a physical force.

"Oh my god," Emmy kept saying. She tried and tried to make the cries stop, cramming the babyish plastic bottle into its dumb plastic lips over and over, but it cried for five, ten, then twenty minutes, and then she was crying, too, she was overwhelmed, and her mother knocked on her bedroom door.

"What the hell is going on?" And then, when she saw Emmy crying, "It's OK. It's OK." She took the doll from Emmy, squinting in the near darkness. "Did you … try to smother it?"

"I just … it was so loud."

"Maybe it has some sort of censor? Or you jostled something?" Her mother ripped the tape off the doll's body, and as soon as its torso was free it went silent in her arms. "Let's get you a glass of water, OK?"

Emmy nodded. The two of them sat on their balcony overlooking the parking lot, sipping water. Everyone was asleep except for some teenagers playing chicken in the pool.

"I don't like this," her mother said. "I don't like this at all. I should complain to Hartley. You're a kid, for Christ's sake. Teenagers need their sleep. Fuck. *I* need my sleep."

Emmy didn't say anything. The water felt cold in her stomach. "Mom? I don't think I got the same kind of doll everyone else got."

"What do you mean?"

"It … talks."

Her mother went silent, and the sounds of the teenagers playing, their shrieking, became ominous.

"And it knows things about me." It made her want to vomit the water in her stomach, remembering the things the doll knew. "Like it knew I'd been wearing the same bra for two weeks straight. Things like that."

"I knew I hadn't seen it in the laundry lately." Her mother laughed. Emmy felt small. Maybe her mom hadn't heard what she'd said. Maybe she didn't want to. "This really is a stupid project. Doesn't take taxpayers' money to tell you getting knocked up in high school fucks things up, at least for a little while. I've taught you better."

"Yep."

"And it's not like you were this fucking … awful. I mean, it was harder in some ways, like, teaching you good and evil and stuff, but if you'd cried this much, I would've hurled my ass out the window. Yours, too."

"No jury would've convicted you." It was almost as if there were four discrete beings in the apartment—herself, her mother, the doll, and the hidden part of herself that the doll seemed to know. Her mother had only a fractured view. "I hate this. I hate her."

"Is it a her?"

"I don't know. I'm tired."

Her mother kissed her cheek. "Good night, pookie."

Emmy knew she had to finish her story. This reading was important to her for reasons she couldn't quite articulate, and even though the library wasn't exactly a worldwide audience, it was an audience. This fucking baby doll wasn't going to keep her from it.

There was a sunrise in her window as she put together an ending, hard-won but not exactly right. She fell asleep with her laptop open, the doll on the floor beside her bed.

"Emmy?" Her mother shook her shoulder, and Emmy knew that she'd overslept. "Oh no," she said.

She had thirty minutes to get to the library. She hated how greasy her hair was. She didn't look like a writer. Halfway out the door, she heard the doll's screams. "No. I don't have time for this." She threw the doll in its seat and ran down the stairs, the car seat banging against the rails. Passersby looked at her with alarm. "It's not … it's not real," she said weakly.

It was ten after by the time her mother pulled up to the library. "Good luck!" She called after her. Emmy tried not to think about why she'd been up so late. There would be time to handle that later. God, she *hated* being late.

As she entered the library, she made her way to the makeshift stage where a crowd was already gathered. One of the readers was reading a story about coming out to his parents and eating so much popcorn shrimp at Red Lobster that he threw up on his mom's lap. The audience applauded when he was done, and when the event organizer introduced Emmy, she tried to look confident and well-rested.

From the podium, she could see a few nice old ladies smiling at her. "Hi," she said. "I'll, umm, be reading a story I've been working on." She pulled up the document on her phone. God, why had she agreed to do this, what a stupid idea, but it was exciting, too—her mouth opened in a big, nervous grin. She started reading, and it excited her that nobody seemed bored or confused. She was nearing the end, reading over what she'd put together the night before.

"*A shot to the head was too easy. She'd seen the pain in those girls, the ones who'd survived. A bullet was too quick. She found a candle lighter. She held it up to his face until he wept, and a burning smell filled her nostrils. It blistered while she watched—*"

Somewhere in the audience a baby's sad coo started. *No, no, no.*

"*And he begged her to stop, but she pointed her gun at his face and told him to shut up. She pushed him into the kitchen and told him to choose the sharpest knife he had. His hands were shaking as he opened the drawer—.*" The baby's coo was louder now, and a few old ladies were whispering. "'*Listen,' she said. 'I'm going to cut off one finger for every girl you raped and two for every one you killed. You don't have enough fingers to pay that debt, but we'll start there.*'" The baby's cry was so loud now that some of her words were drowned in the pulsing shrieks, and she had to keep raising her volume. "*HE LET HER SLICE INTO HIS FINGERS, BECAUSE HE STIL HOPED HE'D GET OUT OF THIS ALIVE.*

THE BLOOD FROM HIS VEINS SPRAYED HER IN THE FACE AND SHE TASTED SOME OF HIS BLOOD—." Some of the older ladies had disgusted looks on their faces. *"BUT IT STILL WASN'T ENOUGH. 'I'M GOING TO CUT OFF YOUR DICK—DO YOU UNDERSTAND ME?' SHE ASKED—."* The old ladies were leaving, and now people were standing around the car seat, alarmed at the noise, and she noticed the event coordinator rushing towards her with a panicked face. "You know what? Fuck this." Her face was burning as she ran off the stage, snatching up the car seat. "It's a fucking doll, people, get over it." She'd never been so humiliated.

The event coordinator found her outside, head between her hands. The doll was silent. "Emmy," she said. "That was—that was incredibly inappropriate. I don't know what you were thinking."

"People write violent stuff all the time. Way worse than that."

"Well, *yes*, that may be true." The woman fiddled with her hands— Emmy noticed there were daisies painted on her thumbnail. " But this wasn't the place."

"I just wanted to read my story. I was excited about it."

"Well, next time, if your story is appropriate—and I'll have to check it beforehand, please—you'll have another chance."

Emmy nodded so that the woman would leave. She glanced down at the doll. "You stupid motherfucker," she said. "This is all your fault." She kicked the seat. A young mother sitting across the way gasped when she saw the doll fall to the concrete, and looked confused, then embarrassed, when she saw it was only plastic. Emmy didn't care if the sensor went off and caused her to fail. Let it.

The boy who'd read before her came out of the library. "Hey," he said. "I liked your story." Emmy only smiled. "I could drive you home, if you need a ride." She bit her lip. She really, *really* didn't want to call her mother. This kindness from someone who didn't even know her that well made her feel the weight of the day; she was so exhausted she felt like when she was a kid, going along with her mother to clean rich ladies' houses, spending all day in the car.

When he dropped her off, she saw her mother's car was gone— she must have picked up an extra shift at the rent-a-maid company. Emmy realized her mother had probably kept her day open because of the reading, and that made her feel like an Emmy-sized vortex. In her room she fell into a deep sleep, one she felt she deserved, and hoped nothing else would happen.

She woke up because she was hungry, but she realized, upon waking, that the baby hadn't cried, not for hours. It was already dark out. The doll was probably dead. She dragged herself out of her room.

"Hey," her mother said. "I didn't want to wake you, but dinner's ready. There's spaghetti in the fridge."

"Thanks." She ate the pasta cold over the sink. Her mom paused the TV. "How'd your reading go?"

"Good. I think they really liked it."

"That's great, pookie." Her mother smiled. "I'm so glad. It's good to explore the arts."

Emmy was happy to comfort her—*See, Mom, look how well adjusted I am*. Emmy thought, *if I were a food I'd be cold spaghetti*.

"Any plans tonight?"

"No. Can't do much with the stupid baby."

"That's too bad. We could watch a movie, if you want."

That sounded nice to Emmy. She almost told her mother the truth about the reading, about everything—the secret the plastic motherfucker seemed, inexplicably, to know, despite the fact Emmy had never told anyone, not ever—about how all those people looking at her that way made her feel like an idiot, how she thought maybe she'd never try to make anything again, never try to tell anyone anything, ever. But she didn't. She leaned against her mother's shoulder as they started a movie, something silly.

"Mom," she said. "The other day, that stupid Infant RealLife video, they kept talking about teen moms like they were these tragic losers. And I guess that upset me, because I don't think you're, you know, tragic."

Her mother pursed her lips a little. "That's sweet, pookie. Thank you for saying that. But ...." She took a sip of wine. "I also think it would've been different if I'd had you later. You know what I mean? Like if I could go back in time and say, hey, give me the *exact same kid*, but ten years later, I would. I sometimes think ... it wasn't fair to you. It wasn't fair to me. It wasn't fair that my mom didn't teach me the same things I've taught you. And I've tried really hard to make things right for you. But sometimes I feel so fucking guilty."

"Why?" She was alarmed to see that her mother's eyes were red; this wasn't at all what she'd intended.

"What if you would've had a better life if I'd gone to college, got a decent job? If we weren't bouncing from apartment to apartment? I know we love each other, I know we're pals, but I also know I wasn't there a lot of the time. I had to leave you alone when you were so little. Remember? You were eight when I first got that job at the warehouse. You were too young to be making dinner alone, putting yourself to bed. But I was a dumb fucking kid still, Emmy. I was backed into a goddamned corner."

"I know, Mom. There wasn't anybody to help us. Just you and me."

From the corner of the room, a voice: "Tell her, you fucking coward, what do you have to lose? Tell her about that day, about that greasy little boy. Tell her whose fault it was." And then Emmy knew the doll had only been waiting, quiet—nothing she could do would ever silence it. She felt her chest heave—she wondered what the symptoms of a panic attack were.

Emmy scanned her mother's face for any indication at all that she had heard the voice. But her mother was looking sadly, a little shyly, into her wineglass, and Emmy knew: only she could hear the doll.

"You did everything right. OK? Anything bad that happened had nothing to do with you."

Her mother looked at her—really looked at her. Emmy panicked. "Like, hypothetically. Like missing a recital or something."

"I never missed any of your recitals."

"I know, I'm saying *hypothetically*."

"All right." She wrapped an arm around Emmy and kissed her head. "What do you say we finish the movie, huh?"

She un-paused the movie, but Emmy couldn't focus. Even though Emmy could tell she tried not to, her mother fell asleep before the movie was over, so Emmy turned the television off and shook her mother awake. The baby had begun to cry.

"Go on to bed, Mom."

Her mother squeezed her hand and they departed to their rooms. Emmy shoved the bottle to the baby's face and it quit crying.

"I hate you," she said. "I really hate you."

"I don't think you do," it answered. It pushed the bottle out of its mouth. "Why didn't you tell her?"

"I don't know what you're talking about."

"I'm sorry. You do. You were, what, ten? And your mom was at work, and had left you alone?"

"Stop."

"And that neighbor boy knocked on your door, asking if you wanted to play video games?"

"Shut. Up."

"And even though your mom told you to *never, ever* open the door for a stranger—"

"Please—"

"You opened it. And that was your fault, kiddo. Your bad. But you know, and I know, that you never should've been alone in the first place."

And then the worst, the most terrible thing: The doll no longer talked, but played, as if it were a recording, a boy's voice. *Come over.* She heard the sounds of the video game, its happy little pings, and then, *Come closer.* And then, *It's OK.* And then, *Don't tell.*

Emmy had never been more afraid in her entire life until she realized she wasn't angry at all: only a blank where there should be a person, a carbon copy of a girl who something terrible had happened to.

Why she did this, she couldn't say, but all of a sudden it was like the story she'd written, and the candle lighter was there, and she held the flame up to the baby's face, watching the rubber blacken and curl away from its blue glass eyes, watching its lips shrivel away into melted drippings that burned her hand, and as the room filled with smoke—*Oh, shit, the smoke detector*—she panicked: She opened her window and threw the baby outside. There was a mechanical kind of crunch, and then, nothing.

"No," she said to herself. "No, no, no." She was going to get a zero, she'd have to look her mother in the eye and tell her she'd made an F in *child development*, she was never going to get a scholarship, never going to get accepted to any school, and their whole lives up to this point would've been for nothing. She had to do something, quickly. Her mother could not see what she'd done.

What she chose to do—and this, she was not proud of—was look up Mortenberry's address in the faculty roster her mom kept in her desk drawer.

She lifted her mother's keys off the entrance table, slowly, so they wouldn't jingle, and inched herself out the door. On the ground below, she found the doll. She was surprised at how sad it made her, to see its mechanical guts spilled in the dawn light. She picked it up carefully and wrapped it in her sweatshirt.

She took her mom's car and prayed that she would never, *ever* find out, and drove to Mortenberry's. There wasn't a plan, not really, but she would think of one. She *had* to. She felt a deep, nauseous despair, something that wanted to strangle her from the inside. How could the doll have known? But maybe that wasn't important. Maybe that wasn't the question worth asking.

Mortenberry's home was the normal kind of red-bricked one-story she saw on sitcoms. The sun had risen—there was already an old man out watering the lawn. She grabbed the doll by one of its rubber wrists and made the walk up the drive. She knocked. A little girl in a unicorn-covered nightgown answered the door. She could hear cartoons playing inside.

"Hi. Is Mortenberry—umm, your dad—is he home?"

"He sleeping."

"Oh. OK then, I'll just head—"

"Cady?" She heard Mortenberry's voice, and then he lumbered out, shirtless and yawning. He froze when he saw her. "Emmy? What the hell—."

"Please, Coach, I need to talk to you." She couldn't tell if he was furious or confused. "Please."

"Well ... fine, but let me ... let me get settled." He gestured vaguely at his naked chest and seemed instantly to regret it. "I'll be right back."

She didn't want to cry. She would *not* cry in front of Mortenberry. She would state her case as clearly as she could, he would help her, and it would all be alright. She heard a woman's voice in what she guessed was the bedroom, and Mortenberry's murmuring; she could only imagine what he was saying to his wife. He returned looking more composed and invited her into the kitchen. "Girls, go play somewhere," he yelled. "OK, Emmy ... what in fresh hell are you doing at my house?"

She unwrapped the doll from her sweatshirt and placed it on the kitchen table. It looked even more gruesome against the lacy tablecloth. Mortenberry made a sound like a belly laugh, or a gut punch.

"Jesus Christ, do you have *any* idea how expensive that was?"

"Please, Coach, *please*, I can't fail. I have to get my grade up." She felt the inside of her mouth getting dry. "Can't—can't you maybe just get me a new one?"

"You want *another one*? So you can, what—." He lifted the doll a little to see its face clearly. "Burn its damn face off?"

"I wasn't thinking."

"You're right, you weren't thinking, and now I gotta call Hartley on my day off—"

"You don't understand. The doll, it wasn't *right*." A tear trailed her cheek and she wiped at it, furious. "It was *talking* to me. I know you won't believe me, but it was. And it knew—and it knew—"

Emmy will never understand why what happened to her when she was ten years old spilled out in Mortenberry's gold-lit kitchen; she only knew that she had felt too much in too little time, and that she was scared that the anger that kept her buzzing like a hive was now silent, and he was an adult, a teacher, and he was *there*, so she told him.

A boy. I was scared. I let him. It hurt. It still hurts. When she finished, she wiped the snot from her nose with the sleeve of her sweatshirt.

"Christ. I—." He cleared his throat. "Why me?" She looked at him with such pure venom that he corrected himself. "I mean, why tell me, specifically?"

"You're a teacher. You're supposed to help."

"I'm ... I'm sorry, Emmy. That's ... wow."

Emmy shook her head. What an idiot she was. Mortenberry didn't want her story; now it was a burden he had to deal with, a complication of his cozy Sunday morning. World's biggest idiot. She grabbed the doll—what she meant to do with it, she had no idea—and turned to leave.

"Wait." He stood up and his stomach pushed at the edge of the table. "Don't leave. OK? Shit. It's just I ... I never had ...." He rubbed his palms over his temples. "I'm sorry that happened, Emmy. That's not how I meant it. I just ... thank you for telling me. That was brave of you."

"I'm not brave, OK? I just had to tell someone."

"Have you told your mom?"

"It's not her fault." There it was—a flash of that old feeling. How dare he.

"Of course. It ain't yours, either. Just his." For a moment he looked human, like just some guy. He sighed. "Tell her. Then we'll go from there."

Emmy bit at her nail. They both looked at the charred thing on the table.

"I'll tell FamilyWorks I left it on top of my truck and drove off. OK? I'll say you did everything you were supposed to."

She blinked. "Thank you." And she meant it. "I think I'll go now."

"All right." He stood awkwardly, and she almost felt sorry for him. "Anything else I can do for you?" he said.

"I'm really grateful," she said. "But it was still pretty fucked up when you said periods were gross."

"I didn't."

"Yeah, but you didn't correct the guy who did."

He looked like he might try to argue with her. "You're something else, kiddo." The way he said it sounded affectionate, maybe kind. "Listen—I don't know if you saw, but I got two girls."

Emmy nodded. "I hope you get what you need," he said.

As Emmy drove home, she thought, Mortenberry really still was a fuckface. And yet. He had helped her. And there was something to be said about letting her words slide out onto the table like so much phlegm, out of her body and somewhere she could look at it. She regretted telling him, maybe, but she didn't regret telling.

She eased the car into her mother's parking space. Going up the stairs, she felt the lightest she had in days; she didn't miss the doll and all its weight. It was still so early there was no chance her mother was awake, so she slowly, slowly turned the key in the lock.

"Where the *fuck* have you been." It wasn't a question. Her mother's face was tear-stained. "I get up, your door is open, you're *gone*, the car's gone, I thought … I don't know what the fuck I thought, but … I was scared, Emmy." She collected herself. "So I repeat, where the *fuck* have you been?"

Emmy looked at her mother, huge in her rage. She saw her mother was also angry, about the way her life had crystallized around her until she could hardly breathe, about the things she couldn't quite make right, and Emmy wondered if it was arrogance that made her believe she knew all her mother's secret pains. Of course it had to be her mother she told. It was to her a small share of Emmy's story belonged. Emmy had been giving it to the wrong people. The sunrise through the window was still pink, and in its light both women looked soft and alive, like something becoming, like something newborn.

Fuck it, Emmy thought. And she told her mother everything.

Jo Brachman

What I Worry About at the Aquarium

For you, I want to love
the sea creatures,
the sideway eyes,
the quick movements,
the undulating grass,
but I worry they feel trapped.
Up against the glass,
I worry the enormous tank
will explode from their wild
sadness and longing for home.
It's been four years
since the court ruled
in our favor, and still I worry
if I'm not vigilant,
your biological parents
will snatch you from me.
We move along the corridor
behind a group of older kids.
I hold your small hand
too tight. You complain,
My hand is catching fire.
Instead, I hold on
to the back of your T-shirt.
You're stretching my shirt.
I worry my worry
will seep into you. I let go.
You dive into the noise

of the taller crowd.
You're suddenly up ahead,
and then nowhere.
Just when the panic
in my throat begins rising
to a scream, you emerge
back at the glass
looking for me. We wave.
You dive again,
my slippery fish to watch.

JO BRACHMAN

I say goodbye wraparound, but linger

on the wicker with our dog. I say goodbye
house-ghost. She's the sad, haunted one,
but when I leave, she must stay.

I should've said goodbye kitchen stinking
of marigolds, red mailbox twined
with purple clematis. Should've said goodbye
back stoop, tin roof, chimney's crumbling brick.

I wave to the blurred conductor shaking
this crossroad town. I should wait. I should say
goodbye dear husband,
tell you how the long nights shook

the moon from the leaves, breathed
life backwards from the trees. I should tell you
how for hours I tried to divine an escape.
The train's faint signal droned:

Dead summer, raise up your thin limbs and go.

WENDY BARKER

After Pittsburgh

Where can I go when the world overburdens us, not
     with Wordsworth's "getting and spending," but with bombs
         and gunfire, though I still want to turn to that poem, his
twilight, "calm and free," but now, another mass
     shooting, this time eleven Jews gunned down in their own
         synagogue. Though not observant, my husband's Jewish,
so I turn to Eliot and the "stony rubbish" where
     the "cricket gives no relief," and then I walk outside to fill
         the bird feeders and yes, Wordsworth, it is a "beauteous
evening," all "tranquility," not even the neighbors' dogs
     yipping. Once back inside, I learn the neighborhood
         of Pittsburgh's Squirrel Hill where the white supremicist
opened fire is the same neighborhood where Mr. Rogers
     lived and filmed his television show that calmed my little
         son when he was crying and always reassured me, too, as
we cuddled on the shabby green sofa. But we're backed
     into "The Waste Land"'s "rat's alley." Eliot, I remember,
         was anti-Semitic. Now the dogs are snarling by the gate.

Andrea Marcusa

My Unfamiliar City

March 17, 2020, NYC
Out of Air

I've been holding my breath a lot. I can hold it for forty-five seconds. My husband says to stay inside. But it's 11:15 in the morning, the time I've decided it's safe to walk the New York City streets. I've read if you can hold your breath you don't have it. But a Facebook post declared this more fake news. I'm siding with my lungs. I hold my breath when I hear the soaring death counts, case numbers. I hold my breath to the sound of wailing ambulance sirens in the dark.

I find my shoes where they sit outside our door. I put on my mask, feel my pocket for the baggie filled with three Clorox wipes and extra pumps of hand sanitizer. My front door closes. Then silence. Only ten of the families filling this building of fifty apartments have remained in the city. They've fled to upstate or the Hamptons, or across state lines, and left us here in an echoing absence. No smells of stews simmering from next door, or dog yaps below, or high heels clacking on bare flooring above.

The elevator arrives. Empty. I fill my lungs, step in, and watch the doors close. Despite the dearth of tenants, the air filling the car could be riddled with someone's viral droplets, suspended there, waiting. My lungs press against my chest—four, three, by two they burn, and finally in the lobby I let out a gasp. It is possible that Tony, the handyman, slouching too close to the elevator, is an asymptomatic spreader, so I take just a tiny mouthful of fresh, cool air. So many things about Tony make him suspect. His swagger, his youth, his invasion of my six feet. But the pecking order in the building sees it another way. He's one of the super's favorites, so I'm stuck with him in my space. Perhaps our mayor is right. We're all going to get it anyway. I scoot past Tony, then Bill at the door, who's usually bubbling with tidbits about the Yankees, the weather. But today I look away. So does he.

On the street, the Fresh Direct and UPS trucks teem with activity; their drivers are grave-faced or masked, mountains of cardboard cartons beside them. From the sidewalk beds, pansies smile violet and golden; trees sprout soft pink blossoms that reach toward an unbearably blue sky. I stare down Lexington Avenue and wonder what we are all doing—all of us behind millions of panes of window glass, in this city, called by some the greatest city in the world.

Today, all of us are hiding, news on, phones out, thermometers handy, trying to breathe.

March 25, 2020, NYC
Now We Have Shortages

I felt grief stricken yesterday after receiving my Instacart order and finding no fresh ginger or garlic bulbs. Who knows when a delivery spot will open again? Maybe in a week, when luck or the Divine lets me click past the luscious photos of plums and pears and green scallions to the word PURCHASE, and a delivery time slot finally drops onto my computer screen.

Did you know, there's no yeast anywhere to make bread? Not on Amazon, eBay, or Fresh Direct. Yeast—the thing that has kept us going in huts or caves or tents, huddled around fires for millennia—now nowhere, not even the shelves of my New York City neighborhood grocery store this afternoon when I (ignoring the surging death count and my oncologist's warnings) left my safe, Upper East Side apartment to search. I stepped into the pouring rain, masked and gloved. Then a man beside the shop entrance hacked and spat at my feet.

Back home, I was afraid to touch my hair. And what about that young woman who nearly clipped me as I trudged home carrying my precious cargo—my manna or last supper? Streets deserted, she jogged past, earbuds in, eyes blank, unafraid. Breath poured from her lungs, her youthful gait bold.

All around the neighborhood the pigeons look stunned. They flit about the emptiness everywhere—the barren Madison and Fifth Avenues, the crosswalks, the subway station entrances, wondering where we all are in this great human absence. They peck and scour our sidewalks, search gutters, hunt empty trash cans. Not a soft pretzel piece, roasted peanut, old sandwich crust, anywhere.

Soon they'll learn to survive without us.

April 2020, NYC
Tents

I don't know why I glanced down 77th Street with its drab brick brownstones and scrawny bare trees. But white tents had sprung up on the sidewalk outside Lenox Hill Hospital. They shined in the sunlight, roofs flapping in a stiff spring breeze. I stared at the shelters, trying to make sense of their sudden appearance, in a time when everything around me had emptied and shuttered. Triage tents, I told myself. One entrance for the regular patients, another for the COVID-19 ones. I decided this in the haphazard way I'd been filling in blanks, as I tried to understand abrupt changes in my neighborhood—the vacant avenues, the averted gazes as pedestrians passed, sirens howling far into the night, a fleet of strange medical supply vans double-parked on streets.

Others stared at the tents too, as we strode on daily walks for fresh air and sunlight—masked, separated, cautious. We were still imagining help, kindhearted care, the latest treatments readily available. That's how things had usually gone in our first world lives. Smiles in the morning from the woman writing out my dry-cleaning receipt and the shopkeeper who rang up my coffee and everything bagel. Stores brimming with the banal to the exotic. Medicines a quick hike down the street. Surgeries to improve vision, fix hearts, replace hips, erase wrinkles, just ten blocks away.

A day later, a tractor-trailer truck appeared on the same street. Delivering needed supplies, I thought, proudly telling myself that hospitals in Manhattan were among the best in the country. The place where my two children took their first breaths, my husband and I fought the flu and infections, and had limbs repaired.

The next day more white tents appeared. They looked like the street fair structures under which summertime throngs feast on empanadas, cotton candy, and wet slices of pink watermelon. But the shelters had no windows or entrances. The white tenting covered a hospital exit door, turned, and traveled to the mouth of the vehicle.

The truck's cooling equipment hummed hour after hour, a steady, low wail. The vehicle stayed parked there for days, then weeks as the tsunami of cases hit.

One night, while the whole city worried, I walked. The dark streets were quiet, the sidewalks empty, with only an occasional cab whizzing by for company. At 77th, there stood the tents, a blemish of shadow and yellowed white roofs under the weak amber glow of a few streetlamps. And the truck. It sat low to the ground under its weight.

I said a silent prayer to the sound of the vehicle's hum. The truck's din rose through the shuttered quiet, past the dark brownstone windows and rooftops, and hovered over the nearby streets with its persistent call.

Or was it the sound of departing souls, whispering to the stars?

August 2020, NYC
Now It's Just Turko and Me

There's Turko, my eight-year-old Cockatiel, resting on her perch in the kitchen glued to the news, preferring this spot to the quiet of her cage in the spare bedroom. This summer of 2020 in New York City, which in any other year I'd refer to as "the city that never sleeps." But that was back when the city's avenues were stalled with Ubers and restaurants crowded with fancy high heels.

The city where I now reside is inside my apartment's world of kitchen, living room, dining room, office, bedroom and where I wear flipflops. Turko is here keeping me company, and I note to her about the good old days of nights filled with crowds in Village jazz clubs and that place on Lexington with the best hamburgers where you had to wait for a table because they didn't take reservations and afternoons crammed into the Starbucks at 87th where I sipped the foam of a latte to the pitter-patter of laptop keyboards all around me. Days when I traveled to the gym for Pilates class and never thought once about using the club's mats, and those Saturdays spent at the Metropolitan Museum strolling about overhearing conversations in languages from distant spots across the globe as we leaned forward to read the display labels. The Met with its Egyptian mummies, Japanese koi pond, Mayan statues to joy, knowledge and fear, European masters, and Senegalese twelfth-century gold pieces. The place where I spent hours moving with other curious beings from room to room, culture to culture, civilization to civilization.

I was so spoiled by the pulse of my thriving city, I put up with its smog and grit on my windowsills, its six-dollar lattes and all the pushing and shoving, like that woman behind me at CVS, unable to stop herself from pressing her cart into my hip as she impatiently waited. I squeezed onto buses seizing the bar above or rushed down subway station steps, grabbing the banister, and then jammed into a crowded subway car, wrapped my fingers around a pole, the doors closing, sealing us in together.

All of us racing, sprinting, careening, through days, weeks—maybe years—until suddenly looking up from a street corner, or from driving just when the skyline comes into view right before the toll at the Triboro Bridge. In that skyline each dot a window to a story with its own characters, waiting to be told, discovered, from a chat with shopkeeper, or at a book signing, or by a seatmate met during intermission at an off-Broadway show where patrons were placed practically on top of each other.

I was so confident, sure of tomorrow back in those days, so safely unaware of the precariousness of it all. No problem taking Turko for a walk in Central Park for some sunshine, she on a perch in her small carrier, while I paused to allow a child to push her face against the mesh and speak to the bird. Turko looking curiously at the child, her eyes full of wonderment. Or the way the bird hesitated for just a second when I took her from her carrier and she hopped onto a tree's low branch, her wings newly clipped so she couldn't fly away, allowing her to feel a limb underfoot stirring and swaying in a gentle breeze. I, so delightfully oblivious, and Turko, too, never once considered the possibility of a pathogen lurking on that branch or the ground that she soon fluttered down to, and how easily the pathogen could jump from a mouse or squirrel or an itinerant bat from upstate to her tiny, unprotected body. So easy it would be to make a jump from her to me. Birds can do that, like with bird flu.

Eight months ago, I innocently relished our city, its density, intensity. For more than thirty years I'd rushed from coffee to meeting to lunch to gym to salon to drinks, to 8 p.m. curtain, to a late-night walk through a bright-as-day lit-up Times Square, and hopped a train back uptown. Criss-crossing the city, north, south, east, west, my beloved glittering town. Now it just Turko and me in the evenings, watching the news or Netflix, until she tires and settles down in her cage for the night. Outside the streets are quiet, the nightlife still switched off. I stare at the dark streets, devoid of traffic, the only glitter before me, the light of a few dying stars.

ALYSE KNORR

WOLF TOURS' Official Statement on the Apocalyptic Summer Forest Fires

Forgive us our garbled syntax
     and give us our daily air, for
     the trees can't make enough.
Wretched, righteous forest-city,
     with its pitiful nests and self-
     effacing brush flames—
for years we've meant to scratch it
     from the route. We apologize if guilt
     has tainted your Tour experience.
We did not include guilt in our itinerary.
     If the forest offends,
     remove it with your ax—then the one
in your neighbor's eye.
     Your neighbor has beautiful eyes:
     careful and ecological.
Your neighbor is a forest with forest eyes.
     Now do you feel better? You've
     truly done nothing wrong.

Jonathan Greenhause

A Makeshift Ark

I shelter several honeybees in my cupped palms, a makeshift ark
to guard them against CCD, against this shitstorm

of mites & pesticides & the steamrolling of their habitats;
they'll reside here 'til I discover how to feed them

with a modicum of pollen, a drink from dewdrops, with sweat
gathered in my lines & furrows. I'm careful

not to antagonize, one absentminded sting assuring their destruction,
my words honeyed, my lofty intentions

quick to take flight. All around us, colonies collapse, queen bees
reigning over the ruins, abandoned hives bearing witness

to the tragedy of ten million Roanokes. A lost world is in the works,
the bees' diaphanous wings clipped, their dried-out honeycombs

split apart. Even while writing this, my own home
splinters, the sea seeping in through the basement, my body

resting against the rotten planks of a rowboat;
&, for us, no gracious palms will be large enough to offer us flight.

GABRIEL WELSCH

Why We Count the Birds

I once thought we wrote about leaves
and trees and the creatures that run
at night because the politics and the wars
and the culture bristling with fright
all stunk so richly of their time. The people,
the movies, the sound bites would all pass.
And then the bees' buzz murmured, I read
the ladybugs are fewer, the rivers
rise and take with them a park bench,
a precarious house, a morsel of land no longer
to appear on a map. I thought we wrote
about timelessness to share our hurt
and joy anchored in something rooted thick,
something dependable. I thought we wrote
a place that always would grow,
that nothing so permanent could die.

KIM ALLOUCHE

You're the Broccoli

The day starts out regular: us kids hunched over the breakfast table, Dad, outside, poised against the frame of the sliding patio door, only half-open to keep bugs out, a towel, thankfully, tucked around his buck-naked loins, pool water snaking down his copper chest hair that makes me look down and sip the glass of milk I hate. As he speaks, Burt stuffs his face with buttered grits, while our brat sister, Peaches, who understands nothing, nods like a fool. At least this time Dad keeps the lecture short, bellowing, *Remember, that which does not kill you makes you stronger*, a statement I highly doubt. I mean, Burt's no superhero, and I can tell that today's lesson is mostly meant for him as some kind of strange apology or warning.

"Hurry up, Burt. We don't want to be late for school," I say, which is only true for me.

We grab our stuff.

Bent over the kitchen counter in her teensy nightie, Mom calls out her favorite joke, the one she's repeated to us since *we split her wide open* thirteen years ago. "There are two things in life for which we are never truly prepared."

Burt slams the back door behind us when she's midway through the punch line: *Twins*. Again, I wonder, apology or warning?

I say to Burt, "That which doesn't kill you ..."

"Also kills you," he says.

We hurry along the bayou decapitating cattails.

A half-hour before the afternoon dismissal bell, the principal, Mr. Cotinsky, a jumpy, sausage-shaped man, calls an emergency assembly. He clears his throat into the mic, and none of us stop talking. Teachers pull on ears to hush the whole middle school in their perfunctory fashion. (Perfunctory: one of tonight's vocab words, as in the sample sentence about *moi-même,* "Lia preforms even perfunctory tasks with zeal.")

"There's been a change in direction. The hurricane's headed straight for us," Mr. C. announces, wiping the sweat from his bald head with a hankie. "She's gathering speed and we're told she could make landfall well before the weekend. As early as—"

The mic goes out.

"Hold on now," Mr. C. squeals, "School could remain in session tomorrow. So far, Ole Dutch said squat about closing and not a peep about evacuation. Never know till the last minute, though. Y'all tell your folks."

I scan the faces around me. Everyone's taking in only a *part* of what Mr. Cotinsky is saying. My friend Peg giggles, her hand pressed against her buckteeth. Burt high-fives his clan, all of them forced to sit in the front row "due to poor comportment." Then Mr. C. contorts his face before belting out one of his melodious farts, which, of course, Burt stands and imitates, his posse shaking with laughter. Me, I sniffle and dab my eyes at the inevitable forces of destruction. Tomorrow, September 26, 1968, could be our final day. There's a premonition I have that lives inside my body and escapes whenever unexpected things happen. Technically, I guess, it's not a premonition at all.

Like he's talking to himself, Mr. C. adds, "Though getting out early might be the smartest move."

Everyone jabbers.

"Go 'head home," he cries, "and you're welcome," like he's doing us a solid when it's already quarter to three.

The thick air crushes Burt and me as we trudge down the levee bathed in sweat. By the time we reach our carport any urgency about the storm has vanished and we can't muster it up again, as if all that heaviness jells our blood the moment the backdoor slams behind us. We plod through the laundry room, machines bouncing with blue detergent that I pray hides our house smell. Every house has one, but it's pretty impossible to know your own, though I fear the worst— dog shit, feet, and peanut butter like Peg's. Probably not, though, 'cause we're not even allowed to have a pet since that thing with Peaches' goldfish.

Burt and I dump our book bags on the first free spot, the *Formica* kitchen counter. (Mom loves to say Formica.) Everything's new but meant to look old, like a miniature plantation. *French colonial.* I hate hearing Mom's words inside my head. Same as every day, the minute we drop our stuff, she calls out from somewhere, *Get those books upstairs—they don't belong in the kitchen,* and we do not obey; we let ourselves believe there are no consequences. Immediately, goosebumps rise on my limbs, the central air set low for Dad, who runs hot.

Stooped over the counter, Gertie pounds a platter of pink cutlets into compliance using a metal hammer. Loud and clear, last night Dad told Mom to *tenderize,* the word itself grossing me out to no end—surely some stray cooking tip he read in the *Picayune*; I'm guessing this is how it's done. Gert's lived in our attic since I was born, though I've only ever seen her in her XXL uniform. She's so big, I feel protected when she's near, though this is foolish. Sometimes, late at night, I rest my cheek on the top of her arm where her doughy skin falls the loosest, the softest skin I've ever felt.

"Hey, Gertie-pie," I say.

She stops thumping, "An' how you doin', sugar?"

"Just fine, I thank you."

Bunions split her worn work shoes on the sides. I can't help but stare. Same as every day.

"I've worked my whole life, standin' on these feet, child," she says, her voice smooth as syrup.

"And you, Mr. Burt?"

"Cal—hooooon," he yells, his voice rising at the end.

Just to bother people, Burt says things that are senseless. His friends egg him on or copy, but I don't like it when he does it to Gertie, seeing as she's my favorite person.

"Look, Gert."

Burt holds up his arm next to hers to compare the shades of their skin. He's clearly darker now from spending summertime outdoors; plus, unlike me, he has the advantage of starting out olive. Gertie, an octogenarian octoroon, nods like she's pleased—*pleased as punch,* our mother would say—while I flinch at his way of apologizing.

I linger at the fridge and pull out a plum, and Burt slides out Dad's hidden tin of Charles Chips from the back of the pantry. Mom calls out what she always calls out, *Don't spoil your supper*. From the doorway, I watch her narrow silhouette glide from the den to her bedroom, still in her teensy nightie. It takes her a while to dress. Ha.

Next, Burt and I traipse into the den where Peaches is snuggled into the smallest possible ball, hypnotized by the Flintstones, her hair done up like Pebbles. At *Yabba dabba doo,* Burt grabs the remote from her hand, changes the channel, and he and I sink into velvet sofas to watch *The Twilight Zone*, my favorite, and then *Dark Shadows*, his. Peaches pouts, exaggerating her lower lip, and I want punch her even though, technically, she's right. She goes to tell Mom. She knows better than to complain to us, and it's true that I do feel a little bad for her, but by now she should be used to the routine. Plus, when I was in third grade, I didn't act like a baby, and, plus, plus, she's by far the favorite, something that's easy for me to see in every family I've ever known. She has my mother's doll face, with a small nose that points up. Could be why my mother loves her so, but Burt has the same face and he's the least favorite and that's a nice way of putting it, and even though he and I are twins, I ended up looking exactly like Dad, who's a true pinkler, and it's a known fact that throughout all history no one has ever once wished red hair and freckles on their worst enemy. Burt reminds me of this sad truth, lest I forget.

At a commercial for Frosted Flakes, the phone rings a million times and Mom shouts, *Get the phone,* and we don't budge. Big mistake. The heavy door to her bedroom swings open and she's right there blocking the TV, hands on her hips, her face half on, Peaches posed at her side, fake-innocent and vindictive.

"You, mister," she says, pointing to Burt, who is flexing his biceps under his leftover baby chub. "That was Mr. Cotinsky."

"Who?"

He knows the principal's name, as well as I do … if not better.

"Oh, you mean Mr. Cunt-insky?"

"Yep," says Mom, not even noticing. "Not back at school a full month, not a whole month, and four demerits! Are you crazy? It's been proven time and time again that Super Glue can kill people, smarty pants. You're going to write an apology to that woman. It was your homeroom teacher, right? Miss Herbert?"

"Hebert. Not Herbert. It's pronounced '*A bear*,' Mother. She's Cajun," I say deferentially. "Think about … *a bear* walking through a classroom."

Burt turns to me chuckling between his words while he talks. This is when I love him best.

"You got that right. Miss Hebert dragged her chair from her fat butt all the way to the chalkboard without even noticing it, and then, and then, when she finally swung around to yell at us for cracking up, she yanked it off so hard her skirt ripped wide open and she went over hard, like a lassoed heifer—"

He laughs so hard he spits.

"Wait, wait, and then … the whole class saw her blubbery ass."

"Do you want to be held back again, son? Do you want to go to elementary school next year with Peaches? You're already a full year behind Lia. Look at her grades, why don't you? And you've failed every single spelling test. Every one."

"I can't see the board."

"What do you mean you can't see?"

"I mean … I need glasses." He mutters, "Genius."

"Then you just scooch your desk up close till you can see it."

"Cal-HOOOOON!"

"I'm telling Daddy when he gets home."

She sounds just like Peaches.

"You're the home," he says.

He doesn't mean anything by this. It is just another annoying thing he does. He says, "You're the …" and adds whatever word you just used to end your last sentence with, like if you say, *Looks like thunder*, he'll say, *You're the thunder*. Still, though I know it's random, there seems to be something true about his comparisons. Or maybe that's just me looking for connections where they don't exist.

Mom rolls her eyes. "What, you think I won't?"

I think she will. It's something she does.

"But Mom …," I say, trying to change how everything stays the same every day, which again, I realize, is me doing the same thing, too.

"Well, what do you want me to do?"

She's sincerely asking me this, and I'm thinking of what to say 'cause I do have some ideas, and I'm starting to feel bad for her, like she's *my* child, but I know she won't listen to a thing I come up with because she never does. I think, *Maybe go ask Gertrude*, given that Gertie's got half a century on her, but I shrug 'cause there's no way Mom's gonna listen to her, either.

Burt turns his face to one side, sticks out his tongue, as if to catch a fly, curls it up, hesitates a sec, and then flaps it right back in. It makes the most repulsive sound imaginable. He's *tickled*. *Ew*, Mom's word. Quickly, his head shifts on an abrupt, reptilian angle and he does it again. We're all used to the lizard.

"I *am* gonna tell Daddy. Just as soon as he walks in."

Mom's getting to us now; this is supposed to be *our* time. Burt and I know how to stretch it. We pretend that afternoons go on and on forever, that they belong to us. But Mom, trying to barricade sizzling meat fumes from the kitchen, saunters over to the door and shuts it with her hip, mumbling, not-so-under-her-breath, "No matter how many times I tell her …." Then she marches back and, sure enough, blocks the TV *again* just when the doctor with the pig face unwraps the girl's bandages—the best part of the best episode of the best show of all time. I don't even try to lean over and look around her. I try to be good and not just so that she'll leave me alone, not just for that. She points at me.

"And you, Lia, why didn't you stand up for your little sister?"

I shouldn't have corrected her pronunciation of Hebert, but I have a stubborn streak that likes when things are right. I say, *I will next time, Mom, sorry,* and for a minute, I think I really might, but she just says, "Well, miss."

Peaches stands there grinning. "Mommy, bathe me," she whines.

She damn well knows how to bathe herself. But the image of bathwater awakens sausage-man's announcement at assembly, and I stop myself from saying, *Well, if Peaches does skip a day, Mother, it'll be just fine, 'cause come tomorrow night, she'll be bathed, all right—more like drowned. When that hurricane hits.*

Mom's mouth pulls all the way to the left, which means she's torn because she wants to suds up li'l angel-face, but she can't; there's not enough time before Dad gets home. I know this because I know how to read faces, and that's why, in spite of my looks, I'm pretty popular at school. Dad always wins.

Mom murmurs to Peaches, "Sweet love, I've got to get a move on and dress for supper. *And* fix the *mezze*. Daddy will be home in … *twenty-three minutes!*"

"Want me to set the table?" I offer, thinking about folding the linen napkins into fans like Gertie showed me—something she learned at a ranch outside Texarkana where she had to make three dozen pecan pies every morning before breakfast when she was only nine years old.

"Yes, dear, go help Gert. Thank God I don't have to worry about you."

Mom always says that. That's something, I guess.

When I stand up, I notice she's not wearing any panties under her nightie and there's a clump of hair where I hardly have any (not like Peg's bush), and I think of the lock on my parents' door and always having to knock. Even Peaches has to knock. One time, after one of my parents' fights, the one where Mom wrote swear words on the mirror in lipstick, and Dad punched her twice in the stomach and she fell over, Dad followed me upstairs. He sat real close to me on my bed and used his teaching voice. "Lia-doll, you don't know what goes on behind that bedroom door and trust me, you don't want to," meaning something about how they make up afterwards—which is the same as saying, "You don't want to know about that pink-and-green zebra" because what else are you gonna do but think about that damn zebra? And now, with Mom standing there like that, all I'm thinking about are those watermelon stripes.

I have to change my thoughts. And I know how to. It's the main thing Mom taught me. You just have to think about something else; you force yourself. Like when I was little, and I'd wake her after a nightmare, she'd say, Lee-Lee, think about pretty, pink, buttercream cupcakes and the smell of gardenias and what kind of birthday party you want. I guess she imagines things like that when she has her own bad dreams. So, I think about Annette Funicello, my favorite movie star, who started out around my age as a Mouseketeer. Actually, she looks just like Mom, the youngest mother of all our friends' mothers—only twenty-nine—and even Burt is proud of that. *Proud as a peacock,* she'd say. Still, he prefers Ann-Margret, a red-head, though definitely not a pinkler.

After I've set the dining room table, put the ice in the glasses, filled the crystal pitcher with water, and set out the Kleenex box for Dad's after-dinner sneezes, I fold paper napkins for "the kids." I give Burt two because he's a messy eater and right then Mom peeks her head in and says, "You're a good girl." Her familiar smell lingers as she walks away. She doesn't exactly smell bad, but not good either, kind of like a new puppy. "Oh, and Lia," she says from the doorway, "You know how sometimes I can get these little flecks inside my nose? Just between us girls, let me know if I need to go blow it." She winks.

When I go out front to cut azaleas for the centerpiece, the quick, warm wind blows my hair into an orange halo, and a tree full of Japanese plums tosses fruit all the way to the braided magnolia roots. The lawn is speckled with color. Everything feels magical and scary at the same time. Back in the den, I hand two fat plums to Burt. A bit of juice falls from his chin to the sofa, which he rubs right in.

The honk from the two-tone Silver Shadow in the driveway is our four-minute warning before the front-door lock clicks and he's inside. Dad won't use the garage door like us. Burt slams off the TV, and we grab our books, run up to our rooms and put slippers on our feet. Next, of course, Dad is on the couch that's warm from Burt's butt, sipping his scotch on the rocks and eating pickled peppers, beet-dyed turnips, and crushed, spicy wheat. Same as every day.

"Norma, are these mushrooms from a can?" Even this is not a surprise. Why can't Mom get the simple things right? From upstairs, I crouch at the banister and hear it all.

She says, "They didn't have fresh ones at the Piggly."

To get his narrow eyes off her, she says what she's gotta say, 'cause that's how it is, and I know all the rest.

"Well, guess what; I got a call about your son from Mr. Cotinsky, the principal. He glued Miss Herbert to her chair. He's glued another teacher."

Dad doesn't answer like he doesn't hear.

From his room, I hear Burt yell, "Cal-hoooon."

I go lie down on my bed until Mom screeches, "Suppertime."

At the table, right away Dad brings up the big news, our news, the news Mr. C. announced at assembly. "Expecting another storm tomorrow. Supposed to be the big one." From his seat at the head of the table, Dad turns to his right to face Burt and me for an instructional moment.

"See, they name hurricanes after women. If the last one started with an 'A', this one will start with a ...?"

We don't say anything cause c'mon.

"A 'B,'" he finishes," nodding his head.

Class dismissed. Burt looks at me like, no shit, and I half-smile back.

"A hurricane. Is that so?" says Mom as if Dad had said, "There's a bluejay on that willow."

As I clear the salad plates, Gertie brings in the hot dishes: rice and lentils, spinach pie, pulverized meat, and broccoli. Everyone serves themselves while Mom's doe eyes dart from plate to plate to make sure we don't starve to death, her main motherly role as far as I can see, and then I erase that thought, not with pink buttercream, but with what Gertie says to me every time I say wicked stuff out loud. "You lucky you even got a mamma; mine died when I was only five years old." No matter how many times I ask her to tell me more, this is all I get, as if this is all anyone would need to know or maybe it's all she has, so I'm left to fill it in for myself and I always end up real sad.

"Well, we need to prepare," says Dad, his mouth clenched. "You still got the tape, Norma? If those windows blow out, all that rain and floodwater—"

"Rolls and rolls in the laundry room, dear. I'll quick double-check." She calls out, "You still got tape, Gert?"

"Sound like a fishwife. In this house we don't yell from room to room," says Dad.

Except we do.

Gertie plods in. "Yes, ma'am. Sho do. The water bottles, too. We still got all them bottles from last time."

"Can't have those windows bustin' up," Dad says.

Then Burt whispers, "Watch Mom chew."

It's gross, her mouth circling to one side, slow like a cow's, lips heavy and open, a ball of brown gook churning, a glob of spinach on her pointy chin. I'm laughing on the inside.

"Gotta weather the storm," Dad says.

"Dang," says Burt, blurting out what Mr. C. told us like it's his own. "Maybe we should evacuate."

Dad lets out a guffaw like it's the stupidest thing he's ever heard and I'm thinking two things at once. If it is the big one, if it really is, shouldn't we get out? Couldn't that save our lives? At school we've been told countless times, today included, about what could happen if the levee floods. Our city is a fishbowl and we're not fish. I picture poor Moishe, Peaches' goldfish, sliding down Burt's throat. At the same time, I'm thinking, children should be seen and not heard; I don't say a word.

Chewing noises give me the chills and for a while that's all there is. With her fingers, Peaches eats one lentil at a time and then one grain of rice and on and on until Mom leans over and spoon-feeds her. More disgusting chewing until Mom says, "Son, please pass the broccoli." (We are a polite family, always please and thank you, and if someone sneezes, we say, *God bless you*.)

"You're the broccoli."

Burt can't help it and I can't help laughing and even Peaches giggles, showing me, yet again, that all her baby-ness is a big act and while she seems so pathetic, and her grades are barely average, she's winning. We're all watching Dad from the corner of our eyes. Like every night, his food is all clumped together on his plate and he's patting it down with the back of his fork like a drummer, pat, pat, pat … pat, pat, pat, and a revulsion rises in my groin that feels a little nasty and it rises up through my stomach to my face, which feels warm, and I have to look away, feeling sorry for him or loving him, which seems like the same thing and also, there's something else, something much more unkind. Like, it's only fun in the slightest when he's not home and what if he were dead? And then, pronto, I change that thought.

Quietly, so quietly, to Burt, Dad says, "Respect!"

When dinner's done, he sneezes and I hand him two tissues for each one.

"Godblessyou, godblessyou, godblessyou, godblessyou."

"Time to clear, girls," says Mom.

Dad presses the buzzer beneath his foot, a little lump hidden under the oriental rug, signaling Gertie to clear up.

"May I please be excused?" says Peaches, "I have a teeny bit more homework left."

Miss Independent.

"Wait," says Burt.

He can never leave well enough.

"Dad, Dad, can I try to make a basket?"

He crumples his napkin into a tight ball, his wrist flexed back and aimed at the wastepaper can that sits between my parents.

"Absolutely not," says Dad. "That's a NO, N-O."

"Dad, please. I can make it. Lemme just try."

Let it go, Burt, I think. *Not tonight.*

"C'mon, Dad. One shot, just one shot."

"Did you hear me?"

No one says a word. Peaches stays glued to her seat, even though she's officially excused, and Gert lurks in the corner.

"How 'bout this, Dad? If I don't make it in, if I don't, you can punish me. You can ground me for a week."

Dad doesn't make a sound. A vein rises in his forehead. Even for someone who can't read faces like Burt, this means something.

"A month. You can ground me for a month."

"Burt," says my mother.

How much protection is that?

Gertie moves in to clear the food. Dad holds his hand up. She stops and hovers.

"A year. You can ground me for a year."

Dad's hand relaxes around his own napkin, his face still glowing like fire but his jaw loose, shifting right and then left. He leans back into his chair and we all sit nice and quiet, waiting for what he'll say. His nostrils flare. He can't resist.

"One shot."

Burt smiles wide, his lips stretching over his two front teeth showing the big gap between them. He crumples the paper ball tight and stands.

"From right there," Dad says.

"From here," Burt answers and there's a serious pause. Then he says, "On three ... one, two and a—"

On the count of three, the wadded napkin-ball flies in an arch over the table. We all stand, except for Dad, who, like Mom, can see perfectly well from where he is. Burt doesn't have to see; he knows.

"Swish," he yells, and then, "and he scores!" Dashing to fetch the napkin from the trash can he says, "Gimme five" to Dad.

Before I can see how Dad reacts, all us girls, meaning females, start to clear up, our high-pitched chatter intentional, hoping that whatever we just witnessed is done with—wishing to make it so. I return to the dining room for the water glasses and the rest of the plates. Burt and Dad are talking football. It's like spy code. I wonder, did Dad start this little chat? Maybe he needs a friend, just one? Maybe he began the whole conversation with, *How 'bout them Saints?* Or maybe it was Burt who started it off, making it all right in the only way he knows, as in, see, we're on the same team. And I let myself pretend that everything's gonna be fine.

"No, it was Kilmer's *last* play that scalped those Redskins, scalped 'em good."

"Will all due respect, Dad—"

Burt catches me roll my eyes. He usually says this when he means no respect at all, but this time his eyes are huge and I can see he's earnest.

"It was all 'cause of the *de*fense. They got Steve Stonebreaker, the meanest linebacker of all time. Quickest, too. He's like the quarterback of the *de*fense, Pops. Can't win diddly without that kind of *de*fensive protection."

"That so?" Dad tilts his head back. "That so." Rubs his chin. "Well, if you're so dang smart ..."

Here it comes.

"Why'd your mamma get a call from Mr. Cotinsky today? Huh? If you are ... indeed ... so smart?"

"It was just a—"

"You come with me into my room and let's settle this man to man."

I'm standing there, frozen, holding their dirty dishes, one in each hand, 'cause we're not allowed to stack, it's low-class. Man to man? Sure, Burt's pretty big and strong for a thirteen-year-old, compact, not bony like me. Kinda like a shrunken linebacker, and he's real good at fishing and trapping animals. Mostly rodents. Gross, and frogs. He knows how to explode them in bottle rockets but he's nowhere near a man in anyone's book and I wonder why Dad always says that, like if it makes him feel better about what he's about to do. They're walking together through the den to my parents' room and I can hear Burt still at it.

"It was just a joke, Daddy. I'll do makeup work. And I'll tell her I'm sorry. I already did. I'll tell her again. I'll—"

The heavy door closes behind them and I go upstairs to start my homework, which is another way I change my thoughts. But then I hear it, the steady rhythm of the drummer, the paced smacking, *sheeeh, sheeeh, sheeeh ... sheeeh, sheeeh, sheeeh*, straps of warm leather cracking against the only place skin is baby-white. Breaking it open. Needing it to break. My thoughts aren't budging. I try my science book: *A light-sensitive emulsion on a photographic plate ...*. Not working! Try vocab. It comes easy. *Perfidy: a base breach of faith or trust. Pernicious: harmful, damaging, detrimental. Precocious: one mother fuckin' curse.*

Sheeeh, sheeeh, sheeeh.

I dig my head hard into my pillow for as long as it will take, trying to remember the English poem. *Some say the world will end in fire, some say in ice* .... *I think I know enough of hate, to say that for destruction, ice is also great* ... fire, ice, fire, ice, fire, ice, fire ....

I am walking down the hall to the bathroom when I see Burt come up the steps, his face flushed and pretty as a girl's but he isn't crying and he never does. Still, it feels like I'm seeing him naked and he's gotta get his clothes on quick.

"What are you looking at, ugly," he says.

"You're ugly," I say.

"You're so ugly, if you go to the zoo, they won't let you out, you cunt."

"Shut your trap, fat-ass."

"You're so ugly, your doctor's a vet. Ginger twat-face."

"At least I'm not *stupid*." Nope, I'm my daddy's girl.

Burt's eyes narrow into slits and he's coming at me and I run down the hallway to my room for cover. *I'm in*, I think, my pink canopy bed just behind, but he's pushing the door hard before I can lock it. Then he's on me and hitting me and I'm hitting him back as hard as I can, not caring if I get injured, not caring if I die, as long as I hurt him, as long as I *kill* him. Positions shift, no rules in this fight, only inflict pain. We're glued, there's this breathing, a clenched fist escapes to land a punch, punches, a loose hand manages a chokehold, a knee finishes a headlock, a foot makes a solid kick, bruises and is bruised. But only *my* nails sink deep, draw blood. Soon I'm mostly pinned and there's nothing I can do but grab a bunch of his thick, black hair, Mom's hair, a hunk of it in my hand and I can't let go and I pull hard; it's all I have. My grip tightens and slackens with the thrusts of his fists pummeling into my chest, the pain most brutal where my titties have started to sprout.

Now his eyes are empty. We're in another place, this place we go, a place that's black-blue-red, a place that smells like firecrackers and sweat, but it's hard to remember and hard to describe, those two things being connected, a place that brings absolute closeness, surely the closest either of us have ever felt—might ever feel—to any other human and then, finally, when time has disappeared and there's only this, grunts and struggle, there are some small surrenders, a release of my grip on his hair, his blows slowing down before ... before what?

I never know why it ends. Is there a signal? Do we read or misread a pause? Are we satisfied? Or do we just tire out? I can't say. I can't even answer why a good girl like me would fight back at all. When Burt leaves, I open my hand to find a fistful of his silky hair and I stroke it like a pet before I watch it float into the wastebasket and for a few minutes I want to die. I lay breathless under my canopy thinking about tomorrow, the *whoosh* of racing waters, shattering glass explosions and our house, filling up and floating away.

There are times when it is too much, when I tattle like a sissy to an evil fairy godmother, and then my wish is granted and he is, again, beaten to a pulp.

Next morning Gertie's frying bacon and Mom's in the kitchen, too, her one day to drive Peaches' carpool and she's standing in her miniskirt cutting the crusts off her sweetie's Velveeta sandwich.

"Triangles, Mommy," Peaches says. "I only like triangles."
Freak.
Mom nods as she slices the sandwich on the diagonal.
"Mornin', sugar," Gertie says, as I take my seat.
"Good *afternoon*," Mom says, 'cause it's like 7:21 and I'm six minutes late 'cause I hate breakfast.
Burt's wolfing down the meal they always show on commercials, a stack of perfect pancakes, syrup dripping down the sides. He looks up, does three lizard-tongue flaps. Peaches says stop, I say gross, and he goes back to chewing like nothing.
I know not to look out the sliding patio doors while Dad does his morning laps naked. Still, sunlight pours in yellow through the glass. I can't help but glance at the treetops, the sugar maple, the hickory, even the oaks, swaying hard, hurling leaves, acorns and wigs of frizzy-haired moss. No one even mentions the hurricane.
"What can I get you, dear?" Mom says to me, chipper and carefree. *You don't know what goes on in that bedroom*, rings in my head. I switch the thought to the best and most mysterious song on TIX, *Cheer up sleepy Jean, oh, what can it mean, to a … daydream believer and a … homecoming queen?* and I'm filled with a new and desperate kind of longing. I know right then and there, for a fact, that my life won't always be like it is now.

"I'm not hungry." I say this every morning. I'm not hungry in the morning.

"You have to have something."

"Mom, really, I might vomit. I'll vomit if I eat."

"At least a glass of milk."

"A half. I'll drink a half."

Gertrude pours it and Mom sets it on the table like she's done something.

"Y'all get home right after school, case it hits early," says Gert. "Storm's supposed to hit after midnight but a ways back, when I worked at the ranch—"

"Meanwhile … back at the ranch," Mom mocks.

"Cal-hoooon," Burt yells as we leave for school.

Together, we head to the levee, pathetic as the Siamese version of what we are.

"Wanna see something?" Burt says.

The humid wind is filled with tantalizing whiffs of ozone, which Ms. Hebert claims is toxic. Hard to believe that one, it just smells so damn good. Beyond the cattails, muddy bayou water swirls. Every now and then bubbles appear on the surface, a catfish, a frog, some secret life underneath.

Burt opens his book bag, dumps it over in the tall grass. There are no books, just rolls and rolls of masking tape. I nod. We might still be enemies but we are the kind who respect one other. There are other kinds.

"I dumped out all the water bottles, too. Last night. In the pool," he brags.

Together at the bayou's edge, one by one we toss the rolls into the murky current. On and on, they float then sink, float then sink, float then sink.

I say, "What's gonna happen to the windows?"

"You're the window."

We amble on, stopping to picking up bleached oyster shells, tossing them, when we want, *plunk, plunk, plunk,* not scared of anything— no—hoping for something real big as we make our way.

BLAKE KIMZEY

The Fantasy of Things

Thing is, you don't expect to take a motel room for three nights in Moriarity, New Mexico, with a woman who has never shown interest in metal detecting, a woman you've only known for two days. But there we were, on our way from Truckee, Nevada, to Marfa, Texas, when the Buick LaCrosse broke down.

I was with Cheryl, the girl I'd picked up outside of Lake Tahoe. She'd been thumbing a ride along Highway 39 out of the mountains. I'd parked the Buick on a turnoff so that I could wand along the banks of the Truckee looking for lost bits of metal, engagement rings, or expensive fly lures I could claim for resale. I didn't look up but once and there was Cheryl, walking towards me, her backpack a tortoiseshell. Her face was sun-scorched from taking in too much sun at altitude and she was coming right for me. I went back to wanding under a copse of green-brown evergreens, and before I knew it she was off-loading her backpack and it hit the loose gravel and kicked up a mist of elevation-dry dust and road sand.

"I'm headed anywhere you are," she said.

Up close she couldn't have been more than twenty-five and she wasn't too thin from smoking a mess of bathtub chemicals, not the way I figured a woman hitchhiker might be. I'd seen gangs of hippie kids from the Pacific Northwest who rode freight trains around the West, letting their gums go black and their teeth fall from their mouths all the while playing Hacky Sack or some such. No, Cheryl had the sinews and veins of a rock climber even though she looked like she didn't know how to hold onto much.

"I'm going to a funeral in Texas," I said. I'd let the wand go slack at my side, the way my jaw must have looked after it lost its hinges. My wife had died a decade ago in a car accident coming out of Reno and

I hadn't so much as talked with another woman outside of the grocery store checkout line, and so I was startled.

"Who died?" she asked.

"My brother, Marven," I said, and explained I was heading to Marfa. Said she could go if she wanted.

"I mean, up to you, but I don't mind," she said. I'm not sure why I extended the invitation, but she accepted and I wasn't gonna rescind. My wife and I were unable to bear children and looking at this young woman on the side of the road outside of Tahoe I saw something of a future that we were never able to conjure: being aged with grown children who need things from us. Everyone assumed that it was Joanne who was barren, but it was me. No motility, the doctor had said, and that was it.

In Moriarity we played solitaire and ate at the hotel diner for each meal and slept in separate twins. The mechanic called and said the LaCrosse was ready, and we made Marfa the next day and smoked Marlboros and chewed Freedent as the mile markers streaked by. Cheryl said she wanted to come to the funeral with me. Was the least she could do, she said. I hadn't been estranged from Marven but I hadn't seen him in a long while. He'd moved to Marfa in the early nineties and wanted to make his name as a sculptor but died managing a hacienda-styled Tex-Mex restaurant.

We went to a thrift shop in Marfa and Cheryl got a black dress that reminded me of the 1980s with the shoulder pads, puffed and padded. When we got to the funeral Cheryl introduced herself as my daughter and everyone knew that was a lie, but we were happy to live in it that afternoon. I had been alone for more than ten years, but for an afternoon I had a dependent. When you bury people it is easy to be won over by fantasy, especially with the smell of turned dirt hanging in the air.

That night I said goodbye to Cheryl in a Dairy Queen parking lot. I watched her walk along Highway 67 until she thumbed a ride in an F-150 heading south. I watched the taillights until they hit the horizon and were snuffed out. The sun was orange and then it was gone. The next day I gassed up the LaCrosse and hoped to make it back to Nevada in three days.

Some years later and on the mend from gallstone surgery, I found myself back on the banks of the Truckee wanding for lost metal. I can say every time I looked up I hoped to see Cheryl on approach. We'd both have stories to tell, and I thought it would be nice to catch up.

CATHY ALLMAN

October Cyclogenesis

We tend to our rhythm
despite winter's early advance,
walk our dog through the mar.
I try to explain how scared
I get in the dark,
how my heart gallops.
My husband says, "We're safe,"
as if he will remind me
of what I should already know.

My husband slept through
the worst of last night's storm,
though our dog barked
when the ladder fell
and garbage splattered.
The for-sale sign dangled off its hook,
potted ferns spilled,
and the howl wouldn't calm,
even when morning split the clouds,
and my husband reached for my cold hand.
The shade on our window
swayed with the draft through
the part cracked and not painted shut.
"I know," I told our dog
as she growled at what
we heard, but didn't see.

RONDA PISZK BROATCH

If the Dream Isn't Ripe Someone Will Advise You to Pluck It

A longing of bees will make your head roar.
Write a letter to the pandemic with no return address.

Greet the sad things wilting in pots by the door
as if you were the UPS driver, and they were

your long-lost relatives. Leave your mind at the door.
Listen to the frog in the drainpipe, until she becomes a dove.

Read how acrimony is a bitterness on the tongue,
how agrimony avails itself upon gallbladder, corns, and warts,

fights feelings of disaster in the lungs. Donate your brain;
you've grown accustomed to its tendency

to wander. Know a big asteroid will fly by Earth on Wednesday,
but don't be fooled into thinking there's zero chance

relief will wash over you in the foreseeable future.
Midwife a swarm of gone-to-seed salsify, hang star-honeyed

objects above the bed. Fly to the moment before the storm.
Get bewitched by ladybugs on the ceiling, waltz through sky fires

until you learn how seraphim swing, the way an insane God
has lost her brass knuckles. How the snakes of the apocalypse

console her without weeping, offering every apple blossom
on all the trees.

NOEL SLOBODA

Online Chatter

Like that sweltering July
it was too hot to breathe

and our windows remained
open every night

and Dad resolved
he'd had enough of listening

to Bob next door
cavorting with strangers

every other evening
in the hot tub built

after his wife left him
back at Christmas

and the cedar privacy fence
Dad started one weekend

had not been finished
when bald-faced hornets

descended to claim material
perfect for a new hive

and my brother and I learned
hornets work in the dark

as we eavesdropped from our beds
to chewing drudges

louder we swore than Bob
and somebody we never met

roaring as if they had not been
already kicked out of Eden.

ERICA PLOUFFE LAZURE

Why My Dad Got Me an Xbox for My Birthday

All I wanted was my blowup unicorn. My giant, rainbow, pool-within-a-pool float unicorn my Auntie Jojo got me as an early birthday present for the pool block party this year, or whatever they call this stupid Hawaiian luau thing, because every year they pick my birthday for the block party and the lady who runs it, Mrs. Secondo, doesn't want cake in her pool and so I have to go home after the party's over so my family can sing me "Happy Birthday" and I can at last make my wish and blow out my candles. Only this year, Kori got sick on account of the tiki torch fumes and so we had to leave all in a rush and only later that night did I remember that my birthday unicorn, which Dad inflated special for me so I could ride it in the pool and all the kids would be jealous, was back at the Secondos and so Mum sent Dad back to get it before my cake and presents. And then, when he didn't come back after a half hour, she sent me out to get him.

"Everything'll be ready when you return," Mum said. So off I went, still in my swimsuit, the lawn water spinners spinning and jetting, and I jumped through each one as I got closer to the Secondos' pool and the fumey tiki lamps were still lit, and all the neighbor kids were gone from the pool, and no one seemed to be home but I could see on the lawn the horn of my unicorn, like those old blacked-out profile pictures you can get done at the mall, only his profile was moving, his head nodding yes-yes-yes. And as I got closer, I could make out a person lying on the unicorn, inside the pool-within-a-pool, making the entire unicorn move like it was listening to music, only the person wasn't alone and the other person sounded like they'd been hurt or something. And before I could call out "Dad?" from behind me, Mr. Secondo yelled, "Frieda? Are you out here?" The unicorn stopped bobbing its head. And before I knew it Mr. Secondo ran past me and leapt onto my unicorn, as Mrs. Secondo sat up, screaming with her top down, with two white patches of skin that were her boobs, and then up popped Dad, his face grim and hair mussed up, like after a shower. We all started yelling as Mr. Secondo hurled the tiki torch at the unicorn, like a spear, and it made a loud pop before it burst into flames, and then, before Dad could even stand up, Mr. Secondo called him a "fucking shit" and socked him clean into the pool.

When I got home, I told Mum that the unicorn float popped, and that Dad was still at the Secondos, trying to patch things up.

ERICA PLOUFFE LAZURE

Don't Look Back

I almost made a bet with Hal last week that you can't drive a half-hour on the Pike without hearing a damn Boston song on the radio. He said I needed to get Sirius if I wanted to control my sound environment, and I said, "Hal, are you serious?" and he didn't even get it, because that's how stupid Hal is. In fact, Hal is so stupid he thinks I'd spend good money on satellite music when I can easily just change the frickin' dial for free.

And of course he's waiting in that idiot lawyer's office right now, probably calling *me* the stupid one, because I'm running late, even though it's not my fault I'm stuck in traffic with the rest of New England funneling into Fenway on game day. Nothing else to do but fiddle with the radio, because if that twangy opener for "Let Me Take You Home Tonight" shows up it'll take everything in me not to rear-end the car ahead of me when the song hits that full-throttle hoedown finale. I read somewhere that Boston wasn't even a band—the guitarist made the whole album alone in his basement, guitar and keyboard and all, and then scrounged for a singer and a few other musicians when the album sold. But I guess he's entitled to the royalties for his shitty fake songs, just like Hal thinks he's entitled to more than half of Mom's estate, because he convinced some snoot-ass lawyer that you can put a price on caring for her during her last months. It's true I didn't come by the house much, but even if I did I sure as shit wouldn't claim it like some expense account on her will. But Hal kept his receipts. I guess that's what they teach you in college, that you are owed money when you take care of your dying mother. I feel like telling him some people have jobs that you can't just take "family leave" for, that someone has to install plateglass windows in America's future suburban corporate parks to make sure the windows seal up right and don't pop out in cold weather.

And once this traffic clears, I'll cruise down Landsdowne and show up late in my work uniform, and the lawyer'll go through my brother's receipts, one by one, and hand me my ass on a platter before he cuts us each a check. Maybe Hal's right. Maybe I'll get Sirius for the van so I won't ever have to hear Boston again. Maybe with the money I'll just blast out of here, like that crap-ass opening to "Third Stage," where the guitar sounds like a rocket. But sure as shit, the radio's got their "Bossin' in Boston" Power Hour, to celebrate the Sox, and when the first few licks of "Don't Look Back" come through the airwaves, something in the lyrics catches me and I figure, just this once, I'll crank it loud, full throttle, all the way to Fenway.

ERICA PLOUFFE LAZURE

The Seamstress Bride

What's left of my mother's things are set up on the lawn and open for business, when this girl comes flying up the street, driving so fast I'm sure she's gonna crash into something, and then, when she sees me see her, she pulls over onto the wrong side of the road, and I'm sure what she's gonna crash into is me.

Before I unclench my eyes, I hear, "How much for the bodice?"

She's wearing gym clothes, but her hair is done up, curly-stiff, and there's a strand of pearls like Silver Queen corn curls around her neck, like she's on her way to a workout prom.

"It's called a form," I say, recalling Mom's phrase. "A dressmaker's form." I work the knobs, stalling, to come up with a good price, making the chest of the form expand.

"It adjusts to different sizes, see?" What would Mom want for it?

"Great," she says, stepping out of the car. "So how much?"

The word "twenty" leaves my mouth before I can catch it, and I can't tell if it's gonna be too high or too low. Before the arthritis got her hands, Ma was the best seamstress in the county—the form is top shelf. But the girl barely blinks as she pulls out a sweaty twenty from her waistband pocket and hands it over.

"Thanks," she says, her jaws working the gum in her mouth. She grabs the form, unscrews the stand, and embraces it with both arms. Then she hoists it onto the passenger seat and straps it in with the seatbelt. The backseat of her car is filled with white balloons.

"Out running errands. I'm getting married today," she says, glancing back at the balloons, as if she'd just remembered. "But I've always wanted a bodice. For sewing."

"Well, enjoy the form," I say. Another car pulls up. "And congratulations!"

And as the bride zooms off down the street, an image of the form dressed in a tuxedo pops into my mind, a string of balloons battling the wind, as they drive off together toward their honeymoon.

"Excuse me," says the next customer, breaking my spell. I turn to her. An older woman, clutching Mom's old birding kit. "How much for these binoculars?"

María Alejandra Barrios

Pimiento Season

When Mamá's apron catches fire, my first reaction is to grab Mamá's body and share the fire with her.

Pimientos en nogada is a dish that people eat in México at weddings and important occasions. Mamá is set on making it on our special day since she wants to prove to us, but mostly to herself ,that despite her curled fingers and the ache in her knees, she can still cook. The night before the fire, she makes the nogada. She leaves the unpeeled nuts soaking with milk, mashes the nuts with fresh white cheese, a pinch of sugar, cinnamon, salt, and white wine. The mixture, after straining, is fragrant and creamy.

Mamá starts the dish with the fire, a set and steady flame that turns blue at the tips. She puts the pimientos on the stove. "How long on each side?" I ask, half looking at her and half looking at my phone. "You have to look to see," she says, her bare hands turning the pimiento to the other side. Although they must be hot, she doesn't say so.

"Mamá!" I yell, far too late, as the fabric of her hand-painted apron she had bought in México D.F. gets consumed by the flame.

Two days later, when we come back from the hospital, the nogada is still sitting on the table with the rest of the pimientos all over the floor, some blackened and some uncooked—the remnants of our kitchen incident, as Mamá would call it. Roberto, my soon-to-be husband, in the rush of paramedics and sirens, hadn't put the food back in the fridge. I touch my stomach, which is covered in bandages, and think about flies.

☾

Mamá, who rests in bed days after the incident, predicts that rain will appear midceremony and soak us all.

"Rain is a good omen," I tell her, my fingers covered in the thick white odorless matter I use for her stomach burns.

"How did it feel for you?" she says, trying to sit up after I am done with her stomach. "I didn't feel it," I lie while carefully applying the salve to my middle, which is covered in purple blisters. "My skin must have been numb from the pain."

She turns to the wall, smiling as if she were seeing it for the first time. A flash of the flames engulfing the carefully hand-painted flowers on her apron comes to my head. The same flames that traveled to my cotton shirt.

I had poured a pot of water on both of us. I can still hear the panic in her raspy smoker's voice. The way that her voice addressed me in one word: "Corre," her delirious tone convinced that we could escape the flame.

I removed the blackened apron and her shirt first, afraid that it would get stuck to her skin. My hands acted quickly as howls of pain escaped my mouth.

"The wallpaper. It's starting to crack," Mamá says.

I nod without looking. Every night after the fire, the smell of our leathering gets stuck to my nose.

Roberto, who comes to visit Mamá every day, swallowing his I-told-you-so about Mamá in the kitchen, Mamá at the stove, Mamá doing anything, is the first to be against the idea of postponing the wedding.

"I can't wear the same dress," I say, thinking about how the corsé will press against my skin.

"We will buy you another one."

"My mother will not be able to go to the beach. Her skin could get infected."

"So we marry here. Problem solved," he says, sitting on the couch and putting his feet up on the table since Mamá is in her room and can't move to tell him that he is not an animal and he is not in his own house.

I sit on his lap. Kissing his forehead, his cheeks, telling him not to press on my stomach—not now and not in the six months that it will take to heal. We start kissing, and for a while we don't check on Mamá, who after going to sleep, will miss the start of the rainy season that will stay long after the pimiento season is over and long after Roberto and I get married in the rain, my baggy wedding dress and his going-out shoes soaked by the aguacero and the water that leaks from the top of the house, Mamá with her flimsy blue umbrella and with her water-resistant camera will take blurry pictures that will mark one of the first bad September storms.

When Mamá goes to sleep that night, I cover Mamá's burns in the thick mixture. In the dark room, I hear Roberto calling for me. The taxi is here, he says. I lift Mamá's shirt. My fingers get lost in her tender skin.

By next September, our stomachs will burst in a sea of scars.

María Alejandra Barrios

Afterlife//Dear Daughter

In our family of witches we have a tendency to collect spirits just as we have a tendency to follow bad men around and to drink too much aguardiente chased with light beer after two in the afternoon when we are convinced we'll never love again and then bam! someone else falls in our net, we love and we love a lot and we love spirits too and they visit us to tell us things about your aunt who everyone thought was crazy because she was scared of the beach but ended up drowning on a calm summer day, and mostly I'll visit you, my daughter, just to gossip—so know that you'll hate me for hearing me in your head all day, and most nights you'll finally fall asleep after praying to the god we never believed in to please make me go away, "Diosito, por favor," you'll say, "make this vieja pendeja live in someone else's head," and I'll try to, at least for a while, but it will get boring hanging out with my dead sisters, and I'll come back to just chat a little and make you choose better than I did—not a drunk like your father or another drunk like the man I married after, someone more fun, light, like a little paper boat that floats on a beautiful vibrant green lake, untouched, better than we ever were—so know that I'll stay with you and that you'll always remember my recipes, even the one topped with the smelly burnt cheese, and you'll smell my sweet scent of mud and cinnamon everywhere, even in places you think I could never find you, places that I never visited when I was alive, because in the afterlife there's always a tomorrow and I've heard even that crazy aunt of yours finally learned how to swim.

KATHY GOODKIN

Pedagogy

Over time, the forest
becomes our lungs.
We breathe, and light

through the leaves
writes words at our feet.
Your hands are alchemical

as thought. Black snakeroot,
sassafras, a snail on the path.
I learn the names for plants

because I want
to show them to you
with whom I walk.

Naming is one way
to hold the world
against the self, to feel it

pulsing. Today, I hold nothing
but the forest
between us. The syntax

of the forest unites
your name and mine.
We breathe with

our forest lungs,
and your thoughts
are as tangible as a hand.

KATHY GOODKIN

Climate Change Cinéma Vérité

I sat in front of the Starbucks window
for hours, but I never turned my head that way.
And rising to leave, was surprised

to see across the street
a stand of old oaks clumped close
like mourners, behind a Walgreens

and a storage facility called "Bee Safe."
There was a picture of a bee
on the sign. As though bees

have anything to do in this landscape,
except die. Except fall into drifts
of little corpses for me to collect daily

from the pavement. Except lie
hollow, immeasurably light,
scatter like dry leaves

during the burial rites
I hold in the funeral parlor
I once called my yard.

VIVIAN EYRE

What's in Front of You

On Instagram, a diver swat-swims through a mess of jellyfish,
swollen domes adrift, their limbs stinger-thin,

except the caption insists: *Plastic bags under the sea.* In the Pacific,
the *Island of Debris* is twice the size of Texas

floating, woven solid. I don't look at the quilt of sun
over Southold Bay—only at seaweed's clutch

of straws, cups, Doritoz bags, a red net bag
that I knot into a rummage sack.

Shaking sand from a blanket, a mother says: *Hurry up,
we're going.* Next to the sandcastle, a blue toy shovel.

What's left behind ghosts the crevices of the heart.
I keep company with my thoughts of Indonesia

where a list of one thousand items includes flip-flops
found in the belly of a whale. The sandwich wrapper

sunbathing in a parking lot also swims
through rain and gusts into sea-foam.

Stopping at the grocery a few blocks away, shoppers
buy plastic bags, a nickel apiece. My cart is full

when I remember the reusable bags in my car
next to the red net sack.

After all I've seen, I can't believe the temptation
to pay the pittance, to wheel my cart to the end of the line.

MATTHEW PITT

Boat of Books

While moving to a new state, I misplaced a box of books. It remained vanished—in my possession, yet adrift—through two more moves. Its absence stung, my whalebone prosthesis, my *Moby-Dick* (one book lost in the box's belly, though a book which, at that time, I was yet to read). It also stung that I could not precisely recall which books the box contained. Which words had gone missing.

I was on a thwarted dragnet team, dredging rivers for lost companions. If I could only hunt them down, their knowledge would, I believed, instantly reunite with and flood my brain.

At the time my box strayed, I first read Cheryl Strayed's, "The Love of My Life." In her essay Strayed entreats readers to imagine a boat at sea that can only hold (and thus save) four cherished people. Who, she asks, would comprise your quartet? Which lives would you allow in, and which would you permit the sea to swallow?

I began conflating which four lives I'd save with which books. What people to bring onboard my hypothetical raft was a problem, in fact, more easily solved. My last surviving grandparent, born on Armistice Day, was at that time ailing mightily. Maybe best to let him go. But in 1918 *My Ántonia* was published. If I could tow both book *and* relative, might reading Willa Cather aloud wring from my taciturn paternal grandfather some details about his farming life? Then again, would he honestly spill more of his Polish immigrant life on the Midwestern plains than Cather's carefully wrought sentences? And if he were to maintain his present course of silence, wouldn't his raft spot be better served by someone more apt to spill secrets? Wouldn't *My Ántonia* be more likely to render my grandfather's life to me then the grandfather himself?

Each year, I read several dozen books: If actuarial tables hold, I might manage 2,200 in total—both an estimable sum and a feeble drop in the ocean. That doesn't even count beloved childhood books—and how could I exile from the raft all titles that reared my love of books? Something wonderful might happen if I read Judy Blume alongside *Mrs. Dalloway*.

Selecting an unread book would offer surprise, though if the foreign book disappointed, I'd have to carry its tedium forever. Or toss or eat the pages.

Could I sneak in a story? James Baldwin's "Sonny's Blues" would make a fine stowaway, easily folded and hidden. If it wound up counting against my book total, though, I'd let it go, like clothes from a person I tried to tug onto the boat, but who slipped my grip.

Possessions don't carry to the afterlife. Perhaps knowledge does. Comforting thought, that gold and jewels are nontransferable, but insight can be banked in this world then spent in the next.

Does acquiring knowledge *only* bolster a brain? Or can excess breach its hull? As if taking on water—the very substance lifting and conveying you now tugging you toward uneasy, icy depths?

My books finally surfaced in our current home's backyard shed, beneath a crate of unused ornaments and tinsel, the box labeled "Bedroom Belongings," a mark that did and did not fit. After all, my wife and I often read to each other in bed. A raft of thought and beauty to steer us toward sleep.

I celebrated finding my long-lost books but did not reread a single one.

I keep a clearinghouse file filled with favorite, retyped sentences from books. I rarely check it, though. It's a storage unit filled with unused ornaments and tinsel—keepsakes barely kept.

I imagine the lingual spare parts will nudge me to reread books they came from, though retyping them usually disposes me *not* to reread. As if, once my prized sentences are safe in my computer lifeboat, abandoning the books they were borne from becomes easier.

Other than the Bible, my paternal grandfather rarely read. Perhaps any other narrative seemed threadbare. Or he feared a secular book offering as much sustenance and light as his holy one would cast daunting shadows on his faith.

If he were a passenger in my boat, could I use any extra space he neglected to fill with books?

My daughter once demanded I read aloud four books to her nightly. Now she rarely shares what she scans in her beloved books—two boats passing. She stows these things in her heart. Clutching tight to this keepsake, this love of words, she is drifting away.

Ryn Haaversen

Stained

The kitchen had always been a sacred place. It was the room I thought of when someone said "home." It was where we would all gather, on the stools and the floor. The pleasant aroma of freshly baked goods would drift throughout every room. The white tiled floors were stained from years of family, friends, and food. It was this room that was responsible for my most vibrant smiles and fondest memories. Christmas cookies would be stacked by piles of unused cookbooks and baking magazines. This was where visions of Mom grace my memories. Now beetles creep up my spine when I think of the pale yellow counters dusted with wheat flour.

Dinner Bread Recipe

5 cups flour (4 ½ bread, ½ wheat)
1 ½ cup warm water
4 teaspoon yeast
3 tablespoon butter
1 egg
⅓ cup sugar
½ teaspoon salt

For Rolls: 375 for 15-25 minutes
For Loaves: 350 for 25-35 minutes

Flour flew from Mom's crimson apron as she turned on the tiled floors. Even during Thanksgiving it would be "Jingle Bell Rock" that echoed through the house. She would softly sing along, pausing only to count her ingredients and double-check the recipe card. Her bloated feet were shoved into ratty old shoes that were caked and crusted with old food. New flour would be added to her laces as she kneaded loaves of bread for the holidays. She would brush her dough-coated fingers against her apron, letting bits tumble to the dirty floor and gather there. White specks now stained the red cloth. Smiling, I waited for fresh knots to be taken out of the oven. I would try to lend a hand, brushing melted butter across golden crusts.

I had avoided his touch for years, never walking close enough for his hands to reach me. Walking away when he would talk about my body like it belonged to him. My sister and I were making dinner, something Mom had always done. Shaking hands fiddled with the paring knife as I chopped. It was there that Carl, my father, came up behind me. He asked for a hug. A simple request, but it was never really a question to begin with. I never replied. I wanted to say no, but it was my job, wasn't it? To comfort him after Mom's death? That's what the narrative had been ever since I came back to the house on White Street. That's what was expected of me, so I shouldn't say no. People kept telling us to take care of each other. It became my responsibility. No matter how much I wanted to say no. No matter how much I wished I had. No matter how much I wanted to be anywhere else.

Vanilla Maple Butter

1 pound of butter
½ cup powdered sugar
Real vanilla to taste
Real maple syrup to taste

I used to sit on those white tiles, lean against the floral walls, and watch Mom move around the kitchen. Carl would occasionally walk through, on his way to the garage or work. He never stayed in the kitchen long. The TV would continue playing quietly in the background as Mom and I talked—about school, skiing, theater, college plans, moving, anything that came to mind. Sometimes, I would end up at the yellow counters next to her, chopping a bowl full of russet potatoes or whipping up a sweet butter. Slowly learning how to cook like she did. Always talking—we chatted even as we worked.

His hands were lower than they should have been, resting below my waist. He held on for too long and it felt like I was suffocating. I was trapped there. Between him and the pale counters. I had nowhere to go and nothing good to say. Of all the things to come out of that kitchen, his touch is what I remember the most. Even after he let go, his touch lingered on my hips. I squirmed for hours, his calloused hands still crawling up my back. They held crevices of black from the mines that had seeped into my skin. I didn't stay at the house that night. I grabbed the bag that lived by the stairs and went out into the cold night again.

Fresh Basil Pesto

2 cups fresh basil leaves, packed
½ cup grated Parmigiano-Reggiano cheese
½ cup extra virgin olive oil
⅓ cup pine nuts
3 garlic cloves, minced
¼ teaspoon salt
⅛ teaspoon ground black pepper

During high school I would walk home for lunch. I'd find Mom surrounded by my friends and hers, all here for wonderful food. The TV would be turned off at times like this, its usual background noise replaced by boisterous laughter that echoed from the White Street house. Even on cold winter days, her food would warm us. Everything from mac and cheese to sandwiches on focaccia bread with homemade pesto warmed in our rusted oven. This was where we would gather for a midday pick-me-up. A place where no one had to knock and all were welcomed.

His fingers continued to dig into my waist during the family photos. Photos that were taken as the family gathered in Mom's memory. No matter how hard I tried to stand anywhere else. By anyone else. To escape the photo all together. His fingers dug deeper, holding me in place. He never noticed the look I had on my face— the pain I wore in my clenched jaw or the void he would have seen, had he only looked me in the eye. He continues to ask for hugs when he sees me now. Can't he see? The answer will always be no.

Orange Cranberry Bagels

1 cup plus 4 tablespoons water, divided
½ cup dried cranberries
⅓ cup packed brown sugar
4 ½ teaspoons grated orange zest
1 teaspoon salt
¼ teaspoon ground cloves
3 cups bread flour
¼ ounces active dry yeast
1 tablespoon sugar
1 large egg white
1 tablespoon cornmeal

My favorite days were when Mom made bagels. Her lively voice would waft through the white halls to announce the first batch was done. I would clamber down the carpeted staircase and slide into the kitchen with haste. No matter how hot it was, I would devour the first bagel on sight. The orange zest coated my tongue, popping with juicy bursts of cranberries. She would laugh at me when I complained about burning my mouth, fully knowing that I'd never change.

I tried to talk to him about it a couple times. What he had done to me, how his subtle touches affected me. The first time it all started with him wanting to see my tattoo, something that wasn't for him. He demanded, said he had the right. He had always been domineering, insisting on forced respect. I got the tattoo as a symbol of Mom. It was for me and me alone. I turned to explain, but he had already stomped away. He thought he held some right to my body, simply because I carried his DNA. I threw on my blue coat that was ripping at the seams. Brushed the salt off my brown moose-hide mukluks and rammed my feet inside. I took a final look into the kitchen before walking out and into the steadily falling snow.

Years later you still pretend it's all fine, ignoring all the times I've told you it's not. You still sends birthday cards, but they aren't in your handwriting. You still invite me to holiday dinners, only I'm a thousand miles away and you only tell me a week ahead of time. No matter how hard you think you're trying, you're still missing the point. All of these gestures are a slap to my face, because when someone tries to hug me it's still your touch that crawls up my spine.

The last time I set foot on those light tiled floors, nothing of Mom was left. The whole kitchen had been cleansed; memories and stains were erased. He had boxed up her memory, put her away, sold her to the highest bid, and replaced her with a new face. Cookbooks and baking magazines overflowed from the trash can. Recipes lost to the purge of his old life. I walked out the back door a final time, carrying another box to my car. The sight of the for sale sign is still imbedded in my brain.

The taconite dust from your hands still stains my body black.

M.A. SCOTT

After My Mother and I Discuss Her DNR

They're deflating the ice cream cone in front
of Rita's, ready to close for the night. The Sprint
store glows pink as a cellophane Easter basket.

Still a spotlight on the billboard of an American flag-
wrapped fetus at the Knights of Columbus hall, where
it leaned by the door on Election Day, in illegal proximity.

Flower Moon rises blurred, yellow. There are roses
and votives on the bridge over Beaver Brook
where a young (no, not young, my age) mother

chose to end herself last Saturday. Some last breath
of lilacs in the dark. We used to cut their branches
for Memorial Day; now they crumple weeks earlier

in eager rush at bloom and rot. By June the lindens
will fill us. Our front walks, the neighbor's, mine, all
staked with cheap solar lights, holding last teaspoons

of sun up to phlox, irises, dandelions. Next
door, a Trump placard still stuck in the weedy lawn,
and two hollow plastic Santas chained to the gas pipe.

ROY BENTLEY

Teratology

Everything is as expected, April arranging itself
as what happens in dim cattle barns in west Texas,
until a Janus-headed calf is wrenched out and the vet
lets off monologuing about Texas Longhorns football.

Again, a washing of hands and looking away as if some
are judged unfit or ugly chiefly for reasons of their rarity.
Again, a cumulus of epithelial matchlessness of a design
neither intelligent nor sacred but at least somewhat new.

One dog watches as if seeing stars fall for the first time.
Another is wrapped in dry, grassless dreams of summer
but wakes to the noises of birth on some straw in a stall.
Tonight a freak, and you see the risk in loving anything.

At least there is initiation in the way the vet is talking—
regardless, it's standing. Which is not to say it can be
saved from dogs who spring from the backs of trucks,
slipping their chains to roam an American darkness.

SHEVAUN BRANNIGAN

Wildwood

We ride your pickup truck through a Jersey Shore town
in November, a star or two above, the roads abandoned
as ice cream parlors. *If this was all driving was,*

I say, meaning no people, no bright lights in the rearview,
no fender benders, no steady rotation of staring in mirrors,
no turn-signal clicking, no sudden brakes, no radio crackle,

yes your hand on my thigh, yes the lazy veer of wide lanes,
yes the brights on, yes the deer's eyes reflecting at the road's edge,
yes every cup holder full with coffee cup singing the engine's song,

if a traffic jam were an angry goose, if the traffic light swinging
a flashing yellow was the only sun, if squinting was to see your silhouette
sharper, each bristle of your beard, *we would be on time*, we would

take our time, ahead of us this night a two-star, seventies hotel
where I'd hear the fight outside, two bodies grappling each other,
thudding against the cement, and you would sleep through it,

or I dreamt it and I slept through it, while the lava lamp thought steadily,
like the concierge downstairs at the desk, open all night, *No hurry,*
she said on the phone, *we'll be here as long as you need us.*

Robert Brian Mulder

Right Things Left Undone

Unlike most things, the job isn't complicated. Weekdays, and every other Saturday, I put on a Day-Glo vest, drive a flatbed truck, and pick up roadkill off WY–390, or along Highway 191, a two-lane, twenty-mile stretch that runs the gap between Jackson Hole and Hobak. Mule deer mainly, but also elk, badgers, coyotes, porcupines, red foxes, striped skunks, the occasional black bear or bison. And moose, of course. Somebody will call—supposed to, at least—or I'll spot something from the truck on a daily run. In winter, when plows cover the carcasses with snow, you look for crows. Sometimes we'll euthanize. It all depends. The occasional hunter will stop and cut the antlers off a big buck for rattling, a trick that mimics the sound of two bucks sparring. Works as a deer call. In parts of the West, a dead deer can be harvested for its meat. Not in Wyoming—though, of course, people being people, some do it anyway, despite the risk of contamination from a ruptured bladder. In August, the meat can cook down to the bone. Winter work is preferable. It means less smell, though the hide of any animal can be stubborn if frozen to the ground. It's like scraping day-old grease off a cast-iron skillet. Makes for a long day, and a dangerous one if there's heavy traffic.

A sort-of buddy of mine, Dale, who works for the National Park Service, got me the job. Or the connection, at least. Felt guilty, I guess, for dating my ex not two weeks after we finally called it quits. Me and Dale both worked construction off and on for years, mostly hanging drywall on condominiums in Jackson Hole, where there'd been a steady fever of development. "Bloated as a deer tick," was Dale's verdict, though we both knew the bloat was paying our bills. Last summer, he was seeing this anarchist-vegan type, a monkey-wrencher with legs and arms skinny as PVC pipe. Anyway, one night this girl persuades Dale that what he needs to do is gas and torch two bulldozers parked on the site leveled for a T.J. Maxx. "Popping the tick," is what Dale called it. "Make it bleed." If I ever make the mistake of buying him a beer, he'll get riled about the old fuckers with their road-hog, half-million-dollar RVs. About the fat-ass kids feeding candy bars to even fatter squirrels that'll climb straight up your pantleg to beg. About the fool-headed devilry of spending budget dollars on plastic containers devoted to dumping plastic bags full of dog shit. About the drones. "These goddamn drones," Dale says, poking his tongue into his cheek like a drill as he traces a finger around the neck of his empty bottle. "The other day I'm out at Elk Ranch Flats and hear this loud buzzing noise. I look over and spot one," he says, "hovering in the air like a fucking prehistoric insect, not more than five feet above a bison."

Anyway, when Dale mentioned the WYDOT opportunity, I figured I'd rather pick up roadkill than get myself into a position where I'd need to start eating it. Hanging drywall had burned out my knees and back, and I hadn't worked for six months. I told myself I'd do it for a spell, save up, then find something else. Maybe quit altogether—quit building people's vacation homes, quit watching ranchers sell out to developers. Get out, go wherever it is people aren't going. But a year passes quick, then another. I can't say why exactly, but sometimes it seems right that I end most days standing at the edge of a carcass pit carved from the east ridge of Horsethief Canyon, site of the Teton County landfill, staring out at a rotting sea of garbage. Over 788,000 cubic yards of waste. Coyotes and crows scavenging like hungry ghosts. Black clouds of bulldozer smoke. The slow swell of the stinking heap as it chokes the canyon like an advancing glacier.

A few years back, at the end of my first day on the job, one of the old-timers caught me staring stupidly at my hands. My work gloves already had holes, and blood had dried on my knuckles and up under the nails. He pointed me toward the smallest of three nondescript buildings that border the pit. I stepped into a mostly bare room. Bloodstains—some old, some not so old—covered the concrete floor. All different configurations, like some grisly map of the underworld. There were two rows of severed deer heads, maybe a dozen total. Fur bristle-stiff, eyelids shut. Antlers sawed off and piled in haphazard fashion along the far wall, beside rusted tanks of propane. I never asked. Though I later overheard it had something to do with testing for CWD, a.k.a. zombie deer disease. It was midwinter, bitter cold, but all the windows were open, which made the stench, cut with petrol, tolerable enough. I walked to a small sink in the corner, began to do what I could to scrub the bloodstains from my hands with cold water and a filthy sliver of soap. On top of the wall-mounted towel dispenser, the old type with a small metal crank, some wise-ass had balanced a formidable rack of antlers, all the tips sharp as hawk talons. And they'd pencil-sketched two large black eyes, slightly crossed, demented-looking, and a long black tongue that hung out at an obscene angle.

I shook my hands dry and left.

Nearly every night that week, I'd dream about those severed deer heads. In the dream their eyes were all open wide, unblinking—black, like wet stones pulled from a creek bed. And their lips were parted, as if ready to speak. Strange enough, after that first week, I never had that dream again. Not once. As if a deafness, a numbness had settled in. It was like those ghost deer haunting my dreams had been spooked off by too much contact with the real thing.

Four o'clock. Friday. An hour before sundown. Heavy snowflakes falling like singed moths in a reddening sky. I unload the half-frozen carcasses of three adult deer—legs outstretched, stiff as signposts. Rigor mortis sets in quick. Three is unusual, but not unheard of. The largest, a female—struck by a school bus—twitched and shuddered in a shallow ditch while children wearing bright-colored coats pressed pale faces to windows that soon began to fog with their breath.

A new recruit—Jim, or maybe Tim—comes over to help. My shoulder, the left one, isn't good anymore, especially in this cold. Clicks and locks, like a bad hinge on a busted door. "Ready?" he says, staring down into the carcass pit, a pulled-tooth gap in the blood-red mouth of the canyon. We each grab an end, me at the rear. As we lift, I feel a heavy bone in the right hind leg grind before it slips loose. We swing, toss—the pain in my shoulder humming.

Heading south on Highway 191 towards Hobak. Population 1,176. December cold in the valley. Car wouldn't start—probably the alternator—so they let me take a work truck for the weekend. I rent a place, a little guesthouse on an old widow's farm. Small, but clean and quiet. Fields with low hills to the east. Cottonwoods down along a creek. Warblers, meadowlarks, the occasional white-headed woodpecker. The widow leaves me a loaf of sourdough bread inside the screen door every Sunday morning—still warm—a scripture verse attached with a red ribbon.

It isn't the most charitable thought, I recognize, but with her kindness, sometimes I catch myself looking ahead and hoping that, when the widow dies, being childless, she just might do it—might leave me the place in her will. Or at least arrange it somehow so I can stay on as caretaker.

It's still snowing—fat, lazy flakes—but the road is clear. Almost zero traffic. A motor home, Class A, black as buffalo shit, blows by— Jeep in tow, heading north, at least 60 mph in a 45 zone. On this stretch of Highway 191, known to locals as the Splatter Speedway, WYDOT puts up these big flashing signs: DRIVE SLOW! SAVE WILDLIFE! People ignore them, of course. Tourists, or locals, distracted with directions or mobile phones or just the scenery.

I jam two fingers deep into the throbbing ache in my shoulder, rub the offending tendon crossways. Check the rearview. Reach down to adjust the rubber floor mat. When I look up again, a red Dodge Ram is drifting into my lane not thirty yards ahead. I swerve to the shoulder, straight into a road crater that rattles the truck's frame like a dropped box of tools. As the oncoming truck passes, something pops against my windshield. I jerk back in my seat so hard I hear the recoil of rusty springs. Slowing, I pull all the way off the road, hit my hazards. Hunched forward, squinting in the twilight, I run my thumb along a clean bright crack in the glass. My chest tightens like a bolt turned too far. And the feeling of something unspooling at the base of my spine.

Bastard.

Checking both directions, I torque the wheel, do a U-turn and start back, heading north.

Soon I'm riding the bumper of the Dodge Ram. Tinted windows. California plates. A Teewinot bumper sticker. I rummage blind in the glovebox for some paper. Nothing—just a greasy tire gauge, a large black marker, a pair of binoculars. After a quarter mile, as dusk nears full dark, I see movement off to the right, at the edge of the woods. A dark shape. Tall as a man. Then another beside it, smaller. Both still. All this in a second or two before I hear a muted hollow thump, see the outline of something up ahead tumble off the road, disappear down an embankment. I lift my foot off the gas—expecting brake lights—but the fucker just keeps rolling on. I follow for another hundred yards or so, then abruptly pull off the highway and begin to back the truck along the shoulder—the sound of fresh snow crunching beneath the tires.

From the truck, I can see her—a moose calf, lying motionless on her side in the snow, like a discarded doll. The mother is there, head low, sniffing the length of her calf's underside. After a time, she lifts her head, looks down the darkening road, then turns and begins to move, unhurriedly, back toward the trees—each step in the deep snow precise, deliberate, as if testing unfamiliar ground. Before long, I can hear the dry snapping of branches as the mother and her remaining calf move deeper into the woods.

An hour later, in a dark corner of the lot, I park near two dumpsters enclosed by a brown fence with a green metal sign that reads PROPERTY OF TEEWINOT CONDOMINIUMS. The Dodge Ram is up ahead, down to the right a few spaces. Almost no one coming or going for a long while. Around eleven, I start the engine, pull forward, drive past the rear of the red truck, then back up till I'm just a few feet away. Headlights off, I get out, lower both tailgates, slide a board from the bed of my truck so that it rests between the two like a plank. Grabbing the moose calf by her skinny hind legs, I pull her onto the board. She is small—ninety, maybe a hundred pounds, her thick rust-red coat smelling faintly of pine bark and willow shrub. I make to slide her gentle on the board, but the loose fold of skin under her neck catches on the edge of the wood so that I have to push her back before hoisting and tugging quick, which works, though the muscles in my shoulder feel newly cattle-branded. When the calf is all the way in, hid beneath a black vinyl cover that runs the length of the bed, I push the board back into the work truck, lift and secure both tailgates, return to my spot by the dumpsters, cut the engine.

If, at some point, I had a clear idea of what to do next, it was to leave. To go home. But I don't leave. Though I can't say why exactly. Maybe I just need to see it. To see him see it.

I think it was last Friday night when Dale told me about a story in the news. A boy who'd been granted his wish to hunt and kill a Kodiak bear in Alaska. "A dying boy's dream," Dale said, "made possible by the Make-A-Fucking-Wish Foundation." He grinned a drunk's grin, grabbed the underside of his jaw as if he meant to reset it, then tracked the hustle of a tight-ass waitress as she scooted past our table. "But enough of that bullshit," he said. "Tell me something good. Tell me about your little brother. The Saint of South Dakota. How's Kern? Has that boy gone full Lakota yet?"

Kern teaches geology at Sitting Bull College. Spent his sabbatical trying to persuade the federal government to give the Black Hills back to the Lakota people. We get along, though I haven't seen him for going on twelve years—probably more my fault than his. One thing about Kern, he's always seemed to have this irksome knack for knowing what's good and how to get there. Like the line between right and wrong is straight and true as a roofing nail.

Anyway, for some reason, I started telling Dale about a time a while back, when Kern was living in Boise and helping out with a program at his church. Friday and Saturday nights, church leaders and a few lay members would drive a kind of circuit, checking dumpsters for discarded babies. It wasn't a regular occurrence, but if they found one still alive, they'd take it back to the home and family that had disposed of it. Then they'd ask the mother or father to take back the child. One man, now a leader himself, a deacon in the church, had previously been a father who'd dumped his boy in a bin behind a Super-K. "The point is for them to face it," Kern said with his usual confidence. "To confront them with what they've done. To bear witness. Give them a chance to do what they know is right." He almost made it feel like he meant to recruit me. Like my sorry ass was just sitting around waiting for something better to do.

Past midnight. Moonlight.

Two raccoons scratch at the dumpster lids crusted with ice. A shrill whistle of insistent wind leaking through gaps in the insulation around the door. It's fucking cold. I crank the engine, pull off my gloves, blast the heat on high, rub and flex my hands in front of the vents till I can feel my fingers again.

I try to sleep but can't. I try not to think about babies abandoned in garbage bins, or about the way the calf's broken neck bobbed as I dragged her up that embankment. I try not to imagine the driver of the Dodge Ram in his king-size bed, warm, sleeping peacefully next to his attractive wife in a condo I probably helped build. I try not to think about how most people are selfish bastards. Try not to consider all the ways I'm a selfish bastard. The wrong things done. Worse. The right things left undone.

Morning. Clear sky. Nine o'clock.

Two high-pitched beeps. All the lights flash on the red Dodge Ram. I look up to see an old man and an old woman making their way down a flight of stairs, stepping sideways in the snow. The man wears a black cowboy hat and holds the woman by the elbow. The woman holds the rail with one hand and a cluster of red balloons with the other. Halfway down, they stop. The woman turns to say something. The man crouches, fiddling with a wire by his left ear.

As they make the slow, stiff effort to climb into the truck, I grip the cold steering wheel, hunch forward, squint up through the cracked windshield to the top of the stairs. Expecting to see the old man's son or daughter. Maybe a grandson wearing snakeskin boots, a cocksure grin.

Headed north of Jackson Hole on Highway 191. Along the shoulder, a shredded truck tire. A half-gutted recliner. An orange plastic bag blown about like tumbleweed. Any doubt that he was the driver last night evaporates when I see the way the old man hugs the center line—drifting over from time to time—taking us up to 55 mph in a 40 zone. Only easing off when we get stuck behind a logging truck.

No turn signal before the Dodge Ram makes an abrupt left into a development along the Snake River. Ten-acre plots that border a wildlife refuge. Massive homes on snowy hills. All big timber and stone.

A half mile in, the old man brakes suddenly, then turns and starts up a long unplowed driveway. He doesn't get far before he stops and slowly backs the truck down the hill and parks beneath a fir tree, along a tall row of holly bushes. I pull off the road, grab the binoculars out of the glove box, wait. The couple eventually gets out, the old man reaching for his wife's elbow as they begin to shuffle up the driveway to a house with a red door and a wreath the size of an inflatable pool toy. Two Land Rovers—one black, one silver—parked under a stone portico. In the big yard out front, half a dozen children playing in the snow. One of them, a dark-haired girl in a yellow coat, runs down the hill toward the couple, waving her arms. As she hugs the old woman and takes hold of the balloons, a large white dog appears from the far side of the Dodge Ram. It doesn't bark. Seems intent on not being seen as it lifts its lanky front legs up onto the rear bumper, stretching its neck toward the top of the tailgate. When the girl sees the dog, she claps, calls for it to come. The dog looks over at the girl—whimpering, straining its neck up once more before giving up and racing toward her.

I wait nearly an hour for the kids to tire out and go inside, but no luck. Soon I'm yawning nonstop till my jaw muscles ache, so I give in, let myself nod off—ten, maybe fifteen minutes. When I wake, I grab the binoculars—no sign of anyone. Everything quiet. But when I look over at the red truck, I see them. Crows. Three perched on the cab, three hopping along the black vinyl cover. Then four more up in the fir tree, cursing as they bob their black heads up and down like pistons. Suddenly, another flying up and off with something stringy and red in its beak. And at this point, I don't know. I don't know if it's the fact of the old couple being so goddamn old, or if maybe it's the dark-haired birthday girl with her yellow coat and balloons, or just the sudden uneasy feeling of watching the dead calf being picked at by hungry crows. Whatever the reason, I find myself reaching for the keys to start the engine, pull past the drive, back up till the rear of the truck is close, checking to make sure I'm well hid behind the tall row of holly bushes. Then, stepping out, hissing, waving off the crows, I lower both tailgates, set the board between them as before.

When I reach to take hold of the moose calf's hind legs, I spot something twenty or so yards downhill—a red, heart-shaped balloon floating a few feet above a neatly stacked pile of firewood. Perfectly still. Then, it moves—a slight jerk—like a tugged lure at the end of a fishing line. I leave the calf in the bed of the red truck, raise and push the tailgate shut. Wait a moment.

"Whose birthday?" I say, glancing up toward the sprawling house on the hill where a bloated funnel of smoke is rising from a red-stone chimney.

The boy stands, slowly, his face a blanched potato. "Not mine," he says. "My sister's. Sophie." He starts to walk out from behind the woodpile, the fabric of his bright blue snow pants swishing. The boy is wearing the old man's black cowboy hat, and he holds the arm with the red balloon out horizontal, steady, like a falconer.

"My sister is twelve," he says, stopping a dozen feet from me, one boot swinging, kicking a divot in the snow. "I'm almost seven."

"Almost seven," I say, leaning back against the tailgate of the Dodge Ram. "Almost seven is good." The boy shrugs, eyes on the ground.

"Do you know my grandpa?" he asks, eyeing the red truck, his expression serious, one eye squinted hard against the glare of sun and snow.

"I do," I say. "Wears a fancy black cowboy hat." I lift my chin toward the boy. He goes stiff. I cross my arms and smile. Then he smiles, steps forward.

"He tried to rub it off," the boy says abruptly, pulling up the sleeve of his sweater. "See?" He holds up his forearm, pale as a toad's belly. "Grandpa scratched at it hard with his fingernail. He thinks it's dirt," the boy says, pointing to a black mole. "See?"

"Doesn't look like dirt to me," I say. "That must've stung." The boy shrugs. He is staring at the mole as if maybe he isn't entirely sure about it.

"So, what did you do?" I say.

"Me?"

"Did you just let him scratch away, or did you tell him to stop?"

"I don't know." The boy looks down, kicks the snow with the toe of his boot, his leg swinging like the loose-hinged leg of a toy soldier. When he looks up again, he points behind me.

Four of the crows are back. One, the biggest, wings fully extended, glides down, ruffling the cold air, disappearing into a corner of the truck bed where the black tarp came loose. The boy suddenly rushes toward the truck, crouched, making a screeching noise, flapping both arms, the red balloon bobbing wildly. The crows fly off again, one up to a branch of the fir tree. The boy smiles, then walks over to my truck. He tilts forward slightly, studying the green decal lettering on the door.

"Horse. Thief. Canyon." He turns to look at me, shyly pleased with himself.

"That's right," I say. "You like horses?"

"They're OK, I guess."

"Just OK?" The boy doesn't respond.

"Ever heard of horse thieves before?" Now the boy's right hand is on his crotch, squeezing, as he stares up at the giant fir.

"Well, horse thieves, like regular thieves, are bad people," I say, raising my voice a bit to hold the boy's attention. "They'd steal horses and hide them down in that canyon before smuggling them across the border to Canada. Many of the horses died. The townspeople eventually got fed up and started hunting the bad people down. They'd hold midnight trials on horseback beneath a large tree near the rim of the canyon. They called that tree the Courtroom. If they decided the people on trial were bad, they'd hang them with braided rawhide ropes. Let them dangle there till sunrise."

The boy's gaze is fixed on one of the crows. It is standing on something, tugging at it repeatedly with its beak, like an angry man trying to start an old chainsaw. He leans down, picks up a rock, hurls it at the crow. The crow flaps its wings but stays put, cawing defiantly.

"Grandpa says when I do a bad thing, that I get a black spot on my heart." The boy glances up toward the house. "He says that if somebody does lots of bad things, their heart turns black and they could die."

"Well," I say. "Do you believe that?"

"Maybe. I don't know." The boy stands there in his blue polyester snow pants, kicking a deep divot in the snow, like maybe he is searching for something he lost.

"Well. Do you want to be good? To be one of the good guys?"

The boy reaches down, grips his crotch, squeezing. "Maybe," he says, glancing around. Then he raises the arm with the red balloon out horizontal before rotating it around like a water sprinkler till it stops, pointed directly at me.

"Hold it," he says, pushing the balloon at me before hurrying over to the opposite side of my work truck, where he pulls down his snow pants, unzips, and starts pissing on the right rear tire. I can hear him making large circles around the outer rim of the hubcap. He giggles. The little bastard seems to be amused with his ability to produce different sounds.

That tendon in my bad shoulder feels torn like the seam on an overfull bag of grain that splits and I find that I'm walking over there and I tell the boy that you can't just piss on something and walk away and that now he'll need to get down on his knees and grab a chunk of ice or a handful of snow and rub it good and thorough around the rim and the side of the tire till everything is clean and good and back the way it was before. The boy stands there, frozen, his face like a fish. Before he does anything, another boy's voice calls from somewhere far off down near the river, and the boy's head turns in that direction, then looks back at me, his pants still unzipped as he pivots and begins to run a crooked line down the hill, his dark little shape getting smaller and smaller in all that beautiful whiteness until he looks like the spit-out pit of a fruit.

Without any hurry, I open the door to the work truck, grab the black marker off the passenger's seat, pop off the cap—proceed to draw a black spot the size of a half-dollar in the center of the heart-shaped balloon. Next, I unfasten and pull back the black vinyl tarp, folding it up over the cab of the Dodge Ram. I use the string to tie the balloon to the calf's left hind leg. Then I step back to admire how it floats nice and high and visible in the still air.

Before I refasten the tarp tight to keep out the crows, I look down at the moose calf, seeing her now in full light—lying on her side, head and body and limbs stiff and covered in a fragile lattice of frost. All a ghostly grayish-white, save for the upturned eye—black with a trace of silver, like the backside of a mirror. I place a hand on her broken neck. Let it rest there.

Maybe it isn't enough. Maybe it's more than called for. Maybe it's foolish. Futile.

Kern would know.

And Dale? I suspect Dale would torch the Dodge Ram, and probably the two Land Rovers, and maybe the house and the entire goddamn neighborhood if he could get away with it.

Pop the tick. Make it bleed.

One thing I know is that when I drive the stretch of highway that leads from here to Hobak, and pass the widow's house and park the truck and pull off my boots and drop my weary body down on the bed to finally get some sleep, that I will stare up at the shadows on the ceiling and wait for the calf—her frost-webbed body and black mirror eye—to haunt my dreams.

Ace Boggess

Train Tagging

Wish I could know what the symbols mean
as they scroll slowly east before me
like a bottom ticker on CNN:
what eyes see while watching something else.

There are stars & monochrome rainbows,
wolf heads, checkerboards, jagged names
as if chisel-struck on rolling headstones.
What was the artist trying to say

with these corporate logos
for the spray cans of youth?
Letters sealed in Atlanta or Charlotte,
passed along by West Virginia,

I watch as their messages blur into a tide
with breakers, whitecaps, sediment, kelp,
flotsam pulled by unseen forces.
It's like hearing a dead language—

Aramaic or Mayan—spoken:
strange as poetry to ignorance, &
I am an ignorant man, waiting,
trapped with others in a lengthening line.

JENNIFER POPA

Morsel

I was reared among meat
except on Fridays, Lent,
when we ate fish sticks. Sea-meat
I suppose. I blamed Jesus
for many things: house fires,
permitting wasps to make homes
in mine, denying an unbaptized
baby. I learned the way
meat sways from its hook

in my garage, the doe's hollow—
a closet laddered with ribs, fat
tongue loosening. With rolled shoulders
I might have fit inside. I wondered
if her people looked for her,
considered my own untouchable spaces,
gallbladder, spleen, an appendix.
I had no explanation for this

distress—for the knowledge of my own
innards, or the way my cat spun
to reach the bloom of her rump
on a tattered towel in my closet.
Her appetite for her lover delivered
the mouths of five kittens. Each arrived
in a jellied sac. How still they were.
I suspected the first dead—

another Baby Jessica in a well.
How easily the small

become stuck, become a song
in a well or womb until born

again, by a mother's tongue
animating each to life, to mew,
& when the wound between
her legs produces a placenta, it is
a wad of bloody Bubble Yum
she eats without pause.

RUTH BARDON

Chicken

I didn't see how a truck of stacked crates
could carry such a wallop of a smell
until I saw the feathers floating
in front of my car.

City girl that I was,
I hoped there was a structure in the middle,
but then I thought about it, seeing
that it was chicken tall,

chicken wide, and chicken deep,
a honeycomb of birds,
the ones in the very middle
facing bird upon bird.

I rolled behind it down the highway;
we were one row of marbles
shooting down a narrow lane,
and I wondered

if they felt any panic
as the cages shook around them,
the rhythm steady
or sometimes jerky;

then, as it happened,
we both pulled to the right,
the distance between us
getting very small,

the feathers getting thicker
and the smell increasing
as we slowed down and headed
towards the same exit.

ALLISON FIELD BELL

Darwin and Everything

Immediately at dusk, Eva was in front of the adobe restaurant in Old Town, its purple archway open to a pleasant tiled courtyard. Standing there, surveying the wire dining furniture surrounded by bright painted pots of cacti, she thought, *Chickens*. She imagined them feathering their way between the collections of the yard: rusted bits of metal in one pyramid; the smoothed glass bottles to be saved and beside them, the ones to be disposed of; her piles of bricks, sorted according to size, shape, color. The bricks would eventually become a patio slab—designed by Eva, set in place by James. The chickens would be scouting out a good roost. She imagined their panic when, lost from their proper roost and therefore still roostless, the day would commence its rapid ending, dropped now, as it was, into that softer light, desert evening light, the last light of a sun stuck for hours against a cloudless sky, a swift blurring of edges. Their day of pecking between aloe and cooling themselves in hen-sized dust pits, an entire day of this, collapsed in only a fade of colors. So unlike the sunsets over the Pacific, slow and chaotic, light thieving between bundles of clouds and fog so that sometimes the actual orb itself was discernable— yoked whole and gold and then broken right there at the sea line.

Eva had spent her day in productive boredom. Trips to different stores, hunting for acceptable end tables and the little things one forgets to anticipate in a move: toilet brush, bathtub stopper, potting soil, spare batteries and light bulbs, spices, all the types of oil needed for various cooking heats and dishes—canola, olive, sesame, coconut. So much stopping and going, cash registers, fluorescent aisles, her palms full of crumpled receipts, and after, she had just needed a moment to really move, a brisk walk in the descending dusk.

And then, in front of the restaurant, breathing in the odor of spice and roasted meat, an odor of Tucson, of desert, she noticed the blackboard easel. Hand-chalked across it was the happy hour special: MARGARITAS—HOUSE & PRICKLY PEAR.

Eva pushed through the swinging bar doors. She did not sit at one of the wire tables in the courtyard despite it being a good temperature and still a novelty to be outside in the evening. In California, the passing of the day—the time from office to apartment, from Embarcadero to Muni to Cole Valley—was often chilled by fog streaming over the city from the Headlands, spilled into her neighborhood from Tank Hill. She brought extra layers to work but the damp was ruthless, and she always arrived home chilled (James: poor circulation, inherited maybe).

Here, even with the night approaching, she still wore short sleeves and would have liked to embrace the new climate by dining at one of the wire tables outside, but it seemed rude and strange to eat by herself. The state of being alone so acute and obvious: Is it just you? Will someone be joining you this evening? Or, even worse, the perfunctory removal of the second setting, a busboy or server completely indifferent to her aloneness, asserting in his quiet way: You look like the kind of person who dines alone. No explanation necessary. The kind of person who is accustomed to occupying more space than she needs because no one is willing to share that space, even for the brevity of a meal or a cocktail at happy hour.

A bar is different. A person can be alone at a bar. A woman can sit at a bar at happy hour. This is a working woman, the bartender may think; this woman has been at work all day and now she is in a bar for a drink, to unwind. Later on in the night, of course, a woman alone in a bar is confusing. She becomes a receptacle—an empty thing to be filled with words or salutes from across the way. Men trying to buy their way into conversation. Her drink's on me, the heroic man will say. And often, the woman (Eva) will (used to) accept the drink because it is free and will potentially make the subsequent conversation more tolerable or interesting or possibly fruitful. Even if the woman (Eva) refuses to accept the drink, the heroic man (James) will understand this to be an invitation of sorts, a challenge: This woman is a difficult woman playing a more difficult game.

Eva entered the adobe bar uninterested in conversation or games, however easy or difficult. James would not be back from his rotation at the clinic in the White Mountains for another day, so Eva, alone, slipped onto a bar stool and ordered the prickly pear. She chose the short end of the L-shaped bar top, away from where the servers stood and collected drinks to bring to the various tables. She put the whole corner between herself and the closest patrons—a young couple—and they in turn had put one barstool between themselves and two older men, obviously regulars. The young couple seemed lost in their own world of infatuation, a state that triggered, in older couples (James and Eva), a feeling of nostalgia and disconcertion: We were never so naïve, so young and so relentlessly affectionate. We were never so. And even if we had been, we would never be so again.

Eva's drink arrived. Pink. In a short, stemless glass. "Is this—?"

The bartender nodded. "Prickly pear, sí, señorita. The house specialty."

"It's just so"—she blushed—"pink."

The bartender was a short older man with black hair. He had a generous laugh.

"That's the fruit," he said. "Almost purple on the plant, but the juice is pink."

She pressed her hot cheek with one hand. So lost she had been in her own private thoughts and then jarred into speaking: Her voice was ugly and critical. Even for a tired, lonely, working woman at a bar. Beside her, the young couple laughed together at some private joke. The young woman's voice was all light and music.

The bartender tilted his head at Eva and said, "It doesn't taste pink, I promise."

"Of course. I have that cactus in my yard, I think. But I didn't know about the fruit, what it looks like and all."

It had sounded so exotic, she half-expected it to come with spines, the glass itself a cactus, like a tropical rum drink in a coconut. She'd ordered one of these in Maui—last winter, with James, her first trip (spontaneous, brief) to the islands (no presents, just experiences: hiking, surfing, mai tais at midday)—and since Tucson was still equally unfamiliar, she had desired a drink of equivalent novelty. A new experience, some specific small thing she could eventually make familiar. Instead, it was punch at a child's birthday party or a cosmo with ice cubes.

Eva sipped through the straw. It was tart and boozy, not pink at all. "Good," she said, her surprise obvious. "Delicious. Thank you."

The bartender picked up a glass and a rag, occupying his hands in the way that bartenders do, always prepared to abandon conversation should the customer wish it. "If you don't like it," he said, "I'm happy to make you the house."

Eva took another long drink, this time from the glass itself, catching flakes of salt on her lip. The young woman of the couple laughed again and Eva fought her desire to look over. "It's excellent, really," she said, reexamining her drink. "I've just never had this kind. I've never had prickly pear anything, actually."

He smiled. "Where are you from?"

"Here. I mean, I live here now. California originally—San Francisco, actually. But I grew up right outside, north."

The bartender held a polished glass up to the light and hummed, "If you're going to San Fran Cisco—"

The young man of the couple picked up the bartender's tune and continued humming. The young woman drew her hands over her head: a flower crown. "We adore San Francisco," she said, to Eva or the bartender or the young man.

"Very beautiful, I hear," the bartender said to Eva.

"Yes," Eva said with an unintentional sigh.

The bartender took this as a dismissal. "Welcome to Tucson, señorita. We are happy to have you."

Eva smiled, "Thank you," she said again. "This is very good."

He nodded and moved off down the bar, leaving Eva alone with her drink. The young couple had ceased humming and the woman now draped an arm across the man's back, her unadorned left hand resting on his shoulder. Young and unmarried: Who knows what would pass between them.

Eva folded and refolded her napkin, sipping in measured intervals. She pulled her phone from her purse and again thought, *Chickens.* No window was near her, but it was surely dark by now. In the days past, they had roosted in the mesquite tree, which dipped over the fence into the yard next door. The neighbor dogs were locked up, but in the morning, they would be out, and the chickens would be fluttering down from the tree. The chickens will have panicked, she thought. They will have panicked and scattered into the mesquite tree, and Eva will have failed in this thing, this one little thing that she had sworn to James ("They'll be my chickens, my pets, I swear it"), and to herself, to succeed at. Chickens. Such a simple, easy animal. ("It's still responsibility, Eva.") She had raised them as a child, a constant battle with her brother about who would feed and water and lock them away at night. It was an excuse to battle though, the chickens themselves being easy and manageable. But her childhood chickens had always found the roost in their coop, responsibly corralled themselves. Perhaps, then, James was to blame. He had constructed the coop ("I'll build it; you'll raise them"). Eva knew that this was unfair, inaccurate. Even chickens needed time to adjust, acquaint themselves to a new home. And maybe by now, tonight, they had learned to retire into their coop. It had been almost a week; animals adapt, evolve. This is how they survive—Darwin and everything.

Nevertheless, she resolved to finish her drink quickly. She chopped the red straw down between the ice. The couple ordered another round and a basket of wings, the young woman emphasizing that she wanted them "spicy-spicy." They were drinking Mexican beers, two used limes between the newly emptied bottles.

It occurred to Eva that she should request her check.

But James is the one who requests the check, she realized. Intuits, actually. He intuits the check. Not because of maleness, but because of him. James. He is capable of affirming camaraderie with his body—a nod, a raised eyebrow, a precise pressing together of his lips. She folded her napkin in half until it could no longer be folded. If he were here, Eva would still fold the napkin, but it would be a mindless occupation, background to their conversation. Like the young couple, she thought, noticing the way the young woman now threaded her fingers through her long, straight hair. If the young man of the couple had been elsewhere, in the mountains or on a rotation, the young woman might focus on her split ends, pinching and separating them with dramatized care. Or the woman might have simply stayed home. This was the easiest option. They were an infatuated couple and young, and young and infatuated people cannot justify visiting a bar or other public place without a companion or a predetermined occupation.

"Have you ever been to Pancho Villa's?" the young woman said, and it took Eva a moment to realize she was being addressed.

"Pardon?" As though Eva were trying to appear older. Grandmothers said "pardon," not working women at bars.

"Pancho Villa's," the woman said again, though seeing her now fully focused on Eva, it was clear she was girl more than woman. "I think that's the name. The revolutionary, right? In the Mission on— what was that street, babe?"

The man—a boy, really—shrugged. "Valencia?"

The girl smacked him playfully. "That's just the only street name you remember."

The boy began reciting streets: "Market Street, Haight Street, Ashbury—"

The girl pressed her finger to his mouth, and then to Eva, she said, "Anyway, Pancho Villa's. The best hang-over veggie burritos on the planet. Next time you're there—go. You won't regret it."

Eva forced herself to smile. "Thank you." A young, foolish girl recommending a restaurant in Eva's city, and she was saying thank you. She unfolded the napkin again, rubbing it between her fingers. Eva should be the one making recommendations: How about the benches near the marina under her favorite slanted cypress tree, or the corner café actually on Valencia with the sourdough bread smell and the bicycle racks constructed of bicycle parts? Have you been there, infatuated couple?

But before Eva could say anything, a man occupied the space between her and the couple. The two men at the far end of the bar nodded at him and the bartender brought him a cheap American beer without taking his order. The man wore a faded red baseball cap, a white Longhorn logo. He did not take the hat off. The bartender brought him a basket of chips, too, which he did not touch. He simply sat, drank, gazed at the wall of bottles behind the bar.

Which shape had drawn him? Eva wondered. Which color of glass or color of liquid or emblem of quality? And did he have the same thought that Eva often had: If I could steal one, which one?

Or, in her home sometimes, back in San Francisco, if an earthquake, which thing would she choose—what is it she would rescue? Sentimental or financial. She liked to think sentimental— the irreplaceable portraits of her mother, deceased, and her father, demented. But she couldn't really know. In that half-second of panic, she could instead reach for her purse—the expensive one James had given her, turquoise, and with wallet and sunglasses inside.

Eva supposed, however, that living things would always be prioritized above the rest. If she had a child, for instance, it would be the thing rescued. But what if, at that moment of instinct, it wasn't? What if she chose cat instead? And is this enough of a thought to prevent children?

It is. Or Eva is. Or James.

And the young couple: What would their thought be? The boy, stupid in his memory of streets; the girl, too willing to talk to strangers. Would there be an affair? A monsoon? The thing that would drive them apart—what would it be?

This new man in the baseball cap—a Texas team—would choose tequila, she decided. Not the nicest bottle with the gold foil and the frosted glass in its odd beveled shape, raised above the rest. He would choose the fullest bottle, the closest.

And how would he respond to this choosing game? No fucking way, he might say. I think that same thing all the time! Always, in a grocery store, I imagine what I'd get if I were on one of those game shows—the ones where you get the free cart and a minute to stuff it with everything you possibly can. What if I just ended up in frozen food? Ten bags of frozen peas and not a single six-pack.

The young couple's wings arrived, and Eva, for the third time, thought, *Chickens*, thought perhaps now it would make sense for her to try out vegetarianism. The girl tore into the meat of one without decorum, wiping a napkin ineffectively against the orange smears on her face. The boy dabbed his napkin to her cheek and she shoved his hand away, embarrassed maybe or feeling that he had condescended.

The man in the baseball cap finished his beer and the bartender brought him another.

Eva smiled and sipped more of her own drink. The pink had paled, diffused by the melting ice. And suddenly, the image of herself: a woman at a bar alone on a Friday (it was Friday, she realized) with a watery, pink margarita.

This was the image of a lonely woman.

As if to emphasize this point, the young couple was giggling now—the boy forgiven.

But Eva was not lonely! She had James. A doctor. Her brother had not failed to recognize this good fortune. As if Eva had somehow chosen, from a lineup, the most successful suitor. As if Eva had been practical. Be practical, she should advise this young couple now. And practical does not translate to doctor. And brothers are not privy to the more intimate moments, the ways in which a surgeon, by necessity, must be a certain kind of person who might not be chosen from a lineup for a sister.

A surgeon does not think: This scalpel must be hurting in this way or will scar in this particular shape, which may be unattractive to a husband or terrifying to a child. A surgeon does not think: This will be a scar that *I* put there. No, a surgeon decides mechanically: A scar is a scar is a result, a consequence, not a thing to fret over. Therefore, a surgeon is an excellent lover—physiologically. Controlled. Accurate. Anatomically perceptive.

Be practical, young infatuated couple. Wait until the infatuation—the anatomical novelty of each other—wears off, and then decide accordingly.

And what would this man be like—the one beside her with the Texas cap and the cheap American beer? What kind of lover was he? The man removed a chip from the basket in front of him. "Some salsa, Martín," he said.

Less successful, Eva decided.

The bartender—Martín—returned with the salsa, and the man curiously dumped the salsa on top of the chips and began eating them. Eva watched as he selected one smothered chip after another, crunched down on them, and then licked his fingers clean.

In her distraction, Eva had finished her drink and had therefore exhausted her purpose there at the bar. *Chickens*, she thought again. Here was her purpose, a reason to leave.

"Another round?" Martín asked.

Eva shook her head no, removing her wallet from her expensive purse.

But then: Why not? James gone, the chickens already either properly or improperly roosted, the house empty. Eva rested the wallet on the counter. "Actually," she said, "how about a shot? Tequila, whatever's good. Your favorite."

He inclined his head to her and smiled. "Salt?"

"Please."

He turned to the bottles.

Then, unexpectedly, she said, "Two, actually. One for him," and nodded at the man beside her who angled his head to look at her.

He was older than she would have originally guessed, or maybe he had not aged well. Too much sun or cigarettes or cheap beer. And she could tell right away that he was not at all interested in conversation. "I don't take shots alone," she said.

Eva waved her hand casually at the bartender who was now watching her more sharply, perhaps thinking: Is this woman drunk? (And perhaps she was.) Or is she so desperate and lonely that she needs to throw herself at any man nearby? (Was she? Did she?)

Eva corrected her order again, "Actually, shots all around. On me. Top shelf, please."

She felt like a child saying please, like she was too small to reach the thing on the top shelf.

To the man who was now scooping up another chip, she said, "My husband's a brain surgeon."

His eyes were very dark, impossible to distinguish the pupil from the iris. "Oh?" he said. "That's lucky."

She hid her ringless hand. James was not her husband. He could have been, provided they lived in a different century or had met in a different city. But James and Eva had decided that marriage was an antiquated formality, and San Francisco agreed. Eva didn't really need a ring or silly overpriced dress to feel satisfied with his commitment to her. Did she? ("Do you, Eva? It's a useless expression of insecurity. We're above that. We don't need a public declaration of fidelity. I trust you, you trust me.") That's love.

Martín searched a few bottles before pulling one to present to Eva. "That's a lucky doctor," he said, winking.

The young couple: the boy's hand on the girl's lower back, the intimate space there.

Calling James her husband was understandable, but James was not a brain surgeon. He was an orthopedic surgeon, or at least he would be once he completed his residency rotations. Orthopedic even sounded more impressive. No respectable wife of a doctor would call her husband a brain surgeon. Neurosurgeon. He's a neurosurgeon, she could have said.

Eva agreed to the bottle Martín held out to her: 100 percent agave. Gold.

Or maybe it would have been better to not offer any explanation. She didn't need an excuse for buying a round of drinks, did she? The man next to her would not have found it necessary to explain the purchase of five tequila shots for strangers.

To the bartender and the man's profile, she said, "Yes, a neurosurgeon. We moved here for his practice. So he can be close to the trauma center here. One of the best in the country. He's very good."

She had no idea about the state of the trauma center here or anywhere.

The man stretched his neck, twisting away from Eva, and Martín said, "Sounds like a smart husband you got there. I wouldn't mind a surgeon's salary myself."

The man grunted. In agreement? In ridicule? Were they laughing at her?

The young couple now chimed in. The girl said, "I've always wanted to be a nurse."

Of course, Eva thought, why isn't she the neurosurgeon? Why must it be her husband? A surgeon to a person who isn't a surgeon's spouse is surely enviable. Impressive. Intelligent. Powerful. Instead, Eva had become the woman in the bar spending her husband's money. Eva wasn't the surgeon, but it was still Eva's money. Her savings. She earned it. Teaching in Japan and then managing those afterschool programs in San Francisco—at twelve different high schools, and weekend programs for toddlers, too! It is my money, she could scream. It's my money, earned and saved, and soon all of the things in our house will be mine because I will have spent my days purchasing them, picking them out, very particular because James will not tolerate a poor-quality comforter. ("If you're going to spend money, Eva, be practical.") Be smart about it. Do not be impulsive. Do not purchase a thing that you'll need to purchase again so soon. It's just common sense.

This was why she had requested the expensive tequila. "Because if you're going to be overcharged at a bar, you might as well get the most out of it" (James). And she valued this in James because he had not been this way as a child; this had been something he had cultivated later in life—a desire for quality. He had earned it. He had been poor, and he had earned his way out of it, his way to a good comforter and expensive tequila. Unlike Eva, who had always been privy to the middle of things. Adequate everything, never wanting for necessities. And her father so frugal—no bad whiskey, only better whiskey. But James chose to do certain things expensively and certain things himself because he could. Because he could choose with precision. James could decide beforehand: sentimental or financial. And there would be no hesitation, no doubt.

Martín arranged the shot glasses along the lined lip of the bar and slid a lime slice onto each before pouring the tequila, a light gold color—bronze. He set two in front of the old men, who nodded their casual thanks like it was common for a woman to buy them tequila. When he placed the shots in front of the couple, they smiled, delighted but not surprised. Couples like these felt entitled to delight, and rarely did they question who had provided it. Still, the bartender made an explanatory gesture towards Eva. The couple smiled big, pretty smiles and held up the drinks, suspended in mid-cheer, waiting for her to join them. "To California," the boy said.

"To San Francisco," said the girl.

The boy: "Van Ness, Embarcadero—"

Eva held up her glass to them. "Tank Hill," she said, and they pretended to agree.

The young couple tapped their glasses together, Eva promptly excluded from their celebration. She looked to the man beside her. He was without a doubt less successful with sex, somewhat aged by sun. He took his shot and swallowed it immediately, disregarding both the salt and the lime and Eva's own shot outstretched to him.

"Thanks," he said, his Texas hat bobbing in an insincere nod.

She had purchased the shots. He should be more grateful, physiologically.

She slid across to the stool next to hers, next to the Texas man, close enough to smell the day on him—he had spent it outside, in the sun.

"Martín," she said, her voice stronger than before. "Another please. For us two."

Texas Man looked at her: a lonely woman buying expensive shots with her husband's money.

"Not for me," he said. "No, thank you, ma'am."

And he held up his left hand—a thick gold wedding band. He returned to his chips, only a few remaining.

Martín poured Eva's shot and she took it quickly without lime or salt.

"I'm not a homewrecker," Eva said, angry suddenly. She was the very definition of *homemaker*. She should tell them of the yard, the little house in progress. The chickens—the ways she'd been worried sick over them, the way she would, without a doubt, in an earthquake, choose chickens over purse. "You shouldn't make assumptions about strangers," she said.

The Texas man glanced at Martín, then they both looked to Eva. "No, ma'am," the man said, tilting his hat at her.

"Good," Eva said. "I'm very happily married to a doctor."

Then Eva laughed, and the men looked at each other, while the young infatuated couple seemed to be staring at her now, appalled.

"Oh, don't look so surprised," Eva said to the young couple. "You're not the only couple on the planet."

The young man of the couple made an attempt at laughter and then cleared his throat twice. Martín seemed desperate to intervene. "Another round?" he asked the couple, as the young girl attempted to peel the label from her beer.

Eva was making people uncomfortable. Again. This was something James had discussed with her in the past: "Now, Eva, you can't just say whatever the hell is on your mind. It's not right."

The Texas man gestured to Martín. "I'll take the bill, Martín," he said.

Eva couldn't help herself: "Don't you leave on my account. Afterall, I'm just a woman."

And then she laughed again. Now the two old men were staring at her as well. The whole bar, it seemed, found her unacceptable.

Eva sighed her best young-girl infatuated sigh. "I'm sorry," she said. "Tequila and me—it's been a while."

The bar seemed to understand this: a woman drunk and angry on tequila. Still, without being asked, her bill was brought.

Outside, the city had fallen into full night. The walk home was short, and Eva did not mind being alone for it. All the spaces between houses were dark, and the starred sky hung clear. The air had cooled significantly, a strange neutral sensation—weightless, detached. Physiologically. Bodiless.

Inside the house—no, inside her home, her new place of living—it was still and warm. She walked through the living room with the half-packed boxes and the brick fireplace that had seemed so essential when they accepted the place as is. Eva had imagined them in there—she and James together—with the fire, in the winters, which were never too cold. The fire would just be for comfort, for the living room to feel lived in. Beside it would be the metal tool collection and a box of newspapers and wood peels for kindling. In San Francisco, their fireplace had been sealed with granite, a useless mantel in the middle of the wall. Eva had made it into something pleasant, a shelf for the little things that pleased her: pictures and polished shells and a few vases from her mother's collection.

Eva had been so confident about the fireplace here. A sign, she had thought: James, this is it, this is the house, our home. The imagined woodsmoke smell and all the additional tasks to share. Light the fire, build it up, keep it going, douse it, clean out the ash and sweep the bricks free of it. They could buy a cord of wood and together, and with good quality leather gloves, they could stack it beneath a tarp outside to preserve it.

This was another thing to tell the young infatuated couple: Do not think of wood cords and tarps. And if you do, do not think a city will change it one way or another. A fireplace is not a sign, boy. Chickens cannot anchor you, girl.

Because now, on this night, Eva alone and worried about the impending sight of the chickens, the fireplace an empty, sad mouth between the two windows that faced the neighbors' yard. The dog neighbors with the tire stacks and the disintegrating couch. And half of Eva's mesquite tree hung over the fence.

James would blame Eva for the chickens.

Plus, there were all the other things that Eva was always neglecting. Her sometimes-depressed posture ("bad for the bones") contrasted with his very correct spinal alignment. ("Mild scoliosis, Eva; you should be mindful of how you move.") How you hunch or don't hunch. And the other problems: replacing the empty toilet paper roll with the full one. ("Do not just set it on top. Such a little easy thing to remember.") But it was this kind of detail that made a surgeon a surgeon. Nothing could be forgotten. There was a correct way to slice a zucchini or open an avocado, a more efficient way to hold a knife and mason a patio. Ways to maintain consistency, control.

But there were the things wrong with James, too, Eva thought, flicking on the kitchen light with the hope of making the outside dark more manageable. For example, there was the way he looked after a haircut—too groomed and young, ears stuck out too far from his head. And the throat-clearing, unconscious, that happened sometimes when he was reading, reviewing patient files or scrutinizing a sports magazine. There was the fact that he dried her blouses—all of them—but always hung her underwear, unable to understand that lace is not what makes an item delicate.

But these were not important things, not really, not to her. Eva, who was not a surgeon. Eva, who had moved here for a man who was not her husband, a man in the White Mountains doing important work. Eva, who had so recently been imagining another man, so obviously a kind of man whose body could not intuit anything, not a check or a woman's pleasure. Eva, who had been foolish with her pink margarita and her expensive tequila. Eva, who had desired chickens, desired their nostalgic presence, the sentimentality of them, the responsibility of them. A woman, who now, stepping directly under the mesquite tree, was rather obviously akin to the chickens, pathetic in their inability to properly roost, to mount their tiered ladder and shuffle out across their well-crafted perch.

But the chickens did not want to be in the coop. They wanted to be in the tree. Even if there was the risk of the dogs and the chicken hawks which could surely swipe them off a branch at sunrise. They wanted the tree, and who was Eva to deny them?

Inside the house, her phone rang. It would be James calling to check up on her. And if not for James, it would have been her brother: Has Eva wandered out alone in a city she doesn't know? Alone and helpless as a child? Doing foolish, irresponsible things like a woman, like Eva, tended to do?

James would be on the phone waiting, worried.

She should answer it. She should forget about the chickens, leave them to their idiot tree. They're just chickens, after all.

MARNIE RITCHIE

I'd seen Susan Sarandon do it in Atlantic City

I couldn't just flick the feeling
away like a spider

The situation called for ritual
and a carefully assembled
mise en place of juice and skin

In an M pattern

mouthing each
letter of my name aloud

I swept a lemon half
over my arms,
collarbone,
nipples,
stomach:

following the procedure
passed down to me
after the casino oyster bar

burning off
the imprints of men
their fishiness

flavoring my body,

meat and more,
prepared (for what?)

Bless you, lemons
Bless you, Susan
Bless you, Louis Malle
Bless you, fingers
for this

CHARLES HARPER WEBB

What's That Red Thing in the Middle of an Olive?

—*Boy at Safeway*

Pimento is no answer, any more than *God* is
            to the question, "What created the heavens
and the Earth?" To name a thing does not
      explain it. (*Photosynthesis,* the teacher states,
as if the word feeds the planet.) Are pimentos

irises that help those green-eyeballs-stacked-
            in-a-jar to see? Did you know that *pimento*
means, in Portuguese, a large, sweet red pepper
      shaped like a heart? Caesar's slaves jammed
pimento plugs into olives like corks into amphorae.

To save time, we moderns make machines
            that stuff pimentos in at the same time
they punch out the olive pits. Pimento
      and olive bond like bagels and cream cheese.
Some say a falling pimento, not an apple,

knocked loose Newton's insights into gravity.
            Yet, did his equations stop one sunflower
from toppling when its time was done?
      Did they keep the Sheriff of Thrombosis
from evicting life from one sweet mom?

Today, pimentos are pureed, then molded
                 into plugs. Pimento shards embedded in *cheese-*
food create *pimento cheese*. Pimento mixed
      with ground-up meat creates pimento *loaf—*
a different *loaf* than just lying around,

which the pimento loaf Mom won at her book club
                 did in the fridge until Dad tried a piece.
"Decayed," he gagged, rushed into Mom's
      bathroom—still full of her stuff and his grief—
and slice by slice, flushed the sad old thing away.

LYNN PATTISON

Mise en abyme

*(In which the image contains
a smaller copy of itself)*

Giotto paints a grand triptych as altarpiece
the cardinal who commissioned it on his knees
offering a miniature of the work to St. Peter.

Picture within a picture, the Droste Effect, identical images
shrinking to infinity. High art or not, we love
recurrence: the Morton Salt girl, the nurse

on the package of cocoa powder, the blooming patterns
in our grandmothers' quilts. What yearnings
are satisfied by Hamlet's play within a play,

the moon's faithful diminishment and return?
Is it that the heartbeat we learned
in our mother's bellies taught us

to love the perpetual? Something in our evolution
selected for those who would fashion pantoums,
Tommy Tippy Cups, the Book of Hours.

There can be too much of a good thing:
tortured men who wash their hands
until raw or women who require

an exact number of swipes of broom on floor
each day. But it must be a crucial survival
skill. Maybe it's why we can press

on after loss, aware of how patterns repeat,
the world renews. Morning dawns. Loons
return in spring to our northern lake.

CAITLIN FELDMAN

Replica

Four months before my then-boyfriend and I broke up, we sat across from each other at a rooftop restaurant in Bangkok, and he gave me a tiny, porcelain cat. Orange and striped, it resembled a cat named Tiny that his former roommate owned; Tiny had gone briefly missing only to turn up at the neighbors' house renamed Shrek and newly adopted—or kidnapped, depending on who you asked. In miniature porcelain form, it's had just one owner and currently lives in triangulated space on a shelf in my apartment, shielded from the forces of clutter and loss by journals whose pages are largely devoted to the boy who impressed the cat upon me in the first place.

At the end of six months traveling Southeast Asia together, Angst gifted me the cat for two reasons. The first was that we'd talked about getting such an animal when we returned home. Our trip had been emotionally tumultuous—we were struggling to find answers to the questions that returning home forced us to consider: whether to live together and in what city, and what that would mean. The figurine served as an unspoken offering. *We will be together*, it said, *and we will get a cat*. The second reason for this specific gift was its size: about one inch long, fully stretched, as if swatting at a fly. Following the standard rule of miniatures, this means that the cat is an ideal size for its form. Any smaller than 1:12 of its original size, a miniature object loses detail, becomes abstract. Of course, Angst wasn't thinking about this when he bought the cat for me at the Chatuchak Market nearly four years ago. He just knew that as a decades-long collector of all things tiny, I would appreciate its smallness. A true miniaturist probably wouldn't be amazed by this particular miniature—there is nothing especially lifelike or impressive regarding its rendering—and yet it is the final remaining relic of that boyfriend on display in my apartment.

I remember deciding to find a visible home for the cat when decorating my new bedroom after we broke up. I thought it was OK for the cat to avoid the confines of a drawer or the garbage because it looked innocuous enough just sitting there, and also because it reminded me of something that wasn't quite Angst and wasn't quite us. It was a representation of a certain time, a certain place, a certain state of being, and I couldn't let that go. Though I've wanted to move beyond that era—and have tried to cover up the memories, to desaturate and make them flat—I often find I'm still attached.

A dating error I made last winter picked up the cat once. He held it in his hand and looked at me as if about to say something, as if he *knew* something, but then just took a breath and returned the cat from whence it came.

I feel about tiny things the way writer Alice Gregory does: "It is difficult for me, in the presence of miniatures, not to feel like a pervert. Tiny things have always filled me with a devious and urgent covetousness. 'Delight' is too casual a word to describe it, and not at all physical enough."

The first tiny things I collected were miniature books, most often Disney princess stories printed on glossy pages between textured hardback covers. But my grandma had a habit of buying me any small book she found, so I ended up with a handful of pocket-sized adult comic books whose jokes I am only recently capable of understanding. The second tiny collecting binge I embarked on was focused on miniature tea sets for reasons unknown, though it may have had something to do with an aunt who collected teakettles. From there, I moved into the more predictable realm of Barbies, American Girl, and porcelain dolls. Arguably, these are not tiny, per se. They definitely sit outside the purest definition of what it means to be miniature, but I loved their small accessories, especially those that belonged to my American Girls. (I had Kit and Samantha, if you're wondering.) I rarely coveted their traditional garments, and instead spent birthdays and Christmases asking for more modern accessories: lunch tray replete with cardboard milk carton and plastic spork; ice skates; Weber charcoal barbeque; thermos, crutches, and leg cast presumably earned during a skiing accident; violin with functional, horsehair bow and rosin; working karaoke machine. I liked the utility of these items, how they perfectly mimicked their life-sized counterparts. In one particularly creepy childhood photo, seven-year-old me crouches down next to Samantha; we tuck our violins beneath our chins while exhibiting close-mouthed smiles.

Gregory writes that, "The tacit philosophy of miniaturists— celebrate all entities, neglect no details—is at once ambitious and laughable. To mimic the known universe as it is, not with imagination but with rigor, allows for an uncommon kind of pleasure: One notices, with some sadness, how rare it is to be purely impressed." My miniature obsession, then, is perhaps impure. I do ogle functional and accurate miniatures, but do not reserve my awe for items that could be catalogued in a museum. Governed by no miniature laws, I am less miniaturist and more tiny-thing enthusiast.

As an adult, this obsession focuses primarily on ceramics and art, for which I've begun running out of flat surfaces and wall space. This collection was born of practicality—as a thirteen-year-old visiting Ireland with my family, I wanted to buy something at the Waterford crystal factory, but the only thing I could afford was the smallest vase they offered. Back in Ireland as an adult, I bought a painted canvas less than two inches tall.

"Miniatures are practical—like mementos they can be carried out of a burning house or by immigrants to the new world; they can be held under the tongue like contraband and smuggled past border guards," writes poet and essayist Lia Purpura. "Miniatures are made to travel."

I once mailed a tiny vase home from Chiang Mai, carried another around New Zealand in a backpack for two months and managed not to break it. Several more I had bubble-wrapped in Hanoi. At a market in Melbourne last year, I almost bought a miniature terrarium, maybe an inch tall and filled with succulent rosettes. Worried it would get confiscated at customs, I left empty handed. But I still think about how perfect it was. How small.

I recently knocked a small but not-quite-miniature mug to the floor from its place on my bookshelf. It didn't shatter, but it splintered beyond reasonable repair. I had bought the mug at a Portland market with a friend who was then a functioning alcoholic and is now a nonfunctioning one. I haven't seen him in over a year, but when I bought the mug several years ago, he was still one of my closest friends. He was someone who helped me move, encouraged me to enjoy singledom after Angst and I broke up, and who, before Angst and I left for Asia, gave me the sweet and impractical gift of a small electronic picture frame. *You can put pictures of all your friends on it*, he said, *and we'll be with you wherever you go.*

That friend was one of the last remaining threads between me and Angst, a thread I've since detached from, thus losing whatever connections I'd spent time convincing myself remained. When the mug broke, I almost went to the top drawer of my nightstand, almost pulled out ex-boyfriend letters, almost lost myself for a few hours to the memories of people who used to know everything about me, whom I'll likely never know again. Instead, I practiced some breathing exercises, mumbled some expletives, and threw away the remains.

"In miniature," Purpura writes, "everything is significant."

I keep trying to make this universally true. When Angst and I first met, I thought nothing could have been more significant than our shared Taco Bell order of Mexican Pizzas or that we'd lived around the corner from each other our senior year of college but never met. When I met a Belgian man while traveling two years ago, I thought we were meant to meet because we'd experienced similar heartbreaks at similar times and had a mutual habit of overdrinking without reason or cause. I thought it serendipitous that a Tinder match I never met had a mom who'd worked as a social worker, just like me. When I met my current boyfriend, I found it problematic that I couldn't find meaning to latch on to; I wondered if he was the wrong guy because without coincidences I could point to and call significant, we had to be more grounded. We simply had to be.

Gregory argues that one of the allures of miniatures is precision and order in an imprecise and disorganized world. I am inclined to believe her. Who among us doesn't hope to find meaning in the items we collect and keep? Who can look at the remains of a broken object and not see the remains of the people we associate it with? Who doesn't want order, for the things we hold closest to be true?

My best friend once gave me a tiny clay cup, perhaps twice the size of a thimble, with a lopsided, melancholic face painted on it. It is a replica of nothing, and so it breaks the traditional rules of miniature. It is small for the sake of being small, serves no purpose except to spark my joy at its existence. Although perhaps its replication simply lives in the abstract, a representation of the love between the giver of that gift and me. Over the years, friends have given me spoons and spatulas one-fourth their regular size, which I've never bothered upgrading to life-sized versions; a smaller-than-palm-sized bowl brought over from New Zealand; a sample-sized jam jar that I use as a weed container; an inch-tall plant pot complete with succulent leaf attempting to root.

Yet another friend painted me a miniature scene of a back road just outside my hometown. It's on cardstock she cut into a circle, and measures maybe three inches across. The road is lined with telephone wires scooping across a sky that's turning violet around a haloed sun that's been covered by the moon. She gave it to me for my birthday two years ago, which fell just a day after the total solar eclipse passed across the U.S., stopping for less than thirty seconds above my parents' backyard.

If day must become night, what a beautiful way, she wrote.

I could attempt to find the core of how seeing the eclipse made me feel. I could wax rhapsodic about frogs croaking at 10 a.m., wind fluttering through previously still and silent trees. I could try to figure out why darkness at an unusual hour rendered a country speechless, brought people to tears, made me want to believe in anything. I could try to blow the feeling up until it's too big to hold, until the meaning becomes warped and twisted in the grandness of it all.

Or I could leave it to the words on the back of a painting three inches tall. I could find order in the simple. Accept a marvel for what it is.

I could return to the painting hanging on my wall, peek behind it and read the part I didn't hold in memory. *Remember the beautiful things and how they guide you through, always. Yet another year.*

On our last night in Bangkok, Angst handed me a card. *Thank you for showing me that it's always better to do things with someone you love.*

At least, I think that's what the card said. I know it said much more—I trained that boyfriend to write me love letters of the most verbose variety, cards that were hard to read in the presence of another because it took so long to reach the end. I could find out for certain what it says. I still have it, and I know what drawer it's in (top of nightstand, next to photos, awards, more cards from him and others, vibrator, unused journal, half-smoked joints). But I don't really want to check. Every time I pull that card out, I become incapacitated for half a day, end up sitting on the floor surrounded by the detritus of a relationship that lodged itself under my rib cage or between my toes or something. It's stuck somewhere in my body, but not in any of the obvious places. Trust me. I've looked.

Then again—it's easy to overlook so much.

Recently, I realized my cat figurine resembles transfigured Professor McGonagall much more than it resembles Tiny, the cat I used to know. It has markings around its eyes that look like glasses, just like McGonagall does. And on closer inspection, it's more brown than orange. But I didn't know this until I held it most recently; in my memory, it's tangerine.

And yet I can still see Angst and me sitting on that rooftop, remember how the sun set rose gold over the smoggy horizon, how we asked the waitress to take a dozen photos of us but nothing visually captured how it felt to spend six months traveling with another person at age twenty-four, how six months felt like a lifetime. And, in a way, it was.

"Time, in miniature form, like a gas compressed, gets hotter," writes Purpura.

Of Bangkok, Susan Orlean writes, "[It was] as if the world were the size of a peanut—something as compact as that, something that easy to pick up, shell, consume, as long as you were young and sturdy and brave."

My image of myself from that time feels farther away than any other part of me. I wonder if this has something to do with the compression of that miniature era, that place. I wonder if that time was so singular, so compact, that the distance between it and everything else has since magnified. Or maybe its anomalous nature is more like an opposing magnet, forever pushing against that which does not match.

After we returned from Asia, Angst and I once drove down the same back road that my friend later painted for my birthday. We were living at our parents' houses in different states and broke up a couple months after that visit—we would've broken up while driving that evening if either of us had been capable of making decisions. Instead, we pulled the car over and I took a picture of our faces against a backdrop of glowing wheat fields, another rose-gold sun. I look at that picture now, two squared inches on my phone, and am transported.

In miniature, everything is significant.

But there's a difference between miniatures that contain resonant memories and mementos that do not. I often find myself looking at the items that fill my apartment and wondering if the meaning I've attached to them is real or imagined. Is there still meaning here, or did there just used to be? Is it truly a replica, or do I just want it to be? It's the difference between being given a gift and being given a *gift*: that perfect thing that only this person could have given to only you.

We attach meaning to items when they are more than the sum of their physical parts, when they contain the essence of a person, relationship, time. Even more so in miniature—so condensed, so weighted—nestled in our hands. The cat was never just a cat. It always meant to sink its miniature, porcelain claws into me. And yet I hold out hope, however futile, that maybe someday I'll pick the cat up, and it will have lost its heat.

SAMANTHA PADGETT

Hauntology

I'm twelve.

I'm in the passenger seat of your car. We're parked on the shoulder of a two-lane highway. The ignition is turned off and all four windows are rolled down. It's late September or maybe early October. The air is sticky with the residue of summer.

On either side of the highway, there are cornfields freshly harvested. Endless rows of stripped-down stalks stretch out around us—each of them bent over at the waist like a child holding onto their ankles waiting for the belt.

I'm waiting for you to speak.

I'm not twelve.

I'm twenty-three.

I'm sitting in a paisley-patterned chair across from my therapist and I'm telling this story for the third time.

Why am I telling this story for the third time?

I don't know. You tell me.

I'm twelve.

I'm looking for my mom's car in the parking lot after volleyball practice but I can't find it. I'm about to call her when I finally see your car.

You're parked at the back of the lot under the shade of an elm tree. I force my feet to move towards your car. When I open the passenger door, I find you pouring a Miller Lite into a coffee tumbler. As I climb into the passenger seat, you toss the empty bottle down at my feet. You don't bother to tuck it under the seat with the rest of your collection.

Foam oozes from the mouth of the bottle onto my shoe.

With your foot on the brake, you put the car in drive before bringing the tumbler to your lips. I watch your Adam's apple bob against the skin of your throat. As the car moves forward, you keep the beer in your right hand while steering with your left.

Without looking at me, as we pull out of the school's parking lot, you say, *We're going for a drive.*

I'm still twenty-three.

I adjust in my seat just to feel the rough fabric of the chair scratch against my thighs.

Were you afraid? my therapist asks.

Yes.

Because he was drinking?

No, I was used to that.

Why then?

I'm twelve.

The shower is running and steam is slinking catlike into the hallway. I'm listening at your bedroom door. Mom's already at work so it's just you in there.

You and whoever you're speaking to on the phone.

You put her on speaker when you think I'm in the shower—when you think I can't hear you.

I hear you.

Your voice is low and your laugh is deep in your throat. She laughs high and often. I wonder if that make you feel good.

I can't make out the words of your conversation over the sound of the shower but I listen to the rise and fall of your voices. I don't know how long I stand there—only that, when I get into the shower, the water is frigid against my hot skin.

I listen to you talk with her for weeks.

The night before our drive, I tell Mom.

I have to be twenty-three.

I'm here. I'm sitting across from the therapist. I can see her. She's stopped taking notes. She's waiting for me to say something.

I'm here. I'm not there.

You are here, she says, *but you're also there.*

☽

I'm twelve.

I don't know where we're going but I do know that you're drunk. Or maybe I only think you're drunk.

With each exhale, the beer on your breath permeates the air in the car.

You must know that I told Mom about your morning phone calls. Why else would you pick me up from practice? Why else would we be going for this drive?

I try to remember the last time I was alone with you, and nothing comes to mind. Even now, I don't feel like I'm alone with you.

In this car, there's me and you and that woman—that woman you speak to every morning after Mom has gone to work and I'm getting ready for school.

Who is that woman?

I say nothing as we pass by the turn that leads to our street— to safety. We leave our neighborhood and the suburb behind. Soon, we're surrounded by cornfields.

Am I twenty-three?

I feel like I'm still twelve, enclosed in a snow globe. Shake me up and this memory plays out again and again.

I don't know how to finish this story.

My therapist says, *Start at the end.*

I'm twelve.

I'm in the passenger seat of your car. We're parked on the shoulder of a two-lane highway, and I'm staring out at a cornfield.

I'm not looking at you but I know you're drinking. I listen to each rhythmic swallow as you consume the rest of your beer. Soon, I can no longer hear the liquid crashing against the stainless-steel walls. I know the beer is finished when you let go of the tumbler for the first time, setting it into the cupholder standing between us.

I won't look at you, but I feel you staring. I wonder why you brought me here where no one can see us.

No one can stop you from leaving me here.

Looking out into the cornfield, I can see myself decaying there— my skull crumbling in on itself or else the skin of my throat blooming indigo like bluebonnets lining the interstate in the spring.

Samantha.

Your voice is cool and steady as you say my name. I know I have to look at you—I have to pull my eyes away from the image of my corpse nourishing the earth.

When I finally turn my head toward you, I stare at your moustache. I watch your tongue dart out to lick your lips. I can't look at your eyes. I'm so focused on watching your mouth wrap around the words, I don't hear them the first time.

What?

Your lips become thinner still.

Why would you do this to your mother and me?

I'm twenty-three but I'm also twelve.

We are the same.

My skin is raw and inflamed from trying to scrub away this memory, but I need it to be me now.

You are you now, but you are also you then.

I'm twelve.

I'm staring past your shoulder at the cornfields on the other side of the highway. The shadows have descended and I watch as their fingers stretch out towards us inching closer and closer with each passing breath.

Why would you do this to your mother and me?

I'm twenty-three.

I know your infidelity is not my fault.

I know your infidelity is not my fault.

I know your infidelity is not my fault.

My therapist reaches out and places her hand on my knee. She rubs soothing circles there before she says what we both already know but it has to be said aloud.

You don't know it's not your fault.

I'm twelve.

I'm in the passenger seat of your car. We're parked in the garage. Neither one of us has spoken since we left the cornfield.

Finally, you move—pull the keys out of the ignition, unbuckle your seat belt, and step out of the car. You pause long enough to grab another beer out of the outside fridge before going inside the house.

I remain seated in the car for a few minutes.

Or maybe it's a few years.

In the corner of the garage, I can see my therapist sitting in a lawn chair.

She's stopped writing.

She's waiting for me to say something.

I adjust in my seat—the paisley-patterned chair scratches against my thighs.

MUZAFFER KALE

Death Whistles Like a Bird

They were twelve young men, gathered from the village and two of its hamlets. Rüstem was eighteen, the youngest of them all, and he had large black eyes. The commander and deputy who'd come to take them to the mountain regiment were dressed just like guerrillas from head to toe. Between them walked the twelve unarmed men.

They hadn't been trained yet. The only ones in the column carrying any weapons were the commander and his deputy. One in the front, the other in the rear, they seemed to shoulder enough ammunition to dispatch an entire army. Live ammo, as the saying goes. That's exactly what they were.

They stopped. A minute later a decision was made. They would put the garrison up ahead to their right and climb the hillside unseen. The slope was covered by an oak forest, with junipers and hornbeams peeking out here and there. Farther up the valley you could see where the sage maquis shrubs began. Advancing wouldn't be very difficult at all.

When they came to a small clearing, the commander in front ordered them to kneel. They did. He spent a long time watching the garrison through his binoculars. "What's going on?" his deputy said. "Is the place infested?" "They're slouching, the lazy bastards," the commander said. He didn't lower the binoculars when he spoke. "The sentry in tower number three is asleep. That idiot must have a death wish." His voice was weighted with contempt, as if he were discounting the sleeping sentry's very humanity. To him, those soldiers looked more like lice.

Everyone in the region knew where the garrison's sentry posts were. Which meant the sentry in tower number three really had fallen asleep.

"We'll crawl up," said the commander, "towards that rocky part of the forest."

The commander was somewhere in his forties, the kind of man who did his job well. How else can you put it? He had that broad, easy manner that people of many talents tended to possess, as if he could do anything. He inspired confidence. How the elders in the village had watched him as he spoke: a hero! Anyone would have wanted to be in his place. Beside him his deputy paled in comparison, although he too had the same courteous and candid demeanor.

About an hour later the commander in front said, "We're here."

He listened carefully.

Then he whistled like a bird and waited for a reply.

They all waited for a reply.

It didn't come.

"We're the first ones," he said. "We'll wait." So this was where they'd meet the recruits from the other villages before continuing on their way.

He gave a sign and they all knelt in the maquis shrubs. They were practically invisible now. The metallic screech of a sooty falcon rang out overhead and echoed around the hills. No, it wasn't her sound they were waiting for. She was a falcon on the hunt. If she started circling, it meant there were partridges nearby; that's what they did— they circled the partridges. They waited for the perfect chance to dive. And when the time came they gave their bodies over to the void, hurtling through it as if from the barrel of a gun.

The deputy commander took a pack of cigarettes from his backpack. He unwrapped it with painstaking care.

He couldn't have opened it any more methodically with a pair of scissors.

He closed his eyes, pressed his nostrils to the open pack and breathed in. Then he slid it into his hip pocket. Rüstem watched him. It didn't make much sense. Sniff them all you want; at least take one out and light it up! The only expression on his face was anticipation for the arrival of the others. He occasionally looked around without much interest, but that was it. He was calm. They might come from anywhere, so he kept pricking up his ears in every direction.

After a while, a noise sounded from the forest up above: a whistling bird ....

The commander sat up.
But he didn't get excited.
He whistled back.
It was the same sound, like the call of a bird.
The others had arrived.

A column of eight recruits appeared out of nowhere, strung between an armed man in the front and a second in the rear, just like before. These boys didn't have any weapons, either. The two commanders shook hands. The one who'd just arrived explained why they were four men short. Apparently, they'd agreed to come with the next group.

They ordered all the recruits to dress right. The younger ones looked at each other. Then the deputy commander of the second group showed them how to form a line. Some of them started laughing. It was obvious, and in every respect, that the commander of the first group carried the most clout. He spoke to the recruits steadily in a kind, firm voice. "Get a hold of yourselves, gentlemen," he said. "We're not going to a wedding, quit laughing."

"OK," a few of them said. Rüstem said, "OK," as well. He didn't know why, but an uncontrollable desire to laugh was welling up inside him, and he felt a mischievousness playing across his face, which he tried to turn into a more serious look.

Hadn't he always wanted to be in the mountains? Well, here he was, right where he wanted to be. There was just this thing that he couldn't name, which stemmed from a lack—or was it an excess?—of something. Either way it was inside him now, this feeling of uncertain origin thundering in the depths of his being, a force not very different from when a fear of heights sucks downward on your soul.

"Pass around the cigarettes," the first commander told his deputy.
The line broke apart. The deputy commander began to hand out the cigarettes, but some of the recruits didn't want any. "It's protocol," he said. "Everyone lights a cigarette! If you don't want one, don't inhale!"

The lighter passed from hand to hand, and the air filled with smoke.

Some of the recruits chuckled.

Rüstem coughed. As he did, tears came to his eyes.

☾

As if startled by a noise, the four commanders suddenly reached for their guns and jumped to their feet. Their faces had changed. Before anyone knew it, they'd leapt three or four steps backwards. Then they readied the mechanisms of their guns and turned them on the recruits, who still sat on the ground.

The recruits went quiet. They looked at one another. Their mouths hung open.

"All right," the first commander shouted in a shrill voice, "to hell with all of you!"

The barrels vomited their fire.

The stench of gunpowder, strong enough to burn the nasal passages, spread everywhere.

Then the deafening sound of the guns fell away, followed by a heavy silence.

Rüstem toppled over where he'd been sitting and met the gaze of the deputy commander who had handed out the cigarettes. His dull black eyes stared at him, as if they'd never forget what they'd seen.

The deputy commander took a new pack of cigarettes from his backpack. He didn't open it very carefully this time. Nor did he sniff. He pulled out a cigarette and lit it. The commander of the first group glared at him. "You smoke a lot," he said.

"Never mind," said the other. "It's been more than two years since I've gone on leave," he carried on. "I need a little break! I need to go on leave!"

Translated from the Turkish by Ralph Hubbell

Salgado Maranhão

Fractures 2

In them what is there
overflows with viscera (and

bits of memory
without a home).

The fractures
turning them to night
come from days

that never have been born:
                        from a house
built among snakes;
from an umbilical cord long lost.

Now,
when the jungle opens its door
to them,
it isn't birds that sing,
but vipers.

Translated from the Portuguese by Alexis Levitin

ANDREW BERTAINA

The Space Between Us

Shana and I are in Italy: twenty-eight, unmarried, drinking, and sad, still young enough to believe people should stay in love. We're at a party in the San Vitale Quarter of Bologna with newly minted friends, the sort you make when you are traveling, saving money on food and spending it on alcohol. Our new friends are good-looking blonds from some Nordic country we'd never visit. If we've learned anything in our eight years together, it's that we both hate the cold.

I'm standing against a gray wall beneath a print of Rubens' *Samson and Delilah* and watching the nylon-covered legs of women pass through the artificial light of the patio. I am in a sea of unfamiliar faces, and everyone is speaking a language I don't understand. It feels as though I have returned from space to find the whole world changed.

Shana and I pass the time with sweating drinks in our hands, reminiscing about our first night in Bologna. That night, under the influence of gin, we'd wandered dim streets with broken cobbles, past fading pastel houses, black grates on windowsills, mauve pottery that held bouquets of flowers. It was cold; the cement smelled like winter. We walked down Via Independenza beneath the porches that line the main street—stores offering harbors of light. We entered a large town square of red brick, walled off on our right by a castle, crenellations intact. I thought of telling her about Henry VIII, how he'd killed all his wives because they wouldn't bear him sons, and how we know now that it is the man's responsibility to father sons and how sad it was that so many English women lost their heads.

A statue of Neptune stood in the center of the square, bravely nude, cobwebbed in a feathery yellow by lamps hanging from brick walls. Four statues of mermaids flanked Neptune, water shooting from their nipples. We sat on a rectangular bench by the statue as stars appeared.

"Do you remember how we both wanted to be astronauts?" she said, turning to face me, the light caught in her eyes, a stray hair, caressing her cheek.

"How could I forget?" I said, turning away from her and towards the stars.

"We talked about it on our first date," she said, and I could hear it in her voice, the yearning to have me turn toward her.

"Now that, I have forgotten," I said, not wanting to talk anymore, content just to be there. The same way we'd been in our third-grade classrooms, a thousand miles part, but still beneath the same light of the sun, watching *The Challenger* take off from Merritt Island.

"I still think my version is right," she said.

"When have you ever thought you were wrong?"

I swore that I remembered *The Challenger* leaving the Earth's atmosphere, a meteor that parted the clouds like the prow of a boat through water. She remembered it falling faster, barely reaching the blue of the sky before arcing down towards the sea. It was in the air for seventy-three seconds, our brief dream. They say that the crew disintegrated over the ocean, or died from the impact. Both of us remember that day the same, though—the quick shifting of childish dreams in the aftermath of the explosion. We were not meant to leave this Earth.

"There's the Great Bear," I said. Then, I moved my hand across the blackness at the speed of light and pointed to a new spot. "There's the Little Bear." Shana rested her head on my thin shoulder and closed her eyes. We remembered that first night as our best because that's the way of things; they always feel good at first.

The night she told me she was pregnant—seven months ago—I drove up the dim road into the brown foothills behind our apartment complex. I parked and walked through a field of dry grass, burs sticking to my jeans, to a black pool of water reflecting stars. I thought of my childhood, the days with my mother in church, of God promising Abraham descendants as numerous as the stars. I dipped my toe in the water. The stars wavered and faded as little waves broke on the loam, and I thought that if I could make all the descendants of Abraham disappear with my toe, then maybe we could make it work.

We'd spent two weeks walking the cobblestoned streets of Bologna—naked statues pissing eternal rivers, bars with circular tables, and restaurants, where old men scribble bills on tablecloths to avoid taxes. We'd walked through the open-air market where fresh rabbits hung, folds of pink skin and white muscle, only the eyes remaining, staring at nothing.

"That's so sad," Shana said, pointing to the rabbits. She told me about the pet rabbit—Chocolate Charlie—she'd had as a child. They'd loved him when he was new, when he fit in the palm of their hands, his breath a feather on their fingers.

"But he got old, less cute. He sat in the corner of his wire cage on a pile of shit like it was treasure until the day he died."

"Is that something I should be worried about?"

"What?"

"You locking me in a cage with a pile of my own excrement when I'm no longer cute."

"Oh, honey, the word is shit," she said, smiling, but with a distant look in her eyes. "You know, his funeral was the first of my life. I remember my mother telling me that he'd passed into some other place. I believed her."

"Childhood is about believing in things, though, isn't it?" I said.

Italian socialists are smoking cigarettes on the balcony in the rain. A striking dark-haired girl with a perfectly curved ass is barefoot and swinging her toes through small puddles. She holds a cigarette between her middle and index fingers, ashing on the tiles. It's as beautiful—her gesture, the thin white fingers tapping the railing—as all the pollution-inspired violet sunsets I've seen drop below the hills behind our complex.

"What are you staring at?" Shana asks.

"Nothing," I say. "It's just strange to be in a place where you don't understand a damn word that's being said."

"Sounds like heaven," she says, and her eyes go blank as she pulls absently at a stray hair.

I feel like we are astronauts traveling through the vacuum of space, and I want to tell her everything, but I can't take off my helmet, or I'll suffocate.

"I'm suffocating," I say.

"No sex games tonight," she answers.

We haven't been talking since the morning of the miscarriage. That day, I came back from the park and lay on the couch in front of the television, pretending to sleep. She didn't ask me where I'd been; she took apart the crib in the dark.

As I lay there, listening to her, blue light poured out of the television through a satellite a million miles away. I thought what a miracle it was that we could speak to each other from across the galaxy, but how sad and strange it was that the words meant nothing.

The next morning, I dug through the trash and found every part of the crib. For the first time in my life, I worked on putting something together. I worked like a man is supposed to, on something that could be completed. I committed my whole day to restoring the crib while Shana slept in the bedroom with the shade closed.

She came downstairs once and shook her head at the mess on the floor. "What the hell are you doing?" she asked, eyes, red-rimmed.

"I'm working," I said, putting the screwdriver carefully back into the case, the way my father used to.

She sighed, and went into the kitchen, opened the cupboard, took crackers into bed.

I finished putting the crib together. As I tightened the last screw and stood to behold my work, I was filled with a strong feeling of satisfaction. I had shown my son how to build something. I walked into the back yard and sat in the lone chair. A stray cat walked along the fence line, tail-twitching to keep balance. The light drained from the sky. I looked at our cherry tree, green buds showing months too early to avoid frost.

In the morning, Shana and I are hiding from the sun in a boxy room on Via Romita. We're renting it out on the cheap from an Italian babushka or whatever. The curtains are closed, and we're lying in the dark on an old stained mattress as roaches scuttle across the floor. It smells of old semen and burnt hair. I trace the sharp angle of her hip bone, where it rises, like a dorsal fin, from beneath layers of skin.

I've got a headache; my tongue is thick in my mouth, and I'm daydreaming of water. Shana's stomach rises and falls in the half-lit room. Her tits are spread apart and flat. I lap water from the faucet like a dog. On the way back to bed, I put a cigarette out on a roach's back. He lies there, and I wonder if he is in the space between life and death, between the stars, then scurries toward the wall. "What noise is this? Not dead? I that am cruel am yet merciful," I say, trying to put heel to roach.

"No fucking Shakespeare when I'm hungover," Shana says.

I lift my foot and brush the half-broken body beneath the sink.

"You look horrible," she says.

I throw a pillow at her. "Your nudity offends my puritanical proclivities." I say, facing the water-stained wall. "Let me know when you're all tarted up so I can speak to you properly."

"Did Shakespeare ever use the word 'tart'?"

"Prodigiously."

Shana throws her underwear into my back. "It strikes where it doth love."

I climb into bed, and Shana rolls to face me. A line appears on her forehead, and I become scared of what she might say, so I start naming the roaches scurrying across our floors, throwing my shoe at them, extinguishing them early, like light on a winter's day.

"We can't use the same name twice," Shana says, slipping on her shirt.

"That one's Magellan," I say. "He's circumnavigating the room."

By the end of an hour, we're calling them He That Rides the Pale Horse at Noon or Shitonya, names we'd heard on television talk shows or read in history books when we were less afraid of ourselves.

We eat at a bar on the corner of Via Independenza beneath terra-cotta arches with peeling paint. A sudden rain falls in the street. We let time pass. Long-haired men ride by on mopeds over wet stones, and underfed Italian waifs clop by on expensive heels. A pigeon hops by, a piece of garbage held in his beak like prize. Above him, his brethren shit on a fading mural.

"Where are we going?" Shana asks, stirring the coffee with her finger. "Maybe we should climb the Torre Degli Asinelli today," Shana says. "It's one of the tallest towers in Italy."

"I didn't realize I was traveling with an official guide. Somebody boned up on their Jeopardy before leaving California."

"Alex Trebec is a sex God," she said.

"Those Canadian men: always fucking our best and brightest."

"Can you think of any other Canadians?"

"Not offhand, but I'm certain they exist."

I tell her that I've been dreaming of water, and that we're being called to Venice. We take the bus down Via Independenza passing exposed brickwork and expensive stores on the way to the station. The sky is cigarette ash, and neither one of us believes in dreams, God, or each other.

We board the train and sit in a car by ourselves. Beyond the window, businessmen read the newspaper and smoke. Trash blows from concrete onto the tracks.

"Italy would be great if it weren't for all the dirty Italians," I say.

The train idles, and Shana sleeps. Beautiful, long-legged foreign women board trains to places I've never been, and I think of leaving Shana—sleeping on the train—and following them to a distant place, where we could make the indescribable love of people who know nothing but each other's body. I imagine Shana sleeping as the train passes through the countryside, until a dark Italian man puts his finger on her lips. When she wakes, they will talk for hours, and he will find all the beautiful things inside her that I'd lost.

Shana wakes and smiles at me in the innocent way of a child freshly returned from the world of dreams. The train hums and moves out of the station. Green hills appear and rivers run through tall grass. We pass through tiny hamlets where houses dust the hillsides like snow. I get up to pee but walk slowly past the other cars: Two men sleep, arms touching, with backpacks on; a bored woman stares out the window at cows and vineyards; a father, gray hair at his temples, reads to his son. All this domesticity comes to me through a barrier of glass, thick as a hospital window, where fathers dream lives for sons. I go back to Shana and watch her sleep, and I want to wake her, but she is as far away as those childhood dreams of reaching the moon.

We don't speak for miles of rails. I read out of a guidebook, and she drools on the window. The harbor of Venice appears lined by the skeletal outlines of ships; the grzy sky spits rain. I run my finger across the ghostly veins on Shana's hand; sunlight appears on the prow of a schooner.

"If we are in space, we have finally found the sun," I say.

She smiles at me again, her face, suddenly light as though the shadows have passed.

The brick walls of the Santa Lucia station are covered in graffiti. Outside, the clouds have lifted to reveal an unimaginably vaulted sky. We stand in the sudden light on wet stone steps, looking over concrete to the Grand Canal. The boats move through the water and part green water like silk. Exhaust pours from their tailpipes and fades like ashes into water. I shield the sun from my forehead with my palm. "Mine eyes have seen the glory," I say.

"No politics," she says, and pulls a laminated map from her backpack and asks what I'd like to see.

"I'd really like to see some more men's penises," I say.

"I don't think they have a lot of sculptures here. Besides, that's all you ever want to see. Pick something new."

"I've got nothing," I say. "I came to Italy for the express purpose of withered penises and have been sorely disappointed thus far."

We buy tickets and board the number one vaporetto. We push through the mob of people, armed with digital cameras, to get the best view of the drowning city. And I wonder what makes any of us here feel unique, staring at the same few things, but maybe that's the point, that we're all sharing it together, like all the stars of Abraham casting distant light that still falls on this same planet.

Mansions line the water, hemming in the gondolas, vaporetti, and water taxis, like ancient guards of some long-dead city. We coast over the green water beneath a ribbon of blue sky. The palaces have bricked-up bottom floors and moss-lined steps. The water rises on all sides, staining the siding. Buildings are veiled in thick curtains, too blackened by the exhaust of passing boats. We float past fading Byzantine structures whose windows are lined with crosses. We coast past thick gothic structures with porticos for street vendors to hawk fresh vegetables. Everywhere, brick is turning to chalk.

"How did they build this?" a fat guy keeps asking his bored kids.

"By hand," one of them says.

The wind is rushing in our faces, and Shana is standing at the railing, a hand keeping her hair in place.

"Can you believe that little bastard?" I asked.

"I didn't realize your powers of deduction were so shrewd, Dear Watson."

"Oh yeah, there's no way that handsome little devil came from him."

"Postman?"

"I was going to go with gardener, but I'll accept postman."

A woman with short dark hair and thin glasses reads to her children from a guidebook. She points to the Ca' d'Oro, noting that the brilliant facade still remains; water laps at the porticos lining the bottom floor. The children look on with mild interest, shading their eyes from the sun. Her husband's hand is wrapped tightly around a stroller.

We pass underneath the brilliant Via Rialto—the first bridge in Venice—lined with people taking pictures of other people.

Shana leans on the white railing, listening to the speech as the wind stirs her hair. The woman describes the Baroque architecture exemplified by the massive octagonal crown-shaped Santa Maria della Salute, which is made of white brick and two massive double domes with a statue of the Virgin ruling over the sea. I notice that as the woman has been reading she's forgotten her purse, which rests between my feet. I lift her purse from the ground and move to the center of the boat. I stand in the same sea of unfamiliar faces, happy to blend in, waiting to disembark at St. Mark's Square.

Shana slips to my side, and we drift off into the current of people. We hear a commotion coming from the boat, a woman has lost her purse. I pull Shana's hand to my chest; I want her to feel it beating furiously. She pulls her hand away, unsure of the gesture.

We walk out of the main square as light begins to settle on the water. We turn onto narrow, winding streets with worn-away facades, pass houses, brown shutters open to the alley.

"Do you think brown is my color?" I ask her, turning a leg in what I think is a girlish manner.

"No, and where the hell is this city park supposed to be?"

"Because I really like how it matches my shoes," I say.

She turns, and her eyes are bright, alive. "What the hell are you doing with a purse?"

"Accessorizing." And there is a strange difference between what I mean to say and what I've done.

"What is wrong with you?" she asks.

I think of asking her the same thing, but silence is best. When we reach the park, Shana sits on a redwood bench beneath a canopy of dying trees.

"Are we criminals now?" she asks. "Is that what we're going to do? Go around stealing from the rich and giving to ourselves!"

Her lips are shaking, and a strand of hair has broken free and is bisecting her face.

"I found it on the ground," I say. I feel a surge of feeling towards her; I want to brush the stray hair from her face and wrap my arms around her. I want to touch her.

"If we were in Pakistan, you realize that's what they'd to you?" she says, gesturing to the statue of an armless woman across from us.

"Turn me into a woman?" I answer.

"This is serious," she says. "This is not some fucking childish game."

"Are you going to turn me in?"

"I should," she answers, and we sit in the cold. An elderly man tosses flakes of white bread into a flock of pigeons. A small white bird with a yellow plume on his head darts among them, stealing what he can.

The sun is lying on the canal where it widens in some dazzling way that reminds of a trip from years ago. Shana and I drove up to the lake above her house. We'd dipped our toes in the water, and she'd lain on top of me for hours as we looked out over the water into the incandescent light of our futures.

"I'm going to be Buzz Aldrin," I'd said, watching leaves drop in lazy circles towards the water.

"Buzz Aldrin?"

"You know, the guy who almost made it to the moon," I said, rolling over, kissing the space the space on her skin where neck met shoulder.

"Couldn't you set your sights a little higher?" she asked, arching her eyebrows.

"Higher than the moon?" I asked, pinching her brown arm, still warm from summer light.

"Almost the moon," she said, giggling a little, and rolling onto her back and away from me. Her hair was wet, and her body was as thin as a reed. I do not know if anything in life will ever match that afternoon at the lake.

We walk down a tree-lined street scattered with yellow leaves. A statue of Garibaldi stands at the end of the street on a stone dais, circled by a black iron fence. Beneath the statue is a winged lion: the symbol of Venice. Garibaldi was covered in pigeons.

"They're shitting on the founder of Italy."

"Do something about it then," Shana says, releasing my hand.

I run toward the pigeons and shout, "I'm a scarecrow, you sons of bitches; be scared." The pigeons hop off the statue and drop into the street, standing dumbly among the leaves.

"Are you going to help?" I ask, and Shana shakes her head.

It's just me and Garibaldi now. His whole face is covered in white shit, and we stare at each other as though we are brothers. I slowly raise my hand and salute him.

By the time we leave, the pigeons are back on Garibaldi, shitting everywhere, because that's the way of the world.

Shana and I walk down the narrow shaded streets of Venice towards squares of light. We pass small houses—water-damaged bricks, statues of women's heads, bouquets of flowers on the balcony— all that fading and decadent beauty. We cross little bridges over slow water and pass thousand-year-old buildings.

As we walk along the filthy canal, an aqueduct appears—the face of a lion—spitting water into a moss-encrusted basin. Shana puts her head underneath the spout and then her whole body. Her bra is visible, and her shirt cleaves to the small curve of her stomach. I put my head beneath the flowing water; it is clean and cold.

"I have been anointed," I say, slapping Shana's ass. She spits a mouthful of water in my face, and I grab her narrow hips and pull them towards me. We kiss like people who are still in love. I think that this moment is perfect, like when Buzz was watching Armstrong plant the flag on the moon. I wonder if he loved him from behind the glass of the shuttle window. We wrap our hands together like lovers.

We arrive back in St. Mark's Square with a thousand other tourists. The wind swirls, blows papers from the sky, catches and holds them. We stand in line for what feels like hours.

"We should talk sometime," Shana says, bumping me with her hip and smiling.

"What do you think we're doing?" I ask. "Exchanging guttural growls of apes?"

She lowers her eyes, and her shoulders drop.

Inside the basilica, we stand underneath the ceilings, incredibly vaulted like all the churches in Europe, and look at the Apostles and Disciples on the ceiling. I think of all those Apostles who spent their whole lives doing the right thing, and how they died just the same. And maybe Buzz had been jealous at the window; maybe he'd wished that Armstrong died.

We walk to the top of the building and stand on a balcony overlooking the courtyard. The wind blows trash from the square towards the canal, and Shana's nipples poke through her shirt. The pigeons and people flock to a patch of light in the center of the square. It is cold, and we stand together like that, just watching for a long time.

"Where did you go?" she asks. "I needed you that day. I don't know if I can ever forgive you for leaving." She keeps staring straight ahead, though, watching light crumbling from the sky.

I remember the afternoon she told me about the miscarriage. She'd been crying in the bathroom, wanting me to hold her, but I'd left instead. I spent the afternoon in the park, drinking beer, watching kids play on swings, falling back and forth into the arms of their fathers, praying for no reason.

We look down at a three-pronged lamppost, pigeons winging above piles of trash. The sunlight starts to fade and everything—the water, the sky, the light—turns the shade of blue of Picasso's *Old Guitar Player*.

We walk across the square, still dotted with tourists. The smears of exhaust are cloaked in dark, and the buildings are like gargantuan sentries on some ancient Roman highway.

"Do you think we can still fix things?" Shana asks as we walk towards the sleek black gondolas that patrol Venice at night.

"I don't know a hell of a lot," I say, remembering how we'd talked about floating above all that dark water, above the bones of all the men who had built this dying city, how it would be like space. That it would be like traveling inside a black hole and looking back at the stars. How foolish we were; how foolish we have always been.

The gondolier has a tattoo on his right biceps that he flexes slightly as he smiles at both of us.

"How much?" Shana asks.

"Ninety," he answers, trying to catch her eye.

"I think we've got that much," she says, digging into the purse that I'd stolen hours earlier. She squeezes my hand, as if to reassure me, and steps into the swaying gondola. And as she settles into the red satin interior, moonlight seems to be caught in strands of her hair.

The morning after I built the crib, I wandered through the house in a vague green light towards a banging sound. I opened the bedroom door of my dear little boy, the one who I'd built the crib for, and there was Shana, smashing it with the end of a hammer. She was crying, and I wanted to hold her. I wanted that shuttle to pierce the veil of clouds and drift off into the dark cold of space where we could be alone.

"What the hell are you doing?" I asked, trying to grab the hammer from her shaking hands. She leaned forward and sobbed into my chest. I stroked her hair, and held her tightly against my chest. But no, that never happened. I walked away then, too

The moonlight has left her hair. I run as fast as my legs will carry me, and it feels as though I am the wind, as if I am faster than the sound of her voice. I run through the square and into the side streets, heart pounding, shoes burning. I run through the night until I reach an empty street lined by flowers. The crickets are silent. I stand on a bridge overlooking dark water, which reflects the stars. It feels good to be alone again. Perhaps that is all any of us are fit for.

The sky turns black, and I am in a steady rain. I walk down a narrow street—exposed brick, graffiti, bits of trash, and puddles, a pink checkered dress blowing in the wind and rain. The stars are dead things hidden by a curtain of clouds. We are all empty planets in space separated by fathomless darkness, and it's a miracle, like this city of water or the flag on the moon, that two people ever understand each other.

The rain is starting to freeze. A stray dog—thin slats for ribs—licks water from where it collects between stones. I walk down the wide tree-lined street, and the branches bend in the wind, pointing me toward Garibaldi. I stand in the dark at the foot of the statue, watching it rain.

"I'm sorry," I say, to the statue. I lift my arm to salute him for a second time. I shiver; rain runs down both our faces, falling from our chins. Here we are, me and my shat upon brother, standing in the rain, waiting to come clean.

JAMES ELLENBERGER

They Taste on the Air the Rich Red of Roses

Students stand around the room
as the autopsy continues. A woman
wearing gloves but not a mask
lifts the heart from the chest
and sets it on a digital scale. A number
flashes blue. The students write it down.
The liver, the mother of ponds,
seems podunk in her hands. The left lung.
The right. The drawing of radials
and the sound of a saw. The pens
can't catch up with the body
growing empty, yet the books
shaking in their hands
flourish, hooking and curling along faint red lines
until each page bears a latticework
of black stems. Nothing is missing
nor exceptional; the remains, accounted for,
to be incinerated. Drinks will follow.
The washing of hands. The washing of hands.
The annotations in their books
like black stems
rush towards the margin as if to bloom.

ABBY CAPLIN

Tumbling Through a Faucet

At heart we are innocent as
molecules tumbling through a faucet,
or a paltry eight billion caught
for a fraction of infinity in the lab's
glass beaker, sometimes knocked over, contents
flung, the school custodian fast mopping up,
wringing out thirsty tentacles of capillary action
into Earth's blue bucket—
 bottomless combinations spun
through plankton, dinosaur, ladybug,
redwood, pelican, peach, coffee.
Or peed onto the floor of a Neanderthal
cave seventy-five thousand years ago—
this morning in my garden,
misting a rainbow with once-indecipherable
permafrost, the mud teeming
with hoary flesh, bacilli, viral load.

AMANDA AUCHTER

Gardening

My sister trims her pots of mint
in the white Colorado sun, and there is

no storm brewing for her, no blizzard, no
avalanche or mudslide coming down

the mountains near her home, but
she cannot turn on a television or radio

(and who listens to radio anymore)
because it's fake, she says, and she says *fake*,

a curse, a scissored snip, another
cut of mint, a hacked weed

invading her little garden. *I don't know who
to believe*, she says, and here is her fear—

it flies inside her, bangs the screen doors,
the open windows. Here is another night

in a world of thick woods and her rope
getting thin. She repeats what she hears,

weeds the garden. She collects the clippings—
the brown stems, leaves, a curled rootball—

and it's difficult for her to recognize their beauty,
how brave they are in spite of the clipping,

the culling, the fingers that sweep them away.

KIM MAGOWAN & MICHELLE ROSS

Oh-Oh-It's-Cruel

When my son frets over the lightning bugs my nephew has trapped in a plastic bin that used to hold individually wrapped biscotti, my brother Shane says in his son's defense, "I don't give a flying fuck about insects." Then he says, "I think a lot of people care more about animals than they do people. They're all oh-oh-it's-cruel-to-eat-animals, but meanwhile, do they care about the homeless guy sitting on the street corner? Do they care about their own family?"

We're here at Dad's house for the weekend to be educated about his and our stepmom Gillian's will. Dad wanted us to "know in advance what's what so there won't be any arguing" after he and Gillian are dead and gone. I laughed when I read that in his email. He sent me a separate, private email asking if I would agree to be executor of the will. When he announced that detail this morning, my brother Shane blurted, "But I'm the oldest!" My sister Lorna and my stepbrother Mike said nothing, but their bodies visibly stiffened, making me think of royal icing when you let it sit for too long and it dries and forms a wrinkly skin.

My husband, Grant, is inside helping Dad and Gillian hook up their outdoor stereo speakers while the rest of us sit out on the back deck, drinking mojitos—all of us except Lorna, who's in AA and made a big fuss earlier about how she couldn't miss the local chapter meeting this afternoon. Our drinking mojitos means we have to put up with Lorna's cigarette smoke without a word of complaint or else she'll launch into a mumbled soliloquy about how all her life we've conspired against her.

"Oh, like I want to do this," Carrie says. "Like I'm jumping up and down to be the executor of his will. Do you realize what a pain in the ass this will be?"

Mike nods in his sedated, bobblehead way. Everything moves slowly with that guy. Being stoned for ten years straight has thickened all his reflexes. He's a human mashed potato. But Lorna looks at me, cigarette clenched between her fingers, and her look is as legible as if she passed a note. We both know Carrie.

When we were kids, Carrie was a dictator. She sucked on grievances like they were jawbreakers. When we played Monopoly, Carrie insisted on being the banker, because she claimed I once stole $500 from the bank. She would hold up the game to make sure that exactly a third of the house-purchase money went each time into Free Parking: $67 precisely, Carrie thumbing out the bills while Lorna and I moaned and groaned. She's anal as hell, which my parents always mistook for responsibility.

I remember Mom giving her a bag of potato chips to divvy out. Once Mom got sick, she was always sending us out to the lawn with various snacks. "Go have a picnic," Mom would say, so she could nap. Not only did Carrie deal those chips as if they were cards, making sure that Lorna, she, and I got the exact same number, but also she decided that one of my potato chips was too large, and gave Lorna a bite of it to make it even. "Just this much, Lorna," she said, tapping the potato chip.

When Mom was alive, she called Carrie "My little hammer," because of the way Carrie would go apeshit playing whack-a-mole. There are people who venerate fairness because they have an authentic sense of justice, and then there are people, like Carrie, for whom fairness is an excuse to cudgel everyone into submission.

"I call your bluff," Shane says, and I'm transported to high school when I complained to Gillian and Dad that it was sexist to always put me in charge of watching Lorna and Mike when they went out to dinner alone. They'd say, "It's because we trust you. We wouldn't trust Shane to keep a fern alive through the evening." Then as soon as they left the house, Shane would say, "You're not fooling me with your cries of unfairness. You eat that shit up."

Shane's kid Lenny already has more lightning bugs in that container than one can count, but still he's running around the yard looking for more. He reminds me so much of Shane. Greedy as hell. He won't stop until he captures every damn lightning bug that makes the mistake of crossing the property line. And his demented glee when he captures one! "Don't even think about getting away!" he yells at the insects as he scoops them out of the air, floating flakes of gold.

My son Robert is in full-blown distress over this. He's got a chunk of hair wrapped around his finger, and he's tugging like he's trying to unearth a stubborn turnip. If Grant catches him, he'll launch into another lecture about how Robert's going to develop a bald spot like I did as a kid. Grant isn't particularly fond of Shane, but when he's irritated by my stressing over something, sometimes he'll say that my brother's coolness is admirable in a certain way. "Like how a psychopath's lack of empathy for his murder victims is admirable?" I say.

"And what the hell is that supposed to mean, Steve McQueen?" Carrie says. "'I call your bluff': Are we gamblers? Are we in some bad Western? Because if so, get me out of this shitty movie."

In the back yard my son, Lenny, zooms around pretending to be a velociraptor, his arms extended wings. Lenny tries to get Carrie's son Robert to play with him, but Robert is a crumpled-up hedgehog in the hammock. He keeps pulling his own hair: a weirdo like his mom. "Baldy," I used to call Carrie.

"It means if you think being the executor is such a drag, then politely decline the job," I advise her. I emphasize "decline": I'm communicating, to Lorna, smoking madly, and to Mike, who looks like he wants to suck his thumb, that I, at least, am behaving like an adult.

In reaction, Carrie's eyes bulge. Mouth open too, she looks like the girl on a horror movie poster. If Dad could see her now, his illusions of Carrie-the-Competent would finally fall away. He'd see Carrie for who she really is—a passive-aggressive freak who always has to be in charge.

When Mom was sick, Carrie drew up a visiting schedule, turning our own house into a hospital. She had one of those fat pens where you can change the color cartridge by clicking, and she assigned different colors to Lorna, me, and her. When I complained to Mom about Carrie dictating what time we spent with her, she said, "Oh, hon. It makes her feel better, having something to do." Then she tousled my hair and said, "How about not arguing with your sister?"

Arguing: We heard that verb a lot as a kid, often hissed by our father. "Don't argue! Your mother is trying to sleep!" To this day, Dad acts like arguing is calamitous, something only savages do. When I asked, composedly, why he'd chosen Carrie to be the executor, he looked aghast, as if I'd poured gasoline on his chair and torched it.

Six months ago, Dad's and Gillian's Christmas card had contained a check for $15,000. The typed letter wrapped around the check had read rather cryptically, "If this card contains a check, the money is our attempt to even things out, to treat our children fairly. If this card does not contain a check, consider our loans to you forgiven."

I wagered that we were the only ones to receive a check, but Grant thought Lorna might have received a smaller check, say a couple grand at least. "What could she have spent $15,000 on?" he said. "Doesn't she buy everything she owns from secondhand stores?"

"Booze. Marty. A DUI," I said. The DUI is a conjecture, but it's not wild guesswork. Lorna's only been in AA for about eight months now, since November, and Dad was clearly worried about her at Thanksgiving. Lorna bounces between problems the way Shane's ex-wife Sherilynn did fashion trends. When Lorna was a kid, the rest of us shared a secret candy stash behind the waffle maker in a high cabinet Lorna couldn't reach. This was for her own good, Dad said, because Lorna had "self-control issues" and also it was mean to eat candy in front of her. Then in high school, she became bulimic and so thin that one time she was wearing these drawstring pants and they came untied and literally fell to her ankles when she stood from the table at breakfast. After high school, she stopped vomiting and gained the weight back, but she moved in with a jackass named Marty who played video games in his boxers while she worked at a yarn store. Then there was that time she called Dad from Mexico because she lost her ID and couldn't get back across the border.

Neither of us doubted that Shane and Mike had "borrowed" $15,000 plus from Dad and Gillian over the years.

And now Shane has the gall to suggest that I should decline being executor of Dad's and Gillian's will? As if there's anyone else in this family who is responsible enough to take my place.

Feeling a little feisty from the mojitos, I say, "And what? Nominate you, Shane? Or how about Lorna? You think she'd make a good executor?"

☾

The thing about the number three: Someone is always being left out. Oh, there are isolated moments that can be harmonious—say, the three of us would briefly have a good time playing Monopoly— but twenty-five minutes in, Lorna would be crying about landing on Waterworks and rolling a twelve, and Carrie would be commenting on the irony of crying about Waterworks, and Lorna and I would be united, again, over what a pretentious, pleased-with-herself shithead Carrie was. Or, every so often, Carrie and Lorna, though normally as compatible as a cactus and a kitten, would be bonding in some dorky girl way—baking Toll House cookies, knitting these ridiculous beanie hats—and I would be the little match girl stuck outside in the snow, peering in.

It's not just siblings, either. Every time I get together with my friends Todd and Ollie, sooner or later, it ends up two picking on one and that one sticking his lip out. Something about the number three: it's like a law of nature.

You'd think that when Dad married Gillian and Mike got introduced into the mix, that would have resolved our triangulation dynamic. But Mike is too much of a potato to count as a full-fledged entity. His entry into our lives was less like converting a three-legged stool into a stable, four-legged chair than like sticking a wad of rolled-up newspaper under one of the stool legs to make it that much more tippy.

Though I have to say, it's not so much that Lorna and I choose each other than Carrie shoves us forcibly together. Like when we used to play badminton and Carrie would always want to be solo. "You and Lorna be partners!" she'd trill. That's how I feel when Lorna straightens up from her hunched vulture posture and says, "And why wouldn't I be a good executor? For fuck's sake, Carrie!"

Lorna's mad as hell when she says it—her wedge of a face has gone red, like it always does when she gets mad. We used to call her Heat Miser. But "for fuck's sake" cracks the three of us up. Not Mike, of course, who sits there looking back and forth among Lorna and Carrie and me with his mouth half open. If there were subtitles to Mike's thoughts, those subtitles would all say, "Doh?"

"Fuck!" I say. "Poor Fuck." Fuck was what Shane and I used to call Lorna's hamster Chuck. Because after her first stroke, Mom struggled with pronouncing various sounds. She developed this weird way of pronouncing "ch" so that the sound was more like "f." So when Mom would get on Lorna about the hamster "Lorna, did you change out Chuck's wood chips?" what we heard was "Lorna, did you fange out Fuck's wood fips?" When Mom wasn't around, Shane and I would say to Lorna, "For Fuck's sake, fange out the wood fips, Lorna!"

Then one time Mom overheard us. Her face turned red as fast as flipping the switch to turn on Christmas lights. That's where Lorna gets it from. She has super-pale skin like Mom did. Any bit of blood rushing to the surface stands out like blood on snow. When Mom overheard us, she turned red, but she didn't say a word for a long moment. Then she said, quietly and without emotion, "I'm going to be too busy with medical treatments to stay on top of making sure this hamster stays alive. You're going to have to remember to take care of him, Lorna. Or you two are going to have to help her. Either that or he's going to end up dead."

One might think that moment would have been the kick in the teeth Lorna needed, or Shane and me, for that matter. But Lorna was five at the time: I was ten, Shane eleven. Even if it weren't for the distraction of all of Mom's medical issues, we probably wouldn't have been responsible enough to keep a hamster alive on our own.

A Paul Simon song blares out of the speakers, startling every one of us. Robert comes running over to me, his palms pressed so hard against his ears that he looks like he's trying to squeeze something out of his skull, like his head is a giant pimple he's trying to pop.

The volume is quickly reduced, and Grant steps out and apologizes. He's followed by Gillian, who is carrying a tray with guacamole and chips and grapes. The guacamole, we all know, will contain sour cream. Because that's how Mike likes it, Shane has said. But maybe it's just because that's how Gillian's always made it. Maybe Mike liking it that way is secondary.

"Where's Dad?" asks Lorna, and Gillian makes the strangest face—it's as if someone goosed her behind. That's an expression of Mom's that always killed me. I could never figure out what a goose had to do with pinching. Geese don't have fingers.

"Doug's resting. He'll be out in a second," Gillian says. "Who needs another drink?" She takes everyone's orders and heads back to the house.

Carrie's husband takes a seat in that strange, swamp-creature way Grant has, like sitting is a ten-step process. He's three years older than me, but he acts like he's seventy. Do not get that man talking about composting. Seriously, your ears will slide off your head.

"You all should be less focused on the fact that I got assigned the thankless task of being executor, and more on what the job actually is," says Carrie, speaking double-time. "If you were listening to Dad actually describe the will, you'd know this is basic. Gillian inherits everything when he dies, and then when she dies, it all goes to the four of us, in equal quarters. All I am is the knife slicing the cake into four equal pieces." She makes a slicing gesture.

"Well, that's a revealing metaphor, that you're a knife," I point out. I reflect on how coolly Carrie just referred to Dad's and Gillian's deaths.

"A knife slicing cake, not a knife stabbing you," says Carrie, rolling her eyes.

"What about that percent of the estate executors get?" I ask, because I actually know a thing or two. Grant looks like he wishes Dad and Gillian would assign him some other complicated task—rewiring their electricity, shingling their roof—so he could vanish.

"I'll gift that one percent back to the estate. That will be part of the cake."

So I'm momentarily at a loss for words, but then Lorna shakes her head. "Guys. You're like the White House reporters, getting distracted because of some stupid Trump tweet and forgetting the real issue." Lorna was always a basket case, one problem after another as a kid; she could hardly put on her own socks. But when she applied herself—Mom's word, again, as if Lorna were some kind of robot—she could be clever. "Why is Dad so sure he's dying first? Did you hear him say, 'When I pass away,' like that's a given? Why haul us all here in the middle of June to talk about his will? He's sixty-three. Whence the urgency?" She pauses. "Why the fuck is he 'resting'?"

Carrie and Lorna and I look at each other. I remember that year and a half after Mom died, before Dad started dating Gillian. To call us latchkey kids puts it way too mildly. We were feral. Dad would come home late, leaving it up to us to do our homework, take care of poor doomed hamster number two (the first, Fuck Chuck, died, of starvation most likely, a couple of months before Mom died), feed ourselves dinner. The shit we had for dinner! Carrie would try to establish some semblance of order—iceberg lettuce with Paul Newman's ranch dressing, or she'd fry up Steak-umms or boil ramen—but half the time, dinner was popcorn and Moon Pies. I will never forget the chaos of trying to get Lorna to brush her teeth, Carrie holding her down while I squeezed toothpaste and Lorna turned a shade of tomato.

"Spy club," Lorna says, and sticks out one freckled arm. Our code from the bad old days, trying to figure out first what the hell was going on with Mom, why she was talking like her mouth was full of mashed potatoes. You hear about kids being raised by wolves, but the three of us for a while there were raised by kitchen cabinets and vacuum cleaners—nothing sentient. Carrie sighs, and sticks out her right arm, too, and I do as well. Even Mike does, though with that guy, he's probably just stretching.

Of course, it's entirely normal that Dad's tired still from the hip surgery two months ago. The man fell off a ladder pruning a tree, gave himself and Gillian a serious scare. I mean, surgery to replace his bone! There's the limited mobility as he recovers. The pain. And no doubt he's a little depressed too, which is also perfectly normal. He hasn't missed a run more than two days straight in all his adult life. For Dad, six weeks without running is kind of like six weeks without seeing the sun in the sky or six weeks without laughter or six weeks without the taste of something sweet. And while he's gone on a couple of short runs this past week, they were anything but pleasant, he told me.

For years Gillian has been on him about not pruning that tree himself. She even called me once and asked me to talk sense in to him about calling a landscaper. But Dad, always stubborn, kept right on pruning the tree. And then this. The man's a fucking cyborg now.

Shane and Lorna have never seemed particularly attuned to Dad as a whole person, though, as someone more than simply their father. Strange, given how absent he was after Mom died. Sometimes I wonder, too, if they think the man is immortal. Again strange, considering Mom was only thirty-seven when she died. And don't they recognize that men collectively die younger than women? That Dad outlived Mom is already atypical. What are the fucking odds he's going to outlive Gillian, too, when in addition to women in this country having a life expectancy five years greater than that of men, she's also three years younger than him?

Not that I plan to say any of this to Shane and Lorna. Finally, they're focused on something other than my being executor of the will. Let them spy on Dad. Maybe they'll bring Lenny into their spy club so that he'll finally have something better to do than imprison lightning bugs in his overcrowded penitentiary. Then while Lenny's peeking through bedroom windows or pressing his ear against Dad's door, Robert and I can free the unjustly incarcerated.

It bums me out to think about Dad being really sick, but of course it makes all kinds of sense—really, it's the only possible conclusion. That's the reason for that fucked up "Consider our loans forgiven" card at Christmas; that's the reason we are summoned to Fairfield, like Dad's some old time English king. When Mom was sick—well, once she really accepted dying, and wasn't so cranky and aggrieved about it—weirdly enough, those were some of my nicest memories of her. I'd lie in her bed, and while she napped, I'd blow up *Space Invaders* or thumb through a stack of comic books. Sometimes when she'd wake up I'd read them to her. "That guy looks like a thug," she'd say. Like, no shit, Mom, that's Two-Face; he's an arch-villain. She cracked me up.

I picture Dad, lying in bed, and, for once, peaceful and softened. I picture straightening the covers and folding them neatly over his chest. I could make him toast and cut off the crusts. We could play chess together. He would be still, for once: actually present.

I catch Carrie looking at me. "We'll figure it out," I reassure her.

She says, "Hey, go for it." Bossy and difficult as Carrie can be, she's scared for Dad, I can tell, and grateful that I'm on top of this. In the end, Carrie wants to be looked after. That's why she married boring Grant, instead of that dude Ted with the Harley and the tattoo of a jellyfish on his biceps. Carrie wants someone dependable. Which makes sense, given all the craziness we grew up with, having to practically raise ourselves. Our sheets would smell so bad because no one ever washed them. I remember lying in bed, wondering what smelled so funky. Every so often I'll walk by a homeless person and that smell wafts back to me.

Carrie's OCD, according to my ex-wife Sherilynn—Sherilynn is always diagnosing people, like being a psych minor in college gives her the insight. Carrie's son Robert, Sherilynn maintained, was on the spectrum. Who knows, with that weird kid? Constantly deflecting my son's efforts to play with him, to get him interested in nature. Lennie keeps trying, though; he's a good kid, inclusive.

So I smile back at Carrie, to let her know I've got this. That she can lay down her burdens, like it says in the hymn, because her older brother's here.

Gillian comes out with a tray full of refreshed mojitos, and limeades for Lorna and the kids. As she hands Mike his mojito, he says, "Mom, any speculation as to just how much we stand to inherit?"

Shane gives Mike a look like he just suggested we murder Dad in his sleep, then search his pockets. But I know Shane's curious too. I can almost feel his ears stretch, like a vine creeping up a tree trunk to reach more sunlight.

Gillian says matter-of-factly, "We've agreed to not discuss figures. One, you can't account for the unexpected, as you all know. I don't want to tell you one thing and then have to disappoint you if our situation changes. Two, we think you're better off not counting on some future inheritance. We think it's for your own good."

Then she says, "I brought out brie and crackers, too." She smiles.

Shane says, "Hold up. By unexpected, you mean like medical expenses?"

"Well, sure. Or if the cost of living greatly increases. Or our government seizes everyone's bank accounts." Gillian laughs.

One time we were all making fun of the dumb family decals on other people's automobiles. Then Lorna got serious, said, "What happens when someone dies? Do they scratch her off the car?" I remember her pinching the skin on her neck so hard she left fingernail indentations, like tally marks all over her neck. Tally marks that I imagined represented all the things she worried about. Gillian's reply: "Or what if advertising the contents of their families like that only helps ensure that when they're targeted by a psycho killer, he can be sure to pick off every one of them? Not overlook the one hiding under the bed or in the closet?" Then Gillian cackled.

Now Lorna is picking at her neck again. "Seize our accounts?!"

What I think: Does Lorna have any money for the government to steal? Talk about getting distracted from the real issue.

Shane says, "What's going on with Dad? If he's sick, that's something that is most definitely not in our best interest to withhold. We deserve to know. We have a right to know."

Everyone's eyes are on Gillian. Even Lenny has stopped swinging his arms in the air like King Kong. He's still and quiet for the first time all day, the first time in his life, maybe.

About a year after Mom died, Dad started, for the first time, going to church. I thought it was about trying to find solace, to be in a place where he could more easily imagine meeting Mom again someday—a place at any rate where he'd have company in that kind of fantasy. Once, Lorna asked me where Mom was, and Dad overheard me say, "Rotting in the ground." He got all kinds of bent out of shape.

But Carrie's theory—and I have to give her credit for coming up with it pretty much immediately—was that he started going to church to find a new wife. "You've watched *The Sound of Music* too many times," I told her, and she scoffed and pointed out a church was not a convent, and no reasonable person went to a convent to find a wife. "Anyway, it's better than going to a bar," she said. Eleven-year old Carrie, already world-wise. And sure enough, two months later, Dad was dating Gillian.

On the whole, we were thumbs-up on Gillian. She was funny. She made cool desserts, like rainbow Jell-O—that was a twenty-four-hour procedure, where she'd use a glass bowl and make one color layer at a time, pour in the lemon when the lime had hardened and so forth. She even put in canned fruit that was the same color palette— mandarin oranges in the orange layer, sour cherries in the red layer. Carrie called it white-trash food, but Lorna and I were appreciative, after having spent a year scavenging, eating s'mores for dinner, but terrible s'mores, saltine crackers instead of graham crackers because that's all we had.

But Gillian did have what we all called the Death Stare, and she aims that at me now.

"What an odd comment to make, Shane," Gillian says, crisply— when I say "crisp," I mean if you bit that comment, it would make a loud crunch.

I stare back at her. "What a non-answer, Gillian," I say.

And there's an electric-static silence, before Grant coughs and says, like a grandpa, "Now, now." I have never understood that reprimand. What's it supposed to mean? To call one back into the present, reorient one to now, like pushing a "refresh" button? I suspect the expression is code for "Let go of the past," but that's another concept I've never understood. The past is what composes us. That's like telling a house to let go of its nails and wood.

I write a mental Post-it note to remind Grant to please never ever say "Now, now" again, that I can only take so much of that terrible phrase before I reach my limit and detonate like one of the little Christmas ornament-looking explosives in *Candy Crush*.

Then there's the sound of the sliding glass door, and there's Dad. He's got a cake in his hands. He's grinning.

Gillian says, "But we haven't had dinner yet."

Dad says, "So? Anyone else object?"

Grant objects to cake on pretty much all occasions—people and their processed sugar, he says; why not choose fruit if you want something sweet?—but he doesn't say anything. Neither does anyone else. Dad's recently become a fantastic baker. When I say fantastic, I mean like baking-show fantastic. When I said something about picking up a cake for Robert's sixth birthday, Dad was all I've-got-this. He had a "consultation" with Robert, and then the day of the party he showed up with a cake replica of the *Titanic*, complete with an iceberg, both which sat on this glittery blue glaze that included fondant rafts and people. The people all looked terrified, which to be fair is probably accurate, but it also made me wonder if Gillian had a hand in their crafting.

Robert's friends went nuts over those fondant people, though. They played with them like they were action figures. Enacted scenes, which basically boiled down to screams of mass hysteria. "Women and children first! Women and children first!" Robert yelled.

Shane was icy in his comment on the photos on Facebook, clearly stung that Dad hadn't offered to make Lenny's cake a couple months earlier. My pointing out that I lived forty minutes away from Dad versus his six-hour commute didn't do much to ease his mind.

The other thing that pissed Shane off was that when we were kids, the only thing that man ever cooked was hamburgers. And then after Mom died, not even hamburgers. "What the fuck was with that?"

Shane messaged me. "We could have starved to death! And now he's making a cake *Titanic*?!"

This cake is no ordinary weekend's baking either. It's a stack of freaking crepes. I count sixteen. Layered between the crepes is some kind of cream like you'd find in an eclair. The whole thing is covered in chocolate and decorated with raspberries.

As we're chewing, I feel Shane's and Lorna's thoughts ticking. Cake before dinner? Crepes? What does this mean?!

Then when I compliment the cake, Dad says, "I made it early this morning before you guys got here."

Gillian shakes her head. "He was up at five a.m. making crepes! I couldn't sleep with all the clatter in the kitchen, and then he slapped my hand when I went to grab one!"

"Wow, this is really good, Gramps," says my nephew Robert. I shoot Lenny, gobbling up this bizarre IHOP cake, a look: He is not to be outdone by his weirdo spectrum cousin. Lenny swallows—he has so much cake in his mouth that the effect is of an ostrich swallowing a watermelon—coughs, and says, "Yes, excellent cake, Gramps. Thank you so much." I grin at Carrie, to communicate that my kid has better manners. Even if he does have chocolate all around his mouth like Bozo the Clown.

Carrie surprises me by smiling back. Our smiles are a rope ladder between us, something I can climb and finally reach my sister—she has some unflattering salad bowl haircut that makes her look like a toadstool. Cake before dinner? My eyes communicate to her. Her smile widens, but it's an inviting smile, not a malicious one. So what if we have cake before dinner? Her eyes flash back. Dinner will be something weird with sour cream. Enjoy!

I look at Dad, daintily forking a raspberry into his mouth. His cheeks are pink, but in a flushed-with-pleasure way. He's proud of his cake.

When we were kids, Dad used to want us to open our big Christmas present Christmas Eve. "Wait until tomorrow, Doug," Mom would say, and he'd say, "The kids want to open one now, though!" But he was the one; he wanted us to open it right now.

Cake before dinner: It occurs to me that my life is like a film where they get the reels mixed up, and everything happens out of order. When I was a kid, I had no real parents to speak of—one dying, the other absent. I scrounged for everything, including affection. I was like a filthy, gobbling pigeon. And now I have a pink-cheeked father who bakes cake. I was a father before I was a husband—Sherilynn and I married when Lenny was almost two—and by the time he was six, she had taken off. We got along better when I was in the military and I saw much less of her. "Familiarity breeds disgust": The parting words of my ex-wife. But Lenny is doing much better without a mother than I did—well, a mother in California, versus permanently distant. He has a father who cooks and reads him books. He drew his family for second grade, and I have to say, it pleased me to see that "family" consisted of me and Lenny, holding hands—these fucked-up hands that looked like rakes. Partly because Sherilynn didn't deserve to be in the picture, but also partly because it made me feel like, Yeah, we're doing OK.

Now, if I were drawing a family, it would have to include this whole clown car. I look all around the table, taking them in. My dad, with his very pink cheeks; Gillian, patting a napkin to her mouth; caved-in Mike, the posture of a koala bear; messy Lorna, the human tumbleweed; Carrie with her funky toadstool haircut; Grant, with his round glasses—I'd make those glasses look like bubbles; Robert, for the first time today cheerful—I'd draw a big blue smile on that strange kid; my son, with his plastic bin of lightning bugs. I'd draw each bug—curls for wings, a yellow dot for every mystifying chemical reaction.

LAURA LEE WASHBURN

Ritual

*"Better beans and bacon in peace
than cakes and ale in fear."*
—*Aesop*

Butter beans—don't ask,
just eat. Don't tell
if Granny sliced fatback
thick as your wrist
into the pot. Here, I eat
one plate, two plate, dessert plate,
whatever's served as side dish.
Let it all work in me as it will,
raw cabbage rooting
through the fat macaroni,
cheddar unmelting itself,
vinegar bracing greens,
cornbread crust crisp as tortilla,
Granny's cornbread,
                              always the cornbread.

We've seen the health class film,
the shocking lardful demonstrations:
a pound of pure fat unappealing
dished into a bucket, stuffed into tubes.
White globs and blobs may as well
be the arm of your mother.
The latest embalming trend
can show you the artery
that closed a life, the relentless

war Wednesday dinner makes
against an organ.
                    This is my family:
Granny calling her children
and their children and theirs
to dinner one night in every week,
butter beans, meatloaf, green beans,
coleslaw, flank steak, macaroni
and cheese, cornbread, cobbler, pie, cream,
and what can we do but eat,
embrace the fats, the love,
the cakes, the grace.

LAURA LEE WASHBURN

Little Skulls

"… the vertebrae are absolutely undeveloped skulls …"
—Moby-Dick

We say, *My back,*
Oh, my neck. We say,
Bone spur, pinched nerve,
nerve, but the spine
knows better. Each bone
pieced in its column
is a skull not quite finished
forming. The little heads
must have their language
of desire. If only I, one
might think. If only I,
says C2. *Arrarow, arrarough,*
they whisper from the bed,
pressed flat into the sheet
again. Each not-quite
mouth is death plucked
from the graveyard,
Hamlet's foil in his palm,
Tibetan yak bone beads
pressed into hands
for prayer. The body
simpers along, one more
dampened life form
in the long line of planets,
swirl of galaxy, world
within world, aborted
head, turned corner. We pay

with pain for selection,
that simple word
for denial, that flip
side of unformed, reused,
up- or downcycled,
needed, but unfortunate
as any thing aspiring.

MARTHA E. SNELL

I Have Tremors

that ripple out
from my womb

when I remember
those rarely discussed

mechanics, clinical
yes, but wondrous

workings inside
that dark chamber

with its certain
warmth. An ovum's

descent and exit,
predictable as Mars

cycling 'round heaven
and sun eclipsing

the moon—finished
now. Hormonal

drip gone dry.
My hair is gray.

Martha E. Snell

Both times my womb
filled, oh the miniature

bodies floated and
shimmered in that

moss-lined cave.
The fluttering like

no other sensation.

ED FALCO

Millat's Altar

Millat's father was a refugee from Syria. He was raised Muslim, though by the time he met Millat's mother in Huntington, West Virginia, where he was a professor in the Engineering Department at Marshall, he was an atheist, as was his wife, a locally well-known sculptor. Millat was the first of their five children. By the time Millat was a teenager, his father had rediscovered the religion of his childhood and prayed five times a day. He kept a prayer mat rolled up in his study, on a shelf with his books. His mother, too, had given up her atheism and replaced it with a pagan spiritualism that mostly involved a reverence for nature and faith in a goddess rather than a god. At her funeral, her pagan friends spoke of a gateway through which all must eventually pass "to the shining light of the unity that is the mother and father of us all." That phrase had carved a place for itself in Millat's memory. He could still hear the words issued from a tall, elderly woman, addressed to the small gathering of friends. A year after the funeral, his father, too, passed through the gateway.

Millat identified with no religion. He had faith in a presence that was everywhere and unknowable, and he offered up prayers regularly throughout the day and always in the morning and before bed at night. In this way he was an amalgam of the faith of his mother and father.

Most of Millat's parents' possessions had gone to others in the family. He had kept only a couple of things for himself: his father's prayer mat, which he draped over the night table on his side of the bed where he slept with his wife, and a smooth black stone, which his mother had kept in her studio and which he had seen her at times hold to her heart as she silently prayed. He placed her stone on the prayer mat, at the center of it, in a white rectangle beneath an arrow that pointed to Mecca.

It was only after he hung one of his mother's sculptures over the night table that he understood he had created an altar. The sculpture was a large, shimmering slice of polished black hematite with indecipherable lines and figures carved across it in a kind of hieroglyphics. That night, alone in his bedroom, after staring a long time at one of the deerlike figures in the hieroglyphs, he took a step back and saw the prayer mat and the stone and the sculpture as more than relics of his parents he kept at his bedside, more than objects they had once touched and that once had been part of their spiritual lives. He saw the configuration itself as a kind of prayer, a gateway to a place that is always present, is immanent, is always. He thought to kneel and say a prayer but didn't. Instead he stared until he felt as if he were in the shadow of his parents, as if they were right there.

ED FALCO

Millat in Union Square

He's seated on a low brick wall outside the green Union Square subway entrance and its nearby matching green newspaper kiosk. It's a summer day and Millat is wearing white linen pants and a black knit shirt that highlights the bright streaks of gray in his close-cropped salt-and-pepper hair. He's a handsome man, still, with sixty speeding at him, youthful enough to attract the glances of young women. He's waiting for Stav, his Jewish Irish girlfriend of several years, who lives nearby in the West Village. They're going to see Anna in *The Tropics*, a play about Cuban immigrants in Florida. It amuses Millat that he, with his dark-skinned, Mediterranean looks, is native born and a Southerner at that; while Stav, white as the Puritans stepping off ships at Plymouth Rock, is the immigrant, her family's roots in Ireland reaching back to the nineteenth century.

Stav is the great gift of Millat's later years. They live apart but have made a life together. It's not an ordinary relationship, but it works. Stav is the cure for Millat's vexations: the fury that boils up in him night after night as if released by sleep; the everyday anger at the world as it is, so full of hatred and ignorance; the violence, everywhere the violence. It's the beginning of the twenty-first century and in the Middle East, land of his heritage, peace is crushed daily by bombs as the death count spirals into the hundreds of thousands.

In New York, Union Square bustles with life, as if everyone is hurrying in pursuit of a dream. When Millat sees Stav approaching, he stands and brushes off his pants. She hasn't seen him yet and so he gets to observe her, the easy way she strides at the edge of the sidewalk, her eyes on the crowd. She's on her way to a night of theater with her boyfriend. When she sees him, she'll take a few quick steps and smile as if meeting a loved one she hasn't seen in years. It's the way she is and it always amazes Millat, the kind of joy that is so natural to her and so unnatural to him. In bed some nights he sleeps with his arms wrapped around her, as if to pull her into him, as if to be sure she won't slip away.

When they meet at the entrance to the subway they embrace, and for Millat the rest of the troubled world spills away. They're a couple in the city. The son of a Syrian refugee raised in the coal country of West Virginia and the daughter of a Russian Jew raised in Catholic Ireland. They're on their way to the theater, here, at home, in America.

ED FALCO

Millat and the Anger of Men

It's 2004 and Millat is fifty-eight. His olive skin suggests a Middle Eastern heritage, though he could be Italian as easily as Syrian. There are mornings he wakes up furious, anger pushing through his body. He wonders if this is a male thing, this seizure of anger, if it's common to the sex. His father was an angry man, but then his father was a Syrian refugee in West Virginia, where the shade of his skin marked him as other. Millat lives in Brooklyn, New York, in Williamsburg. He fits in easily among the array of faces on the L. On the way to the city the train rattles and screams. Millat works as a director of human resources. He's flush. He owns a two-family house on Leonard Street and rents the upstairs. He'd like to strangle someone—but not really. He'd like to punch someone in the face and knock him to the ground. But not really. He doesn't know why he's so angry. It feels like hate. He wakes up some mornings and his skin is smoldering. Is this part of what it means to be a man? He wants he wants and he can't stop wanting, more and more and more. More respect, more recognition, more honors. More love, more friendship, more power. More things. More time. He's an idiot of want, a fool of give me. More. He despises himself. But not really. He laughs at himself. But not really. The train is hurtling into the city. It's rattling and screaming. There are men all around Millat with dark faces. All of them soaring underground. Who's on the edge? Who's close to unleashing? When the lights go out, Millat is one man among many hurtling through a tunnel in the dark. When the lights come back on, he's one man among many hurtling through a tunnel in the dark. If he could, he would take everyone's hand, bow his head, and ask for forgiveness.

ED FALCO

Millat's Brothers

Karim, the one who died at age fifty-five from a stroke after smoking two or more packs of cigarettes a day from age eleven.

Nasir, the one who died at seventeen, drowned in a quarry on a summer day.

In the morning and at night, in his daily prayers, Millat asks that God hold his brothers "close to your heart, in the light of your love."

He doesn't know what that means, though he speaks the words day after day, year after year.

He heard someone say once that heaven was the light of God's love and hell the absence of it.

The Prophet Muhammad assures believers there are things in Paradise "which no eye has seen, no ear has heard, and no human mind has thought of."

That appeals to Millat. He can't imagine an afterlife of any sort—and yet he prays for Karim and Nasir.

It gives him comfort. He believes in the mystery of what no one has ever seen, heard, or thought of.

And he misses his brothers.

ED FALCO

Millat Dreams of Karim

Karim, their mother's pride: like her, an artist. Rebellious, dropped out of high school in West Virginia, followed Millat to Manhattan and found a job in advertising, worked his way up to art director before starting his own firm—but always laboring at his own art, principally sculpture. His house was a gallery: He sold nothing and made no efforts to show or sell. He collected and produced. In his late forties, he started working in marble, chiseling figures out of hunks of stone, his studio filled with white dust. Millat can close his eyes and see Karim roughing out a block of marble with a point chisel, see the swing of the hammer, hear the quick, sharp impact of the chisel against stone, see the marble chips fly, the white flash of them through the sunlit studio. Sitting behind him on a stool, Millat watched his brother for hours, fascinated by the intensity of his gaze, the hard labor married to faith in something that could not be seen, the figure within the stone that the blow of the hammer searched out, the shape the eye of the artist trusted was there, within that bone-white block of marble, to be worked toward, to be crafted and shaped, to be revealed by hard labor, by persistence and faith.

A gentle man full of passions that would now and then explode, Karim spent hours every morning reading *The New York Times*. His politics were liberal. He was sympathetic to the Palestinians but not unsympathetic to Israel. He acknowledged complexity. On September 11, 2001, after the attacks, he closed up shop and watched his business fall apart. He didn't need the money and so he started telling people he was retired. He spent day and night in his studio. When Millat visited in those last months before the stroke, Karim was working on two tall blocks of marble. He never told Millat what it was he was sculpting. He didn't have to.

In his dream, Millat is talking to his daughter. They're at a family gathering and Karim is in the kitchen out of sight. His daughter, who loved Karim especially and is herself an artist, hugs Millat and tells him how wonderful it is that Karim is alive and healthy. "Remember?" she says. "Remember how sick he was and how close he came to dying?" Millat agrees and he's wonderfully happy. He tells his daughter, "I'm so grateful he's well." He hugs her. He says, "I know we both are."

When Millat awakes, it stays with him for a moment, this unexpected happiness.

When it dissipates, he has to steel himself before he can step back into the world as it is.

THE MISSOURI STATE UNIVERSITY STUDENT LITERARY COMPETITIONS

As a literary journal published by the Department of English at Missouri State University, *Moon City Review* publishes one poem, one fiction work, and one creative nonfiction essay by the university's students in an annual competition. Finalists are first nominated by our creative writing faculty, and then a winner is chosen by a guest judge in their respective category.

In this year's fiction competition, Pablo Piñero Stillmann—author of *Our Brains and the Brains of Miniature Sharks* (Moon City Press, 2020)—selected Mackenzie Morris's story, "Death of an Acquaintance," for publication. Regarding Morris's entry, Stillmann states,

> This story does a remarkable job capturing that late-adolescence/early-adulthood phase in which one begins to discover the seriousness of life, but doesn't yet have the tools to deal with it. The writer mixes such topics as sex, death, *Mario Kart*, and Facebook in a seamlessly organic way that makes this quite an enjoyable read.

Among the other fiction finalists are Morgan Allen, Morgan Dame, Janel Haloupek, John King, Audrey Lutmer, and Jared Scribner.

In the poetry competition, Karen Craigo—current Missouri Poet Laureate and author, most recently, of *Passing Through Humansville* (Sundress Publications, 2018)—selected Habeeb Renfroe's poem, "The Moon. The Moth" for first prize. Craigo expresses the difficulty of choosing a winner, and her reasons for selecting Renfroe's poem:

> It was challenging to make a selection because the group of my top poems were all so very good, but ultimately, 'The Moon. The Moth' by Habeeb Renfroe takes top honors. The poet shows excellent command of both line and form, but it is the use of specific details and bold imagery that made me fall in love. Moth as windup toy. Flight of the moth as eulogy. "Fiery swan of folded paper." "A rival lighthouse to the moon." This

is what I read poetry for, and although Missouri State appears to be bulging with poetic talent and artistry, I'm riding this flaming lepidopteran straight to the nearest convenient satellite.

The following poets were chosen as finalists by our staff: Charlie Crane, Rachel Earl, Trevin Foxwell, Ryan LaBee, William LaPage, Jueun Lee, Katie McWilliams, Sujash Purna, and Grace Willis.

Brenna Womer—author of *Honeypot* (Spuyten Duyvil Publishing, 2019)—selected Alyssah Morrison's flash essay, "Daryle Wayne Orr: 2019 Circle of Honor Inductee for the United Parcel Service, 25 Years of Safe Driving Award," for publication in the creative nonfiction category. On Morrison's nonfiction, Womer comments on the descriptions of father-daughter relationships:

> This flash essay is replete with unexpected, evocative descriptions—UPS trucks like "brown turds in the slush" and napkins folded into sweaty-summer asscracks—and it's tender, too. The author, the eldest daughter of the titular Daryle Wayne Orr, reflects on growing up with the complicated man receiving an award twenty-five years in the making. She asks, "What is restrained in each man with a temper"; she says, "Power and control are two sides of the same brown leather belt." In these three pages, the author looks her father in the eye, not from above or below him, but as an adult: a child, grown, with perspective and a life of her own; a fellow human being.

Finalists in the creative nonfiction competition include Kyra Cook, Katherine Coulter, Anna Edwards, John King, Emily Lewandowski, Alexis McCoy, and Annaliese Schroeder.

Congratulations again to our winners and finalists of the MSU Student Literary Competitions, as well as all the students who entered this year's contests. We are thrilled to share the selected works in the following pages.

MACKENZIE COLLEEN MORRIS

Death of an Acquaintance

No one ever prepares you for the death of an acquaintance. The girl you say "hi" to in the hallways but never have a conversation with. The girl who does theater with you, but you're an actress and she's on the crew. The girl who's there when you smoke weed for the first time but only because she's friends with your boyfriend. The girl you don't know very well at all, but she's just always been around.

When you get the text from your ex on a Monday afternoon that she was killed in a car accident, you think it's a joke at first. Once he assures you that it's not a joke, you say, "Damn, that's wild," but you never expected to see her again after graduation anyway, so you push it out of your mind and move on with your day. It's not until you're in your night public speaking class midway through your speech that it really hits you. You remember your best friend who was also her best friend. Then you realize that almost all of your friends from high school were friends with her. How did you never get close to her when everyone around you was? How is it that only now that she's gone do you realize you would have liked to know her?

You finish your speech with a twinkle in your eye.

That night, Grace texts you.
- *You hear?*
~ *Yeah. You good?*
- *Not really. You coming to the funeral?*
~ *idk. When is it?*
- *Saturday.*
~ *You think I should go?*
- *Up to you. I'll be there.*
~ *All right, I'll come.*

After all, your friends may like to have someone there for support.

The days leading up to the funeral feel like syrup. You wake up, go to class without breakfast, and spend the evenings with your friends. On the surface, it looks like every other week, but to you, it feels like a waiting game. Every second is a countdown. You aren't exactly sad. It's more numbness with a hint of disbelief, and you can't really think about anything beyond this weekend. Is this dread?

"So, when are you leaving?" Your roommate interrupts your thoughts.

"Tomorrow after class, around three," you say. "The funeral is Saturday morning."

She gives you that look that she always gives you when you're feeling down. You think she's trying to be empathetic, but it feels more like pity. She pats you on the shoulder.

"If you need anything, just let me know," she says.

"Thanks, Brenna—I appreciate it," and you do.

When you get back to your childhood home, your parents are on their way out the door. They're going out of town this weekend, so you have the house to yourself. Normally, you'd jump at the opportunity to have the house alone, but tonight it feels like a cruel joke.

You eat pizza rolls for dinner and spend the evening watching movies that make you nostalgic about high school. You're scrolling through Facebook and find the article that pieces everything together. She was driving home from what you later find out was her new boyfriend's apartment. The ice was bad, and she wasn't wearing a seat belt. She slid into oncoming traffic and hit another car head-on. She died on impact, and the other driver walked away unharmed.

The mundanity of her death destroys you. She was always the most reckless person you knew. In your memories, she's untouchable. She was the girl who worked downtown despite living in the suburbs. She built sets for the plays and would jump off high platforms for the rush. You would look up during rehearsal and see her sitting on the catwalk, sometimes just observing and sometimes drawing or reading. When you were juniors, she found the old abandoned barn that teenagers made a game of exploring, and you were with her when you went for the first time. You only went a handful of times before it burned down last year.

You don't remember much about who she was, only who she appeared to be. She was an artist and always spent her extra time in the art room. At the art fair every year, her name captioned half the paintings, but she never bragged about it. It was no secret that she was every art teacher's favorite student. You were amazed at everything she made, but you never told her because you never got the chance.

She loved going to concerts. You remember that more clearly than anything because you always hated concerts, but still felt left out when your friends would go without you on Friday nights. She listened to exactly what you would expect, and she wore this old tattered Joyce Manor T-shirt at least once a week. She just got a septum piercing not too long ago, and you think it was a fitting look for her. Her Facebook profile picture is a selfie of her with her new piercing, and that's what it will eternally be.

While it feels unbelievable that someone so young and so full of life could be gone so suddenly, you can't imagine what she would be like as a grown woman. What would she be like as a thirty-five-year-old? Would she be a mom? Would she have a desk job? You can't picture her in a pantsuit or driving her kids to soccer practice. You can only picture her as she was: a young, reckless, wild girl who never seemed particularly concerned with the future, at least from where you were standing. You suppose it doesn't matter now what she would have become because she is preserved in everyone's memory as she was.

You fall asleep that night replaying all the things in your head that you know about her. *She's older than me. She's braver than me. She's cooler than I can ever hope to be. She's deader than me ....*

The day of her funeral comes. You wake up early to curl your hair, and you settle on a simple black T-shirt dress with a black lace cardigan and black booties. *Is this right?* You realize this is the first funeral you've been to since your uncle died when you were ten, and no one ever told you what to wear for this sort of thing.

You imagine her smirking at the sight of you, a girl she never really knew getting all dressed up for her funeral. With that thought in mind, you haphazardly apply your mascara and leave without looking in the mirror again.

I'm only going so I can support my friends who were close with her, you lie to yourself. You think that story will keep the judgmental eyes off you, but you're going for yourself as much as for anyone else.

When you arrive at the funeral home, it's teeming with old memories and familiar faces. You see the girl who moved to Arizona sitting out front, smoking a cigarette. You hug her.

"It's been a while."

"I flew in last night," she says.

The silence is heavy. You're ready to have this day over with, so you wave goodbye to the cigarette and climb the church steps. Inside, you see people you've never met and people you know all too well. You hug old teachers, old friends, parents of friends, exes.

The event is in a small church that feels too much like a conference hall. In the foyer, there are tables and chairs set up, but people just hover around them in clumps. There's coffee, and you notice it's from the shop she worked at, that just so happens to be your favorite brand. *Well, I guess Kaldi's is ruined for me,* you think, but you get a cup anyway. You doubt anyone will have the stomach for the untouched pastries sitting on the adjacent table.

You walk around the foyer looking at her art and family pictures. One painting catches your attention over the rest. It isn't the flashiest piece or even the best. It pictures a young girl, who you can only assume is her, hanging upside down by her knees on one of those playground bars that were at your elementary school. The strokes are messy, and there aren't any details on the girl's face besides the cigarette hanging out of her mouth. The rendition of the girl's auburn hair flows as if it were actually there, blowing in the slight breeze you feel coming from the air conditioner. The rest of the painting is still. Despite the whimsical subject of the painting, there is an element of sadness. The girl is not playing. She's coping. You stare for too long. It feels intrusive because you know you would never have seen any of these if she weren't dead. You know more about her now than you ever would have, had she survived the year. Over the speaker, the Strokes are playing, a bittersweet high school relic. Smiling to yourself, you step away from the display. That's the last time you hear the Strokes without thinking of her.

Finally, you venture into the nave of the church. The room is larger than you expect with three sections of pews, one large middle section and two smaller ones on either side. There isn't anything special about this church. There are no windows, and the lit stage is full of flower arrangements and more trifolds of pictures. At the front of the church is a painting. It's a portrait of her, lying in a field of flowers like she's sleeping. You learn from another friend that she was an organ donor, which comforts you for a reason you can't quite put your finger on, and the family chose to have her cremated before the ceremony. This painting takes the place of an open casket. It's fitting. She always seemed more like a work of art than a human, anyway.

The visitation line wraps around the left side of the room and feeds into the right where people have huddled to talk and cry amongst themselves. You recognize some of them. You see her new boyfriend at the front, *Elijah*, you think is his name. He's weeping quietly, mourning the death of the relationship that had barely begun. A few rows back is her ex, Jack. She'd dated him while you all were in high school. They broke up about six months ago, but Jack has regretted it since. He finally told her how he felt a few weeks ago, but she was already seeing Elijah. His loud sobs sit with you. Your heart aches for the boys who loved her.

Everyone around you is in tears, and the harder you try to keep it together, the more you begin to lose the battle. Dabbing your eyes, you curse yourself for wearing that damn mascara, and you curse yourself for breaking in front of all these people who loved her so dearly.

When you reach the front, you shake her father's hand, then her mother's. They are both crying. It feels like a lie to accept their comforting gestures, knowing your pain pales in comparison, but you thank them and move on.

Her little sister stands near her parents. She is just two years younger than you, and you remember seeing her in the hallways and even spending the occasional morning with her in high school when she stayed to mingle with her sisters' friends before class. She was always much more reserved than her adventurous sister. Now, she is void of any emotion. Her expression is polite and unfeeling, not a stray tear in sight. She dutifully hugs each guest with care, comforting you as if you are the one who just lost a sister, and she is the stranger offering polite condolences. You are ashamed of your inability to control the tears flowing down your cheeks.

You are relieved to have reached the end of the line and you retreat to the foyer of the church where you join your friends at a table. The conversation is polite, just catching up. Miranda is in nursing school. Josh just got a job at a car dealership. Dylan tells you that Bailey is on probation for possession. You don't care much, but the chit-chat keeps your mind off the dead girl who seems to permeate every moment of silence.

You decide you cannot be alone with your thoughts tonight.

"If you guys aren't doing anything tonight, my parents are out of town. You can come over, we can drink, watch movies, hang out, so we don't have to be alone. Invite whoever you want."

They all take you up on the offer.

The funeral is about to begin, so you find a pew near the back of the church, letting her friends and family fill in the seats up front. A pastor heads to the podium and takes a solemn look at the crowd.

"Good afternoon, everyone. Today, we celebrate the life of a woman who has left this world to be with the Lord." He continues speaking, but you don't listen. You remember that she was never religious, so you know this is mostly her parents' doing, and it fills you with irrational rage. *She wouldn't want it to be like this*, you think as if you even knew her well enough to know what she would want. You stare at your hands blankly the whole sermon. You don't look up again until the music starts. The band playing is one you recognize, the Dragon Beats. You went to high school with everyone in the group, and they were good friends of hers. You appreciate that her family at least cared enough to have this small comfort for those who knew her.

At the end of the service, her mother brings out a box of her clothing. "I brought these so you all can have a piece of her." You watch from your seat as her friends rifle through the box, teary-eyed, remembering the clothes they'll never see their friend wear again. People come and go, each taking an item from the box—sweaters, shirts, hats—as one last reminder of their friend. When the crowd thins, you venture to the box, curiously. You glance at its contents, and you see the Joyce Manor shirt.

That evening, Grace is the first to arrive. She has always been good at hiding her feelings, so you are surprised to see her swollen eyes. She hugs you, and you feel close to tears.

"How are you handling it?" you ask her.

"Not well," is all she says. You stand there in an embrace for a long time. Finally, she lets go, and you sit down at the kitchen table. "Today didn't feel real. I still can't believe she's gone," Grace tells you, reaffirming what you have been thinking all week.

"Do you miss her?" you ask, uncertain of how you would even answer that question.

"I don't know. That's the worst part. It was just so sudden, and I only saw her a couple of weeks ago," Grace replies, more to herself than to you. "I know I'm supposed to miss her, and I know that I will, but right now, I just ... don't."

You feel a familiar ping of guilt. Grace was her best friend, and you can't fathom how she must be feeling right now. Desperate to escape the shame, you suggest, "You know, I don't think she would want us to be sad right now. She would want us to remember her how she was, so let's have fun tonight. For her." There you go again, acting like you actually have any idea what she would want. Your suggestion served to lighten the mood, though, and Grace smiles at you.

"You're right. Today was heavy. Where's the music?" Grace stands and moves towards the stereo. While she adjusts the music, playing the Front Bottoms (another classic), you fix a couple of drinks and set out a bowl of pretzels. You pass the time reminiscing over old stories and drinking your parents' liquor.

As more people show up, the tone is surprisingly lighthearted, the alcohol making the giggles come easily. The volume of the gathering grows throughout the night, and you aren't even sure how many people are in your house. Everyone is solemn when they first arrive, but they quickly join the rest of the party, eager to drink the tears from this morning. Groups quickly form and disperse throughout the house. You and your closest friends retreat to the basement where you share stories from your first year of college. This is the first time so many of you have been together at once since high school, so the stories of classes, friends, hookups, and parties fill the silence all night.

A few hours and drinks in, you're in the kitchen for a refill, and her boyfriend shows up. *Ex? Widow?* His light ripped jeans, plain T-shirt, and green flannel are a stark contrast to the black suit you saw him in earlier. You notice now that he has long hair that was pulled back in a bun this morning. He looks kinder this way, more real.

"Hey! Elijah, right?"

"Hi, yeah, I'm Elijah," he responds, appearing as puffy-faced as the rest of you. He looks around. "Wow, a lot of people showed up."

"Yeah, I guess we all needed something to do tonight to stay sane, you know?" He nods but doesn't respond. "Well, here, let me get you a drink. Beer?"

"Sure, yeah, that's fine," he responds, and you hand him a bottle. "So ...."

"What do you do?" you interject, wanting to steer the conversation away from his dead girlfriend. You think that would make it easier for everyone.

"Right now, I'm in school, but I work at Crooked Tree on the weekends."

"Oh, I love that place! They have the best lattes," you reply, happy to find a shared interest.

"Yeah? We get that a lot." His tone lightens, and he gives you a smirk. "You know what the secret is?"

"There's a secret?"

"Of course!" he says, and leans in close, lowering his voice. "We use drip coffee instead of water to make the espresso."

Heat rises in your neck, and you giggle instinctively. "Wow, no wonder I'm so addicted!"

"They're even better with oat milk." He says it like he's telling me a secret. "Hey, I work tomorrow morning. You should stop by, and I'll hook you up."

"OK, yeah. That sounds great!" *No wonder she liked him*, you think, looking at him fully for the first time. *He's cute, too.* You stop yourself there, though. He just lost his girlfriend. It would be rude to flirt. *Still, we all have to move on sometime.*

Elijah tells you he's going to have a look around and say hello to people, so you head back down to the basement and rejoin your circle. After twenty minutes, he must have made his rounds because you see him come down the stairs.

"Elijah!" you and the few other people in the group who know him shout in a welcoming chorus as he reaches the foot of the steps.

"Ayyyye!" He reciprocates the inebriated excitement and takes the empty seat on the couch next to you. "Nice house," he says quietly to you.

"Did you enjoy snooping around?" you joke.

"Yes, you can tell a lot about a person by their house," he replies thoughtfully. "I think I saw everything except your room?" You can tell he's just teasing, but the thought of him in your room gives you goosebumps.

"Oh, that's down here," you wave towards the door and his eyes follow. "I can give you a tour before you leave."

"That sounds lovely," he says, turning his attention with everyone else to the TV. Grace hands you a controller, and *Mario Kart* lights up the screen.

After a few races, Michael and Sam stand, resolutely. "We're going to J-Box," they announce. "It's taco time." You notice the house above you is quiet. The party wound down without you noticing. Sam and Michael lead the charge up the stairs and your other friends file behind them. Grace and Elijah hang back.

"Yo, you mind if I crash on your couch?" Grace asks, knowing the answer already. You nod, and she starts towards the steps. Instead of following her, you stay next to Elijah. Grace looks back and raises her eyebrow as if to say, *What's going on here?* You shake your head slightly, and she reluctantly leaves you behind. You turn back to the boy.

"How 'bout that tour?" he asks. *He's just curious—it's no big deal.* You smile and lead him to your bedroom. When you flick the switch, the iron chandelier illuminates the yellow walls and the framed pressed flowers that line them. Your bed, the focal point of the bedroom, wears a light green comforter and cream pillows. There's a tall gray dresser in the corner (with nothing in it), and the room is otherwise empty. You took everything with you when you left for university. "Wow, very fancy," he teases, gesturing at the chandelier.

"What can I say?" you reply. "I've always been one for the theatrics."

"I can see that," he says, looking at your corkboard of playbills. "Are these all the shows you've seen?"

"Those are the ones I've been in." You teeter on the edge of your words. That feels like a distant memory. You haven't been on stage in a year. Elijah looks impressed nonetheless.

"Which was your favorite?" he asks, and you can tell he genuinely wants to know.

You look at the corkboard and tug at memories from years ago. You point to the *Into the Woods* playbill. "I played the Witch," you tell him. "It's always the most fun to play the villains because you have to find the good in them to really get their essence across."

His smile fades when his eyes settle on the group picture of the department seniors. You're pictured in the front with the rest of the actors, and near the middle of the crowd is her, all smiles, arms slung around Jack and Grace. Elijah's eyes begin to glisten.

"She was really something, wasn't she?" he whispers.

"Yeah," you reply. "Hard to believe this was only a year ago."

"I didn't even know her a year ago," he says. His voice cracks. "I never even got to tell her I loved her."

"She knew," you tell him. You don't know that that's true, but you think it's what he needs to hear.

He looks at you, and you meet his gaze. You see his sorrow, but at this moment, you know he's happy to not be alone. Without thinking, you kiss him. It's sudden, and you surprise even yourself. His lips receive yours gently. They're soft and kind. *Did he kiss her like this?* Stop. *I wonder if I remind him of her.* You pull away suddenly, shame overtaking you.

"I'm sorry," you say, stepping back and averting your gaze. He catches your hand and pulls you back.

"It's OK." When you meet his eyes, the pain is diluted by what you can only describe as lust. It isn't a gross lust, but lonely like he regrets what he's about to do before he even does it. He pulls you in. The kiss this time is soft still, but hungry. You aren't sure who is taking the lead, but you end up on the bed, your hands moving slowly from his hair to his neck, then to his shoulders and back. You pull off that green flannel, and when it hits the floor, you look at him. The hickey on his neck was hidden until now. You lean into him and put your mouth where hers was.

The next morning, you're glad to see that Elijah didn't stay the night. When you finally leave your bed, Grace is still here, and she helps you clean up.

"I saw that Elijah left pretty late. What were you guys doing?" Grace asks you. You can tell she knows exactly what happened, asking only because she hopes it's not true.

"He wanted to see my room and started asking about my corkboard. We talked for a while. That's all," you deflect, suddenly very attentive to the beer cans you are depositing into the trash bag. You can feel her stare even with your eyes fixated on your hands.

"You are unbelievable," she says under her breath. About thirty seconds of uncomfortable silence pass before Grace ties up the trash bag and drops it by the back door. "OK," she says, "I think that's the last of it. I'm going home." You rise to tell her goodbye, but she turns and leaves before you can get to your feet. You consider going after her to talk things out, but you figure it is probably best to let her cool down first.

Once most of the evidence from the night before is disposed of, you pack your bag. You suppose Elijah wouldn't appreciate you showing up to Crooked Tree this morning, after all. There's nothing left to do but drive back to school and return to your normal life knowing nothing will ever truly be how it was, nor how it could have been, thanks to some ice and an unfastened seat belt.

You still think about her frequently. Some days, you wear her Joyce Manor shirt, and you imagine what she would think of you. You wonder if she secretly wanted to be friends with you the way you did with her, but the awkwardness of adolescence got in the way. Maybe she would be happy to see that you feel her absence, and maybe she understands why you are so affected.

Sometimes you forget that she's dead, and you wonder what she's up to. She must be in art school by now, making experimental mixed-media art and living in a big city. She still drives that old Prius and plays music way too loud. This summer she's road-tripping with you to Yellowstone. In the fall, the two of you are going to Italy for the coffee, but you're staying in hostels because she won't be bothered to book a hotel ahead of time. She isn't anything like she was in high school, but at the same time, she hasn't changed a bit.

Habeeb Renfroe

The Moon. The Moth

In a flash, the kraft-paper wings
of the fungus moth catch fire,
consequence of a kitchen lighter.

Each of them motionless as if to remain
unseen against the heathered grain
of desk, motionless until the click

thumbs each moth, in turn, into fitful
batting—lashing its flight into ashes.
It lands and flits like a windup toy and

alight once again, it lands with less space
between, less distance traveled frantically.
As the burning moth flies, so it lives

each flight a little closer to the final verse
eulogizing its larvaeic appetite
in the syllables of that dead tongue.

The moth's mouthparts atrophy
into adulthood. The great maturation
of the garbage butterfly. Fly away,

fiery swan of folded paper brushing wings
with the selfsame animus
of flame—flicked flint—a butane peony.

Together with the next moths to land,
are we not the bouquet of the afterglow,
the afterward, or at least the afterthought?

Flint twists to lick the dust from every
fire-clipped insect wing. Witnesses vanished
into the noiseless immolation of insect life

caught in the vice—in the restless appetite
of the cosmos—a rival lighthouse to the moon,
bright angel of the transverse orient.

ALYSSAH MORRISON

Daryle Wayne Orr:
2019 Circle of Honor Inductee
for the United Parcel Service,
25 Years of Safe Driving Award

Awarded on December 16, in a warehouse full of brown uniformed men, a few women, everyone shooting the shit like it was just another day, slaps of mittens and gulps of the complimentary milk and orange juice for the occasion. I hadn't been to UPS since I was a kid. It was icy, slick outside, with trucks lined up like pistons or racehorses or brown turds in the slush and snow. My husband and I were the only representatives from my family, "Congratulations, Daryle Orr" on a cake in brown and yellow icing, the same yellow as the Teamsters logo. One lady shook Dad's hand with her meaty, capable hand, large and strong like a farmhand, every hand shaking Dad's hand and faces turning to me and saying what a great man my dad is. His banner was propped up on an easel-like stand and Dad stood by in uniform, wearing a winter hat with brown fleeced ear pads that hung down like he was going sledding. A gray half-zip sweater and a green reflector vest. I could tell he was nervous. When his stone-faced manager spoke, he did not seem thrilled about Dad's achievement, or the fact that Daryle Orr had been at UPS for 32 years, and with my dad standing there grinning I got kind of pissed at that stiff manager with his sweater and his black slacks and his bean-shaped head and secretly wished he would get carpal tunnel in both wrists.

But when he turned the mic over to Dad, I knew Dad was proud. He looked over at us standing there, bundled up and out of place by the vending machine with obscenities carved into the side and our sack of McDonald's breakfast burritos he had brought us, and I couldn't remember anyone in our family ever really recognizing him for driving that truck and loading up dollies and working long hours and remembering the names of each local and each local's dogs. He said, "It's all for yourself and for your family" and he teared up. A funny way to accept an award, even self-congratulating, but he was jumbled and embarrassed. Something so small meant everything. And I think there was some truth in the mixed-up phrase.

In that short speech, I saw my Dad's work history so differently. More than embroidered brown socks and stained brown collars my mom sprayed with OxiClean. I saw that he was a working man who had split motivations: provide for the family and feed the self-serving drive to provide. As I looked around at all the men—young, mostly middle-aged, a few graying—their faces held similar mixed-up motivations. They all sweated through their shorts in the summer with a napkin folded into their ass cracks and peeled long underwear off their bodies on winter nights. I never really knew the struggle of this job, of how hard Dad worked. Even when he collapsed unshowered at night into bed with the TV on as a night light, I did not understand. Because anytime I asked, Dad said he loved his job, loved driving the big brown truck even though I always thought he was too smart to drive a truck. He was a disk jockey in high school, he loves the History Channel and basketball and charming people, and I could think of a million better occupations. But I guess Mom did get pregnant early on, and he always told me he jammed to classic rock radio while delivering packages.

The stress and exhaustion came out in other ways, with slaps and words, but it wasn't the job or anything going on with him. It was the external. It was his five kids or Mom or the dishes or a new dog that wouldn't shut the hell up. What does "having a temper" actually mean? What is tempered, exactly? The Latin *temperare* is to mingle, restrain. What is restrained in each man with a temper and how do they begin to untangle their mingled desires and frustrations? I think power and control are two sides of the same brown leather belt.

When I wrote in Dad's congratulations card, I felt a surge of regret like a sudden slip on black ice. I said he was generous, hardworking, productive, positive, but wasn't the positive production the very mechanism that snatched him up and sent him down country roads until late at night—sent him away? Made him angry? Pressurized him like the sweaty hot dogs he split in the microwave after a long day and smothered in sliced cheese and mayonnaise. 25 years of safe driving, a 25-year no-accident streak. Was it not this very job-business-industry-economy that made him quick to grab my elbow and bite his lip in public when I spilled a drink at the restaurant and yell and yell in the privacy of our unclean home? I remember him calling me pathetic in our driveway as a teenager. I remember him not allowing me to go to the bathroom on road trips as a kid. I remember having all of my needs met.

He looked at me across the concrete floor, his eldest daughter who reaped all the benefits of an upper-middle-class paycheck, and he teared up. It was like he accepted an Oscar in a two-piece suit, and I was standing there as the golden prize. I think he felt thanks and I felt thanks.

JEREMY T. WILSON

Kalamazoo

Jenny misses her son and her husband, even though she's the one who left. All her stories are about them. She feels like an imposter. The other students in her cohort are at least fifteen years younger, still in their twenties, fresh out of undergrad programs, still looking good wearing athleisure wear and flannel and stoned looks of bemusement. They say they admire how Jenny portrays her Floridian characters without condescending or fetishizing. *But what about making them heroes?* someone scribbled in the margin of her last story. She knew who it was, the girl who writes about lesbian wizards from Jamaica.

In Jenny's stories she changes her husband's name, but it always has three letters.

Today Bob's inside binge-watching *The Americans* when his son tells him he lost his stuffed bunny on the roof. Bob's pissed. Don't bother Bob when he's watching TV. His son is ten—too old to be playing with a stuffed bunny. Bob wants to tell him to leave it there, but then he'd have to come up with something else for him to do, and Bob does not have the greatest imagination, which is something his wife would like him to work on.

So Bob borrows a ladder from ~~Keith, Harold, Mike, Ruben,~~ Dan across the street. Bob doesn't own a ladder. Until today he's had no real need for one. But Dan across the street, that guy is always equipped to tackle any obstacle. Dude has everything. His garage is immaculate, and his matching ~~cars~~ (Be specific! something middle-class but not so conspicuous as to make him a type and definitely not a truck ...) Volkswagens sparkle every day with a professional-grade

224

buff. He plucks weeds from his lawn by hand. His leaves are always raked and bagged in proper yard-waste bags. Perfection established.

Dan's in his garage, his arms filled with ~~groceries, basketballs, growlers of beer~~, wedges of firewood, perfectly cut. "Looks like snow," he says.

Impossible! It never snows in Florida, someone will say. But fiction is about making wishes come true! No, that's Disney World. Also in Florida. Yeah, well, Jenny's taking risks! See, Bob wishes it would snow. His son has never seen snow, and if they get lucky and it snows then maybe they can stop being alone and do something together, head to the public golf course and fly down the fairway hills with snow pelting their faces. But on what? That's the way of things. It'll snow in this story for sure, but nobody in Florida owns a sled, not even Dan. Dan doesn't even have kids.

It definitely snows in Kalamazoo. Jenny sent him pictures of herself in a parka and a brown hat with a yellow pom-pom, the snow almost up to her knees. He wanted to know who took the picture. She didn't want to tell him it was a stranger, because then he would think she was lonely, so she made up a girl named Shelly from Sheboygan. He believed her. Always so content to let things be the way people say they are.

Bob leans Dan's ladder against the house and climbs up. He's wearing gym shorts because it's Saturday and he is in no way prepared for this cold. He keeps his eyes focused ahead and his hands on the cold rungs and concentrates on placing one foot above the other because that is the way Bob is. His son steadies the ladder for him, and he feels, for a brief moment, like a really good dad, one who will do anything for his son, and waiting for Bob high up on the roof to reward him for his bravery and pluck will be ~~a lesbian wizard from Jamaica~~, ~~a cute hedgehog named Rusty~~, ~~Bob's mother~~, Philip Jennings from *The Americans*.

Bob should admire Philip Jennings, not because of all the awesome spy sex he gets to have, but because of the way he's so committed to keeping his family together at all costs. Unlike his commie, ice-queen wife, Philip loves the American Dream, has totally bought into it, and sees in it a way to be his best self, a man with a stable family, a comfortable house, a semi-rewarding job, two beautiful, intelligent kids, a neighbor he can call his friend.

What must it be like to be unable to fully embrace all the stuff you love so much?

What happened? he kept saying. *What happened?* Jenny told him he'd fallen off the barstool, but that's not what he meant. What happened to *them?* Was she having an affair? She wasn't, but she felt like they needed a *disruption.* Admittedly, she'd been listening to too many podcasts. She thought they needed something to shake them out of the everyday and force them to make space for fresh possibilities. She was moving to some place in Michigan called Kalamazoo to go to grad school for creative writing. He did not know she'd applied anywhere outside the state of Florida, and she'd done so because she didn't want him to come (really she wanted him to come, but wanted him to want to come). She did not want their son to come, either. (Yeah, totally not true, but she couldn't take him away from her husband, and she would still come home during breaks, so why would they uproot him out of his school and away from his friends?) *Let's be together without being together*, she said. She actually said! The decision was made, and he did not fight because her husband is not a fighter.

She didn't need him to ~~lay~~ lie down in front of the car as she drove away, but c'mon, he could've at least waved forlornly from a train platform. She should've taken a train.

He had never heard of Kalamazoo. He said it sounded like a magic word. Jenny imagined him wandering around the house muttering the word numbingly to drawers suddenly empty of her things, hoping it would bring her back.

Kalamazoo.

Jenny's proud of him today, this version of him. Here he is climbing a ladder in the cold for his son's bunny, the son she abandoned so she could write shitty short stories that no one will ever read. Although, she had gotten one of her stories published in an online lit mag and sent him the link (no, she hadn't). It was really good (no, it wasn't).

Philip Jennings is not waiting atop the summit of Bob's roof to share a beer with him or to congratulate him for being a good dad. What's up there is …

Hmm …

What's up there?

A whole lot of junk. Why not? A doll head, a slingshot, an old bicycle tire, a blond mullet wig, a horseshoe magnet, a flip-flop, an abacus, one fingerless glove, a badminton racket.

Bob is like, what is all this stuff? How did it get here? Good questions, Bob. Is there a tree in the yard shaking out junk, losing people's shit every autumn instead of its own leaves? Or is it his son's fault? Has he been throwing things on their roof his whole life without Bob noticing?

Well, you could say that.

"Did you find it, Daddy?"

Bob's not the only one on a roof today. There's his next-door neighbor ~~Phil, Robbie, Luis, Carmen, Jules,~~ Roy, up on his own roof. And Roy is not like Dan or Bob despite having an almost identical three-letter, white-dude name. Roy sprays Roundup on his weeds. Roy refuses to recycle. Roy has a half-restored Camaro in his filthy garage. Roy has two wild mutts that he never keeps on leashes and that take enormous, steaming shits in Bob's yard. Roy lets his mail pour out of his crooked mailbox and collect in drifts because he distrusts the postal service. This description is easy because Roy is based on a real-life person.

Now Roy holds the stuffed bunny, its severed head in one hand and its body in the other.

WTF?

Roy dangles the bunny from its feet as white stuffing flutters from its neck hole. "Looks like snow," he says.

Roy could not possibly have done this to a child's stuffed bunny. "That's my son's bunny," Bob says, and immediately regrets using the word "bunny" because now his neighbor Roy is going to think he's a pussy.

"It was on my roof," Roy says.

But Roy can't be a total monster. Jenny does not fetishize or condescend. Maybe he's misunderstood. Roy lost a son in a boating accident back before they were neighbors. He told Bob all about it one blistering summer Friday over catfish and beer in Roy's driveway. He was sitting in a lawn chair with a Styrofoam cooler swimming with ~~Heineken, Land Shark, Yuengling,~~ Bud Lite and a gas fryer frothing with oil when Bob came home after dropping his son off at a friend's house for a sleepover. Roy asked him to join him. Told him to join him because that is the way Roy rolls. *Sit down*, he said. *Have a beer.* Bob told him he couldn't because he had a date with his wife. Really Bob has always been scared to get to know people, especially people who may not be like him. Roy said he knew Bob was lying because he knew his wife had left him. *I'll get you a chair*, he said, and went in his garage and dragged out a one-armed plastic chair. It had four legs, though, so Bob didn't fall out. They sat and stared straight ahead like they were appreciating their view of the ocean or a sunset or a parade, but they were only looking at Dan's house. Roy asked Bob where his son was, and he told him he'd just dropped him off at a friend's, and Roy nodded and finished a beer before tossing the can in his lawn. *I had a son*, he said. And a long pause draped over them like the heat, and Roy scooped out some catfish from the fryer and put it in a paper sack before Bob got the nerve to ask what happened. *Fell off a boat*, Roy said. *I was driving the boat.* He cracked open another beer and gave Bob a piece of catfish.

OK, now how do we feel about Roy?

Bob still wants to hurt him. To get even. He surveys all the stuff on his roof. A jump rope. Yo-yo string. An Elf on the Shelf. Cornhole bags. A glass snow globe with a picture of a woman Bob had once seen living at Roy's on and off for six months.

Jenny never told him, but she'd heard Roy and this woman having sex in one of those ENO hammocks that encased them like they were two peas in a porno pod. That's why Jenny came home with her own ENO hammock, but they never hung it up.

Bob picks up the snowglobe.

"Where'd you get that?" Roy asks.

"It was on my roof," Bob says, and smashes the snow globe on the shingles in a cascade of glitter and glass.

Roy drops the bunny. He climbs down from his roof on to a small stepladder balanced on top of his air conditioner unit. He hops the chain-link fence that separates their property.

But Bob does not like to fight, remember? Not verbally. Not physically. And certainly not on a roof. He hurries to the ladder, to Dan's ladder, and with all his strength hoists the ladder up so his neighbor can't climb.

Roy stands in the backyard staring up at Bob.

~~"Take that."~~

~~"Serves you right."~~

~~"Love thy neighbor, fucktard!"~~

"Now we're even," Bob says.

Bob's son stands next to Roy.

"Your dad doesn't know what's good for him," Roy says. He looks into the sky. Sticks his tongue out like he's waiting for flurries. "You should stop playing with stuffed animals," he tells his son.

His son? But it's not his son, and this could register unnecessary confusion or cause someone to think Jenny is being overly clever by implying that the son here is everyone's son, or Roy's son reincarnated, and probably someone will think he's a symbol for Jesus Christ.

So why not give his son a name?

Because he's the only one here who doesn't deserve this.

Call him JC just to fuck with everybody.

JC rubs the back of his little wrist across his eye in that way that makes him look like he did when he was a baby, overtired and struggling to stay awake.

"Come with me," Roy says. "I've got something better than a bunny."

JC puts his hand in Roy's hand and lets Roy take him away, through the side gate and in Roy's front door. JC does not resist, because he is one of those boys who believes that grown-ups always have his best interest at heart. Why would they lie? Why did his uncle give him the head of a jackalope if jackalopes aren't real? Why would his mom move to Michigan to study creative writing if it wasn't so she could write a big book that would pay for a bunch of Legos and a bigger back yard?

Don't let this happen, Bob. Go save the bunny, Bob. Go fight for what's left of your family!

He drops the ladder and climbs down, lifts it over the fence, props it against Roy's roof. He tries to jump the chain-link fence like Roy but scrapes his shin. Their roof lines are identical, their houses identical, except when he climbs the ladder this time he feels like he's climbing higher than before, like it won't ever end and he'll climb right into heaven, where he'll meet God, who looks just like Beyoncé.

Make it worse.

Bob's freezing now. His shin is bleeding. He really has to pee.

He picks up the bunny's headless body. He wants to yell across the street to Dan, ask him if he can believe what this psychopath did to his son's rabbit, ask to borrow his sewing machine to fix it because of course Dan has a sewing machine, but Dan is gone from this story now, likely hunkered down inside with his wife who didn't leave him and a mug of hot ~~coffee, cocoa, chamomile~~, peppermint tea.

Wisps of smoke curl from Dan's chimney. Bob's never seen it used. All their houses have fireplaces that nobody uses, but now, all across the neighborhood, smoke seeps sweetly from chimneys, and on every roof is more and more stuff. Maybe not on every roof. Certainly not Dan's. Not Roy's, either. But everywhere else. Balls wedged against satellite dishes. Hooded sweatshirts flapping on ancient antennae. Frisbees. Foam fingers. Comic books. Rotten pumpkins. Bobbleheads. Water bottles. A Slip N' Slide. Why? What's all this stuff mean? Jenny will have to figure that out eventually. Or someone will mansplain it in workshop.

Bob peeks over the edge of the roof. Bob yells Roy's name, stomps on the peeling shingles. He thinks about peeing down his chimney, but the opening is too high, so he kicks the chimney until a brick falls off. He picks up the brick and bangs it on the gutter, yells again for Roy to come outside.

When he does, Bob leaps from the roof and buries that brick in Roy's head, cleaves his skull like he's Philip Jennings in duty to Mother Russia.

Jenny told him she wished he were more creative. *What do you want me to do, write a poem?* Sure, but he could start with some new socks. She wanted them to grow their own vegetables and shop at used bookstores and try those edibles everyone kept talking about, maybe even go vegan for a month. *Disruption.* She did not want to keep living a false promise, the false promise of safety and security and comfort and Netflix. She wanted to be with him *and* to be with a different him. Did that make sense? He said it did, but she knew it didn't, and that's when she told him he never fought for anything.

But look now, Jenny! Here he is murdering his neighbor with a chimney brick.

No, he's not. No, he wouldn't.

The catfish Bob had eaten with Roy had been really good. Bob had eaten a lot of it. He never thought he liked catfish, but there he sat drinking beer and eating catfish in his neighbor's driveway until there wasn't any more. Roy put the baseball game on the radio, and they listened as the sun finally went down, tempting them to believe in mercy, their fingers greasy from fish, their mouths and heads bubbling with suds, both of them enjoying being close to somebody in the dark.

At the time Bob thought he might become friends with his neighbor. They might end up doing this every Friday night, replacing the standing date he had with his wife. They would hang out and bitch about their women and their losses, listen to ball games, eat fresh fish. Maybe Bob had underestimated Roy. Maybe there was more to him than he knew. But they never did it again. There was no reason why. They didn't talk about it, or talk much at all, really, just a wave, or a nod, sometimes not even an acknowledgment. It had happened once, and Bob regretted not doing more to make sure it could happen again.

Bob must do more.

Stray stuffing swirls below his bloody shin. "Looks like snow," he says.

Bob reaches inside the open neck and pulls stuffing from the bunny's body, digging deep into its arms and legs for every last tuft, and it's like the stuffing goes on forever, flowing ceaselessly from the bunny's insides. Bob tosses the fluff in the air and yells, "Kalamazoo!" He tosses more and yells again, "Kalamazoo!" Again and again, "Kalamazoo!" until the yard is covered and the roofs and the street, the whole neighborhood harbored in a soft blanket of white.

"Roy! Roy! Come outside! It's snowing! Come look!"

The front door opens and Jenny runs out. She's carrying a sled.

SIAMAK VOSSOUGHI

The Grandmother

Her eyes would spring open, and it would be the most alive she looked when they woke her up to eat something. The grandmother was young in the face, and she did not look like a dying person, except in the way she was tired all the time. The moment when her eyes sprang open made her grandson think of the movies. She looked the way he felt at the movies, which was not the same as how he felt on the way to the movies, or how he felt about the movie after they had watched it. She had a look like even happy movies were scary, not even because of the movie itself, but because of the movie's implications about the size of everything in life. She had a look like what he was sure his own face must look like when the movie started, and what he had always felt thankful that nobody could see in the dark.

There was something frightening about an old person looking like that, and there was something beautiful about it, too. He was a young boy, and it was the first time he had seen fear and beauty go together like that. He had always thought that everybody else understood the movies perfectly well. They understood that the lights had to go down and the movie had to start. They understood that the movie was just the story on the screen. It wasn't everything. It wasn't telling you everything of what the world was going to be. He had thought that everybody else knew that you were just going to step outside to the same old world after the movie.

His grandmother's eyes sprang open and he knew that if he were very brave, he would tell her—yes, that is how I secretly am at the movies. Who could ever be that brave, he thought. Who could ever be so brave to tell her that she was right to look at the world like that?

What he did instead was he watched very closely to see when his mother began making something for his grandmother to eat, and he would ask his mother then if there was any work that needed to be done outside. It was spring and there was work to be done in the garden. He would pull out the weeds or till the soil, and from there he could see inside his grandmother's room. It was better if his mother brought his grandmother her food, he thought. She knew how to sit in the movies. Maybe when his grandmother's eyes sprang open, it wouldn't be so much like how he felt at the movies because there would be nobody there to think of it like that.

Once when his mother was preparing soup for his grandmother, he asked her if there was anything that needed to be done outside even though it was raining.

"It's raining," his mother said.

"It is? Well, I don't mind."

"Do you want to catch a cold?"

"You're right. I guess I'll go clean my room."

"Okay. I'll call you when the soup is ready and you can take it to her."

"My room is very messy."

"Clean it, and then take this soup to your grandmother."

Up in his room, the boy tried to tell himself that the moment when his grandmother's eyes sprang open wasn't so bad. It was like the moment when the lights went down at the movies: It was only an instant. Something happened in that moment at the movies though, when the room went dark and the show started. It was like a sudden announcement that life was temporary. It was very quick, and then everybody settled into the story. Somehow part of it stuck with him through the story: These people whose lives you were following on the screen, you were going to have to say goodbye to them. There was a deeper truth in that. He would try to shoo the deeper truth away: It's just a movie. All these people wouldn't be sitting here watching happily if there were a deeper truth like that. He didn't dare look at them, though. He didn't dare look at the other people for fear that the deeper truth might be on their faces.

When he came back down, it had stopped raining.

"I can pull the weeds now," he said.

"Take this soup," his mother said.

Maybe she would be awake. If she was awake, it wouldn't be so bad. She would still be dying, but he knew how to be sad when she was already awake. He just didn't like having to be the one to kill her.

That was how it was when her eyes sprang open. Whoever woke her up was bringing her soup and telling her that she was going to die. It would almost be better if she got angry with him for waking her up. But she didn't get angry. She only looked terribly alarmed, like she had just gotten the news. And then he couldn't pretend that it was only that she wanted to rest more. It wasn't anything other than what it was, that when she was sleeping, whether she was dreaming or not, she wasn't dying.

As he took the soup, the boy thought of how it would probably make more sense if it were the end of the movie that got him. The moment when the lights came back up and the day returned. But he had nothing left by then. That moment was hopeless, but it mingled with everybody's hopelessness, and he didn't feel like he was holding it by himself.

He loved his grandmother for how her eyes sprang open like how he felt when the lights went down. Here she was, finally, somebody who understood how he felt, and she had to be dying. What kind of world was it when you had to be the one to kill somebody to love them like that? He thought of the people at the movies. Something had to die in them for them to love the people in the movie. His grandmother knew. Maybe she had always known. If he had known that she always knew, he would have asked her how she felt at the movies.

He came to her room and she was asleep.

He spoke to her and she woke up. Her eyes sprang open.

"Soup," he said.

"Thank you."

"I'm sorry to wake you up."

"It's OK."

"My mother says you should eat."

"She is right."

His grandmother ate the soup and said nothing. I would not want to talk to me either, he thought. He wanted to tell her that he knew what he had done. He knew he had killed her by waking her up. He wished she knew that he had tried some way around it.

What he hated the most though was the way his grandmother had to settle back into remembering that she was dying when he stood there in the room with the soup. She had to settle back into the story that everybody wanted. It would be OK if her eyes could spring open in alarm and stay alarmed. The alarm wasn't death. The way he felt when the lights went down wasn't death, either. It wouldn't be alarm if they could all do it. They only made you think that it was death because you were alone in it. If they could all look at each other when the lights went down, then the feeling wouldn't be fearful. It would be brave. If his eyes could spring open when hers did, it wouldn't be alarm. But it never went that way. He was alone at the movies and she was alone in bed.

A few months after his grandmother died, his mother asked him if he wanted to go to the movies.

OK, he thought. If his grandmother could sit up in bed and eat her soup after her eyes sprang open, he could go to the movies. He could sit there as the lights went down and everybody began to settle into the story. If she could eat her soup with him in the room after what she had seen, after seeing a world in her sleep where she was not dying, he himself not being able to give her anything so good as that, then he could go to the movies and not hold it against anybody that they did not seem to know that the real moment was before the movie started. The real moment was when the room went dark and they all agreed—all these strangers, men and women, boys and girls—they all agreed that they would dream together, that they were not strangers after all, and that in the dark there was a great intimacy between them. His grandmother had never once looked at him as small for waking her up from not dying. She could have. He knew from the way her eyes sprang open that she could have. She could have told him that he was small and foolish and that he had no idea the size of the world that he was waking her up from. She could have said all that and she would have been right; he would have stood there and taken it. Sometimes he even thought he wanted her to do it, because in that way he would see the world where she was living and not dying. But she had never once done it. She had sat up and eaten her soup.

If she had not seen him as small, then he could go to the movies and not see them as small, either.

"Ok," he said to his mother, "Let's go." And he had a look of such forgiveness on his face then that it was easy for his mother to mistake it for sorrow or grief or something else that was much more in the neighborhood of death.

CHARNELL PETERS

I Imagine You Gone

you'll forget about your death
before it happens so I'll think it for you

when a wasp tucks in a scabbed wood
or a wound crusts over the knee
of a curly-haired child neither of us had

I will think you gone in the nights
we, unheld, look through ceilings

and imagine the white suits and fans
the wailing woman gripping a mic
like a baseball, dragging us down

into a sorrow through our throbbing
bellies so deep we had only dreamed it

I remember there were millions of years
when you were, in fact, not here

and neither was I and neither was here
and this is no comfort, of course,

we are temporary, tender, improbable

and time is not ours, and I memorize you,
face open as a vowel because this, I say,

will help, of course I do not know

I will say "who could have imagined?"
with everyone else and answer me, me

Patrick Holian

My Legacy of Repose

I.

Pleasure: our lips slowly tearing open from cold. What
is my legacy of repose? Recall, we made
love, recounted the mechanics behind buttering
a tub of popcorn. Late autumn next year I built
a cypress guillotine, lopped off my head, which came to rest
among the fennel and rhubarb and golden poppies.

II.

So hear me out: I am the dreams of my surrender,
the dreams of my tongue turning to dust in a cave
lit only by the red, glowing eyes of an ocean
of rabbits. This car's made of the highest quality
car and can fit so much car inside. The snowstorm
knocks on the cabin door: I will love you forever.

III.

The first woman to compose a symphony was twelve
years old, Mexican, wrote about the rites of terror
and horror, dedicated it to her mother, sleep,
and the feral cat that napped outside her window.
Attrition haunts the history of naval warfare
the way weary old men haunt shipping lanes and church pews.

IV.

Heretics and devout alike have in winter warmed hands
at the pyre: an act of sacred obligation
and blasphemy. This is my legacy of repose:
the crowd anxiously awaits the reverberation
of the fireworks in their hearts, in their bones and blood,
the bank of fog pulsing with bruised light. This is my stop.

KATHLEEN ZAMBONI MCCORMICK

And Still, You Choose Denial

When the grammar school nuns chide you that by not finishing your tuna fish sandwich for lunch, you're causing Christ's crown of thorns to burrow more deeply into his already bleeding head, you, intelligently, don't fully believe them. It sounds ludicrous, even coming from a nun, that someone in the present can hurt someone in the past, especially Christ on Calvary, almost two thousand years ago. But it becomes your and your mother's most useful fiction.

Why don't you maintain that healthy skepticism about your Aunt Alice and your father? Probably because you trust your mother so much when she first tells you. But as you get older, you just don't want to see it, and denial creates a powerful lens. Your mother explains that your father's every encounter in the present with his infinitely irritating sister, Alice, yes, even on the phone, literally traverses time and space, that Alice has the power to agitate, even torture him, all the way into the distant past when he and his brother (and Alice herself) were little and hungry, left motherless by TB, and being raised by a bastard of a father. How do you respond? There's no way of putting this nicely. You simply abandon all powers of reason, wonder if maybe the nuns had a point, and readily believe your mother about Alice's capacity for transtemporal travel into the past of your father, her brother David.

We all know Alice is no saint. Her only goal, growing up in poverty, was to marry well, and she succeeded and became "lace curtain Irish," the absolute worst of the nouveau riche, flaunting her money and punctuating her incessant stories with parentheticals of how much everything cost. She can also be patronizing, which she takes as her right because of her wealth. Your father worked for years to get a college education, but glancing at your threadbare couch or your three-family house in need of a paint job, Alice repeatedly points out that David's inability to reach anything close to her financial status is "simply one of life's little ironies." And she rubs things in, so much so that anything she brags about becomes anathema to him.

Just think how Alice shows up, lights a cigarette, French inhales, and starts showing off the tan she got during their latest vacation in Bermuda, from which she says she's still jet-lagged (despite only a one-hour time difference), and he turns as red as a sunburn. As what your father terms "Our Lady of Perpetual Island Tours," the magnitude of Alice's assumed superiority in the vacation department seems to render him incapable of allowing your own family to travel anywhere, except the occasional day trip to a local beach, annually to the zoo, and on the first Tuesday of every month to Howard Johnson's for their Unlimited Fish Fry Night, none of which you think actually qualifies as "taking a trip." You blame Alice for your father's stuckness, and maybe it is her fault. But to reiterate, Alice is perfectly capable of countless annoying actions without having to time travel. So why do you believe your mother that Alice is in possession of supernatural transporting abilities?

Looking back, there are various interlocking explanations. Occam's razor, which you obviously hadn't heard of then, says that if you have competing explanations of something, the simplest one is always to be preferred. So here are the most likely reasons for your father's reaction to his sister: She gets on his nerves—easy, simple, and accurate; he resents her for marrying money while he had to slowly pull himself out of poverty; and if we must be somewhat more psychoanalytically complex, the two boys and the father all probably expected Alice to play mother, given that she was the oldest (about fourteen when their mother died), which she refused to do and they—particularly your father, who was the youngest (only eight)—never forgave her for not abandoning her own life and her own grief in an attempt to assuage theirs. All these explanations are reasonable, fit Occam's razor, and probably some combination of them could be seen as quite accurate. Yet you give credence to something complicated and impossible. Why? Could you have already suspected that a rather Byzantine notion of Alice's capacities could help you rationalize your father's frequent and quite disturbing behavior?

Example: You're visiting Alice in her latest new home, and she passes around one of many platters of food—*lobster thermidor, scallops en croute, veal scallopini*—all, as she points out, from the latest "Gourmet Cuisine" section of *Exceptional Country Living*. Needless to say, she never lives in the country. Wherever she resides and whatever the food, Alice always says, "Take as much as you want and eat up. There's plenty!" Let's grant that she's exasperating since "taking some" and "eating up" are the usual responses upon receipt of a food platter at a dinner table. But there you are, in total defiance of Occam's razor, and under the spell of your mother's story about her, imagining that Alice has whooshed back to the past to taunt little-boy Dad, to whom she used to always announce (so his account goes), "Don't take too much. The porridge" (sometimes a version says "gruel") "has to last three days." So "There's plenty!" becomes, in your young mind, Alice's time-traveling mocking of her eight-year-old brother with visions of her future abundance and his future insufficiency. Thus, when your father erupts from the table after a rather lengthy discussion with Uncle Paul, throws his napkin into his uneaten food, and screams at your mother, "Why are we here, you stupid woman?" it all makes sense to you. And it's Alice's fault for hurling "There's plenty" into your innocent father's "Don't take too much" little-boy face. You even allow thoughts of Christ's bleeding wounds worsened by your uneaten tuna fish sandwich to slip into your consciousness as your mother leads him out of his sister's house, and he slams his car door on her hand as she's trying to settle him in.

There's no question that believing your father somehow exists in a liminal state between past and present causes you to develop sympathy for him. And, let's face it, he's not easy to sympathize with, given how cranky, demanding, and dissatisfied he usually is. Perhaps turning Alice into some kind of witch figure with the capacity to inflict anguish across the ages was part of your mother's plan to wring pity and approval out of you whenever he did something cruel to either of you. If you hold Alice responsible for causing your father endless sorrow, and if this sorrow explains why he's so hurtful to you and your mother, then he's off the hook. Your mother's married a good man, after all, who just happens to possess an evil sister.

Further, while blaming Alice gives your father a sort of permanent GET OUT OF JAIL FREE card, it also offers him insurance that you and your mother are not, by any means, off the hook for any offenses he commits against you. In fact, you're more on the hook than ever. When your father berates either of you or does worse (usually only to her), rather than feeling anger or fright toward a man who's fairly out of control much of the time, the wicked Alice interpretation insures your father against your ire. How could you be upset by a man who's been antagonized both in the past *in the past* and in the past *in the present* by his supernaturally malevolent sister? So if he treats you badly, your mother says, "That's your cue to act kinder and more understanding towards him." His aggression should be interpreted by you both as an urgent imperative to become more generous, compassionate, and sympathetic. Even if you're vomiting with anxiety after he shouted at you or she's nursing the welts on her arm where he gripped her too tightly when he shook her. All because of Alice. Or, as your mother so often tearfully regrets, because you two weren't sensitive enough to him in the first place and brought it all on yourselves.

You've now, of course, learned that abuse victims commonly are in denial and blame themselves. Psychologists argue that self-blame for actions objectively outside victims' control is a way they can feel a sense of power when they really have none. So your thoughts are common enough; it's the reasons you employ to blame yourselves that are uniquely bizarre.

OK. OK. You still want to argue that your belief that Alice passes thought time to hurt your father has nothing to do with his violence. Let's just go ahead and jump into the butterfly buns story.

Your family's been to Easter mass and should have gone directly to Alice's Easter Extravaganza ("E squared," she likes to call it and we can all imagine how that goes down with Dad), but you and your mom have to go home to pick up two large boxes of butterfly buns. Which, because of their cost, you haven't told your father about. Now that you're home, he's trying to avoid going over. He's been angry with your mother all of Lent because she agreed your family would attend Alice's Easter luncheon without checking with him first. All of Lent is a long time. You don't ever think to look for bruises.

"What could I say, David?" she pleads.

"'No,' if you had any sense."

When Alice just "pops in" unannounced the day before Ash Wednesday to invite your family for her Easter Extravaganza, she's wearing a brown subtle tweed suit with a sheath skirt, a silk brown-and-beige striped scarf, a three-quarter-length (both hem and arm) camel hair coat with brown alligator boots, a matching purse, and her seal hat with wisps of blonde (Lady Clairol) hair peeking out. Home from school with a cold, you get to study her every detail. You think (though with some guilt) how beautiful Alice is, like she's walked out of the pages of *Vogue*, which you and your mother study but never dare buy at the drugstore. Your mother looks pretty awful by comparison in her faded pink, flower-print housedress with a large white band holding back her thin gray hair. She acts like the poor and ugly sister-in-law, too—so deferential.

Well, your mom won't be out-dressed today, which is partly why you want to get over there. You both are wearing exquisite up-to-the-minute Easter fashions she sewed for you. She insists it definitely wasn't Alice's invitation that prompted her to create such intricately designed outfits—and, to be fair, she does make new Easter clothes every year. You're dressed in a wool-and-silk blend, light peach, double-breasted coatdress with self-covered buttons she created from a huge remnant she got at Jordan Marsh just after Thanksgiving. She convinces your father to let you go to Thom McAn for their pre-Easter shoe sale, where you buy orange patent-leather shoes with an orange-and-white flower on their front (also in patent leather) and a matching purse. Then you get that shiny orange belt on sale at Zayre's. In your eyes, they all coordinated so beautifully. We won't go any further about the fact that their color coordination doesn't make them any less excessively orange.

Your mother's resplendent in a gray-blue featherweight wool suit. The jacket alone has eighteen pieces, not counting the lining, which led to a fair bit of cursing and seam-ripping during the sewing process. Jacket and skirt are both edged with a three-inch, biased-cut, gently pleated ruffle (which takes way more fabric because it's on the bias, so luckily she's had a huge store of it in the back closet for the last three years from a Filene's Basement end-of-bolt sale). Her blouse is pale gray (silk blend remnant) with pintucks she hand-sewed to be perfectly aligned. The wrists are trimmed with layers of matching lace that slip out at the (shortened) ruffled jacket cuffs. A lovely effect, even if she hasn't thought what she'll do with all that fabric around her wrists when it's time to eat. She even found your father a last-season markdown French blue shirt and striped silk tie combo to offset his cheap charcoal Anderson-Little suit.

So you muse happily that Aunt Alice, Cousin Ali, and Uncle Paul won't be the only ones with fancy, stylish clothes and matching accessories today, even if theirs come from Saks Fifth Avenue or Bonwit Teller. And that's when you mention the butterfly buns.

Alice asked her to bring some over and said to be sure to mention them to David because they were a "good little joke" of theirs. Your mother was suspicious. Alice and David have no shared jokes. You and she looked everywhere for butterfly buns, even some specialty bakeries in the Yellow Pages. No one had heard of them. So, in the end you bought croissants, with and without chocolate, and with and without almond paste. They were very expensive.

"Mom, since we're almost ready to go," you say encouragingly, "I'll get the butterfly buns from the fridge."

"What?" he glowers.

Your mother's eyes grow huge with worry that he'll ask what they cost. But he doesn't seem interested in the price.

"Alice actually used the words 'butterfly buns'?" he spits. You bring in two bakery boxes wrapped in Easter Bunny paper but drop them when you see him. He's gasping and flailing one of his arms at you. So, totally by accident, since of course you've never consciously brought on one of your father's incidents, not that you even imagined you had the capacity—that always being the purview of Aunt Alice—you travel back in time and provoke your little-boy father into some kind of unbearable vision of pastry. You've no idea what the vision is, but he's fallen back onto the couch as if the very force of time's winged chariot has just knocked him over. And then you're all sitting in the living room, where he's displaying the horror of what you, yes, you, Bridget Flaherty, have triggered.

He pants, rolls his head from side to side, and mutters, "GD butterfly buns."

"David," your mother calls, handing him a glass of water, "Alice said these buns were some joke between you two."

"Joke?" he hisses. Your mother starts biting her cuticles and you know she's sending up a quick prayer to St. Anthony, Patron Saint of the Impossible (whom she believes to be your father's personal saint).

Then you think of an angle. If butterfly buns bother him, he should be relieved to discover that you don't actually have any. "Well, don't worry, Dad. They aren't real butterfly buns because Mom and I couldn't find any. They're just cro ...."

Your mother interrupts you. He hates anything sounding French, believes everyone charges more for things with French names. "We bought pastries like iced buns, David." He likes iced buns. Plus on Mondays you can get a "day-old dozen" for a dollar at the local bakery, so even though you don't mention the price, he might imagine you only spent a dollar on Alice, which would please him. But, of course, he isn't pleased. Probably hasn't even heard anything you've said since "butterfly buns."

"That bitch!" he cries out, rushing to open a window, where he takes some deep breaths of the chilly outside air. "A joke, she told you? She's gone too far! She'd no right! Call them and say we're not coming." He bangs the window shut and rushes back to the couch, finger threatening your mother. "You had no right!" You sit next to him, trying to guard him against the past without a thought that you're guarding your mother against him. He starts to talk softly, a sign he's drifting back. Now that you imagine you've inadvertently shared in Alice's powers, you stay silent, fearing that one wrong word will, like the tuna fish sandwich, hurt his little-boy self even more.

"Alice announced with great pomp and circumstance to Joe and me one Saturday afternoon that she was serving 'butterfly buns' after church the next day." Your father's blue eyes travel back thirty years or more in a second. "Joe and I kidded that we wanted food that'd stay on the table, not fly away. Then we laughed and wrestled, thin boned, on that bare and cracked linoleum floor."

He pauses and you know he's flashing through time, remembering when he could roughhouse with Joe. Then when the war came. Then the shrapnel and the endless war in Joe's head. You will him to come back or at least to return to the butterfly buns, which can't be that bad since they're just a confectionary and not like a war or anything. "Have I told you, Bridget, that once Joey got quite a gouge in his leg when he landed on one of those linoleum cracks the wrong way? It bled and bled."

"Yes," you say, hoping your father won't go into his discussion of the painful contrast between innocent childhood wounds and war wounds, though his reddening eyes and that slight swelling in his upper lip let you and your mother know he's already thinking about it. She widens her eyes to indicate you need to remain silent. Your father didn't pass the Army physical because of his poor eyesight, and your mother's told you that ever since Alice exclaimed when he was in one of his liminal states that he was "so lucky to have missed the war," he's felt responsible for Joe's getting hit by that bomb. She'd seen him, right after Alice left, go back to Joe's past right before his battalion was hit, and felt him grab her as he tried to pull Joe out of harm's way, and then double up with guilt and remorse that he wasn't there to take care of Joe.

Finally, he shakes his head. But you don't know where he is until he speaks. Let him be in the present, please, St. Anthony, you silently beg. But St. Anthony chooses not to intervene this time. "After a lot of sighing and arm-crossing and eye-rolling in her phony way, it became apparent I had to go to the corner store to buy the butterfly buns." You glance at your mother and you both shrug, wondering how, with all your father's trips into the past, he's never made this one before.

The next part of the story almost makes you forgive him for all his cruelty. "Probably because Joe and I were so hungry, we believed buns shaped like insects might just be real. Joey imagined butterfly buns covered in different colors of sugar with crunchy wings made of fried pancake syrup. Then yellow jacket buns, filled with butter and chocolate. And strawberry jam and licorice ladybug buns." You father comes back and looks at you and your mother. "Can either of you grasp the gravity of the situation?" he yells. "Joey was always such an innocent. And he was just about drooling with his hopes so high for some sweet food to look forward to."

The idea of anyone's dreaming of buns containing fried pancake syrup or licorice got you sobbing almost instantly, realizing how little Joe and your father knew about normal food when they were young. You extend your hand to your father and he grabs it.

"At first I said I wouldn't go. Then she started flattering me, telling me I was the man of the house, and it was getting dark and wasn't safe in our neighborhood, filled with drunks and perverts, for a young lady like herself to be out walking alone." He stares out, babbling quietly about Alice's malice and phoniness. You wonder if he could get stuck somewhere between back then and now and be lost to you forever. You make an intercession to Mary Magdalene, believing that of anyone in the Bible, she seems likely to be the most sympathetic to an aunt who had once believed in butterfly buns.

"Alice, you loathsome creature!" he wails, and quite unexpectedly hurls his water glass at your mother's head. Her quick reflexes deflect it, and the glass lands on the rug. It doesn't break because it's an old, rock-hard Flintstones jelly jar glass, one that could have given her a nasty cut or, at the very least, tipped and ruined her outfit. The water spills and the carpet turns dark. You move to get a rag, but she motions you to stay still. She must be really worried about time, and maybe about your father, to leave a spill alone, even if it's only water.

"When I went up to the grimy storekeeper, I mumbled at first, but eventually got it out. 'I want some butterfly buns for my sister.'" He nervously intertwines his fingers, giving you a glimpse of him as that child in the store. You imagine him smelling kind of tinny, like he needed a good washing, with dirty ears, wearing shorts that are too small, despite his being skinny, and squinting because he can't see very well.

"When I finally say the words, my eyes sting with tears. I know how foolish I sound. The storekeeper and the men hanging around smoking laugh and make me repeat the words louder and louder."

He's breathing hard and opening and closing his fists. You imagine his once-little chest heaving, his once-small sticky hands, ready for a fight. Fights that he couldn't have then, but he can have now, whenever he wants, with your mother and you.

"They don't sell stupid butterfly buns! Just like I said!" he screams out to Alice thirty years ago. "Look at you, lazing around on that couch, like you're the queen. How could you have done this to me?" that little boy shrieks, his loud, too-high voice piercing your apartment, startling you, and causing some of the bone china cups to shake in their saucers in the dining room cabinet.

For an intelligent girl, it's amazing that you never ask yourself whether this man—who you are convinced journeys back and forth in time—modifies or even invents details as he spins his endless stories when he's caught in one of his spells. Did he really have the nerve to say words like that to Alice, whom he won't confront even now? If he had, would these episodes, or his cruelty to your mother and you, need to happen now? Over and over?

He throws his head back, huffing. "You know what that sister of mine said to me?" His glassy eyes don't see you. Where is he? "She said, 'Oh well,' sighing nonchalantly, 'I guess we'll just have to do without.'" Her indifference then enrages him now. He stands, his left fist rhythmically punching his right hand as he blurts out repeatedly, "Do without." Then he notices you and your mother. He looks like he wants to hurt someone.

How odd it is that he himself so often uses this very malicious and cutting Alice remark—"I guess we'll just have to do without"—when he looks at the price of something you or your mother wants. He'll stand tall, become disengaged, as if he's commenting on the weather. "No, girls, at that price …"—and it can be anything from good Parma ham in the Italian grocery to new school shoes for you—"I guess you'll just have to do without." Even though you have enough money now. But you try to tell yourself that his repeating Alice's words is unconscious and only goes to prove the extent she's responsible for his pain then and yours now.

Your mother's voice pierces the room. "Well, she's made up for it all now, hasn't she?" Her patience is at an end. "Look, David, we have to go," she states with an unusual firmness. "We've been invited, and we accepted the invitation." Your father scowls at her but puts his jacket on.

You and your mother take this as your cue and stand. You decide not to listen to anything else he's saying. She pushes you into the front hallway, where she changes into her Easter shoes. Your father becomes impatient, sighs, goes downstairs ahead of you, and bangs the door, as if you were the ones who've been making him wait.

You grab the boxes of croissants and hold your mother's hand as she finds her way down the steps. She has to be careful not to catch her high heels in the cracking rubber stair treads. Her hand is cold, and she's shaking a little. "Oh, my feet are killing me already!" her voice echoes in the hallway. With the morning your father's had, her feet will be the least of her concerns.

As you climb into the back seat of the car, you realize that, despite everything, you're still excited to be spending an "E squared" with Aunt Alice. She'll have fifty Easter lilies lining the long, sunny flagstone path to her front door, which your father will avoid by using the side door. The house will be filled with bouquets of daffodils and hyacinths because the color scheme this year is yellow and blue. Your father will complain that Alice's ostentatious display of Easter flowers bothers his allergies. The flowers probably will bother his allergies. And Alice may already know that.

You open the back window just a crack so you won't get carsick. You can smell the spring, and to celebrate, you choose denial. You wonder whether Alice will have both yellow and blue plates, and if your father will comment rudely that they don't match. But mostly you worry what Alice might inadvertently say to hurt your little-boy father back when he's malnourished and missing his mother, and how long he'll let you and your mother stay, and how much of it will be in the present, and how hungry he'll be, both today and on the Easters after his mother died when Alice wouldn't play mother.

ANTHONY VARALLO

Today You Are Green

This summer you turn thirteen, and what is a thirteen-year-old girl to be happy about? Don't ask your father, who turns to you now, standing before the mini-golf cashier, and asks, "Which color do you want to be?" Don't ask your father's girlfriend, who selects the yellow ball, an offbeat choice, with red, blue, and green still in the offing, and gives you a playful nudge, the way she sometimes does, to signal that she knows how you must be feeling. But how do you feel? Several contradictory options present themselves. Best bet is to select the green ball, a color that nearly blends in with the artificial grass. It's an idea that suddenly appeals to you.

"I'll keep score," your father says. He's already writing your name on the scorecard with a pencil the length of a spent cigarette. "You can go first," he says, too brightly, a sign that he's nervous about today, a return to the same mini-golf course you've always gone to, every summer, when your family rents the same beach house, but never since your parents split, and never with your father's girlfriend, who is several years his junior, and who used to work in your father's office, and who used to make you mixtapes to take with you to the beach house, and isn't it strange how some things work out?

At the first hole, an embarrassingly easy bank shot against a hippo's side, you manage to guide your ball into a water hazard nonetheless, while your father fails to bank his shot cleanly and must give in to the minor humiliation of straddling the hippo's tummy on his follow-up. Your father talks to himself in third person, the way he does when he's stressed, saying, "Come on, Bob, you're better than this," and, "Bob, use your head," and, "Think, Bob, *think*." Your father's girlfriend takes one practice swing, then expertly ricochets her shot off the hippo's leg for an easy tap-in. You finish the hole with a duffer's four, not taking a penalty for the water hazard. Your father scribbles his score on the sly.

The thing is, you loved those mixtapes. Those tapes were like an introduction to being cool, although you would never admit that to your father's girlfriend now, no, not with everything that's happened since. But, still. You've listened to those tapes a thousand times. You've got whole sides memorized. Today it occurs to you that this year you won't get a mixtape, a realization that makes you feel sort of sad in a vague, empty, shapeless way, the way so many things do these days. Most nights, you cry in private, for reasons that still aren't clear to you.

"It's your turn," your father says, on this, the third hole. What happened to the second? No matter. This one is Western themed, with a pesky wagon wheel that lures your green ball into one of its spokes. Your father talks his way through a cattle yoke—"That's more like it, Bob"—but whiffs on an easy tapper and ends up with a lowly four, while your father's girlfriend sails by the wagon like it's not even there, and cups out of a potential hole in one.

"Oh! So close!" your father exclaims, forgetting to hide his relief.

"Yeah," your father's girlfriend says, then taps the ball in with her flip-flop.

"So, let's see," your father says as he scribbles down the score. "That would be a two."

On the fifth hole, you somehow manage to cross a drawbridge and walk away with a three, your best hole of the day.

"Nice shot," your father's girlfriend says.

"Thanks," you say.

"Just keep lightening up that touch," she says without further explanation.

On some of the tapes, she would record little secret greetings, five-second hellos, or short introductions to the next song. "This next one," she'd say, "is a reminder why you don't actually need boys in your life." Here she had laughed before the next song played, a song that had accompanied you all summer long, your favorite, the one you rewound a thousand times, the one you played so many times it got all mixed up with everything else.

On the ninth hole, your father sends his shot out of play and into a cluster of teenagers who congregate by a soda machine. "This yours?" one of them says, and then the rest of them crack up, like this is the funniest thing they've ever heard. When your father's girlfriend retrieves the ball, you can see the teenagers checking her out. Your father's girlfriend is pretty—beautiful, even. Your feelings on this subject are varied, warring, complex. The teenagers watch your father's girlfriend line up her next shot, whoop and applaud when she sinks a hole in one.

"Nice!" they exclaim. "Sweet!"

Your father makes an excellent shot, too, enough for a solid two, but you can hear him mutter, "That's not going to do it today, Bob," as he glumly retrieves his ball from the cup. The stupid necklace his girlfriend gave him, several years too young for him, dangles stupidly from his neck, but this time you don't want to tear it off and toss it into the surf, as you did this morning, when the three of you walked along the beach. This time you want pull your father in for a hug. Another contradictory feeling, to keep all the others company.

Three disappointing holes later, your father's girlfriend is leaving you and your father in the dust. She doesn't acknowledge her second hole in one, nor do the teenagers, who lost interest a while ago. You are hot and sweaty; your underarms stamp your T-shirt with embarrassing half-moons, the way they do more often now, drawing attention to you, you believe, despite a lack of supporting evidence.

"Do you two want to call it a day?" your father's girlfriend asks, out of charity or boredom or spite, who can tell?

"Never," your father says, intending playfulness. "No way."

Here is something you are glad no one knows about you: Sometimes you get angry for no reason whatsoever, and then get even angrier at yourself for being angry for no reason whatsoever, until it is all you can do to lock yourself in the downstairs bathroom and look at yourself in the mirror, staring down the stranger there. Who is this person, you wonder.

At last, the eighteenth hole: the volcano. The hole where you've posed for a half-dozen family photos. Hit the ball through the volcano's glowing core, then race across the rope bridge to the other side to see where it has disappointingly landed. The impossible hole. Now, you each take turns, sending your shots through, and then for reasons that reveal themselves to you once you reach the other side, you sprint across the rope bridge to see that your father's girlfriend has hit yet another hole-in-one, while your ball shelters behind a lava obstacle and your father's ball rests in a water hazard. Quickly, you toss your father's girlfriend's ball into the water hazard and replace it with your father's ball, still wet, still glistening. "Hole in one!" you surprise yourself by shouting. "Hole in one!"

Your father's expression, upon crossing the bridge? Well, you will keep it with you a long while. Longer than the look your father's girlfriend turns on you as your father shakes water from his ball; now, how did that happen? Your mixed feelings take a little break, for once, which is nice of them. Otherwise you wouldn't be able to tolerate your father's childish smile.

The rest of summer? You spend your days wandering the boardwalk to avoid your father and his girlfriend's silent arguments. Eventually you meet a boy. You begin hanging out. He tries to kiss you and more, and you let him, after a while. And so on.

BRET SHEPARD

Summer Camp

After the bull tutu falls, the herd dissolves momentarily, dust pulled
into air—then a glassy silence, but mostly a slight, unpretending breeze.

Shed of their velvet, his antlers are a full red. Imagine warm
blood setting. What is taken apart   is also reduced to more—

heart and liver like lessening fires
tamped from flame   by the crystal-white outline closing in.

BRET SHEPARD

Last Sunset

Darkness is animal. Hunting hours
nearby it attacks eyelids, rips apart

what weather holds, what it packs
to leave with it. You watch in need

of its contracting edges near a past
you once slept beside. The dark is

not darkness. It is you given leave
from the realness of seeing. Dark

in many things is only one thing
desire hides inside itself. There are

still beginnings that hurt, days you
claw your way back into your body.

JOSHUA ZIMMERER

National Taco Tuesday

Since all the adjacent streets were blocked off, and since a mariachi band had been practicing outside his window all morning, and since he may have preemptively called off work for the day, and since it was National Taco Tuesday after all, Carson decided the girls didn't need to go to school. They all sat at the kitchen table eating cereal, which he couldn't think of the Spanish word for. He knew you didn't just add an O at the end. That would've been offensive. But was it in the Latin root? Maybe it was related to the word for grain. What was that, though? It's not that he ever knew Spanish in the first place, but Julisa would always speak it when she got angry at him, so Carson thought subconsciously he might have picked it up. The worst part was if he got it wrong the girls would know immediately. Their mom raised them speaking the language. When they all lived together, he would play this stupid game before they went to bed where he would go, "One kiss, two kiss, red kiss, blue kiss," alternating between the two of them. Julisa, on the other hand, would give them long soliloquies Carson found indecipherable, only picking up on the rolled Rs and the—what he could only presume were—upside-down question marks. At the end she would say something to their daughters as beautiful as they all were, and then they would say it back like birds calling out into the wild with their own grammar and their own song. It was terrible.

"What does it mean?" Carson would ask her.

"You wouldn't understand," she'd always say back.

Watching his girls meekly spoon up milk, he hoped when Julisa came to pick up the girls this weekend she'd be the one who wouldn't understand. He could almost see it now. She'd be at the front door beckoning the girls to get their stuff together, to grab their pillows, making sure they had all their homework for the weekend—"Do you have your lucky pair of socks? What do you mean they're your sister's socks? What about the socks I got you before the school year started?"—and the girls would be dancing around the apartment squeaking about carnitas, and barbacoa, and how corn tortillas are so much better than flour tortillas. He thought about the taco-themed T-shirts he'd buy them, or a sombrero they could share. Then, in his wildest scenario, Julisa would give him this look, with her hair tucked behind her ear and her eyes flattened from a poor night's sleep, and he'd say to her what she always said to him after their nightly routine. Of course, this was no foolproof plan. There was no way he could predict what kind of sleep Julisa would be getting the night before.

Still, he felt confident in National Taco Tuesday, felt a confidence in himself he hadn't experienced in a while now. He decided to stop taking the Epitol over the past week, worried about what kind of person it was making him. Someone who wasn't his authentic self, filtered and mitigated. Someone, sure, that Julisa felt comfortable having their two daughters for an extra week while she went out of the country for another conference, but also someone who was too tempered to be deserving of his daughters' love and respect and endearment and excitement. Someone who could muster enough energy to ensure their health and safety, but that was about it. He was tired of being a half-empty well, cranking out what little there was left to truly give.

As weekday dad, Carson never had the time for family activities that really mattered. He'd take them to school before work. And he'd take them to karate and science club. And he'd cook them nutritious but delicious meals, such as eggplant parmesan or grilled chicken breasts with broccoli and corn. All the necessary things he was required, but also wanted, to do for them. And as weekend dad, he barely felt the capacity to do more than just the same. He never felt like he fully knew his girls unless it was over summer break, when they'd go on vacations to Wyoming or the beaches of New Jersey. And even then, he'd catch them on their phones, texting Mom.

So, the girls had to be excited. Who wouldn't be? They would get to spend time with their Dad, and there was going to be music everywhere, and there were going to be tons of people, and the police would be on horseback—so the girls would get to see that—and there were going to be tacos. Tacos for every meal: tacos with different meats and cheeses, tacos they could take pictures with, tacos they didn't even know were tacos. It would be like seeing a meteor shower, except they could actually do it in the city.

Most people would be annoyed by the festivities taking place so close to their home, but Carson moved to this apartment in the heart of downtown to be integrated with the culture. He liked all the happenings buzzing outside his door. So many days to celebrate, a swath of ordinary, each with its own holiday. He felt compelled as a father to ensure his children partook in the spectacularly mundane. Only, when he got out into the street there weren't as many people as he expected. A couple of the vendors were still heating up the flat-tops, and food trucks hadn't made their way past the barricade. The Mariachi band blaring outside the apartment earlier took a smoke break against the brick exterior of his building. They were all wearing embroidered jackets with white pearls snaking down their arms and along their collars, and the bottoms were hemmed up above their waists like maestros' jackets. One of them rolled a cigarette on the back of his giant guitar. The girls asked what kind of guitar it was. The musician rolling the cigarette crushed it against his instrument before even lighting it, and flipped it around, flaunting its polished sheen to the daughters.

"It's Mexican," the musician said.

"None of you look Mexican," Carson's younger daughter said.

"Enough of that," Carson interrupted. "Who are you to judge how someone is supposed to look? And it's Hispanic, girls. We call them Hispanic now."

Or maybe there was another term Carson had forgotten about, a newer and more accurate descriptor.

But it was true: All the members of the mariachi band were white guys in their early thirties. One of them even sported the same hipster moustache Carson tried to pull off when Julisa and he first got married.

"You guys mind playing a song for my daughters?" Carson asked. "They would love to hear an old folk ballad. Or do you know any quinceañera songs?"

"The gig actually hasn't started yet," the trumpet player said. "And we mainly do pop covers. Michael Jackson hits. Also, Wonderwall."

"Come on. Just one song. I'll even tip."

"We start when we start," the trumpet player rebuffed, and pointed to a taco stand across the street. "By the time you get your food, we'll be up and running again."

"You've got to do this for my girls," Carson said, his hands waving out toward the mariachi musicians. "You know how much depends on you playing for my girls? Do you?"

"Dad," the older daughter said, tugging at the back of his shirt. "Did you take a chill pill today?"

Carson counted to one with an inhale, exhaled on two, and told the mariachi band that they'd return for some "Man in the Mirror." He and the girls went where an assortment of meats were cooking on the grill, the spices heavy and pungent the way Carson thought they should be. He hoisted one of the girls up on his shoulders so she could see the menu, though both his daughters said they weren't hungry. He understood. He did. They literally just ate breakfast an hour ago. But come on, he thought. It's National Taco Tuesday. You're supposed to push the limits on days like these. He never heard them complain about too many presents on Christmas or their birthdays. And it's unimaginable to think there was such a thing as too much candy on Halloween. When Julisa came to pick them up, they didn't drag their feet across his salvaged, original hardwood flooring, complaining about spending too much time with Mom for three days.

"Embrace the spirit," he said to his daughters. "Embrace the spirit or you'll have to go to school."

"Do they have breakfast burritos?" the daughter not on his shoulders asked.

"I'll find out," he said.

"It's not on the menu," the other daughter said.

"I'll find out," he said.

The lady working the stand told Carson they don't do burritos.

"It's National Taco Tuesday," she said.

She was short and plump with a dirty apron stretched across her stomach. For a moment Carson thought to himself that she was the kind of person he wanted making his tacos—the kind of person who knew authenticity. But this wasn't right. He partially wished one of the girls would say this aloud so he could correct them on this misjudgment. He wanted to give them the whole spiel in front of the woman working the taco stand. Julisa always hammered Carson on not teaching the girls enough, that he put too much faith in the public school system. She maintained the belief that schools were meant to give children facts while parents were meant to give children opinions. Julisa, Carson imagined, probably would've talked to the woman in her native tongue—she'd majored in Spanish and linguistics before getting her doctorate in the same—laughing, sharing stories about the country life in the mountains of Peru where Julisa spent two years volunteering at a shelter for women suffering from domestic abuse. But if Carson asked the woman where she was from, he feared she'd probably say Arizona, or Cincinnati.

He ordered three chicken tacos in hard shells without conveying any of this. He led the girls to the curb where he asked them to pose with the tacos. They refused.

"Pictures, already?" the older one said.

"Can we just eat these?" the younger one said.

But Carson had such plans, such wonderful and memorable photo ideas: one where they held them up like religious offerings. Another where they pretended to take humungous bites, their mouths like sinkholes. He would post them immediately and wait as the world would slowly exalt what a sweet and creative Dad he was.

Instead, they hunched down, chomping away while lettuce and sour cream spilled out onto the ground and their pant legs. Carson wiped the mess off the girls' clothes with the bottom of his T-shirt since he'd forgotten to grab napkins. Neither of the girls looked too ecstatic about the tacos, but he reminded himself to give it time. Give it time. He was glad, however, that he had two daughters and not two sons. They probably would have thrown the tacos at the people walking past or tried to steal one of the mariachi band's guitars. They wouldn't have had the patience for this.

By the time Carson and his girls were done with their first round of tacos, sure enough the mariachi band was playing again—"Horse with No Name," by America, Carson was pretty sure, not the Michael Jackson they'd promised—and hordes of people were crowding the city block. Carson knew he wasn't being crazy. This was a big deal. Other people took days off for this kind of stuff. And if they didn't take the day off, they at least took an extended lunch break. Just that morning, before the girls woke up, Carson had been watching the news and the anchors were all about it. They were talking about how they could already smell it from the station, and how both of them were going to visit, and Carson thought to himself how cool it would be for the girls to meet celebrities on their day off from school. Local celebrities, but celebrities nonetheless.

Over the horizon of other taco enthusiasts, Carson saw a news van's antenna reaching out, beckoning. People had begun to gather around it, or at least seemed to. The event was so busy, the world so loud, Carson lost track of his thoughts. He thought of his daughters, of his ex-wife, of the million other fantastic thoughts that bombarded his head at that moment. He wondered, all too briefly, if this week, after all, might have been the wrong one to change up his mental health routine.

Nonetheless, excited over the girls' chance encounter with minor stardom, Carson whisked them up from the ground, pulling them through the thicket of people, using his shoulder to clear a path. He held onto only one of their hands, and it was small and folded neatly into his own. A couple of people he bumped to the side were coworkers, or they looked like co-workers, and as they nudged off Carson reminded himself to later apologize for his rudeness, and to remember some anecdote they told him last week so that way they would feel Carson was being personable, that his lack of manners was simply circumstance. Carson grabbed more tightly around one of the girls' hands, heaving them how a freight train tugs a line of cars a mile long across the tracks, trampling over pennies kids leave on the iron, believing such a small piece of copper could derail such a massive machine. They almost made it to a clearing when Carson felt the weight he was pulling become half as heavy. He turned around, seeing only one of his daughters standing with him.

"Where'd your sister go?" he asked.

"I don't know. She let go of my hand."

"When?"

"Like, right now. Before we stopped."

"No, I got that, but, when did—"

Hundreds of people populated the city block now. Smoke and steam climbed up the old brick buildings, and a part of him wished he'd taught his daughters how to give smoke signals in case of these types of emergencies. That's what we'll do next week, he thought too quickly. Or the next break they get. The three of us will go down to an Indian reservation to learn the same techniques they taught the settlers. History is an important subject. So is geography. Navigation, specifically.

"OK, sweetie," he said to his remaining daughter. "Dad needs you to help find your sister. Can you do that?"

"I think we should get help," she said.

"No, no. We've got this. She can't be far off. We'll search the—"

"Dad, you need to relax. There's a security tent over there. Let's go ask."

"Hold on, we can do this ourselves," but his other daughter was gone now, too, lost in the crowd, headed somewhere Carson couldn't see.

He did a couple of three-sixties on his toes, peering over people's heads, jumping to give himself a better vantage point. But his daughters were too small. When he took another spin, his hands pushing down on strangers' shoulders, he knocked against a woman trying to squeeze by his gyroscopic searching. She fell headfirst into a crowd of businessmen sipping tequila on their break, but they padded her fall. Carson, on the other hand, was not as fortunate. The people in the path of his pratfall parted and suddenly the world drew nearer, and the concrete blacker, and the world nearer, and the concrete nearer, and the world blacker.

"Jesus," the man looking down at Carson said, his hand outstretched and a water bottle held in the other. The man heaved Carson up. A portion of Carson, somewhere lodged in the back of his head, knew the fall had left him partially concussed, that whatever inkling of him wasn't encumbered by his mania had been squandered. It could only whimper and watch.

His mouth was filled with saliva but when he swallowed, he felt nothing.

Static circled behind his eyes.

"How long was I out?" Carson asked, but the man didn't know. A minute or two at the most. "Did you see a girl with me? Where did she go?" but again the man said he didn't know. Carson searched the immediate vicinity, but there was no sign of either of his daughters, and so he yelled out for them, and then again. He yelled out for them so loud that people began to stare, and he hoped they would all call out for his daughters, too, but instead each one sheepishly returned to their tacos, and tequila, and phones. Then he called out for Julisa. There was no sign of his girls.

The static seeped into the rest of his skull, crinkling against the gray matter, collecting in the wells of his ears. The man offered Carson his water, and he took a huge swig, half of it spilling down onto his shirt. The speed of light began to slow. That whimpering part of Carson, that last bit unfettered by his mania, cried out one more time, but so much had taken over. The fear of losing his daughters, of losing custody when just given the opportunity to prove otherwise, of losing whatever was left of him that wanted to be loved: It all turned outward until the world matched Carson's warped vision.

Each person's step fell into place with the others. Tinfoil peeled back from tacos in accordance to the golden ratio as cigarettes and gum wrappers landed on the pavement with the delicacy of rain. The sizzle of carne fat droned to a white noise, the impeding thunder of everyone talking lifted into the air and dissipated like car fumes, eating away the ozone layer atom by atom. Everything was so dire, so important, so completely out of grasp.

Carson wanted to hold on. But he had finally been overtaken by himself.

Grabbing people left and right, he shook them asking if they had seen his daughters. But before they could speak, he let go since, in Carson's logic, if they didn't have his girls, then they hadn't seen them. The crowd pushed back at Carson's franticness, then pulled him in, then pushed him out again. He violently ebbed and flowed through the crowd until reaching by accident the taco stand where they had started their day.

The mariachi band called out next to him suddenly, above everything else, like a guiding light. If I found my way back to this music, Carson thought, then my girls would have to do the same thing. They were his kin after all; they shared the same blood.

Once Carson turned toward his beacon, however, he was devasted to learn the mariachi band from earlier happened to be a completely different one now. This new group wore green-and-white Nudie suits, faded. They were not those white boys from earlier either. The real deal. Authentic. Carson wished his girls could see him now.

"Have you seen my two girls?" he asked them.

They stared back at him with blank faces.

"Umm, dos femalia. No muchos. No muchos. Havo yes dos femalia, no muchos?"

But he had no idea what he was saying. He wished he hadn't been so combative with Julisa, that he'd spent the time to speak along with his family. To learn a new self through osmosis. The group shook their heads no, although a part of Carson believed in that moment that they were saying no to him, that he shouldn't have been there, that they knew what was happening but wanted no part of it.

He looked back into the sea of human beings, and a sudden wave of dismay overtook him. But before he could dive back in, a cop on actual horseback came his way in respect to dozens of complaints made about Carson. The cop was stern looking, to Carson, but with soft cheekbones—the way he hoped good cops appeared. His horse was stern looking as well. If his daughters were with him now, Carson knew, they would have been ecstatic. He imagined the police officer letting them run their fingers through its mane, or at least pet its nose.

"Sir, we've been getting complaints that—," the officer said.

"I know, I know. I'm sorry, officer," Carson said. "It's just I've lost my two little girls. I have no idea where they went. I need help."

The police officer tilted his head into his walkie-talkie and Carson distinctly heard him say ten-sixty-five, two adolescent females. The officer peered down at Carson through aviator sunglasses. Carson became self-conscious of his appearance: his shirt painted with splatches of water and sour cream and cheese, gravel caked into his arms, his entire visage a ramshackle of desperation and loosened nerves. He tried to look back at the officer, but it was as if he were staring down a well he'd dropped a quarter in and hadn't heard it land.

"What do your daughters look like?"

Carson stuck up his index finger to the officer as if to convey "I've got just the thing, don't you worry," and instinctually pulled out his phone, searching through all the pictures he had taken of them. It needed to be a recent one. Julisa had taken the girls out last week for haircuts, so Carson worried they didn't look anything like the picture. *If only my girls hadn't so candidly rejected my sincere documenting,* he thought. *Though, I think they get the same haircut every time, so if I go far enough back, probably before the divorce, I can—.*

"I don't need a picture. I just need a description."

"It won't be good enough. You could think they're anybody. Give me one second."

There was the picture from National Talk Like a Pirate Day, but that wouldn't work. Both the girls were wearing eye patches and had painted stubble around their chins. Which also meant any Halloween pictures were no good either. Julisa came back that day after being gone for almost two weeks, something she'd been doing more frequently. She was at a conference, or was attending a string of conferences, presenting something on intersectionality and language. She had a new camera hung around her neck. Carson remembered when she'd gone in for a kiss from the girls and their stubble rubbed off on her cheek. She had asked so many questions, so many moments Carson was tired of her missing.

"Simple description will work just fine. Trust me. It's OK. Height. Hair color. Any noticeable scars or birthmarks."

"No. You have to trust me."

There were plenty of pictures from National Art Museum Day. There was another conference, or maybe Julisa's mother was sick then. Carson had brought his girls to the new Rothko exhibit because children weren't exposed to enough art anymore. But just as they'd hit their stride, Carson received a text from Julisa saying she just landed, and she wanted the girls to see their mom immediately. She brought gifts for both of them. She always brought gifts. It was a mad dash. Selfie after selfie in front of those monoliths of color, all of them trying to smile as fast as they could. They probably spent no more than five minutes in the room. Before they went to the museum Carson had read Rothko had directions on how to—.

"I know this is stressful," the cop said. "But I need you to act rationally for me."

"I'm looking. I'm truly sorry."

Definitely not National Lobster Day. They were all wearing those stupid bibs. Even Julisa. She said the girls didn't have to eat any shellfish if they didn't want to. But she also showed up late. An hour late. She had been gone again for a while. It's not that Carson worried about her. But she had been gone again. Almost a full month this time, away on research. He was never clear on the details at that point. "I think you need me here more than they do," she said while dipping the white, almost transparent, meat into a small saucer of butter. Carson cracked a claw and juices splattered all over her T-shirt: "And so what if I do? And how do you know what they want anymore?" The girls stopped covering their ears any time she swore in Spanish.

"Do you want my help or not?"

Carson turned to the officer, his expression flat, yet pained beneath.

"Do you know what I had to do to not become just another worthless part-time dad?" Carson said, and then returned to his phone.

None of the pictures would do: not their first day of school for the year, not National Donut Day, not the trip to Wrigley Field, none of it. Nothing was good enough for Carson, nothing worth showing the officer what beautiful and amazing creatures his daughters were to him—why they needed to be found. Carson knew he wasn't helping. But the urgency fell into his phone, into these images. He wanted to look back up at the officer, to continue the search, but he lost control to himself, the part that needed medication, and therapy, and twice-daily meditation, and exercise and diet, and all those small increments of well-being that allowed him to maintain. He became too exhausted to fight the exhaustion, and for once had felt free of it. But now look where it landed him. He kept scrolling through photos, defeated and ashamed.

The officer took notice.

"I might have a fifty-one-fifty on top of the missing girls," he said into his intercom, but not quietly enough. He reached down from his horse toward Carson's phone, but Carson pulled away, feeling as though a conspiracy were taking place.

"I'll find you the picture," Carson yelled. "I'm not crazy. Is that what you said? I'm trying to help."

The static rumbled out from Carson's brain and down his entire body, through his fingertips and toes, like a pair of shoes in the dryer. At the bottom of the photo album on his phone was a picture of his two girls when they were babies. Carson wanted to show the officer this picture, to show him that his daughters were real, that he wasn't making all this commotion for nothing. *What kind of person would make them up?* he thought about screaming at the officer. Instead, Carson couldn't keep the world straight. He peered up from his phone and everything shifted slightly. He woozed toward the horse, placing his hand in its mane.

"You need to step away from the horse right now," the officer commanded, his hands taut around his belt.

Carson grabbed at the officer, which he knew he shouldn't have done. So much, he knew, was out of his control at this point. The officer had incredible reflexes; Carson had to admit it. The officer blasted him in the eyes with pepper spray and, as Carson stumbled back, he heard the swoosh of the officer swinging around the saddle.

A hard kick to his chest sent Carson hurtling down hard. The world crashed back inside his head, the static now pouring out from him: his nose, the cut at the base of his neck, then out from where he bit into his gums as his jaw bounced off the ground. It felt as though a tiny animal were clawing at his sinuses. He tried coughing it out, sneezing it out, but every time he did the chemicals clung harder into him.

The officer flipped Carson onto his stomach, shoving his face into the sidewalk. Carson wasn't sure if it was the minerals from the curb grazing along his teeth but he swore he tasted earth, the taste of returning after being gone for so long.

"I want my girls," Carson said. "I just want my girls."

"I'm trying to help you," the officer said, his knee deep in Carson's lower back. "But I need you to stop resisting." The officer heaved Carson's arms behind his back, tying his wrists together with a thin thread of plastic.

As the officer hoisted Carson to his feet, Carson saw his daughters, finally, on a giant stage at the end of the city block. A massive stage with tall rafters and giant speakers and overhanging lights, and even from his vantage point Carson got a full view. What were clearly low-grade fireworks surround a giant, plastic, hard-shelled taco. The lettuce was too green, the salsa too red, the cheese the color of golden arches. All the mariachi bands climbed their way up, all playing a gorgeous song in unison, and even though Carson never heard it before he began to hum its ascending melody. Blood still dripped from his nose and lips. Behind them followed the proprietor of the festivities, and behind him were all the cooks, and behind them were Carson's two little girls. He saw them now: wearing their sombreros he was going to buy them with pride, with authenticity; smiling and knowing what kind of day they had. They were so far from him, a dream away. He wanted to take their picture. Post it for the world to see, to bear witness. He saw them now: two National Taco Day princesses, blushing on that grand stage as the crowd cheered their prodigious and well-deserved ascent. Looking at them, Carson understood. He hoped they could hear him, distant in the flurry of so many faces and lives fully lived, singing out their names.

REVIEWS

Quilt Life by Cindy Bosley. Huron, Ohio: Bottom Dog Press, 2021. 105 pages. $16.00, paper.

A poetry collection titled *Quilt Life*, and moreover, one whose cover features samples of quilts designed and stitched by the poet herself, certainly conjures up images of an earlier, idyllic America—a simpler time, a homespun time, perhaps even a pre-modern time. And then if you add that the poet hails from Ottumwa, Iowa (home of John Deere tractors), and attended the Iowa Writers Workshop, well, the image both narrows and expands to include cornfields, Mid-Americana, maybe a bit of Midwest religious pietistic fanaticism like the Amish, the Shakers, and the Amana Colonies, and celebrations like the Fourth of July.

A poem like "To All the Solemn People Living There" begins to dismantle this distinctly mid-American idyll through a series of switches and reversals. The poet's father, who is "threading bolts" at the local John Deere factory, is "sitting like a seamstress," and instead of thinking about his wife, the family dinner, perhaps an upcoming vacation at the lake, he hypnotically repeats (as if a mantra) the name of his mistress: "Donna, Donna." In "Patience of God," in a reversal of the prevailing narrative, the young priest at the local Catholic church becomes the object of desire in the eyes of the nine-year-old poet:

> At Saint Patrick's Catholic Church in Ottumwa, Iowa,
> I fell in love with Father Paul at Sunday Mass when I was nine.
> I married him on my first communion.
> At Dickey's Prairie Home Buffet, still wearing my white dress,
> I broke a plate and dropped cranberry sauce in my lap
> And practiced saying "consummated."

Nowhere is this upending more evident than in a poem about the 1976 Bicentennial celebration at the town park, where the poet, again still a child, parades around (and is paraded around) wearing "a halter top in bicentennial colors, / dainty stars and stripes on my nine-year-old chest." The local school has been torn down and replaced with a McDonald's, and new, modular pods are trucked in to create "open classrooms," making it nearly impossible for parents to make sense of the whole project of learning. The openness, too, "allowed us views / of schoolmates on all sides, no one hiding, no one uncounted for," and thus rife with exposed secrets. And, of course, this was also the 1970s, and parents, too, were carrying out their own small-town dramas, too busy even to distract their kids with attention or puppies:

> [We had] just our enemies—each other—to hustle out
> the cold nights while our friends slept in rotting
> comforters down the street, and all our parents
> played poker and Twister and guzzled rum,
> leaving Uncle Ron to prowl the back bedrooms.

In "Father-Daughter Dance at the Reception," the language itself, with its barrage of plosive Bs and Ps, reenacts the controlled underlying violence and pain—even the smacking sound of unwanted kisses. When the bride's father is a no-show, sentimentality requires the DJ to spin "Daddy's Little Girl"—and her to dance awkwardly with her father-in-law:

> The little girl's shy love-eyes ducked into his
> lapels and the father's suit bucked his shoulders
> with paunchy air and pucker. The bride
>
> blanched, and stared at her own slippered feet
> while he groom grinned, oblivious. The first
> rule of the dance is that you must protect ....

A significant number of poems in *Quilt Life* patch together a strong and moving narrative involving the poet's own marriage—or rather, marriage, children, divorce, and the aftermath. They range from the quotidian to the heart-rending. In "Fuse No. 12," for example, the wife doesn't appear to be especially jealous of other woman who might attract her husband, but his car, which needs his constant attention and gets all his "quality time, / words of affection ... and physical touch." Eventually she realizes, as she voyeuristically observes him from the porch, that he's lying on a blanket underneath the car's jacked-up body, his hidden hands tinkering with her transmission. And that "she might be moaning." The humor here in this perfect extended trope is certainly as revved up as the disappointment and anguish.

A sort of mid-American pop psychology is explored in "Five Years to Recover from a Marriage." The poet finds that she must sift through a whole series of contradictory messages thrown her way—not only by therapists, but also friends, relatives, "conventional wisdom," etc. And, of course, there are those nagging reminders of the once-intact union—an ex who shows up unexpectedly at the bank, the consultations about the children. "Plus, / he is gay, and there is the new territory / that both of you have boyfriends," which can only lead to the realization that …

> Life is an experiment, I am the locust
> in the cocoon inside a jar inside a glass
> aquarium inside a lab inside a politically corrupt
>
> and untenable city inside a firestorm
> which does not value the incubation period
> of the locust in chrysalis ….

That "new territory" soon becomes a familiar outpost, a site of constant negotiation and unease, even in a poem with the seemingly nonchalant title, "My Ex-Husband's Husband." Occasionally, there are issues (usually related to the children): "we iron / things out, [with] lots of messages / sent, received, responded." But sometimes it's "like an autopay," always a surprise, oftentimes resulting in an overdraft with penalty fees. The domestic referents are important here—the metaphors employing ironing and the bank account. It always reduces to some sort of ledger, keeping score.

> When you, man who was
> my twenty-two years'
> husband, touch
> the hand
> of your husband.

One of the more engaging and moving poems in the collection, "Children of Divorce," settles into the long-term ache of divorce, but also its expected solaces. One child snuggles into bed alongside, while "the heat pumps hard." A second child, falls asleep to TV crime dramas, "where every dark and bloody / mystery is solved." A third is away at college, and thinking about her, the poet writes,

... My eyes romp
in the merry-go-round that is her face.
My child three and a half hours away
at school, but hot-air-balloon tethered ....

Throughout *Quilt Life*, the poems are adroitly tethered—and to extend the metaphor, tethered on a string that is long and winding, sometimes knotted or stretched to its limits. But that expansion and contraction always results in an artifact that like a quilt, with its seemingly random patches stitched together, provides warmth and comfort.

—*Leonard Kress*

Extinction Events by Liz Breazeale. Lincoln, Nebraska: University of Nebraska Press, 2019. 121 pages. $17.95, paper.

Prairie Schooner publishes work that responds to the hard stuff, the human stuff, the stuff sizzling across our globe, so it is not surprising that Liz Breazeale's story collection, *Extinction Events*, was chosen to receive the Prairie Schooner Book Prize in Fiction. Breazeale's collection reads like an archaeological dig in dreamland, and the excavated finds are significant, gorgeous, and often surreal.

"The Lemurians," a tender story that follows a sister and her gay brother from childhood to early adulthood, is such a find. Deftly, Breazeale presents this tale by joining the narrative qualities of historical documentation and the soft strokes of a watercolor painting:

The seashell people are everything the Lemurians want. They are demure, or witty, or stoic, or meek, whatever characteristics their creators desire. They move like ribbons of silt trapped in currents and their voices are sounds magnified in conch shells, swelled and echoing.

This story is grounded in everyday pain, too. The sister (also the narrator) tries to keep her brother from the hurt of being a young, gay boy: "My school years were punctured by absence, by suspensions, by the battles of my brother fought by me. He stood to the side, helpless, his sand dune face perpetually shifting, collapsing." Both sister and brother age, become full-blown teens, and the brother's suffering is palpable as the narrator lives a normal life while her brother does not: "So the summer before my senior year was all want. The boys clumsy and quick. ... That summer was my brother's want, too—hanging in the air like decaying fruit, like apples rotting on the tree."

Lemuria is only one of many lost or searched-for lands in this collection. Or is it really the land that is lost or pursued? "How Cities Are Lost" is presented in titled sections such as "Angkor Wat" and "Mohenjo-Dar," and as the narrator travels through these places, it is her mother for whom she pines. Her mother is one of many mothers who choose to walk away from their family when their children are young, who just go: "My mother gave me her map one night as she strode across the study. I asked if she was leaving. I felt it in her trembling arms, the broken bone shapes of her words. ... A week later she was gone."

The quests in this collection are often depicted via a methodical format, showcasing the planned excavation site, the story. "In Devil's Tooth Museum," the storyline is demarcated by exhibits within the museum, such as, "Exhibit 1: A good impact crater is hard to find." The exhibits not only explain the evidence of eradication of life on this planet many years ago, but they also hold memories of lives lost by the museum's owner and family members. A prescriptive approach to storyline is present in "Extinction Events Proposed by My Father" as well, where the story is delivered in numbered sections, each section with a theory of how dinosaurs were eradicated: "1. The dinosaurs gas themselves to death. The emissions of hundred-ton creatures create a planet heavy and toxic." Here is another story in which the loss and searching is twofold, of both the dinosaurs and the narrator's mother. We do not know how she died, and this mystery (to the reader) mirrors the father's self-imposed stance to posit numerous theories of dinosaur extinction except the most probable. He, like many of us, cannot face truth because it is too painful. In "Four Self-Portraits of the Mapmaker," the method of the story's progression is again through numbered and titled sections as the main character maps her relationships with men, beginning with her father in "1. New World," and ending with a romantic partner in "4. Failed Expeditions." There is, again, loss, even in the relationships. Breazeale employs subtle yet powerful interactions between women and men, applying an intensity as soft as an elephant's presence:

> It's not a map if nobody can read it. Her father snatches the pen. He boxes off a corner of the page. This line, make it a continent border. And this, a country. Until they are claw

marks in a soft, vast underbelly. Until she feels them under her skin, lacerating the heart of her made concrete.

The heavy presence of the softly forceful man continues in each section of this brief yet notable story, from father, to schoolmates, to boss, to the man that the main character will probably leave one day:

> I don't want to tell you what to do, he offers in the quiet. She blinks. It's two in the morning, she croaks. The world is made of meandering lines. How about something less abstract. That doesn't sound like a question. Don't get emotional. It's just a thought. I'm not emotional.

The language melding of humans and earth permeates this story and collection. Readers may swoon at the lush intertwining: "The mapmaker charts him in her mind, his tropics and doldrums, delineations of spine and limb she surveys with her lips, tongue, fingers." More often, the spellbinding fusion is of humans and earthly ruination: "He is a field after a flood, vacant, washed away around the edges," and "Waves of moss over walls become stubble and the torso-thick roots clinging to collapsed ceilings and doorways are me, clutching my mother's unshaven legs," and "Her lips, rims of craters. She created stark boundaries—before and after meeting her—in people because she was like implosions and destructions in her bones, in her voice."

Women are often longed-for fragments in *Extinction Events*. Mothers, especially, are painfully absent or not present enough. In "Four Self-Portraits of the Mapmaker," the main character has "a chapel of a mother, meek and still and full of others." Sometimes, the mothers' ghostliness renders their daughters unsafe. In "Ashcake" and "Experiencers," the mothers' absorption in controlling environmental or extraterrestrial events injures their daughters' physical or emotional wellbeing. In "Ashcake," the mother refuses to leave her home and bakery on the volcanic island, even as it is erupting, even as her daughter is staying because she is staying, when it is clear death is imminent. In "Experiencers," the mother believes that aliens abducted her when she was pregnant and, therefore, her daughter is a "hybrid." The daughter's childhood is one of rejection:

> I told her all the time: I'm your daughter, Mom. You can't give me back because there's nothing to give me back to. And what did she say?

The daughter still feels the words under her skin. Hears the monotone indifference of her mother's voice, the chill. All she said was: They tell me I'll miss you.

What these women, daughters and mothers are searching for throughout this collection are things that are lost, be they islands, cities, craters, or something in the skies. Be they sisters or parents who died before their time. Be they ancestors disintegrated in their homeland's lahar. Be they husbands lost to Alzheimer's. Be they choices, as they ache for their brothers' pain and loss of their innocence, of which they are partially to blame. Be they themselves, as they write the maps of their hearts.

—*Thea Swanson*

Field Guide to Invasive Species of Minnesota by Amelia Gorman. Houston, Texas: Interstellar Flight Press, 2021. 64 pages. $11.99, paper.

Field Guide to Invasive Species of Minnesota by Amelia Gorman is a thoughtful and intelligent collection of one-page poems and elegant illustrations that slowly bud from gentle cricket song into a poison-leafed and weedy future. The collection is built around the theme of human-caused environmental change and what that might mean for those not given a choice. In "Earthworm," even the mildest lives are displaced, but triumphant in their perseverance.

> While cities crumble, we clasp
> cast to cast, enough of us even
>
> in them to come up worms
> million mother, vertical father.
> Dumped as so much half-bait
> into brown lakes, algae-stained
> by motors who had no faith
> in our resurrection.

In "Brittle Naiad," we are given the perspective of this titular water weed, and it whispers secrets to us at the end of each stanza. The start is compelling and small-chimed, making me want to go outside and sit somewhere quiet.

Brittle as the snow is gray,
she has secrets for one who will listen
We all miss the old world.
Being can count as an action
at four meters fathomed, she whispers
There is nothing safe about houses.
But if this were a hike beside the choked lake, I'd feel a
creeping sensation of being watched and hearing voices.
Submersed symbol of the Mississippi,
one day a year she rises, saying
Harvesting is hard for roots unwoven.

I loved the slow dawning that occurred to me as I went along poem by poem. The increasing awareness that these are not the pastel flowers of Cicely Barker I grew up on, but a sharper imagining where weeds tell you how to survive when the world is out to get you.

And, Gorman uses the speculative element to show how human desire is fickle and subjective.

"Emerald Ash Borer" is one of the shortest poems, but it flirts and then bites. The first stanza is a shiver:

You always wanted a necklace
that scuttled across your skin.

These poems conjure trickster fairies rather than the round-cheeked babies of field and meadow we all grew up on. This is reality spiced with thorn and bramble. The juxtaposition of hardscrabble and lovely lyric brings focus to the humble and strange. From "Trapdoor Snail":

She was the only one who wanted
to discard the mother-of-pearl
and wrap her tongue into legs.

Some of the poems speak with the voice of the plant, and others are narrated by the humans affected by their presence. The plant usually feels dominant in the power struggle, a nod toward the inevitable inside a speculative framing. We all eventually succumb to the seed. From "Elodea":

In the future, you can choose any death
as long as it's by water.

And from "Buckthorn":

> And soon there will be no you.
> Just endless, reproducing
> thorns.

Not every poem is about a plant; there are crustaceans and fowl and even a lamprey. Each living organism is handled as if by a daring and sun-smeared child, the delight in getting muddy and making up stories proudly prominent, and a refreshing pleasure in a collection of nature poetry.

The longest poem is for the smallest organism, the "Spiny Waterflea." Separated into opposing pages of three acts each, this prose poem tells a story through two points of view: the weird and wonderful fleas in the circus and the owner who works the hardest management gig in entertainment.

> Act II.

> She refashioned their little picks out of icepicks and paperclips. She hasn't seen ice in years, though she hears up north they have more than they can handle. She drinks a moonshine neat as she labors under the magnifying glass.

There is a mix of folk tale, myth, and country living punctuated with dreams of space travel and new forms of survival for humans. The whole chapbook invites the reader to imagine all the ways we could persist. "Grecian Foxglove":

> What good is foxglove
> now that we've removed our bodies?
> We've gotten away from the grind
> the gore and the rats and the crowds.
> …
> and death riding war into the mall.

Gorman shares a long author's note at the end of this collection that is part memoir, part history lesson, speaking to the kindred spirits of those wanting to value all life, not just the pretty or productive bits. The work Gorman has done in the environment brought her to see the world as perfect and persistent, even the parts disturbed by our fumbling, while reminding us to revel in the bracken of our hungry curiosity toward an aware future-present.

—*Julie Reeser*

The Groundhog Forever by Henry Hoke. Santa Rosa, California: WTAW Press, 2021. 184 pages. $16.95, paper.

The prospects of literary revisionism for dizzying, meta-level involution are intensified when the precursor text is one in which its protagonist revises the same day of their life over and over. That is the starting point of Henry Hoke's debut novel from WTAW Press, *The Groundhog Forever*, an anecdote from the author's life that he divulges in the press release: During his time at NYU, he was enrolled in a class on auteur filmmakers, and the instructor arranged one day for Bill Murray to join the class for a viewing of *Groundhog Day* and a Q&A, after which Hoke and his friend mused, "What if this day became our Groundhog Day?" Anyone who has met a celebrity that famous understands how the encounter can have the effect of waking us up to the sense of possibility in an otherwise humdrum routine, and it is this encounter that becomes for Thing 1 and Thing 2—the nicknames given to the novel's protagonists by a teacher—the content of the novel's first section, "*Groundhog Day* Day." A premise that is simple and could have potentially led to a lot of derivative silliness becomes so much more due to the book's structural and line-level inventiveness, its critique of the Harold Ramis film, and the lens it becomes through which to examine post-9/11 America, New York City in particular.

I spent most of my youth in Rockford, Illinois, and among the few things we have to brag about—Cheap Trick, the Rockford Peaches, Aidan Quinn—is that the quarry scene from *Groundhog Day* was shot there. Inevitably I thought of the film on the surreal day that nearly no one showed up to my book reading at the wonderful Read Between the Lynes in downtown Woodstock, Illinois, a small town near Rockford that became for *Groundhog Day* the quintessence of backwater provincialism, of a place where Murray's Phil Connors would not want to get stuck for eternity. Having grown up with a narrative can cause its problems to be harder and more painful to uncover; you've taken the medium into your mind, given it a place there, and allowed it to grow with you. Despite the not-subtle ickiness of *Groundhog Day*, it's important to the project of *The Groundhog Forever* that Hoke seems to be confronting an ambivalence that belies a certain affection for the film. I'm not sure that any literary revisionist project can be successful without some investment in the source material, as the authorial implication in the root problems helps ward off the risk of didacticism. Hoke has responded to the misogyny of Connors, using his contrapasso as a means to seduce Andie MacDowell's character, Rita Hanson, by making Thing 1 lesbian and Thing 2 gay, putting two friends in the situation together. The cruelness and nihilism with which Collins initially insists on confronting his fate receives direct comment late in the novel, after a thousand relivings of Groundhog Day Day: "They decided they'd never watch the groundhog movie again, because it perverted their privilege as plight."

A poignant moment in Laurie Anderson's 2015 documentary *Heart of a Dog* is when her rat terrier, following a scare from a hawk, keeps looking to the skies during subsequent walks. "A whole 180 degrees more that I'm responsible for," Anderson narrates her dog's thoughts. She compares the pet's daze with residents of New York City in the aftermath of the 9/11 terrorist attacks: "Like there's something wrong … with the air." The New York City of 2003 in which the novel takes place is still skittish about the sky, the very air. Like Henry Hoke, I was two weeks into my freshman year of college in the fall of 2001, and I experienced the jolt of such a traumatic global event disrupting the outset of what the contemporary American experience had ordained to be a very you-centered journey. Part of what bonded Thing 1 (Anna) and Thing 2 (Sam) as friends was that they were together in the same deli when they found out about the events that started what the book refers to as the "long bad day." "From that day on, Tuesday was the day of the week that meant the most to them," and *Groundhog Day* Day is also a Tuesday, leading them to refer to everyone oblivious to the repeated day (everyone except them) as "Wednesday people." So, in our two friends' "stuckness" on one calendar day, there's always the resonance of a city and a country constantly reminding itself to never forget what it never possibly could plus a perpetual global conflict mediated by the same headlines day after day, year after year.

Anna and Sam have less work to do on themselves as people than did Phil Connors, and whatever breaking free of the daily repetition that occurs in *The Groundhog Forever* is a more abstract one. They are aspiring filmmakers, and a parallel concern of the novel is their attempt to shoot a film that had been foiled the Monday just prior to the repeated Tuesday by their desired location in Central Park being fenced off. Life, film, and novel are merged and blurred in a few different ways in *The Groundhog Forever*. Part four is called "Dual Projection," but here the term refers to a day that the two friends spend separated—and the novel's portrayal of their, for once, divergent pursuits—after a temporary but dramatic falling out. When their unfailing dedication to one another leads them to an alternate filming location and a mad scramble to complete their project in a single waking day, it is this film alone that escapes *Groundhog Day* Day, attesting to the ability of art to both launch us from the smallness of now and preserve the contemporary moment for future viewers. The film itself, when we "see" it, is a dual projection, and the facing pages of the codex become the two screens. The simultaneity of the left page and the right page is assembled retrospectively—as are all attempts at page-based simultaneity—but this moment represents the diegetic escape from *Groundhog Day* Day with an appropriately coextensive rupturing of novelistic time. That it does so via a medium traditionally made to be played over and over again without change is part of what makes this novel about a forever friendship itself so endlessly startling and complex.

—*Joe Sacksteder*

A Common Person and Other Stories by R.M. Kinder. South Bend, Indiana, University of Notre Dame Press, 2021. 216 pages. $23.00, paper.

Author R.M. Kinder rewrites the definition of "common" in her award-winning *A Common Person and Other Stories* collection. Carefully linked short stories explore lives with an unflinching view of what makes a person common or uncommon.

Woven skillfully throughout are themes and objects that never feel trite under Kinder's pen: dogs, snakes, nature, violence, grief, family, community, aging, awakening, sleep, coming of age, community, sky, earth, death, life, fear. The stories become a census to make sure every person counts regardless of their status. Written over twenty-four years, the seventeen stories are linked with Kinder's strong voice down to intriguing titles that include "Everyday Sky," "Brute," "Recovering Integrity," and "The Stuff of Ballads."

In the titular story, Kinder introduces "Maggie" with the matter-of-fact omniscience that helps define each character in the collection. Maggie focuses on aging, the idea of violence and a Facebook post that draws stereotypical "men in black suits." Kinder builds Maggie's life with layers and lists: birds, family, seahorses, dark matter, non-primates, Victorian dress styles, the smallest dog. Even though Maggie wants to escape, it also feels she may be flattered the government has tracked her.

> This was America, her country. She had done nothing. She was just an old woman who owned guns and made a foolish statement. She would be inconvenienced. As would her companions.

Kinder continues to add matter-of-fact storytelling and world-building throughout with sensory words: austere, heels cliopping on tiled floor. Maggie's attendant is described as "younger, slim with red hair so curly it could have been rolled in corkscrews." Kinder's other descriptors are weighty and memorable as well. In "Tradition," the main character compartmentalizes her emotional responses by literally measuring her sibling's importance and describing herself as "a cool, tall, big-boned, hardhearted gal." In "Signs," William Lee Harper is labeled as "very tall, slim, with heavy bones, he was at most homely: his nose was too large, his hair coarse and long, cut unevenly." These descriptions become character bellwethers in the collection's quest to define and not define "common."

Kinder also infuses the collection with humor to balance grief and loss: a snake prank gone wrong, the frugality of eating green beans, a BOOBS HEADED WEST OF I-70 sign. Purposeful exposition and object lessons shine in Kinder's hands. The opening paragraph of "Everyday Sky" includes words that conflict: home, normal, surprised, bottom, sloping, chained, pale, new, familiar. Main character Milosh's life features another series of objects, including gum, walnuts, an uneven sidewalk, his mother fixing stuffed cabbage and fried potatoes, a trash can trio, dog diets, and a father overindulging.

The omniscient point of view also works as the narrator becomes another characterr—often wryly inserting internal thoughts or observations. We see into Maggie's thought process as she is questioned by the men in suits. "I'm not a violent person at all," Maggie said. "I can't bear violence. Most of my life I've attempted just to stay calm. It's a battle."

In many stories, Kinder has the main characters literally waking up but also in a figurative sense. In "Tradition," there is a repetition of a focus on nature and sunlight but that is only the beginning. The story focuses on more difficult subjects: mother-daughter relationships, partners, abortion, confessions. The main character reveals, "I have to have an abortion and I have to tell my mother about it. I could just schedule the damned thing, clutch my sin to my heart, so to speak, and live it out alone, but something in me—probably my mother—says I have to confess."

In "Tradition" and "Signs," Kinder examines characters with clothing as defining measures. As the story progresses, the mother character "... wears jeans a lot but not today. She has on a long cotton skirt, a white blouse with a high, prim collar, and she's pulled her hair back to the nape of her neck. She's wearing stockings and wedgie shoes her own mother might wear." This description contrasts with the daughter's statement that she dresses "... in a black sheath, with a gold chain around my neck. My shoes have spike heels. I'm tall and commanding. Mark's girl. The bleeding little virgin."

While nature and religion (the author scatters C.S. Lewis references) comes into play in many of Kinder's stories, "Little Garden" plays most with nature and Garden of Eden elements: snakes (rubber and real), a magnolia tree, blossomed lavender, gentle rolling hills, dense trees. Kinder matches those elements with contrast: a character who sings, "Give me young women, wild whiskey, and fresh horses." Kinder manages to infuse humor into loss even as the snake prank turns tragic.

In "Signs," Kinder turns to a waking main character and infuses the short story with poetic phrasing: as if she had binged on syrup, too rich a yellow. Multiple stories in this collection begin with the character waking up. In aggregate, this collection of common and uncommon people becomes a wake-up call to be aware of neighbors, friends, family. Contrasting against prettier prose, the uglier side of determining commonality comes to the forefront with this assessment: "Would he ever have air-conditioning? Was his lot poverty? Did he really care? Maybe he was just a bum. Cosmic bum."

There are many unspoken signs in the collection but also physical signs with maybe the most literal and humorous occurring in the fittingly labeled "Signs." In the end, the main character decides against the "Show Me your Beauties" sign because he is a "Christian man" with a "Jesus Loves You" sign even though the naughtier sign makes "him feel inches from a woman."

The most profound questions and answers come in the opening story that leads the collection: "What does that mean to you? Commoner. Do you see society divided into commoners and royalty?" Through dimensional characters and situations, Kinder guides rather than dictating. Her reader is able to examine their own lives through her characters and their experiences to find their own definitions of "common."

—Amy Barnes

Slaughter the One Bird by Kimberly Ann Priest. Knoxville, Tennessee: Sundress Publications, 2021. $12.99, paper.

Maybe there is no feeling more vital than the sense that we are being seen. In *Slaughter the One Bird*, the debut full-length collection from Kimberly Ann Priest, the poet sees her subject—locks on, in fact, with laser focus—and that's all the more moving as she is writing about herself.

The book is a meditation on Priest's experience as a victim of childhood sexual abuse and its ongoing effects, including her adult experience with a violent partner. The power of these poems comes in the way Priest tries to make sense of the damage that has been inflicted on her by drawing parallels with the natural environment.

One recurring image that stuns with each reoccurrence is that of a deer making its delicate way through a violent world. The animal is first glimpsed in the lead-off poem for the first section, titled "Midwestern Doe Story." The poem has terrible momentum as the reader sees the doe emerging from the wood, then reads of the "slow skate of hooves on pavement—thin legs." It's terrible, something so delicate in the proximity of so much deadly force.

The reader's premonition comes true as the doe is depicted lunging toward a ditch, with the "live kick of tires on ice, sharp pang," and then the driver is seen observing the damage. "Maybe some pieces / could be salvaged for meat," he surmises, and the image comes full circle: What is most delicate in the world is also at the most danger, exactly like the young victim of a pedophile—and so much that is precious is assessed for its piecemeal value.

The doe comes back in the poem "Soft Fruit," which hints of similar danger with its own lush imagery, like "the moon, a bullet hole / in its icy pane." Here, the deer exercises caution against a danger that is not seen: "A doe steps into its solstice, her bones / undressing for the season, // growing desire to give up a life."

In "Soft Fruit," the doe escapes its earlier dark fate through its caution:

> ... And though
> 　　the air is silent—no explanation,
> bird call or breeze—she lifts
> 　　her ears. Swiftly,
> they fly—footprints on the path
> 　　speaking only of she.

We wouldn't be human if we didn't root for the deer and her escape from the unknown threat, but there is always a reminder here that humans are the source of the most danger, for the animal world or for ourselves.

Priest's deer have me completely attuned to her message each time they appear—as a reader, I'm roiling with worry for them, and I know this worry is because of how the actual child the poet is telling me about is sublimated into the cervid. As a culture, we manage to overlook the dangers faced by the actual children around us, but maybe we can understand it in the form of the deer, Priest posits.

And we can. "Six Does Kiss the Fields" brings back the image, this time in the form of six does with their yearlings in a field during hunting season:

> Desperate lick of salt, an open palm, rustling leaves against a
> partly damaged shed. Men roam the woods
> as though gifted with gestation, their eyes, stories
> as tearless as the nights they choose to wander beneath
> a Hunter's Moon—waxing, waning, full—maybe
> ripped open by a bullet or blade. The umber trees wielding
> too many bodies to crows ....

The metaphor is nearly unbearable when considered with those hunters' terms, like "culling" or "harvest," because Priest is writing about victims of abuse. In fact, she is boldly telling her own story of being harvested by an unnamed pedophile—from the supposedly safe preserve of her church, no less—thirty years ago, when she was too young to understand or resist. In Priest's skillful hands, there is not a far distance between hunters who are eager to lift up the still-warm body of a deer and the person who hurt her as a young girl.

Although the pedophile is not named in the collection, Priest identifies him—calls him out—as early as the first poem, aptly titled "Theodicy" (a word that refers to the vindication of the divine, which feels like an accurate description of this book). She writes about the pedophile's gaze—

> the every-other-Sunday gaze
> of a pedophile, third seat, first row, next to
> the pastor's wife,
> smiling like the broken swag of moon draped across
> my bedroom floor, passage to the closet,
> burrow, bed, one finger-width crack between closet doors,
> my labia safely gathered in a hand ....

I retract my earlier statement. There is a feeling that is even more vital than being seen, and it's one that we rarely get to experience. That is the feeling of being vindicated. Priest vindicates herself masterfully, as much through the power of her craft, and particularly her imagery, as through her witness.

—*Karen Craigo*

Shapeshifting: Stories by Michelle Ross. Fairfax, Virginia: Stillhouse Press, 2020. 226 pages. $16.00, paper.

In *Shapeshifting*, Michelle Ross offers us stories of people who just miss each other. Every conversation is punctuated by what is missing, and every relationship is defined by what it lacks. We're hit hard and early with "Pangea," a story about a self-help/parenting guru and the wife who actually does the work he manages to take credit for. In this case, it's living in a van to get their child into a Montessori kindergarten. Pete, the "Daddy Sage," is too busy dispensing easily digestible pills of pop philosophy to bother to unclog the bathroom sink—clogged, according to our nameless narrator, by his nose hairs. Our narrator is the prime mover in every action: She decides to spend almost a week in a van with her school-age son and infant daughter, waiting on queue to maybe get the son, Joey, into school. Pete manages to swoop in and take credit, in spite of the fact that he accused her of overkill. "You're being pretty militant about this campout thing. You're so competitive." In the end, Pete stays in the limelight, having been dubbed "Our Father" by the Montessori campout community, and our narrator sits at home, at the edge of dissociating, carrying the domestic after being told that her dedication as a mother is constantly being called into question because she's always tired and—though it's not labeled as such—depressed.

Multi-generational depression and emotionally unavailable mothers are constant themes in these fourteen stories. In the title story, this cross-generational theme is at the forefront. Our narrator, Jess, is pregnant; her mother, who only communicates through postcards and packages, treats her daughter's condition as something that was clearly forced upon her; her boyfriend Flynn is sympathetic but helpless; Jess's friends immediately behave as if her body isn't her own, even though they all embrace their own agency. Ross's style leaves a reader feeling her first-person narrator's sense of being drowned, with brief moments of air during which we get a glimpse of what the narrator can't express to anyone around her. At one point, in a conversation with Flynn—the baby's father, whose existence she has hidden from her mother even after acknowledging the pregnancy—she says, "Don't kid yourself. There's monster DNA in all of us." Flynn is as close to a true listener as Jess gets, and even with what seems his best intentions, none of it connects.

In "The Sand and the Sea" and "Lifecycle of an Ungrateful Daughter," we read both sides of dysfunctional mother-daughter relationships. In "The Sand and the Sea" we get a daughter's point of view, and her relationship with her mother reads like a victim coming to terms with the narcissist in her life. Part of the way the narrator does this, though, is to compare her mother's mothering—or lack of it—to her own relationship with her daughter:

I've never seen my mother naked. This strikes me as odd now that I'm a mother. My kid sees me naked all the time. She brushes her teeth in my bathroom. She begs to take bubble baths together. She reaches up underneath the sleeves of my shirts to rub my arms as though with enough effort, a genie will emerge from my fingertips.

In "Lifecycle of an Ungrateful Daughter" the narrator is a mother who is only tangentially aware of the impacts of her depression, of the impact her own dysfunctional childhood is having on her children, and her reaction is to blame them—specifically her daughter, who has always been the adult in the family and whose weight is only felt when she finds the first healthy avenue for multi-generational disconnect and depression through writing. And in this one attempt to truly communicate with her mother, the daughter is silenced by the narrator's refusal to read the published story.

Two of the stories, "Keeper Four" and "A Mouth for Teeth," stand out in that they explore the core themes of misconnection and humanity but through a different narrative lens. In "Keeper Four" we have a sort of dystopian story in which a research facility is run through with some virus that kills everyone except Fawn (Keeper Four), a Researcher, and three animal test subjects. The titular character feels compelled to choose to free one of the animals—a bear that has already mauled another human—over colluding with the Researcher, whose selfishness and lack of humanity includes even his view of Fawn. "A Mouth for Teeth" reads like it's straight out of 2020. Angela lives at home, writes a baking blog—that a reader points out is really only about Angela baking other people's recipes—and raises a daughter, making sure to follow "the protocol." The husband/father works and is gone for weeks at a time. Angela seems to be suffering from delusions and hallucinations. Her daughter seems to be suffering from the isolation as much as the mother, but the husband/father dismisses all of it with exhortations to follow "the protocol," a protocol that is never described or given context. At first this lack of context is off-putting. But this lends the narrative strength as we are given a more emotional connection to Angela's world than if Angela herself were to be the narrative voice.

Ross's writing is descriptive and still manages to be spartan; the characters are complex and occupy their pain to a degree that's magnetic and disturbing. Each interaction is a ten-car pileup you can't help but watch. Each piece of dialogue and exposition rolls into the next, exquisite and excruciatingly beautiful.

—*Mick Parsons*

Down by Erin Elizabeth Smith. Nacogdoches, Texas: Stephen F. Austin State University Press, 2021. 80 pages. $18.00, paper.

Down by Erin Elizabeth Smith wakes the reader up like tripping on the bottom stair, as best exemplified by the fifth poem, "Remembering the Name," alternatively subtitled "The Ten-Month Marriage." Here the ex-husband abandons the newly minted nuptials and leaves our speaker … not alone, but left reminiscing about Lewis Carroll's beloved character Alice. In *Down*, the reader is dragged through America's Wonderland, a combination of the sweaty South dripping with jazz and the mismatched towns of the Midwest draped through the countryside like chessboards frozen in fondant. Less like a travelogue and more like a lovesong, *Down* reads like a child of grief born to a woman who keeps a well dog-eared copy of *Alice's Adventures in Wonderland* and *Through the Looking Glass* in her glove compartment in case of traffic or stopped trains or hopeless one-night stands.

Chasing her marriage with every drink in the house—"the freezer of vodka, two warm beers, brandy I use for brown mushroom sauces" —satisfies until it doesn't. After the marriage enters Alice—a redrawn character from a past that once made sense. She is a girl drawn and traced and decorated by men, much like the speaker illustrated and shaped by the father figures and lovers in the speaker's life. The marital separation transforms the speaker almost exactly like Alice in the titular poem, "Down":

> I have grown. I have eaten
> and drank until I'm unsure who I am
> without the slim-necked glass, lanced
> olive and gin. I am no longer blue-dressed,
> pinafored, a girl wrapped like a gift.

Alice starts speaking for Smith. She metaphorically sobers up for Smith. She lives alternate lives for Smith, naming and renaming the anonymous towns passed on the freeways, watching rom-coms and going on dates with men found on *OKCupid*. Alice is as much the character written by Carroll as well as the woman Smith has found herself to be: a little lost, a little hungry and a little out of sorts. Fans of the Alice books will find hidden reviews of famous iterations of the stories as well as not-so-hidden allusions to familiar faces and motifs. Just when you've almost forgotten that you're reading a book about *that* Alice, you might trip over a dormouse or a lawn flamingo.

As in the famous stories, *this* Alice does find her way out of the rabbit hole and back onto our side of the looking glass. Alice helps Smith navigate new loves and kindle a relationship with the woman Smith used to be. She helps steady Smith through night terrors and insatiable appetites. Together they wander the real world after the not-so-happily-ever-after.

Near the book's end the speaker confesses to her new love, "I can't write love poems anymore." This strikes as if it was the fourth act of a book from a different author. *Down* and its affinity for Alice reads as a wonderful book-length love poem from beginning to end. After all, aren't all poetic obsessions an attempt at understanding love of the unknown? Surely, even living through heartbreak, Smith's speaker was at least grasping at some kind of love. But there is a moment of clarity when Smith speaks directly to the ex-husband in "Dear John": "there is nothing in beauty // that makes up for loss." Perhaps we all need to sit back ourselves and wonder if it is always a living love feeding fuel to the poetic obsession, or if it might be the memory of a love lost keeping those beautiful things like Alice alive for us.

—*RJ Equality Ingram*

Death, Desire, and Other Destinations by Tara Isabel Zambrano. Okay Donkey Press, 2020. 200 pages. $13.99, paper.

Death, Desire, and Other Destinations is a sometimes surreal set of fifty flash fiction pieces. Through intricate characters, Zambrano tells us stories of just what she warns: death and desire. Even in the more abstract seeming stories, these emotions are at their core. She varies between narrators and points of view effortlessly, and each story feels unique and interconnected all at once. And through her blending of Indian and American culture and experiences, she sheds light to the universality of these feelings and sensations.

Zambrano writes extensively of physical desire, many stories filled with sex and lust from couples and strangers alike. But her use of desire reaches past the more expected sexual desires. Within expertly crafted sentences and beautiful images, she writes about other desires like the desire to have children, desire to be understood, and the desire to know one's path.

One piece that explores multiple meanings of the word is "Nine Openings." In this story, Zambrano imagines an alien landing in the yard of a couple, who eventually give up limbs of their body in order to be penetrated by the alien. "After our limbs are gone, it's impossible to carry the alien. We push ourselves, inch towards it, crave for the proximity and shudder in fear, thinking what might happen when we have nothing left to offer." When the alien dies and they can no longer use it, they are left shells of what they used to be. This overtaking of desire extends far past the enjoyment of sex and becomes a symbolic representation of the lengths people will go to for pleasure and the easing of suffering.

Often intertwined with her character's desires is death. And with the same complexity she explores the different ways death impacts our lives. In the story "The Fortune Teller," she explores the desire to end life. When a tribe's oracle becomes too old to continue, her son has to make the decision to kill his mother, and welcome death for himself as well. In his final moments he talks about how fate cannot be controlled. "I sense the blade on my neck, my pulse fluttering against the steel. And for the first time in my life, I feel certain as if I have always known this moment."

Then in "New Old," she explores a mourning so great that a husband begins to drink his wife's ashes in his tea. Written in second person as if he is our own father, we watch him slowly transform into his wife, acting out her life in a way that makes them become one. He refuses the need to spread her ashes. "We don't need to, he says, creating anxiety as you imagine your mother swimming in his veins, blooming, rising behind the whites of his eyes, wanting to come out, wanting to stay in." While both of these stories are far away from most of her reader's personal experiences, we can still relate to those overwhelming feelings that come when trying to balance what we want and what we know we need in the face of mortality.

Something else she explores in depth is how death is not only constricted to a loss of life. She often shows us other kinds of deaths, like the death of a perception of a loved one or the death of an expected path in life. In "Hands" a daughter catches her father in the middle of an affair. She must grieve over her ideal image of her father while he is still alive. Then in "Piecing" we see a woman deal with miscarriages and the inability to get pregnant. In these pieces, and others throughout the collection, Zambrano challenges us to think about the ways we mourn more than just people.

Zambrano's ability to create such vivid representations of her characters in the brevity of each piece is commendable. The power of these stories is lasting, and I find myself still thinking of them long after I have read them. She manages to eliminate the threat flash faces, of forgettability, with her sense of detail and endings that keep you thinking about how these stories tie into all our lives. They may be futuristic lesbians getting married on the moon or half-snake people lusting after pop stars, but every story is relatable to the human experience. Any fan of flash, or fan of works that make you think, or fan of beautiful prose, will find great enjoyment in this powerhouse collection.

—*Mary Morris*

CONTRIBUTORS' NOTES

Cathy Allman's work has appeared or is forthcoming in *Blue Earth Review*, *Bluestem Magazine*, *Edison Literary Review*, *Elysian Fields*, *Green Hills Literary Lantern*, *Hawaii Pacific Review*, *I-70 Review*, *The Potomac Review*, *Third Wednesday*, *Valparaiso Poetry Review*, *Word Riot*, and many other journals.

Kim Allouche's work has been published in *The Psychotherapy Networker*, *AlterNet*, *Storyscape*, *The Penmen Review*, and *805 Art+Lit*. A version of a chapter of her upcoming novel, *When Everything Beautiful Was Within Her Reach*, can be found in the Summer 2020 issue of *Shark Reef*.

Amanda Auchter is the author of *The Wishing Tomb*, winner of the 2013 PEN Center USA Literary Award for Poetry and the 2012 Perugia Press Book Award, and *The Glass Crib*, winner of the 2010 Zone 3 Press First Book Award for Poetry. Her recent work appears in *The Huffington Post* and on CNN.

Ruth Bardon lives in Durham, North Carolina. Her poems have appeared in *Boulevard*, *The Cincinnati Review*, *New Ohio Review*, *Salamander*, and elsewhere, and her chapbook, *Demon Barber*, was published in 2020 by Main Street Rag. She holds an MFA from the Iowa Writers Workshop and a PhD from the University of North Carolina at Chapel Hill.

Wendy Barker's seventh collection of poems is *Gloss* (Saint Julian Press, Inc., 2020). Her sixth collection, *One Blackbird at a Time*, received the John Ciardi Prize for Poetry (BkMk Press, 2015). Her fifth chapbook is *Shimmer* (Glass Lyre Press, 2019). Her poems have appeared in numerous journals and anthologies, including *The Best American Poetry*

2013. Recipient of NEA and Rockefeller fellowships, among other awards, she teaches at the University of Texas at San Antonio.

Amy Barnes has words at *FlashBack Fiction*, *McSweeney's Internet Tendency*, *Flash Fiction Magazine*, *X-R-A-Y Literary Magazine*, *JMWW*, *Anti-Heroin Chic*, and other journals. She's a *Fractured Lit* associate editor, *Gone Lawn* co-editor, and reads for *CRAFT*, *Taco Bell Quarterly*, *Retreat West*, *The MacGuffin*, and *Narratively*. Her flash chapbook, *Mother Figures*, was released this year from ELJ Editions, Ltd.

María Alejandra Barrios was born in Barranquilla, Colombia. She has lived in Bogotá and Manchester, where in 2016 she completed a master's in creative writing from the University of Manchester. Her work has been published in *Hobart Pulp*, *Reservoir Journal*, *Bandit Fiction*, *Cosmonauts Avenue*, *Jellyfish Review*, *Lost Balloon*, *Shenandoah*, *Vol.1 Brooklyn*, and *El Malpensante*, and is forthcoming in *Fractured Lit*. She was the 2020 SmokeLong Flash Fiction Fellow and her work has been supported by organizations such as the Vermont Studio Center, the Caldera Arts Center, and the New Orleans Writing Residency.

Roy Bentley has published eight books, including *American Loneliness* from Lost Horse Press (2019), who recently issued a new and selected entitled *My Mother's Red Ford* (2020). *Hillbilly Guilt*, his newest, won the Hidden River Arts/Willow Run Poetry Book Award and was released earlier this year. He is the recipient of fellowships from the National Endowment for the Arts, the Florida Division of Cultural Affairs, and the Ohio Arts Council.

Andrew Bertaina's debut collection, *One Person Away From You*, won the 2020 Moon City Short Fiction Award. He lives in Washington, DC, and has an MFA from American University. His work has appeared in *The Threepenny Review*, *Witness*, *Redivider*, *Orion*, and *The Best American Poetry*. More of his work is available at www.andrewbertaina.com.

Ace Boggess is author of five books of poetry: *Misadventure*, *I Have Lost the Art of Dreaming It So* (Unsolicited Press, 2019), *Ultra Deep Field* (Brick Road Poetry Press, 2017), *The Prisoners* (Brick Road Poetry Press, 2014), and *The Beautiful Girl Whose Wish Was Not Fulfilled*

(Highwire Press, 2003). His sixth, *Escape Envy*, is forthcoming from Brick Road Poetry Press in 2021. He has received a fellowship from the West Virginia Commission on the Arts and spent five years in a West Virginia prison.

Jo Brachman's work has appeared in *The Cortland Review, Valparaiso Poetry Review, Bellingham Review, Cimarron Review, Poet Lore, Birmingham Poetry Review, Poetry East, Tar River, Terminus, Waccamaw*, and other journals. She holds an MFA from Pacific University.

Shevaun Brannigan's work has appeared in such journals as *Best New Poets, AGNI*, and *Slice*, and is forthcoming in *Bat City Review*. She is a recipient of a Barbara J. Deming Fund grant and holds an MFA from Bennington College.

Ronda Piszk Broatch is the author of *Lake of Fallen Constellations* (MoonPath Press). Her journal publications include *Blackbird, 2River, Sycamore Review, Missouri Review, Palette Poetry*, and Public Radio KUOW's *All Things Considered*.

Abby Caplin's poems have appeared in *AGNI, Catamaran, Love's Executive Order, Manhattanville Review, Midwest Quarterly, Salt Hill, The Southampton Review, Tikkun*, and elsewhere. She is a physician and practices mind-body medicine in San Francisco. http://abbycaplin.com

Meagan Cass's first collection of stories, *ActivAmerica*, won the Katherine Anne Porter Prize and was published in 2017. Her stories have appeared in *DIAGRAM, Puerto del Sol, Joyland, Mississippi Review*, and elsewhere. She lives in St. Louis, teaches creative writing at University of Illinois-Springfield, and serves as an assistant editor for Sundress Publications.

Karen Craigo is the author of two full-length poetry collections from Sundress Publications, *Passing Through Humansville* (2018) and *No More Milk* (2016). She recently ended her term as Poet Laureate of the State of Missouri and currently works as a reporter for the *Springfield Business Journal* in Springfield, Missouri.

Pat Daneman lives in Lenexa, Kansas. Her poetry collection, *After All* (FutureCycle Press, 2018), was first runner-up for the 2019 Thorpe-Menn Award and a finalist for the Hefner Heitz Kansas Book Award. She is author of a chapbook, *Where the World Begins* (Finishing Line Press, 2015), and co-librettist of the oratorio, *We, the Unknown*, premiered by the Heartland Men's Chorus in 2018. For more, visit patdaneman.com.

James Ellenberger was born and raised in Chicora, a small town in western Pennsylvania. His poems and essays have appeared or are forthcoming in *River Teeth, Sou'Wester, Painted Bride Quarterly, Hotel Amerika, Hayden's Ferry Review, Third Coast, Passages North, Beloit Poetry Journal,* among other venues. He holds an MFA from the Ohio State University and a PhD from the University of Cincinnati. He was awarded an Ohio Arts Council Individual Excellence Award in 2020.

Renee Emerson is a homeschooling mom of six and the author of *Church Ladies* (forthcoming from Fernwood Press, 2022), *Threshing Floor* (Jacar Press, 2016), and *Keeping Me Still* (Winter Goose Publishing, 2014). Her poetry has been published in *Cumberland River Review, Windhover,* and *Poetry South*. She adjunct teaches online for Indiana Wesleyan University and blogs about poetry, grief, and motherhood at www.reneeemerson.wordpress.com.

Vivian Eyre is a New York-based poet and the author of the poetry chapbook *To the Sound* (Finishing Line Press, 2013). Her poems have been published and are forthcoming in *The Massachusetts Review, The Fourth River, Quiddity, Pangyrus, Spire, Bellingham Review, Asheville Poetry Review,* and *Buddhist Poetry Journal*. She serves as the guest curator for the Southold Historical Society's Whale House museum.

Ed Falco has published short stories widely in journals and anthologies, including *The Atlantic Monthly, The Best American Short Stories, and The Pushcart Prize Anthology,* as well as in four collections. His most recent novel, *Transcendent Gardening,* is forthcoming from C&R Press in 2022.

Caitlin Feldman is a writer whose work appears in *Hobart* and *Blood Orange Review*. She holds an MFA in nonfiction from Eastern Washington University. Having spent most of her life in Oregon's Willamette Valley, she now lives and writes in Spokane, Washington.

Allison Field Bell is a Jewish-American writer originally from California. She holds an MFA from New Mexico State University and she is pursuing her PhD in Fiction at the University of Utah. Her work has appeared in *The Gettysburg Review*, *West Branch*, *Ruminate*, *The Cincinnati Review*, *Witness*, *Shenandoah*, *The Pinch*, *The Florida Review*, *Fugue*, *New Madrid*, and elsewhere.

Kathy Goodkin's book, *Crybaby Bridge*, won the Moon City Poetry Prize and was published by Moon City Press in 2019. Her poems and reviews have also appeared in *Field*, *Denver Quarterly*, *Cream City Review*, *RHINO*, *Redivider*, *The Volta*, and elsewhere. She serves as a manuscript consultant for the North Carolina Writer's Network.

Jonathan Greenhause was a runner-up in America's 2019 Foley Poetry contest, shortlisted for the 2019 Mick Imlah Poetry Prize from London's *Times Literary Supplement*, and shortlisted for the Black Spring Press Group's 2020 Sexton Prize for Poetry. His poems have recently appeared or are forthcoming in *Contemporary Verse 2*, *Lake Effect*, *The Lascaux Review*, *New Ohio Review*, *Notre Dame Review*, *Salamander*, and the Poetry Society website, among others.

Ryn Haaversen holds a BA in art from a Montana college. From growing up in northern Minnesota, to exploring the western wilds while in college, to living in and roaming around Europe after graduating, they have been inspired by many things. Back in Minnesota, they are able to devote spare time to pursue art, in the form of learning graphic design and continuing to write, and adventure, as a recently certified Wilderness First Responder.

Patrick Holian is a Mexican-American writer from San Francisco. He holds an MFA in creative writing from St. Mary's College of California and a PhD in English from the University of Louisiana at Lafayette.

His poetry has appeared in *Gigantic Sequins*, *Oculus Vox*, and *Yalobusha Review*, and is forthcoming in *Whiskey Island Review* and *Bennington Review*.

Shen Chen Hsieh received a BFA in graphic design and illustration from Missouri State University, as well as an MFA in visual studies. Currently, she is a freelance graphic designer, illustrator, and artist living and working in Springfield, Missouri.

Ralph Hubbell holds an MFA from the Johns Hopkins University. His translations have been published in *Words Without Borders*, *Asymptote*, *The Hopkins Review*, *Cagibi*, and elsewhere. NYRB Classics will be publishing his translation of Oğuz Atay's short story collection, *Waiting for the Fear*, in early 2022.

RJ Equality Ingram received an MFA in creative writing from Saint Mary's College of California and is a poet and artist from Ohio, now living in Portland, Oregon. Recent work can be found in *Shrew Literary Zine*, *Rag*, *White Stag*, and *Alice Blue Review*.

Muzaffer Kale was born in 1957 and spent many years teaching literature. He has published twelve books of poetry and, most recently, two books of short fiction. He is the recipient of many poetry prizes, as well as the 2016 Sait Faik Award, Turkey's longest-standing and most prestigious short story prize. He lives with his wife outside of Bodrum, Turkey.

Blake Kimzey is the author of the collection *Families Among Us* (Black Lawrence Press), and his fictions have been broadcast on NPR, performed on stage in Los Angeles, and published by *Tin House*, *McSweeney's*, *VICE*, *Longform*, *Redivider*, *Short Fiction*, *The Masters Review*, and in the *Best Small Fictions* Anthology. He is Founder and Executive Director of WritingWorkshops.com.

Alyse Knorr is a queer poet and assistant professor of English at Regis University. Her most recent book of poems, *Mega-City Redux*, won the 2016 Green Mountains Review Poetry Prize. She is also the author of the poetry collections *Copper Mother* (Switchback Books, 2016) and *Annotated Glass* (Furniture Press Books, 2013); the nonfiction book *Super Mario Bros. 3* (Boss Fight Books, 2016); and three poetry chapbooks. She is a co-editor of Switchback Books.

Leonard Kress has published poetry and fiction in *Missouri Review*, *Massachusetts Review*, *Iowa Review*, *American Poetry Review*, and *Harvard Review*. His recent collections are *The Orpheus Complex* and *Walk Like Bo Diddley*. *Living in the Candy Store and Other Poems* and his new verse translation of the Polish Romantic epic, *Pan Tadeusz* by Adam Mickiewicz, were both published in 2018. He teaches at Owens College in Ohio and can be found at leonardkress.com.

Erica Plouffe Lazure's collection of short fiction, *Proof of Me + Other Stories*, is forthcoming in October 2021 from New American Press. She is the author of two flash fiction chapbooks, *Sugar Mountain* (Ad Hoc Fiction, 2020) and *Heard Around Town* (Arcadia, 2015), and a fiction chapbook, *Dry Dock* (Red Bird, 2014). She can be found online at ericaplouffelazure.com.

Alexis Levitin has published forty-seven books of translations, including Clarice Lispector's *Soulstorm* and Eugenio de Andrade's *Forbidden Words*, both from New Directions. His work has focused on contemporary poetry from Brazil, Ecuador, and Portugal. He has had two NEA translation fellowships, has had translation residencies at Banff, Canada, Straelen, Germany, and Belagio, Italy, and has served as a Fulbright professor in Brazil, Ecuador, and Portugal. Together with Sagado Maranhao, he has toured the United States five times, giving readings at over one hundred colleges and universities.

Nancy Chen Long is the author of *Wider Than the Sky* (Diode Editions, 2020), which was selected for the Diode Editions Book Award, and *Light Into Bodies* (University of Tampa Press, 2017), which won the Tampa Review Prize for Poetry. Her work has been supported by a National Endowment of the Arts creative writing fellowship and a Poetry Society of America Robert H. Winner Award. She works at Indiana University in the Research Technologies division. She can be found at nancychenlong.com.

Kim Magowan lives in San Francisco and teaches in the Department of Literatures and Languages at Mills College. Her short story collection, *Undoing* (Moon City Press, 2018), won the 2017 Moon City Press Fiction Award. Her novel, *The Light Source* (2019), was published by 7.13 Books. Her stories have been selected for the *Best Small Fictions* series and *Wigleaf's* Top 50. She is the editor-in-chief and fiction editor of *Pithead Chapel*, and can be found at www.kimmagowan.com.

Salgado Maranhão has published fourteen books of poetry and has written song lyrics and made recordings with some of Brazil's leading jazz and pop musicians. Five collections of his work have appeared in English: *Blood of the Sun* (Milkweed Editions, 2012); *Tiger Fur* (White Pine Press, 2015); *Palávora* (Diálogos Books, 2019); *Mapping the Tribe* (Spuyten Duyvil, 2021), and *Consecration of the Wolves* (Bitter Oleander, 2021).

Andrea Marcusa's literary fiction and essays have appeared in *The Gettysburg Review, Cherry Tree, River Styx, Citron Review, Cutbank*, and other journals. She's received recognition for her writing in a range of competitions, including *Glimmer Train, Southampton Review, Raleigh Review*, and *New Letters*. You can visit her at andreamarcusa. com and on Twitter @d_marcusa.

Kathleen Zamboni McCormick is a professor of literature and writing at Purchase College, SUNY. Her novel, *Dodging Satan: My Irish/Italian Sometimes Awesome but Mostly Creepy Childhood* (Sand Hill Review Press, 2016), was shortlisted for the 2020 Rubery Award, and won the 2017 Foreword Reviews Gold Medal in Humor, and the 2017 Illumination Bronze Medal for Catholic Books, among others. You can read more of her work at kathleenzmccormick.com.

E.J. Morris is a recent graduate of the MFA program at UNC-Greensboro. She is the former managing editor of *The Greensboro Review* and was runner-up in the NC State James Hurst Prize for Fiction. Her work is has appeared in *Mid-American Review* and *Elephant Journal*.

Mackenzie Colleen Morris graduated from Missouri State University with her degree in economics and mathematics this past spring. She has work published in *The Journal of Economic Insight* for her research on fertility and tax policy. This fall, she will begin her graduate studies at Penn State, pursuing a PhD in Energy, Environmental, and Food Economics.

Mary Morris is a recent graduate of Winthrop University, where she received a bachelor's degree in psychology.

Alyssah Morrison is an essayist and poet from the Missouri Ozarks. She recently graduated with an MA from Missouri State University with specialties in creative writing and literature.

Robert Brian Mulder's work has appeared in *The Sun*, *Cimarron Review*, *Pennsylvania English*, *Schuylkill Valley Journal*, *Evening Street Review*, *Sky Island Journal*, *Sandy River Review*, and *Flash Fiction Magazine*. He was a finalist for the 2020 J.F. Powers Prize for Short Fiction and was shortlisted for the 2019 Fish Publishing International Short Story Prize.

Samantha Padgett is an MFA candidate at Sam Houston State University. She lives in Huntsville, Texas.

Mick Parsons is the author of two poetry collections, several chapbooks, a collection of short stories, and a novella. He's organized open mics and readings all over the Midwest and publishes new work often on Instagram (@dirtysacred) and sometimes on his blog at dirtysacred. com. He is also the host and producer of the travel story podcast, *Record of a Well-Worn Pair of Travel Boots*.

Michigan poet **Lynn Pattison** is author of *Matryoshka Houses* (Kelsay Press, 2020) in addition to three other poetry collections: *tesla's daughter* (March St. Press, 2005); *Walking Back the Cat* (Bright Hill Press, 2005); and *Light That Sounds Like Breaking* (Mayapple Press, 2006).

Charnell Peters is the author of the poetry chapbook *Un-becoming*, winner of the 2018 Thirty West chapbook contest. Her previous work has appeared in *Foundry*, *Hippocampus*, *Crab Creek Review*, and elsewhere.

A St. Louis native, **Matthew Pitt** works as an associate professor and the director of English undergraduate studies at Texas Christian University. He has published two short fiction collections, *These Are Our Demands* (Engine Books, 2017), a Midwest Book Award winner, and *Attention Please Now*, winner of the Autumn House Prize (2010). He also serves as the editor of *descant* and a contributing editor for *West Branch*.

Jennifer Popa is a short story writer, essayist, and occasional poet. She is a PhD candidate in English and creative writing at Texas Tech University. Some of her recent writing can be found at *The Florida Review*, *Bellingham Review*, *Ninth Letter*, *West Branch*, and *Sundog Lit*. She can be found at www.jenniferpopa.com.

Paige Powell is a writer based out of central Texas. Her work has appeared or is forthcoming in *Beloit Fiction Journal*, *The Chattahoochee Review*, *Bourbon Penn*, and others. She is currently at work on her first novel.

Julie Reeser is the author of *Terracotta Pomegranate* (CreateSpace Independent Publishing Platform, 2017) and *Beak, Full of Tongue* (Amazon, 2019). Her short stories have been published in *Daily Science Fiction*, *Bards & Sages Quarterly*, and *Frozen Wavelets*. She runs a Patreon full of small joys and is disabled.

Habeeb Renfroe is an undergraduate at Missouri State University and has work forthcoming in *Bayou Magazine*.

Marnie Ritchie is a writer and an assistant professor of rhetoric. She has an MA from Syracuse University and a PhD from the University of Texas at Austin, both in communication. Her poetry has been published or is forthcoming in *FIVE:2:ONE*'s #thesideshow, *Juked Magazine*, *Yes Poetry*, and *Burning House Press*. She lives in Tacoma, Washington. You can find her on Twitter @marnieritchie.

Michelle Ross is the author of the story collections *There's So Much They Haven't Told You*, winner of the 2016 Moon City Short Fiction Award, and *Shapeshifting*, winner of the 2020 Stillhouse Press Short Fiction Award (forthcoming in November 2021). Her work has been selected for *Best Small Fictions, Best Microfiction*, the *Wigleaf* Top 50, and other anthologies. She is also the fiction editor of *Atticus Review*.

Nickalus Rupert is a Pushcart Prize-winning fiction writer who has spent most of his life near the Gulf Coast. His short story collection, *Bosses of Light and Sound*, won the 2019 Spokane Prize for Short Fiction and is available from Willow Springs Books. Find him at www.nickrupert.com.

Joe Sacksteder is the author of the story collection *Make/Shift* (Sarabande Books, 2019) and the novel *Driftless Quintet* (Schaffner Press, 2019). Recent publications include *The Offing, West Branch, Salt Hill,* and *Ninth Letter*. He's the director of creative writing at Interlochen Center for the Arts and a PhD candidate at the University of Utah.

M.A. Scott's poetry has appeared in or is forthcoming in *Mid-American Review, The Adirondack Review, Heron Tree, Gargoyle Magazine,* and the *Nancy Drew Anthology*. She grew up in Rhode Island and currently lives in New York's Hudson Valley.

From Alaska, **Bret Shepard** has lived throughout the Pacific and Arctic coasts. Currently, he is an assistant professor of English at Cabrini University. His work recently received the Goldstein Prize from the *Michigan Quarterly Review*. He is the author of *Place Where Presence Was*, winner of the 2019 Moon City Press Book Award, as well as two chapbooks, including *The Territorial*, which recently won the 2020 Midwest Chapbook Award from *The Laurel Review*.

Noel Sloboda is the author of the poetry collections *Shell Games* (sunnyoutside, 2008) and *Our Rarer Monsters* (sunnyoutside, 2013), as well as several chapbooks. He has also published a book about Edith Wharton and Gertrude Stein. He teaches at Penn State York.

Martha E. Snell's poetry appears or is forthcoming in journals such as *Ninth Letter, Cutthroat, The Poet's Billow,* and *Streetlight Magazine*. She received the Mary Jean Irion Prize from Chautauqua Literary Arts Friends in 2015 and was a finalist for the 2015 Bermuda Triangle

Prize (*The Poet's Billow*) and the 2019 Patricia Dobler Poetry Award. A professor emeritus at University of Virginia's Curry School of Education, she earned an MFA from Vermont College of Fine Arts.

Melissa Studdard is the author of five books, including the poetry collection *I Ate the Cosmos for Breakfast* (2015) and the poetry chapbook *Like a Bird with a Thousand Wings* (2020), both from Saint Julian Press, Inc. Her work has been featured by PBS, NPR, *The New York Times*, *The Guardian*, and the Academy of American Poets' Poem-a-Dayseries.

Thea Swanson holds an MFA in writing from Pacific University and is the founding editor of *Club Plum Literary Journal*. Her flash fiction collection, *Mars*, was published by Ravenna Press in 2017. Her poetry and essays are published or forthcoming in places such as *Pithead Chapel*, *Chiron Review*, *Spillway*, and *Northwest Review*.

Anthony Varallo is the author of a novel *The Lines* (University of Iowa Press, 2019), as well as four short story collections: *This Day in History*, winner of the John Simmons Short Fiction Award (2005); *Out Loud*, winner of the Drue Heinz Literature Prize (2008); *Think of Me and I'll Know* (Northwestern University Press/TriQuarterly Books, 2013); and *Everyone Was There*, winner of the Elixir Press Fiction Award (2017). Currently he is a professor of English at the College of Charleston, where he is the fiction editor of *Crazyhorse*. Find him online at @ TheLines1979.

Siamak Vossoughi is a writer living in Seattle. His first collection, *Better Than War*, received a 2014 Flannery O'Connor Award for Short Fiction, and his second collection, *A Sense of the Whole*, received the 2019 Orison Fiction Prize.

Laura Lee Washburn, the director of creative writing at Pittsburg State University in Kansas, is the author of *This Good Warm Place: 10th Anniversary Expanded Edition* (March Street Press, 2007), and *Watching the Contortionists* (University of South Carolina at Aiken Press, 1996). She is one of the founders and the co-president of the board of SEK Women Helping Women.

Charles Harper Webb's latest collection of poems, *Sidebend World*, was published by the University of Pittsburgh Press in 2018. *A Million MFAs Are Not Enough*, a collection of Webb's essays on contemporary American poetry, was published in 2016 by Red Hen Press. Recipient of grants from the Whiting and Guggenheim foundations, he teaches creative writing at California State University, Long Beach.

Gabriel Welsch's first collection of short stories, *Groundscratchers*, will be published by Tolsun Books in October 2021. He also is the author of four collections of poems: *The Four Horsepersons of a Disappointing Apocalypse* (Steel Toe Books, 2013); *The Death of Flying Things* (Word Tech Editions, 2012); *An Eye Fluent in Gray* (chapbook, Seven Kitchens Press, 2010); and *Dirt and All Its Dense Labor* (Word Tech Editions, 2006). He lives in Pittsburgh, Pennsylvania, and works as the vice president of marketing and communications at Duquesne University.

Jeremy T. Wilson is the author of the short story collection *Adult Teeth* (Tortoise Books, 2018). He is a former winner of *The Chicago Tribune*'s Nelson Algren Award for Short Fiction, and was recently named one of 30 Writers to Watch by Chicago's Guild Literary Complex. His stories have appeared in several publications including *The Carolina Quarterly*, *The Florida Review*, *Hobart*, *The Masters Review*, *Sonora Review*, *Third Coast*, and *The Best Small Fictions Anthology 2020*. He teaches creative writing at the Chicago High School for the Arts.

Joshua Zimmerer is a writer based in Denton, Texas, but his heart will always be in Columbus, Ohio. His writing has appeared in *Cartridge Lit*, *Hobart*, *Fjords Review*, and elsewhere.

CPSIA information can be obtained
at www.ICGtesting.com
Printed in the USA
LVHW111025110821
694351LV00004B/24

9 780913 785621